Witches Gone Wicked

WOMBY'S SCHOOL FOR WAYWARD WITCHES

SARINA DORIE

ISBN: 1985888025
ISBN-13: 978-1985888029

BOOKS IN THE WOMBY'S SCHOOL FOR WAYWARD WITCHES SERIES LISTED IN ORDER

CONTENTS

ACKNOWLEDGMENTS

I am fortunate to have so many supportive friends and family encouraging my endeavors. From an early age I had a mother who was my number one fan. I appreciated the early years of encouragement and the later years of brutal honesty. I am thankful I have a husband who enables my creative addiction. I wouldn't be able to write if Charlie didn't go in his man cave and entertain himself with World of Warcraft during the long hours it takes to produce a novel.

Thank you Night Writers, Alpha Readers, Visionary Ink, Wordos, and Eugene Writers Anonymous for helping me make this series the best it can be. Justin Tindel and Daryll Lynne Evans, you gave me hope and a writing community at a time when both were lacking in my life. James S. Aaron, your suggestion that I'm writing a cozy witch mystery was brilliant.

Eric Witchey, your classes always inspire me to write better craft. If only I had been born with a witchy last name like you were. But one can't have everything.

CHAPTER ONE
We're Not in Kansas Anymore, Totoro

The moment I learned I was a powerful witch and destined for a life of magic was the best day of my life. Finally, I had my chance to learn to control my powers at Womby's School for Wayward Witches.

Forget my dream of being a student at Hogwarts when I turned eleven. I was going to be an art teacher at a real magical high school. The administration didn't even mind my lack of experience. I had thought that would be a problem since I hadn't completed my student teaching and didn't have an official teaching license.

Best of all, I would be reunited with my high school sweetheart, Derrick, now that I knew he was here in the Unseen Realm. We would live happily ever after.

Assuming I found him . . . and he didn't hate me.

Cheerful afternoon sunlight filtered through the unshuttered windows of my very own kingdom a.k.a. classroom. It was an immense room with a high ceiling over gray basalt brick walls and beautiful hardwood floors that would make a historian drool. Someone had written: *Welcome, Clarissa Lawrence* on my chalkboard in elegant cursive.

My desk was made from scarred wood that looked as though it had been through battles of Witchkin past. I'd spent the morning scrubbing the walls and floor and wiping down tables and chairs with Lysol and bleach. At last I was ready to feng shui the furniture into a harmonizing environment for student learning and effective classroom management.

My favorite composition of tables, which I'd seen in the Morty Realm, was shaped like a U with the teacher's presentation area at the opening. It felt friendly and democratic. By the time I was finished dragging the tables, my muscles were fatigued and my lower back ached.

Still, there was no rest for the wicked, and that was me.

I tried to tape my posters to the walls, but they kept falling off the uneven stone surface. I didn't expect the stapler to work, but I tried it anyway. Tacks weren't any better. Among my office supplies, I unearthed a roll of duct tape. The custodians at my last school had chewed me out for using duct tape. I didn't want to make the janitors mad, but I didn't know what else to use.

There was one thing I hadn't tried. Magic.

I'd accidentally used magic plenty of times, and without my fairy godmother's potions suppressing my abilities in the Morty Realm where magic hadn't been allowed, I just might be able to do magic. It was unlikely I would accidentally turn anyone into a toad. Students wouldn't be arriving until next week and hardly any staff was on site yet.

The custodians would later thank me for not using duct tape, I told myself.

I stood on the stool and held Picasso's *Guernica* up on the wall. The poster was huge, five feet long, and the cubist-style scene was painted in shades of gray. I focused my will onto the corners where I wanted it to stick. I thought about kissing, since that had set my powers into motion in the past.

It felt like I should say magic words, so I gave it my best. "Abracadabra. Stick to the wall." I enunciated clearly and managed not to say any unintended words after the fiasco of saying "abra-cadaver" last summer.

I let go of the poster. It remained against the wall for about two seconds before falling.

Maybe I needed to rhyme. "Poster, I'm rubber. You're glue. Stick to this wall, witchy-poo." Not my best rhyme, but it was all I could come up with on the spot. For good measure, I added, "Presto chango!"

It remained against the wall. Yes! I was a witch! I stepped down from the stool. Ten seconds later, the poster peeled off the wall and fell on my head. As I tried to grab the poster, it gave me a papercut on my finger. The cut was deep enough that I bled onto the paper.

"Aarrrgh! Gosh darn it!" Under my breath I may have added a few choice swearwords. I jumped onto the stool, held the poster up again, and beat it with my fist. "Stupid! Stupid, poster!" Not exactly magical words, but I felt something shift inside me, like my organs were rearranging themselves. The room shimmered and smelled sharp.

The poster held this time. I hopped off the table and admired my handiwork. Maybe I had to get angry to do magic. Or maybe it was the blood.

I was just about to turn away when the cubist-style bull in the painting shook its head and brayed in anguish. The horse writhed as it trampled a man. A woman wailed, clutching her dead child to her breast. People flailed and screamed, the blocky angles of their bodies shifting and shuffling. The explosion in the background beyond the window in the scene shook the interior of the house. The walls crumbled into geometric shapes and rained down on the people and animals. Crimson dripped through the grays of the painting, splattering man and beast alike.

The painting was about a Spanish town being bombed. I had admired the way Picasso had captured desperation and chaos in his angular and abstract style. Never before had I felt their terror this profoundly. This felt like war. Tears stung my eyes.

The lightbulb in the painting flickered and went dark, but the light outside the window grew so intense it washed everything inside with white. Monochromatic flames lashed at the building and the people in the painting. Pigment leached into the grays, the flames turning yellow and orange. Smoke billowed out of the scene, stretching beyond the edges of the paper.

I was in awe of the magic I had done. Then it sank in. I'd started a fire!

Flames licked the stone wall. Ashes from the poster fell on me. Black smoke clouded up to the high ceiling. The fire turned indigo and devoured the dried moss growing on the wall. On the plus side, it also got rid of the black mold problem.

I looked around the sparse room for something to put out the flames. At the back of the room in the nonfunctional sink was a bucket of water. I ran around my U of tables, snatched it up, and flung it at the wall. There was only enough water to douse a section of fire. It sputtered out only to return in full force a few seconds later. The fire kept spreading. Smoke filled the room.

Holy batwings! I had really done it this time. I could see it now. Fired on day one of my new job.

CHAPTER TWO
Oopsie!

I ran to the door of the classroom, shouting down the stairs. "Help!" I tried to say more, but I choked on a lungful of smoke.

"Merlin's balls. What is that foul stench?" said a man out on the landing. Each word was enunciated in such crisp British I couldn't have mistaken the voice if I'd wanted to.

My spine went rigid. Appearing like an unwelcome smell in a crowded elevator, Professor Felix Thatch pushed his way past me. His nose was aquiline and long, his dark hair shoulder-length and far nicer than mine—he probably used magic on it instead of hairspray—and he would have been handsome if he didn't have a resting bitch face at all times. He watched me through heavily lidded eyes, lazily like a predator might watch prey.

My colleague was the last person I wanted as a witness to my colossal mess-up.

"What do you think you're doing?" he asked in his cool monotone.

I coughed by way of answer. A bubble around him kept the swirling arms of smoke from touching his brown tweed suit. He cracked his knuckles and gestured with his hands. An invisible wind forced the smoke out of the room. My breath was stolen along with it, and I thought of all the science fiction movies I'd watched with people's air supply in their ships being sucked into outer space. He raised his hands at the fire, waggled his fingers, and the blue flames extinguished. The moment he lowered his hands, I gasped in air again. Unfortunately, that was the moment the flames returned twice as high, heat radiating off them like the infernos of hell. More smoke billowed out.

"Bollocks," he muttered.

Considering he was a trained Witchkin, his use of British profanities didn't strike me as the best of signs. I retreated closer to the door, ready to call for help again.

He removed a slender black wand made from twisted wood from his breast pocket and punched it in the air toward the wall. Orange and gold ribbons of water shot out and drowned the blue flames. Another gust of wind pushed the smoke out the windows, and again the air was momentarily sucked from my lungs.

He pointed his wand accusingly at me. "Not only did you manage to set your classroom on fire, but you somehow summoned flames of seraphim, which cannot be put out by normal means. If I hadn't sensed magic at work and investigated, you would have burned the school down."

Right. I guessed this was why I shouldn't do magic. Lesson learned. Duct tape it was.

"Sorry. It was an accident." I wiped soot from my sweaty brow and pushed my hot-pink hair out of my eyes. "Thanks."

The wall was charred and black now. Interestingly, the corners of the poster remained. Even though it was gone, I couldn't stop seeing the horror of *Guernica* in the place it had been.

"I'm tired of hearing about your *accidents*. You're a menace." He slipped his wand into the pocket of his old-fashioned vest and straightened his dark cravat.

I edged away.

"You should never have been hired. Obviously, a mistake has been made." He tugged at the bottom of his suit jacket, imperiously staring down his long nose at me. "You are coming to the principal's office with me."

No mistake had been made, but the truth was more awful than I had imagined.

I sat in the principal's office, my jaw dropping as Jebediah Ebenezer Bumblebub told me the news. Unlit candles rested in a row at the front of his desk, stacks of books, a crystal ball, and assorted vials littered the remaining space. Sunlight filtered in through the Art Deco-style stained glass of the double windows to the right, painting the room in the shifting hues of a rainbow.

"What do you mean, I'm not ready to do magic? I need this." The words spilled from my mouth before I had time to censor myself and sound grateful for my new position as the arts and crafts teacher. "I thought that was the reason I was accepted as a teacher at this school—not just to teach art—so I can learn to control my powers." Besides the fact that it would be nice to actually have sex someday without electrocuting someone, magic was cool.

I wanted to be one of the cool kids. Or teachers, anyway.

The principal sat behind his mahogany desk. He leaned back in a century-old chair that creaked under his weight. "Yep, that's it exactly. You got a lot of learnin' to do." Jeb resembled the stereotypical wizard with his long gray robes, the only difference the bandana peeking out from under his snowy beard and the hat on his head looking more like a Stetson with a cone attached than a witch's hat. "The problem is, *we* ain't ready yet. I never seen the likes of your kind of magic." His accent reminded me of a cowboy from a Western. "Think how dangerous it would be for you to be castin' with wild magic when our students are about. They're an unpredictable mess as it is."

All the excitement and joy of being at the school withered away, leaving me aching and hollow inside. Once again, I was the freaky teacher who didn't fit in. I'd already signed the contract, arrived back at the school days before in-service, and had started getting my classroom ready.

Jeb continued on as I studied the messy expanse around us. His office resembled one-part wizard study, and one-part Old West parlor with Victorian settees and a full bar of liquors most high school students would give anything to pillage. To the left of the desk, a fireplace sat between columns of bookshelves. Various other items were stashed on the shelves haphazardly: kerosene lamps, candles, and other fire hazards among them. If there was such a thing as a fire marshal in the Unseen Realm, I was pretty sure he had missed this room.

What I'd first taken to be a cow skull—but I now suspected might be otherwise—decorated the wall between paintings of men wrangling cattle-sized dragons. From the amount of clutter piled into every corner, the room looked like it doubled as the storage closet for extra supplies.

"So that's it? I get to be here, but not *do* anything?" I asked.

"You were hired on as a teacher, not a student," Felix Thatch said from where he stood by the mantle. Had he been anyone else, I might have found his British accent and good looks sexy. The sour-grapes face he gave me, though, ruined any chance of that.

I wiped soot from my cheek, suddenly feeling self-conscious from the way he eyed me.

The principal chewed on one end of his curly mustache. "That's right, partner. You're here for the teachin'. Everything else is second to that."

Thatch trailed a finger along the ledge of one of the locked glass cases that contained books. "What did you think would happen, we would just hand you magic on a silver platter and allow you to use it?"

Jeb held up a hand. "Whoa, boy. Rein yourself in, eh?"

I was high on Thatch's shit list, possibly because my biological mother, former Headmistress Alouette Loraline, had been his enemy. And possibly because I hadn't made the best of first impressions. Or second impressions.

Jeb looked to me. "Miss Lawrence, allow me to explain."

I fidgeted in the wooden chair across from him.

"I need you to understand, I'd be mighty neglectful of my duties as principal if I didn't ensure the protection of the students at our school. You hain't exactly got a record for harmless, predictable magic."

Thatch tossed his midnight hair back in contempt. "The Morties are fortunate I happened to witness your blunders or else no one would have been present to undo them." He paused with the drama of a thespian. "You're welcome."

"Mortals," Jeb said to me. "Morties is our term for the mundane mortals living in your world."

I nodded. My mom—adoptive mother—had told me that much when she'd explained we weren't biologically related. I'd never suspected we weren't since I had green eyes like Mrs. Abigail Lawrence and red hair—only, I dyed mine pink these days. Now I knew she was my fairy godmother, half-Fae and half-mortal—a Witchkin selected because she looked so much like me.

"It's a mighty rare thing indeed to find a woman twenty-two years of age with more powers than all get-out in the Morty Realm, but sure 'nuff, there you were. Usually by this point, an excess of electronics, cold iron, and synthetic doodads would have weakened and deteriorated a Witchkin's ability to produce magic," Jeb said. "That's if the Fae don't claim a Witchkin first."

Perhaps the drain of electronics was why my adoptive mom had budgeted to buy me a new iPhone for Christmas every year. She hadn't exactly wanted me to embrace my powers. Abigail Lawrence wanted to hide magic from me, fearful I was going to get hurt or draw the attention of Fae who would snatch me up. I'd come to realize neither fear was that farfetched.

Jeb drummed his fingers on a messy stack of papers. "For this reason, we're fixin' to teach you to control your powers and help you find your path in our world."

Thatch snorted. "Even if you risk injuring one of the students or staff, apparently. If I hadn't been there to put out that fire—"

"Lord have mercy! Shut your trap. I heard you the first time." Jeb cast Thatch an annoyed glance. "Who's the sheriff around these parts?"

A sardonic smile tugged at the corners of Thatch's mouth. "Principal. I think you mean, 'Who is the principal?'"

"That's what I said, dagnabbit!" Jeb turned back to me. "Where was I, darlin'?"

"Um. . . ." This was not how I had envisioned my first heart-to-heart conversation with an all-knowing, all-seeing wizard. This must have been what Dorothy had experienced after Toto outed the Wizard of Oz. I prompted, "You want to help me find my path and learn to use my powers?"

"Right. Left unmanaged in the Morty Realm, it would only be a matter of time before your powers harm yourself or others," Jeb said. "The energy within you is a big ol' beacon to any Fae fixin' to snatch up an unregistered Witchkin. We could have drained your powers to keep you safe. We could have sucked you dry of all magic, so that no Fae would ever recognize you or abduct you to become a slave in their court."

The memory of the Raven Queen and how she'd tried to claim me as her tithe—as her sacrifice—made ice race up my spine. She'd been beautiful with her liquid black eyes and a gown made of feathers. The lullaby of her voice had seduced me. The very air around her tasted of candy-coated black magic. By Fae laws, I could have been hers. Not only had I used magic in the Morty Realm, but I'd unwittingly used magic on one of her servants. I still didn't know why she'd allowed me to strike a bargain with her.

I could see why a high school like Womby's existed for the half-breed offspring of Fae and Morties. Witchkin needed a place to learn magic that wasn't in the Morty Realm where it was forbidden. A place to learn to hide from the Fae and protect themselves.

Jeb had given me that chance as well. I lifted my chin. "Thank you, sir." More than anything, I needed magic. I needed to understand who I was. I suspected he understood that. "Thank you for not draining me."

Thatch's voice slithered across the expanse between us, so quiet I almost didn't hear him. "It isn't too late for that."

Jeb grimaced at Thatch. "You, shut it. This ain't my first rodeo." He tugged at one end of his mustache, the curl springing back into place as he turned to me. "You don't want no drainin', so that leaves the other option. You gotta stay in our stronghold, safe from Fae and creatures who would do you harm. We'll teach you to harness your powers, but you gotta hold your horses on the magic part. Learn outside of school hours so your charges ain't put at risk. You'll obey the rules of the Unseen Realm like the rest of us and follow our school rules so you ain't puttin' no one in danger. And from what I understand of your past, courtship is out of the question. We don't want this school to get blown to smithereens from some kind of fertility magic. Can you get behind this?"

"I understand. No boys. I'll follow the rules. Thank you." It was hard to hide the eagerness from my voice. "When can I start learning magic?"

Thatch made an insolent tsk. My face flushed with heat. I did sound like a child.

Jeb arched an eyebrow at him. "Felix, you got a bee in your bonnet?"

He dipped his head in mock apology. "No, Jeb. I never get bees in my bonnet."

"Miss Lawrence has got herself an earnest enthusiasm for learnin'. Bless her heart," the principal said kindly. "That privilege for learnin' has been denied her entire life. Are you objectin' to her right to an education when the time is right?"

"No." Thatch lifted his chin. His voice was even and calm. "I object to her presence at this school. If she follows in the footsteps of her mother, all of us are put in danger. None of the teachers on staff are powerful enough to sense forbidden magic. If I hadn't immediately gone to Miss Lawrence's classroom earlier, she would be dead by now. The school would be burned to ashes. Only a Merlin-class Celestor such as myself has the skill to put out a seraph-fueled fire. Imagine what would have happened had I not been around."

"Thank you kindly for makin' your indispensability so clear." Jeb folded his weathered hands in front of him on the desk. "Sure 'nuff, you are the most powerful and skilled of all teachers at our school. I'm mighty pleased how keen you are on the welfare of our students, and I'm indebted to your unexpectedly selfless concern, Felix."

Thatch slouched against the mantle, arms crossed. His eyes narrowed.

"I agree that somethin' has got to be done to ensure Miss Lawrence don't stumble down some dark rabbit hole of evil. As a department head, you surely have more than enough to do. But seein' you're one of the most powerful Witchkin at this school, and you're fixin' to keep her out of trouble, I'll task you with her education until the school year begins." Jeb hooked his thumbs into his belt, reminding me of a cowboy.

Thatch's face remained a mask of unreadable calm. "If she lasts that long."

"Um," I said, standing up. "Maybe I should focus on my job before I start studying magic. I have a classroom to set up and—"

"Yep," Jeb said. "And then *Merlin* here will see to your learnin'."

The principal could not be serious. Felix Thatch was the one person at the school who shouldn't have been teaching me magic. Maybe Jeb wanted me to fail. Or maybe it was a test. Yes, heroic characters in fantasy novels were always tested.

That settled it. The person who hated me most was about to become my teacher. I would do anything to learn magic. Even this.

CHAPTER THREE
Encounters of the Witchkin Kind

I had hoped that once I came to Womby's, everything would be clear to me: I would understand where I came from and how my powers worked. Now that I knew Derrick, my former best friend and high school sweetheart, was in this realm, I would get to see him. We could be together again, if not romantically then at least as friends, and I would know who my biological mother was and what she had done to make everyone hate her—and me.

No such luck. The rest of the meeting had gone downhill from the moment the principal appointed Thatch as my new mentor. When I asked if they'd had a student named Derrick Winslow five years before, Jeb said student records were confidential. He evaded answering questions about my mother.

I wasn't going to learn to control my powers—or anything else—from a kind and benevolent mentor.

I trudged back to my classroom. One thing I hadn't gotten used to during the two days I'd been at Womby's was all the stairs. To get to my classroom from the principal's office I had to descend three flights of stairs, go into the main passage, pass the seventies-era cafeteria/great hall and hang a left, go down another hall with crumbling plaster that probably contained lead, and up four flights of stairs to the most remote tower in the school. It was the farthest wing from the West Tower where the main office, Jeb's office, and administration facilities were located, and several flights higher than the main levels of classrooms. I tried to look on the bright side. My classroom wasn't that far from my dorm room, only two flights up and a hallway away.

I had learned during student teaching that the fine arts and industrial arts wings were usually the farthest from other classes. On the plus side, that meant micromanaging principals, like the one where I did my internship, were more likely to observe classrooms other than mine. I'd probably have a lot of freedom at this school. On the downside, I got turned around in the twisting passages. I could sort of tell the difference between wings by the eras of architecture and their levels of disrepair.

The great hall and the corridors outside it were ancient and made of stone, resembling a medieval monastery. A more recent addition of converted classrooms were built in a Gothic style with arches and stained glass. Another section resembled Frank Lloyd Wright architecture with the same mold problems associated with his designs. The student and teacher dormitories were reminiscent of a Victorian mansion. Each wing snaked out from the main hall in a different direction, like the legs of a spider. The mishmash of styles built on top of each other reminded me of *Howl's Moving Castle*, only on crack.

I hadn't considered the impractical nature of an old building: a lack of running water in many of the rooms, cracks in the walls that were big enough I could see daylight outside, and how large and difficult it was to navigate. The stone of the hallway was covered with black-and silver-banners— the school's colors. Crests, portraits and trophies decorated the walls. The paintings didn't move like in *Harry Potter*.

Already I felt disappointed with the school's underwhelming magic.

It only took me about twenty minutes to find my classroom this time. I knew I was in the right tower when I smelled the unmistakable odor of bleach and Lysol. After I'd arrived at the school the afternoon before, I'd spent over three hours scrubbing the walls and floor to bring it up to my standards of cleanliness. Though, even standing on one of the sturdier tables to reach higher, I couldn't remove all the splatters and cobwebs from the grimy stone walls. The ceiling had to be twenty feet high.

I grabbed my roll of duct tape and turned to gather up a poster. A looming figure blocked my supplies. Startled, I dropped my duct tape. Thatch smirked.

"Sorry, didn't hear you come in." I laughed in my nervousness. I casually inched back.

"Witchkin do not use nonorganic cleaners and human-crafted disinfectants." He waved a hand at my bucket of cleaning agents. "I can smell those chemicals all the way down in the dungeon."

"This wing has a serious black mold problem." I scurried after the roll of duct tape and slipped my arm through the hole like a bracelet. "And there were dark splatters on the wall that looked a lot like blood. It was unsanitary."

"You should have seen the mess the last teacher left it in before Ludomil set the crew of brownies to cleaning." He eyed the sooty rectangle that remained on the wall where *Guernica* had been.

"Ludomil?" I asked.

"Mr. Ludomil Sokoloff, our head custodian." He said it in his don't-you-know-anything tone. "After the last teacher exploded, it was a gore-fest in here. You're fortunate you didn't arrive a week earlier."

"Exploded?"

He waved at me dismissively. "The former art teacher had a little accident."

My expression must have given away my horror. "What do you mean 'accident?' What happened?"

He smirked. "Let's just say the students were tired of learning about postmodernism and decided to demonstrate their version of a Jackson Pollock painting—with his blood. As you can imagine, it didn't go over well." He shuffled around boxes of my art books and files, glancing through the contents. "They never caught the students who did it."

"That's supposed to be a joke, right?" I fiddled with the roll of duct tape on my arm. Thatch was just trying to scare me, I reasoned. He wanted me to leave the school.

He looked up from the box of posters. His gaze followed the movement of my hand spinning the duct tape around my wrist. I removed the roll and set it on the table. I didn't want him to think it was a grubby, Morty accessory to match my even grubbier jeans and T-shirt, now spotted with bleach stains and cinders.

He unrolled a poster with an Albert Einstein quote, reading it out loud. "'Everybody is a genius. But if you judge a fish by its ability to climb a tree, it will live its whole life believing that it is stupid.'" His nose crinkled up in disgust. "I suppose you think this resembles you. That every child is a special snowflake, and you are the most original, extraordinary flake of them all."

I wasn't going to reward his sarcasm with an answer. "Did the students really attack the last art teacher?"

He eyed the duct tape with a disapproving grimace. "I do hope that is for silencing the students." He lifted it with two fingers as if it were something gross, like his underwear. "You can do as you please, but if Ludomil catches you using any kind of tape on his walls, he'll do more with your blood than splatter it across the walls."

Cheery much?

"How do teachers hang stuff up?"

"Spells, of course." He looked me up and down. "Unless they're you and can't use magic."

What an ass-hat! I would have kicked his behind out the door right then and there if he hadn't been so big and tall and able to hex me with black magic. I crossed my arms.

"Is there something I can help you with?" Or had he left his dungeon of doom just to awe me with his wit?

He pursed his lips. "Headmaster Bumblebub requests that all staff currently on the school grounds attend dinner. For some reason he thinks you'll look forward to meeting the other teachers. Six o'clock sharp in the great hall." He said it with his usual unenthusiastic monotone. "There, I've relayed the message."

I gestured to the clock on the wall that was stuck on twelve thirty. "Speaking of time—"

"Something I have so little of, especially now that I have one more incorrigible student to teach." He turned to go.

I ignored that comment. "Do you know what time it is?" I'd left my phone in my purse in my dorm. "My wristwatch went missing from my nightstand and the one on the wall—"

He sighed in exasperation. "A digital watch, I suppose."

"Yes?"

"See rule three in the student handbook regarding electronics." He started toward the door again.

I had skimmed the handbook. Like every school I'd interned at, students weren't permitted to use electronics. That didn't answer my question.

"Wait! Do you know what time it is?" I asked.

He lifted up the long sleeve of his tweed jacket, glancing at his bare wrist. There was no wristwatch as far as I could see. "Five thirty," he said. "By the way, your first magic lesson is tomorrow morning. Seven o'clock sharp. I will not tolerate tardiness."

Ugh. I soooo didn't want to learn magic from him. Especially not at the butt crack of dawn. But he was my teacher. I would try to make the best of it.

"Seven. Great. Thanks."

"If you have the courage to show up."

That irritating way his eyebrow lifted, his bored indifference, the way he came in and tried to intimidate me about my job—I couldn't take it anymore. "Why are you acting like this? What is your problem?"

"You." He sighed in an overdramatic way one usually expected from teenagers. "It's bad enough I have to teach at the same school as you, but now I have to . . . teach you."

"Look, I know you didn't like my mother, but I'm a different person than she was." Being nice to him was more painful than having teeth pulled, each word a struggle to form, but I gave it my best. "I know you don't want me at your school, but I'm here, so you might as well get used to it. We're going to have to work together."

He ignored my attempt to make peace. "Don't think that because Jeb wishes me to teach you, I'm going to make this easy for you. You are a danger to those around you. The moment Jeb catches you using one of the forbidden arts of pain magic, necromancy, or blood magic. . . ." He glanced at the burnt remains of poster on the wall.

My blood turned to ice. Never had I realized getting a papercut could be so dangerous.

A sinister smile tugged at his lips. "He will insist I drain you of your powers, leaving you as a mortal. It will only be a matter of time before you show your true nature and kill someone. I'll be watching you." His eyes narrowed. "Closely."

I swallowed. On the plus side, he hadn't threatened to turn me into a toad.

CHAPTER FOUR
Sweet Dreams

It wasn't uncommon for me to have bad dreams when I was stressed. Nor was it uncommon to dream of Derrick. When magical things popped up in my life, sometimes my guilty conscience punished me with nightmares of the tornado that had whisked Derrick away. Being at a school for Witchkin, surrounded by people who cast spells, couldn't get more magical. It shouldn't have surprised me I would dream of Derrick.

What surprised me was how real it felt.

I lay in my old bed, in my childhood room, surrounded by My Little Ponies, Strawberry Shortcake, and fairy decorations. Part of me knew this scene wasn't right. That room had been destroyed in the tornado.

Warm sunlight filtered in through the window. An arm slipped around my waist under the Tinker Bell bedspread.

Without even looking, I knew it was Derrick. I snuggled closer to him. He smoothed my hair away from my face and kissed the back of my neck. I wanted to savor this moment, but the incongruity of being an adult in this bed tickled my mind.

"This is how I always imagined it would be." His voice was slightly deeper than I remembered.

I turned to look at him, wanting to confirm it was truly Derrick. His blue hair was shorter than the last time I'd seen him in real life, his face leaner and older. He grinned, a mischievous twinkle in his eyes as he leaned closer and kissed me.

That kiss was like falling into the embrace of warm water. I allowed the current to sink me deeper. The tension in my muscles melted away. He squeezed me to him, his fingers sweeping against my naked arm.

Holy cow! I was naked. It was going to be one of those dreams. . . .

I wanted this to be real, but I knew it wasn't. Derrick had never stayed the night in my bed. The one time he had been there briefly in high school was after my sister had spiked my drink with alcohol and he'd put me to bed. He'd told me he would talk to me in the morning, and he would kiss me again if I still wanted to another time. He'd been too much of a gentleman to stay the night. Plus, my parents would have freaked if they'd found him in my bed.

I pulled away just enough to see the vivid azure of his eyes reflecting the brilliance of a thousand cloudless skies. He was so handsome, more so than I remembered.

"This never happened," I said.

"Not yet."

"But it will? When?"

The old mischief returned to his eyes. "When you find me."

"How? When?"

"When the time is right. After you've broken the curse." He rubbed the back of my hand against the rough stubble on his cheek.

"What curse? Your curse? Do I need to rescue you?" I asked.

"No, rescue yourself first. Find out about Alouette Loraline."

My biological mother.

He leaned closer. "One more kiss."

He covered my face with kisses that brushed against my flesh like butterfly wings. His fingers whispered over my shoulders and throat and breasts. A breeze tickled my hair against my neck, bringing with it the perfume of faraway places. He kissed me, and it was like that night when he'd kissed me in real life.

My belly fluttered with magic.

The breeze blew harder. Goosebumps rose on my arms. I knew what was coming. Dread settled in my stomach like a lump of lead, crushing the pleasant sensations of magic that had been swelling. Wind blustered against the covers. I turned my face away from the fury of air. One of the dolls on the shelf fell to the floor. Books crashed from the bookcase. I twisted to hold on to Derrick. I wasn't going to let him go this time. The tornado would not take him away from me like it had in real life.

When I looked again at his face, it was no longer Derrick. It was Felix Thatch.

I flinched back. Wind whipped around us. Stuffed animals flew across the room. The walls groaned like they were about to be torn apart.

Thatch smiled. "Draining your powers doesn't have to be unpleasant." He pulled me closer. His lips inched toward mine.

I screamed.

My own screaming must have woken me. I sat up in the darkness, disoriented until I remembered I was in my new room in the women's dormitory at Womby's. I was sweating buckets and panting. It had started off as such a happy dream. Why did it have to end with Thatch? Sure, my subconscious probably found him alluring in that sexy, off-limits professor sort of way, but there was no way in hell I would want to kiss him in real life.

He wanted to drain me of all magic.

I hugged my knees, remembering Derrick. What had he said exactly? His words were hard to grasp with the more ominous shock of Thatch afterward. I had some kind of curse to break. He didn't want me to look for him. Was this an actual message from him or one from my subconscious mind?

Three seconds later, pounding thundered against my door. I snatched up the cell phone from underneath my pillow and activated the flashlight.

"Who's there?" I asked.

"Felix Thatch. Who else?" he snapped.

His timing was uncanny. I prayed this had nothing to do with the dream. I really didn't want to talk to him right now.

Wait a minute. Had I missed my magic lesson? I glanced at the shutters. No light showed through. It couldn't be seven o'clock. I considered changing the app on my phone so I could see the time, but the ray of light coming from the screen made me feel safe against the bogeyman of my nightmares.

"Open this door," Thatch said.

I looked down at my pink Disney princess tank top and shorts. "Um, I'm not decent."

"I'm not going to shout at you through a block of wood."

No, he'd probably shout in my face.

"Okay. Coming." I grabbed my sweater draped over the chair at the desk and pulled it over my head. I hugged the cell phone to my chest as though it might shield me from his wrath.

I hesitated at the door. "Are you going to drain me?"

The air tingled around me, tasting like electricity and starlight. The wood creaked and groaned ominously. I jumped back. It flung open, smashing against the stone wall with a loud crack. He held his black wand in his hand, light glowing as brightly as a ninety-watt bulb. He wore a tweed suit, his hair as immaculate as ever.

The door leaned crooked against the wall, the bottom hinges barely hanging on to the wood.

"What the bloody hell do you think you're doing?" he demanded.

I flinched back. "Sleeping."

He jabbed an accusing finger at me. "You stay out of my head and stay out of my dreams."

"No, you stay out of *my* dreams."

"I wouldn't be in your dreams if your subconscious didn't pull me into them. Learn to control yourself."

"But how? I don't know how to do magic. You're supposed to teach me."

"You're going to release unspeakable evils upon the school and murder people just like your mother did." He turned away, muttering to himself. "The only difference between you two is she could teach."

I ignored the insults. "Hey, are you going to fix my door?"

He didn't answer.

It wasn't like Mr. Dramatic Entrance had needed to magic it open. I hadn't locked it. I hadn't thought I would need to. Now I did.

CHAPTER FIVE
Daughter of a #$%itch

My cell phone alarm went off at six o'clock. A few minutes later, I realized my iPod was missing from my nightstand. Someone was stealing my things. It wouldn't have surprised me if Thatch had done so in the middle of the night after breaking down the door just to make my life one more level of difficult. I probably would have lost my cell phone too if I hadn't tucked it under my pillow.

I hadn't found an outlet for it in my room yet, and I was going to need to recharge my phone soon. I would rather have poked my eyes out than ask Thatch where to find an outlet. I figured I could ask one of the other teachers I had met at dinner the night before. It was hard to imagine I was missing it, though. The outlets had to be hidden with magic. This school was hardcore about keeping electronics off-limits to students.

My room reminded me of something a schoolmarm might have lived in two hundred years ago. Two single beds shared a nightstand that held an oil lamp and nubs of candles. An empty bookshelf hung above each bed. Two wardrobes filled the space across from the foot of each bed. I'd chosen the bed farthest from the window and placed a few things on the desk underneath the window. The walls were gray stone, and the beds wood with gray sheets on top. It was the kind of colorless, blah room that could drive an art teacher crazy. I had to do something about it soon.

I dressed and prepped in the restroom down the hall that I would be sharing with the other female teachers in this wing, and then wandered the twisting Victorian passageways into the main corridor and down to a kitchen built by hobbits if size was any indication of who worked there. Only being four foot ten, I fit right in.

On the other hand, I really wished the kitchen had been stocked with

Pop-Tarts, granola bars, or some other kind of instant food. No one was there, but breakfast was half prepared on plates as if ready to set out. I sat at a stool at the table, eating a slice of toast I slathered with blackberry jam. The bread was dense, like the yeast hadn't risen properly, and the jam was tart, but it was still more edible than dinner had been the night before. Any minute now I expected a kitchen maid to come in and finish preparing the meal. When she didn't, I left and took my toast with me to munch on the way to the dungeon.

I arrived at Thatch's room five minutes early, hoping to show my teacher how eager and willing I was to learn. He sat at his desk, writing in a black leather book. He didn't crack a smile when I walked in.

The "magic lesson" consisted of a stack of books on the antiquity of the school and the history of Witchkin that I was to read before school started so I would know more than the new students.

"Read the book on lucid dreaming first." Thatch tapped the smallest book on the top of the stack. "I will not tolerate an uncontrolled subconscious mind."

Right. Neither of us wanted another pornado dream.

Coming up from the dungeon, I paused on the landing before the ground floor, resting the stack of books on the banister. Movement out of the corner of my eye caught my attention. My gaze fell on the nearest portrait, one painted in a Neoclassical style.

A woman in a pointed hat and a high-necked gown reminiscent of the Victorian era stared out from the painting. She was tall and regal, her cheekbones high and her nose elegantly sloped. She wore an emerald snake across her shoulders like a feather boa. The head of the reptile reared up with the jaws open to bite a raven gliding into the frame. Another serpent spiraled around her arm, the contrast of green with her black sleeve creating an undulating pattern that reminded me of my striped stockings. Her smile was mischievous, her eyes the pale green of an icy pond. Her fair features were startling against the midnight of her hair.

She held herself with a confident serenity, despite the way the animals around her attacked each other. That was the kind of witch I wanted to be: the calm in a stormy sea of chaos. The slight lift to her chin hinted at a strong will and a defiance she wasn't afraid to let others see. I was like that. I wanted to be a great and powerful witch.

Rembrandt would have applauded the way the artist used the lighting to make the woman's face glow. Transparent washes had been used to capture the subtle hues of veins and blood in the skin tone. The artistry was masterful, though I couldn't find an artist's signature.

When I looked away from the portrait, I would swear the snakes were slithering in the painting, but when I looked at it directly they remained still.

"The resemblance is uncanny," a voice said to my right.

I jumped. I hadn't heard the teacher come up from behind me. "Professor Rohin. . . ." Shoot! I couldn't remember the rest of his name. He wore a navy-blue turban and the kind of full beard that would make a lumberjack envious. I guessed he was middle-aged, if Witchkin aged like normal humans. I'd met him briefly the night before at dinner.

"Darshan Rohiniraman. Everyone calls me Professor Ro, or Pro Ro." He leaned closer. "Even the teachers at my last school."

A nervous laugh escaped my throat. He stood a little closer than I was comfortable with. I discreetly shifted the books on the banister and scooted back. Maybe it was the turban, but I had a hard time not imagining Professor Quirrell from Harry Potter.

"I take it you're related?" he asked, nodding to the picture.

"Well, I don't know." I swallowed. "Is that. . . ?" I studied the face. Was it like my own face?

"Former Headmistress Alouette Loraline." He looked from me to the painting again. "She was your mother?"

"That's what they tell me." Out of the corner of my eye I caught movement from the painting again. It was the raven. I would swear it had moved.

Pro Ro scratched his beard. "You never met her then?"

"No." Yet, the moment I'd gazed at this portrait, I had thought she was beautiful, confident, and powerful, all qualities I wanted as a witch. Somehow I'd missed the evil vibe until now. The all-black attire, raven, and snakes that gave her a sinister air should have been a giveaway.

"I hear she was a formidable woman. I never encountered her up close myself." He eyed me with open curiosity. "Pardon my asking, but what made you decide to seek employment at Womby's of all places, at her former school?"

"What do you mean? Why wouldn't I?"

"She died here, didn't she? Or disappeared under mysterious circumstances, rather."

"So, she might still be alive?" I thought of Derrick. He had disappeared mysteriously—if one considered a tornado mysterious. The idea of seeing him made me feel hopeful. I wasn't sure what to think about my mother. If what everyone said about her was true, the idea of meeting her someday shouldn't have sparked such joy in me, but I couldn't help it. I wanted to know who she was and where I came from.

"Pardon my saying so, but I should hope, for all our sakes, she isn't alive," Pro Ro said. "I think we all have our theories on what may have happened to her. She made people's lives miserable here when she *turned*."

"Turned?"

"To the dark side."

I laughed. "You make her sound like Darth Vader."

"I imagine she made quite a few enemies. I can only guess how unwelcome you must feel."

I shook my head. I was not going to be the unpopular teacher. I'd already experienced my fair share of being an outcast in high school. Things were supposed to be different now that I was an adult. I was with my peeps. Surely they would see I was one of them. Eventually.

Pro Ro readjusted his turban. "I saw how warmly Mrs. Keahi treated you yesterday at dinner. Professor Thatch and Ludomil weren't much better."

That was an understatement. Ludomil Sokoloff, the head custodian, had refused to talk to me. Mrs. Keahi, the elderly secretary, delighted in informing me my budget for art supplies was twenty-five dollars and I would be out of a job next semester if the school didn't receive more funding from the generous pockets of rich Witchkin families.

"Julian Thistledown and I had an interesting conversation about Professor Thatch last night." Pro Ro waggled his eyebrows and stepped closer. "And his relationship with your mother."

"No way!" He could not be saying what I thought he was.

Pro Ro leaned in closer. "Apparently, he was quite the teacher's pet. Or headmistress's pet."

Ew. I puked in my mouth a little. It was bad enough I found him attractive and I didn't want to, but the idea he might have been my mother's lover was icky. That made my pornado dream almost incestuous. What if he was my father?

The stabbing sensation I'd felt in my lower abdomen the night before during dinner returned in full force. Was Pro Ro the cause? I'd been seated next to him at dinner.

He scratched his beard as he looked from me to the stairs. I'd been so distracted by our barf-worthy conversation I hadn't heard the voices.

Felix Thatch strolled with another teacher up the stairs, speaking in a hushed voice. The history teacher, Julian Thistledown, was simultaneously bookish and brawny. As golden rays of sunlight splashed onto the hunky beefcake in his gold-and-turquoise robes, he glittered like a vampire in a Stephanie Meyers novel. His beauty stole my breath away as much as it had the first time I'd met him.

"I'm just saying she isn't—" Julian halted when he saw me. He cleared his throat. "Miss Lawrence, we were just talking about you. My, aren't you a ray of sunshine, as always." He attempted to smile, but he looked too flustered to manage a genuine one. "I found a few sets of colored pencils in my classroom, and I was telling my department head—" He cast an annoyed glance at Thatch. "—how much I thought you would appreciate them, especially considering how limited the art budget is. But he said the rules are to turn them in to my department."

Thatch gripped the colored pencils in his hands, his knuckles white. "If a teacher comes to me with additional supplies to share, I am to divide them between other teachers in *my* department. You can ask your department head if she has come across extra supplies for you. We have separate budgets."

Just when I thought Thatch couldn't get any worse I had to hear this. For the freakin' love of God, would it have killed him to give me those colored pencils? This wasn't about me. It was about the students. Didn't he see that?

I seriously hoped he wasn't my father. There was no way I wanted to be related to such a despicable man.

CHAPTER SIX
Spider Faux Pas

I kept forgetting my classroom wouldn't have a computer. Even a Stone Age computer that ran on magic would have been fine. All I needed it for was to take attendance, enter grades, and calculate the math for the grades for me, send in referrals, send updates to parents, and design worksheets. Doing research on the internet would have been a nice addition. Not to mention all my lesson plans were stored in Google Docs, and I'd just learned how to use Google Classroom. Without the internet, I would be spending hours recreating lessons, my syllabus, and warm-ups instead of studying magic.

I'd never been to a school that hadn't provided a desktop and internet access to the teachers. I had left my laptop at my mom's house, along with everything else I couldn't fit into the two suitcases for my dorm and the three boxes for my classroom. Dust covered the previous teacher's hanging file folders in the corner. I would probably need more.

I resumed cleaning and preparations from the day before, working like a madwoman. If I didn't get this done before the other teachers arrived, they would have even more reason to think I was inexperienced and didn't know what I was doing—both of which would be true.

Josie Kimura, one of the other teacher's I had met at the staff dinner the night before, swung by at noon. Her loose, bohemian-style dress, patched together out of orchid and mauve fabrics, matched the purple streak in her black hair. She was only a few inches taller than I was, but her lavender witch's hat gave her the illusion of height. Her ample bosom was endowed with the kind of generous curves I lacked.

She greeted me with a friendly smile. "Hey, girl. Jeb said you might need some help getting set up." She removed her black rimmed glasses and wiped them off before replacing them on her nose. They made her look like a hipster version of Velma from Scooby-Doo.

"Yes! Thank you," I said. "Do you have time to help me hang up some art?"

She slid a wand made from blond wood out of her long sleeve and pointed at my pile of posters. "Show me where these bad boys go."

I held up a poster of Gustav Klimt's *The Kiss* and pointed to the spot I wanted it. She muttered a string of magic words, her brow furrowing in concentration. The incantation sounded Japanese, and she looked Asian, but she'd said she was from Seattle. I knew from watching too much anime with Derrick that her last name meant "tree" in Japanese. I wondered if she was like my fairy godmother and had a tree affinity.

I tried to memorize the incantation, but it was too long. The poster floated out of my hands and wobbled through the air to the wall.

Her magic smelled like lavender and baking bread. I tasted juniper. My senses suddenly got all confused. Purple spots danced in front of my eyes. Was this what magic was supposed to feel like?

In ten minutes Josie made my room look more like an art teacher's classroom. She even removed the remnants of *Guernica* from the wall, no questions asked. By the time she was done, the perfume of flowers and cozy home smells masked the odor of smoke and Lysol.

Next on my list. "Where are the outlets for the overhead and computer and. . . ."

The mortified expression on her face stopped me.

"What?" I asked.

"There are no outlets. Electricity robs us of our powers."

I pulled my cell phone out of my pocket. "It's off. Don't worry. I know I'm not supposed to use it in the classroom. But I need someplace to recharge it."

She snatched it out of my hand and shoved it back into my pocket. "Don't let anyone see that. Do you know what they'll do if they catch you?" She glanced over her shoulder as if someone might pop into my doorway at that exact second. "That's like bringing a knife to school."

"I just thought those rules were for the kids." When I'd done my internship as a student teacher, I'd always been discreet about using a cell phone. My former school had advised teachers to be good role models by keeping electronics out of sight.

She shook her head at me. "It'll majorly suck away your powers."

Jeb had touched on this the day before, but I hadn't realized how serious of a problem it was. This probably explained why I had always caused electronics to malfunction, whether it was an ATM having a power surge or my vibrator dying at the most inopportune moments.

Josie bit her lip. She leaned in closer. "I tell you what. Today, we'll go into town and get some lunch instead of eating the cafeteria crap they serve here. I'll show you where teachers charge phones and use computers."

"Really? So, I might be able to print out my lesson plans?" My future brightened with hope.

She placed a finger to her lips. "I wasn't the one who told you. Got it?"

Josie was my hero!

She turned toward the door on the far end of the room. "Did they give you a key for the door to the back stairwell? It leads to a supply closet."

"No."

"Of course they didn't." She clucked her tongue. "We'll see if we can sweet-talk it out of the secretary. Ali Keahi is either your best friend or worst enemy, and it's better to be on her good side."

Right. I had a suspicion which side I'd already found myself on.

Josie took out her magic wand again and jabbed it into the keyhole of the door. She muttered under her breath, and it swung open. The air smelled fresh and clean, like springtime in the garden.

"You're going to want to keep this door locked," she said. "If you don't, students will steal your supplies. Jorge—the previous teacher—he was always going on about that last year, not that there was much to steal. Of course, teachers will steal stuff too."

This didn't sound any different from my previous school.

We squeezed down a narrow set of stairs, Josie chatting away about her lack of textbooks. The purple glow of Josie's wand lit the way. On a landing one floor below my classroom, we found another locked door. The stairs continued on into a gloom of uninviting shadows.

I pointed to the bounty of spiderwebs that would have made a giant spider from a J. R. R. Tolkien novel jealous. "What's down there?" I asked.

Josie waved a hand toward the stairs that led to the abyss below. "Vega Bloodmire's classroom is two floors below, and she has storage right below your closet. I think the stairwell keeps going down to the dungeon, but I don't know for sure. One time Jorge convinced me to try the passage with him. We made it as far as Vega's closet before she chased us off, accusing us of stealing her supplies."

Note to self: never descend into the spiderwebs of doom. I had ninety-nine problems already. I didn't need anyone with a name like *Bloodmire* accusing me of stealing her class supplies to be one of them.

Josie tapped the wooden door on the landing with her wand and it popped open. A filthy window let in hardly enough light to see. Shelves lined the stone walls of a walk-in closet. It was dusty, and I tore through cobwebs to get to the stacks of sketchbooks. An assortment of paintbrushes filled coffee cans. A single Tupperware tub contained a variety of broken pencils, colored pencils, and nubs of crayons. All my lessons relied on having a classroom with scissors, glue, tempera paint, acrylics,

28

watercolors, and other supplies. I felt overwhelmed by how much work I was going to have to do redesigning my curriculum. How was I going to study to be a proficient witch and be a rock star teacher at the same time?

Josie blew on a stack of dusty paper. There were about twenty pads of paper, not enough for all the students. Unless I had very small classes.

"How many students are in each class?" I asked.

"It depends on the year. Usually about thirty. Sometimes fewer. You can pick up your schedule from Mr. Puck's office today."

Thirty was a dream come true! While student teaching, my classes at Hamlin Middle School had contained up to forty. Classes in Skinnersville School District ranged anywhere from thirty-five to forty-five. There hadn't even been enough seats for all the high school students in classes I'd observed.

On one of the shelves across from the paper, looking very lonely, was a case of white chalk. Corpses of beetles littered the shelf below and dead flies lined the windowsill. My only magic weapon, Lysol, would be coming to this location soon.

I stood on tiptoe to view the desolate emptiness of the top shelves. "So that's it?"

"Once the budget was used up, Jorge went to thrift shops and garage sales to find cheap supplies to buy with his own money. He told me he got this from an estate sale." She waved a hand at the chalk, her fingers tangling in a cobweb. "He let the kids draw on the back wing of the school until they started drawing penises all over the place. Then he tried mud pie art. Jorge was really into art history and tried to use that to fill the majority of the time, but the kids hated it." She made a face. "You can imagine how *great* it is to teach them Morty Studies when they already have a heavy load in their History of Magic classes."

"That's what you teach? Morty history?"

"Yeah, Mortal Studies to each grade, plus one elective and home room." She swept a spiderweb off her hat.

I remembered what Thatch had said about Jorge's accident. "Is it true Jorge was attacked by students? Thatch implied they murdered him."

"Yeah, I don't know about murder. I mean, they did hex Jorge to get out of class, but that isn't abnormal. The thing is, Jorge was a grown adult. If nothing else, he could perform his wards. It would have taken powerful magic to cause him to explode. Dark magic."

"Something a Merlin-class Celestor could do?" I asked, thinking of Thatch.

She tapped her wand against a shelf. Spurts of lavender and rose fragrance shot out with each tap. "If I recall correctly, Thatch was the one who found him. Or what remained of him."

"Whoa! And no one suspected him?"

"That's a pretty heavy accusation toward a teacher. Jeb interviewed everyone with our dean of discipline, Mr. Khaba—Thatch included—but they concluded it must have been a student spell gone wrong. Kids dabbling in dark arts and whatnot."

I shivered. What had I gotten myself into? "So, what's the deal with the kids here? Is this the equivalent of a Title One school? Or worse?"

She leaned closer. "Kids are at Womby's for one of two reasons. The first is because they're poor or orphaned and there's no one to pay the school fee. We're a charity school."

"Why didn't Jeb just say that when I'd asked him about it the first time?" He'd been evasive at dinner. I'd let my imagination go wild. A charity school was noble.

A spider scuttled across the shelf, and I shifted back.

Josie shrugged. "The other kids are here because they flunked out of the nicer schools, either because of bad behavior or academics. Kids are safe—mostly—while they're at school, but after they graduate and don't live here, they're no longer under a school's magical protection." She dragged the pale wood of her wand against the grimy window, removing a panel of dust with a yellow glow. The air tasted of lemon. Golden light filtered in, brightening the closet and stairwell.

"The children need our mark so the Fae will agree not to touch them until they've come of age. If they graduate from here, they still officially have our mark. Think of it like a diploma. That's usually enough to keep them safe, but really it's up to the kids to fend for themselves—if they've developed the powers to be able to do so. They still have to be able to get a job and figure out a way to survive in the Unseen Realm. Some of them have just enough magic to be enticing to goblins and dark creatures, but not enough to protect themselves—and not enough sense to resist the lure of black magic. Some of them know they're dunces, so they choose to have their powers removed and go back to the Morty world."

"I can't imagine going back to normal life after this." I waved my hand, to show I meant the school, and got tangled in spiderwebs.

"Yeah, magic has its perks." She laughed, the sound high and sweet like Tinker Bell. "And drawbacks too."

I was starting to understand enough of this world for it all to make sense. "So, the reason these kids are snatched up by the Raven Court is the same reason I might be? I don't have a permanent mark of protection and because I can't do magic yet?"

"That's one way to think of it. You didn't graduate from an accredited school that teaches you the magic you need to stop them. It's their right to take the untrained and unclaimed. Well, I don't know if I would say a *right*, but within the law. The Witchkin community lets them collect unregistered Witchkin in the Morty world as a tithe. If we didn't let them collect any tithes, it would be all-out war."

My fairy godmother had worked hard all my life to make sure my magic stayed hidden so I wouldn't be collected as a tithe. Every time I'd unwittingly used magic in my teenage years, I could have called the Fae to me. If it hadn't been for all the telephone poles and cell phones, they might have snatched me up. It had only been a matter of time before my accidental magic caught their attention.

Josie leaned against a shelf, continuing on about the school and past tithes of students. She spoke casually about it, as if this was a normal part of this world.

"Why do teachers just let the Fae snatch the graduates if they aren't ready to face Fae?" I asked. These children were being stolen away and enslaved. Eaten? I thought about that creepy scene in *The Matrix* when the machines had fed on humans like organic batteries.

She shrugged. "You can only hold a kid back so many times. The graduation rate is abysmal. We can't afford to keep them indefinitely."

In some ways, this wasn't any different from a regular high school, only if our students at Womby's failed to meet the minimum graduation requirements, they didn't get food stamps or live in their parents' basements until they were thirty.

They died.

The whole system disgusted me. If this was the way the Witchkin community worked, I could see why my fairy godmother had rejected it. My mom—adoptive mom—had told me some of this, but it had been overwhelming to take it all in at the time. I was starting to feel like a sponge that couldn't hold any more information.

Josie waved a wand over a dusty shelf, pushing the dirt into the corner. Earthy notes of fragrance, like flowers and fruit trees, tickled my nose.

"So, those kids who are orphaned. . . . Where are they during the summer?" I asked.

"There are a couple of summer camps. Well, I think they're work camps from what the kids say. The Amni Plandai don't seem to mind the farm camps, but the ones run by the dwarves and gnomes are the worst because they make the teenagers work in mines."

"That's horrible!"

"Tell me about it. But what can we do, right? We're just teachers." She grimaced. "As a kid, I never understood why so many teachers got burnout and stopped caring. But now, well, I get it."

An arachnid with a body the size of a quarter and the hairiest legs I'd ever seen crawled over Josie's shoulder, standing out against the pale purple fabric.

"Spider!" I said with an undignified shriek and knocked it from her shoulder.

She jumped back and looked around. "Where is he?"

I hopped up and down, pointing to where it clung to the wall. "There!"

I snatched up one of the dusty pads of paper and threw it, but the spider scuttled away. It was the kind of giant, nasty spider that journalists photographed in the Amazon right before it bit them and they died. There was an ominous red mark on the abdomen. I suspected it was a black widow.

I lifted another drawing pad.

"No!" Josie screamed, placing herself between me and the spider. "What was that for? You could have killed him."

"That's what I was going for."

She scooped up the spider and brought it to the windowsill. Her fearlessness of a poisonous spider was impressive. She struggled with the latch before using her wand to open it and set the spider outside.

She turned back to me.

"That was a spider," she said through clenched teeth. Her cute, perky voice was replaced by something dark and demonic. "We are Witchkin. We value *all* life. We don't kill spiders. Black widow lives matter."

A nervous giggle escaped my lips. Did she have any idea how offensive that joke was to minorities? Her eyes narrowed. Oh, she was being serious.

I stood there feeling awkward and uncomfortable. The ridiculousness of her anger made me want to laugh even harder. Really? *All* lives mattered? Except orphaned Witchkin who couldn't use magic. I didn't say it out loud, though. I didn't need one more enemy.

"I'm sorry," I said. "I'm still learning about being a witch."

So far, Josie had been nicer to me than anyone else. I wondered if I'd ruined my chances of being friends with her. I could have kicked myself at how impulsive and stupid I was. Of course witches would like spiders. Duh. It was as if I'd never seen any Halloween decorations before.

Josie cleared her throat, sounding more like herself. "Yeah, well, don't let it happen again."

The warning in her voice told me there would be hell to pay if I freaked over a spider again in her presence. I hoped I hadn't trampled the germinating seed of our friendship.

CHAPTER SEVEN
Unexpected Visitors

Josie was polite as she showed me around the school, but the friendliness that had been there was gone. I kept trying to think of some way to regain the camaraderie we'd had only minutes before, but I was failing.

She took me downstairs to the main hall, and we walked to the West Tower. This was the Art Deco section of the school where Jeb's office was located. The closet outside the counseling rooms contained office supplies.

"Do we have a magical copy machine?" I asked.

"It's on the tour." Her tone was sharp.

She escorted me to the storage room in the basement where I could find tables and chairs if I needed them. The furniture graveyard was piled with broken chairs and desks stacked up against walls. The mess made Jeb's office look organized in comparison.

Upstairs, she showed me a dingy staff room painted in avocado green, a copy room, and a custodial office and closet. She demonstrated how to work the copy machine, a giant contraption closer to a steam-powered printing press than a modern-day device.

"You aren't Elementia—an elemental—so you're going to have to wait for the water to heat up underneath. And you're going to have to hand-crank it," she said with a frown.

A spider scuttled across the machine as she showed me how to use the handle.

I pointed. "There's an itsy-bitsy spider about to get crushed."

That turned her frown upside down. "Well, aren't you a cute little fella?" She picked it up and set it on the floor. She cooed at it like it was a puppy.

"I didn't try to kill it this time," I said.

Her smile was weak. "True. Maybe there's hope for you."

Yes! I had said something that hadn't made someone hate me.

"What's next on the agenda? Do they have schedules printed out yet?" I asked.

Josie showed me the way back to counseling.

Thatch blocked the doorway of the office. "Ladies," he said in a lackluster monotone. He stepped aside and bowed, waving his hand at the door for us to enter.

Josie rolled her eyes.

"Teaching karate again this year, Miss Kimura?" Thatch asked.

Her face turned red. "Just because I'm Japanese doesn't mean I know every martial art on Earth. God!"

"Jeb thought so last year. Maybe he'll have you teach kung pao instead this year."

My eyes went wide. I could not believe him.

"Shut up!" she said. "That's a food, not a martial art!"

"*You kon zahui,*" he said with a bow.

She clenched her fists. "That's Chinese, not Japanese. I don't speak Mandarin."

A small smile tugged at his lips. "It's all the same. *Zai lianxi.*"

From the way her eyes widened and narrowed at his Chinese, I suspected she knew exactly what he was saying—even if she wasn't willing to admit it. Josie reached into her sleeve and flourished her wand. Purple glittered in the air.

"Really? You're going to hex me on school grounds?" He tossed back his long hair. "And with so little provocation, no less. Is that how you lost your position at your last school?"

"No!" The flush in her cheeks drained. "I-I voluntarily left my old school because I wanted to work with at-risk youth, not because I was fired."

"That's what they all say." He glided out of the room, a smirk on his lips.

Apparently, I wasn't the only one he felt the need to pick on.

Josie kicked the wall and growled. According to Josie, Witchkin might have been all about valuing spiders' lives and being one with nature, but they didn't have a problem being assholes to each other.

The layout of the counseling office reminded me of every other one I'd been to, with a waiting area on one side of a counter and offices beyond. Josie led me past the front desk. I glanced into the first room. A man sat cross-legged in a Zen garden. Sunshine shone down from a skylight, bathing the man in golden light. Bright Post-it notes flew around his head in a tornado. Papers shuffled and unshuffled themselves on the ground.

Josie pressed a finger to her lips and kept going. "Come on, Puck is busy with schedules."

Aisles of file cabinets that looked like they went on for miles filled the next room. "The student schedules of Christmas past," she said.

She waved me down to the next room. Past a conference table with archaic, anti-ergonomic chairs made of wood was a chalkboard. Each teacher's name was written on a giant grid, with the subjects handwritten underneath. A magnet stuck an envelope with each teacher's name on it to the board.

My schedule consisted of three classes of beginning level art, and two intermediate art. It showed second semester would be three classes of beginning level, one intermediate and one advanced. Each day I had one prep. First-period homeroom was crossed off.

"A paper schedule will be inside the envelope." Josie opened hers.

A handwritten version inside the envelope included a bell schedule. I would have odd periods on A days and even periods on B days. A rotating block schedule wasn't too different from my previous experience teaching ninety-minute periods. Maybe I wouldn't hate ninety-minute classes if it was my own curriculum.

At the bottom of the envelope was a chocolate bar wrapped in brown paper. Scrawled across it were the words: "Puck's Chocolate Prophecy."

Josie opened hers and bit in. She leaned against the wall and moaned. "It's so creamy and smooth and sweet. It isn't anything like last year's chocolate. Yesterday I had known things were going to be better as soon as Thatch told me I got my own dorm room. The chocolate just confirms it!"

I set down my envelope on the table and peeled back the bar, examining it. "What do you mean? How does this work?"

"Puck gifts us with chocolate at the beginning of the school year. It's his way of divining what kind of semester we're going to have. Last year mine was salty and sour. It got sweeter at the end of the bar, just like the semester did."

I peeled back the wrapping, examining the bar. It was thicker than her bar and coated in salt crystals.

She nodded. "Salty because you're going to cry a lot. Unless those are sugar crystals. If that's the case, it means it's going to be really sweet." Her eyebrows rose expectantly. "Well?"

I set down my envelope and papers. I wasn't sure I wanted to know how my year was going to turn out. Still, if this was the tradition at the school, who was I to refuse it? Plus, chocolate was chocolate.

I broke off a square and placed it on my tongue. Flavor exploded in my mouth. It was so salty and bitter, tears sprang to my eyes. I tasted misery. The chocolate was dark but had a high enough fat content it melted on my tongue. The outer chocolate wasn't sweet at all. The caramel center was sweet, though. Too sweet. The sugary caramel mixed with the bitter chocolate and they balanced each other.

"Dark chocolate and salted caramel," I said. "I guess that means it will be a year of extremes."

Craptacular. It tasted like high school. Why couldn't I have the creamy chocolate that represented fitting in with the other teachers and being liked by my students? What if Thatch was right and I turned out to be exactly like my mother?

"Puck does this each semester," Josie said. "Except last year, second semester, everyone's chocolate got all mixed up because *someone* opened everyone's envelope and switched them." Her nose scrunched up in the same way it did when she was in Thatch's presence. I had a feeling I knew who had played that trick.

"What a jerk!" I said.

"Tell me about it. I walked in on him switching the bars around and gave him a piece of my mind. A lot of good it did me. He'd already eaten my chocolate, that bag of dicks." She removed the papers from my envelope and compared it to the list on the board. "They messed up your schedule. This is always happening. It says you aren't teaching a homeroom, but you are. Everyone has homeroom."

I pointed to one of the names on the whiteboard. "She isn't."

"Grandmother Bluehorse is different. She's a department head." She pointed to all the names with stars next to them. "They only have to teach five classes because the other period is spent in meetings with teachers, parents, and students."

It looked like our department heads were Amadea Kutchi, Ethel Bluehorse, Jackie Frost and Felix Thatch. If the color coding meant anything, it looked like my department head was the P.E. teacher, Amadea Kutchi. Josie wasn't so lucky.

"Thatch is your department head?"

She answered with a groan and a nod.

I examined Thatch's schedule. "I thought you said department heads don't teach homerooms."

She walked the length of the board to study his schedule and then walked back to mine. "Huh. You don't have homeroom. He does. That gives him six instead of five. No wonder he was in such a pissy mood when we met him in the hallway."

She grinned. "Isn't that something? He got your homeroom! Jeb must like you."

"Yeah, great."

I wanted to be happy and count my blessings like I'd always been taught to do. Still, it was hard to do so knowing my new magic teacher had one more reason to hate me.

It was a twenty-minute walk through a copse of trees to the village of Lachlan Falls where the internet café was located. I had a feeling I would be going into town every day to use the computer for printing out lessons and doing research. The school might not have had outlets, but at least I had someplace nearby.

The air outside the school was hot, but not as humid and heavy as it was on the Olympic Peninsula this time of year. The canopy of trees shielded Josie and me from the direct sunlight, but it was still warm enough to be comfortable. We chatted amiably about the upcoming school year. Her mood brightened as we walked.

She waved a hand at the woods around us. "Most of the forest is part of the school grounds, but students aren't allowed in the woods after dark. They have curfew, and there are wards in place to keep them safe so they don't fall into the hands of any Fae should they meet them in Lachlan Falls. Of course, every year students figure out how to sneak off campus, and someone gets snatched."

"But why would students risk it?" Everything always came back to the Fae. I'd only met a few in my life, but I could see I didn't want to meet more.

Something stirred in the bushes next to the dirt path. The shadows in the hollows of the trees suddenly looked more ominous. Were there Fae in the forest? A squirrel darted out from under a cluster of leaves and raced up a tree.

Josie shrugged. "Students aren't here at Womby's because of their brilliant past decisions." She went on to tell me about other school rules and what the staff did, trying to keep students safe.

I didn't know what I would have done without Josie to explain the way this world worked.

The moment we parted from the shady sanctuary of the forest, the sun beat down on us. I wished I had a witch's hat to provide an umbrella of shade. We stepped onto a dusty path through a meadow. A small village of cobblestone buildings was situated on the other side of the tall sea of grass. A shadow blotted out the sun and cast the shape of a bird onto the ground. Josie looked up and gasped.

Another shadow streaked past, the black wings glistening like an oil slick. The bird landed on the path to the village up ahead, the shape shifting and stretching into that of a woman. She was still far enough away for her features to be indistinct and hazy.

My blood chilled in my veins. These were Fae.

"Josie," I said.

"I know." She swallowed. "We need to go back."

We turned. Waiting at the edge of the forest stood two women with black feathers for hair and clothes made from midnight down. Their eyes were pure black. I'd seen them before at the Oregon Country Fair.

Emissaries of the Raven Court.

Cold sweat trickled down my back. They were the ones who had tried to snatch me so the Raven Queen could claim me as her tithe. Or whatever it was she wanted with me.

Josie's spine went rigid. Her step faltered for a moment before she kept walking. She made a wide arc around the bird women, trampling the grass, but they stepped forward to meet us. I glanced around. More birds landed in the field behind us, transforming into the shape of women dressed in midnight feathers.

"You are in violation of school rules," Josie said in a firm teacher tone. "Uninvited Fae aren't permitted to be within a hundred feet of school grounds."

One of the bird women held up a wooden yard stick. "We're one hundred and one feet from school grounds. I measured." Her smile was as ominous as the tips of her black talons.

CHAPTER EIGHT
A Can of Whup Ass and a Side of Awesome Sauce

Back at the Oregon Country Fair when the servants of the Raven Queen had tried to grab me, I hadn't known what to do. I didn't know how to use magic. I still didn't. I regretted my decision not to spend my day studying the thick books Thatch had given me to read that morning. It wasn't that I didn't plan on reading them. I just figured I would organize my classroom and write lesson plans first.

Magic rolled off the two women before us, tasting like winter nights and decaying leaves. The air turned frigid with an Arctic chill, all the heat of the day wicked away. My breath came out in quick puffs of vapor that gave away my trepidation.

Josie's hand slipped into her sleeve. She didn't pull out her wand, but she looked like she was ready to do so.

I didn't have any weapons. Although, I did have my cell phone. From what Josie had said, electronics depleted magical powers. I pressed the power button to turn it on.

"What do you want?" Josie asked.

The emissary's voice was deep and rich, like molasses. "Our queen would be disappointed to hear of such poor manners toward her loyal servants. We simply wish to talk." She looked to me. "Come with us, and all will be forgiven." The words were melodious.

I wanted to close my eyes and sink into her words. She made me forget all danger. The music in her voice painted rainbow oil slicks behind my eyes. My head felt light and detached.

"The queen seeks audience with you. No harm will come of you," one of the emissaries said with a lullaby in her voice.

The invitation tasted like heroin-flavored ice cream, so tempting my mouth salivated. Her words hooked under my ribs, and it was painful to stand there and not step forward. My feet marched toward her of their own volition. I smiled.

"No," Josie said firmly. She smacked me hard in the shoulder.

The pain grounded me in the moment. They'd just tried to hypnotize me! Of all the sneaky, underhanded things to do. I would have fallen for it too, if it hadn't been for Josie.

"You aren't allowed to collect lost souls until after dark," I said. "Not that I'm a lost—"

The two birdbrained women launched themselves at us. Josie whipped out her wand and said something I couldn't understand in Japanese. She zapped the closest Fae to her. I threw my phone at the one on the left and hit her square in the face. She wailed and leapt back. The one Josie zapped had been knocked off her feet by the impact of her spell. Both of them scrambled back from the phone on the ground.

"You foul, half-breed mutt! You'll pay for that!" The one I'd hit now cupped her hand over her eye as she shrieked. Smoke slipped through her fingers.

Had the phone burned her?

The woman whirled and spiraled in a blur, her body shrinking. A black bird rose up from where she'd been and flew into the air. The other woman transformed and followed the first bird.

Josie's face was ashen, and she was out of breath. "We need to get back," she said. "We have to report this to the principal." She grabbed my arm. "Only, we're going to omit the part about the phone."

"Why? It saved me. It's proof I should be allowed to keep it with me at all times."

She shook her head. "Jeb is unlikely to see it that way. That cell phone is like a gun. Teachers aren't allowed to keep guns with them in the Morty Realm, are they?"

I'd heard about gun-slinging teachers in Texas, but that wasn't the norm.

Josie needed to rest several times as we walked back to school. "It's the electronics," she said. "I think it drained me too. It's off now, right?"

I held it up to show her. I felt fine, but I hadn't used any Witchkin magic like she had.

We were both out of breath by the time we made it to the school grounds and found ourselves in Jeb's tower. Mrs. Keahi sat at her secretarial desk outside his door. She was every bit schoolmarm with her long silver hair and conservative attire. The only difference between her and Mrs. Picklebee, my third-grade teacher, was the black pointed hat.

"We need to speak to the principal," I said.

She crossed her arms and scowled when she saw me. "The principal is in a meeting right now. You'll need to come back another time."

"It's an emergency," Josie said. "The Raven Court tried to apprehend us outside of school on the way to Lachlan Falls."

Mrs. Keahi stepped in front of Josie, blocking her from the principal's door. "I'll leave him a message to let him know you stopped by."

Next to Mrs. Keahi's desk, the door to a wooden cabinet full of keys was ajar. If she wasn't going to help us with one problem, I figured I might as well be practical and tackle the next one on my list.

I pointed to the keys. "While we're here, could I get a key for my closet?"

Mrs. Keahi's scowl deepened. That was me, making enemies at every turn.

As I lay in bed that night, reading by the light of a candle, I felt like a character in a Gothic novel. At least the lack of lamp and electricity was romantic, even if it was impractical.

I selected the first book on my to-do list and cracked it open. *Lucid Dreams and Subconscious Messages* didn't sound very witchy, but I suspected it was the most relevant to read after the pornado dream with Thatch. I skimmed the introduction and anecdotes intended to convince the reader why it was important to control the mind. I already understood why I needed to keep Thatch out of my head.

One passage leapt out at me: *Developing the skill to know when one is dreaming versus awake is one of the foundational components of lucid dreaming. Those who master their dream state also find the techniques flow naturally into their waking life, strengthening their intuition.*

This book was what I needed! Not just for controlling dreams, but my magic. I'd been told I ignored my intuition when it nudged me. I needed to let it guide me. My brain overthought everything, and I second-guessed myself. Practicing these exercises would help me with my powers.

Most of the exercises, like keeping a dream journal and observing details in a dream meant I would actually have to go to sleep. I placed a pencil and one of my journals on the nightstand so it would be ready for me in the morning.

My next exercise involved meditating on what I wanted to dream about. I wasn't supposed to think about the things I didn't want to see, or else those might pop up too. I sat cross-legged on my bed, trying to think of calming, peaceful thoughts. A breeze from the unshuttered window whispered across my face. The wooden floorboards creaked. I peeked at the room, making sure no one was in there. Having a door hanging off the hinges and leaning against the wall meant I had less privacy than I would have liked. Thank you, Felix Thatch.

No, I would not think about him. I did not want to dream about him again. I imagined rainbow unicorns and little fairies flitting through a misty forest filled with anything but evil raven shifters.

Darn it, there I was again, thinking about what I didn't want. I cleared my mind. The floorboards popped. I resisted the urge to open my eyes. I visualized deer prancing between trees and red-capped toadstools. Although, weren't those the poisonous ones? I didn't want to dream about that.

The breeze brought with it the odor of musty laundry. Something scraped against the floor near the wall. I couldn't ignore the feeling of someone else being in the room any longer.

I leapt to my feet. "Who's there?"

I snatched the candleholder from the nightstand and waved it around, splattering hot wax onto my fingers. The shock of heat jolted through me.

Golden flames illuminated the room. Movement caught my eye. My reflection in the large freestanding mirror stared at me with wide, terrified eyes, the colors in the glass bluer than the gold of the flames. My mirror self wavered like water, but only for a second. I smoothed my fingers against the solid surface, reassured it had been my imagination.

No one was there in the room besides me.

There was no way this exercise was going to help me have happy dreams now. It might be easier to start my meditations in the morning when every shadow didn't resemble Thatch's spindly fingers stretching out to drain me of my magic.

The next morning my day started with a rude awakening. At first I thought I was dreaming and my before-bed meditations had gone astray. Then I realized, this was my new waking life.

"What are you doing in my bed?" a deep voice growled.

I blinked my eyes. I felt like Goldilocks and standing over me was a bear. Or someone with a bearlike personality. I sat up.

She was dressed in 1920s flapper attire, complete with a short bob of glossy black hair. I would have mistaken her for Catherine Zeta Jones when she'd starred in Chicago, except that this woman was so emaciated and pale.

"You," she said. "What do you think you're doing here?"

"Hi, I'm Clarissa Lawrence." I yawned and extended my hand, trying for politeness despite the circumstances. "Good morning. It's nice to meet you."

"Out of my bed!" She pointed at the other bed with a long-lacquered nail.

I vacated my bed and sat on the other one closer to the window in case she tried to slash at me with her nails. She seemed the sort that would.

She waved a hand at the door, still falling off the hinges and leaning against the wall. "What did you do to the door?"

"Nothing. Mr. Thatch did it."

"That fucktard!"

My eyes widened at her language.

She turned away. She gestured with her hands, pushing and pulling at unseen forces. The door thudded closed. The metal hinges groaned in complaint before mending. The air smelled burned and sharp with fruity undertones. I stared in wonder. It took me a moment to remember to breathe.

"That was cool. Thanks. Um, so, you're my roommate," I said. I tried to figure out a way to broach the subject of who she was without epic awkwardness. "So . . . what's your name?"

Her high heels clicked on the wooden floor as she paced, ignoring me. "It's bad enough I didn't get the tower. Jeb promised me the private tower. I've put in the years. Josephine Kimura has no right to that room." She threw up her hands in disgust. "To make matters worse, I then find out I have a roommate. Not just any roommate, but little Miss Raven Bait herself. What was that senile old bat thinking?"

I rubbed my eyes. It was too early for this.

"So, I'm glad you're here, actually," I said. Okay, not really glad, but it was convenient. "I wanted to talk to you about furniture and decorations. It's kind of plain in here. I thought I would put up some paintings and—"

Her eyes glowed red. "If I have to look at anything else pink, I will tear out your heart and paint the walls with your blood."

Instinctively, I shrank back. I glanced around. There wasn't any pink in the room. Except my suitcases in the corner.

And my hair. And the Disney pajamas I wore. What could I say? It was hard to find adult-sized pajamas for a four-foot-ten woman.

She stormed out. I sighed in relief at her departure. My roommate made Bellatrix Lestrange look friendly.

The sky was gray with the coming of dawn, but I decided I might as well get up. I considered jogging on the school grounds where it was safe, but I had too much work to do. Because I wanted to fit in and look like an authentic witch, I dressed in black-and-white striped leggings under a black dress.

The clothes I had set in my laundry basket next to the large standing mirror the night before were gone. I hoped the roommate from hell hadn't burned them.

On my way to my classroom, I stopped by the kitchen. I heard chopping and stirring before I stepped through the door. I thought I caught sight of someone at the stove, but the moment I set foot inside, the busy sounds of cooking ceased.

"Hello?" I called.

No one answered. Eggs sizzled in a pan on a wood stove. I wondered if I'd scared someone off. I grabbed a biscuit and munched on it as I wandered toward my classroom. The bread was so dense and dry I had to guzzle half the water from my water bottle to keep from choking. Along the way to my classroom, I decided to stop in the principal's office to see if Jeb was available to discuss the Raven Court's presence so close to campus. I hesitated in the doorway, seeing my new roomie at Mrs. Keahi's desk.

"I don't care if he's busy. How dare he do this to me!" my roommate shouted.

Mrs. Keahi sat behind her desk, scowling. "You're going to have to talk to your department head, dear. Professor Thatch is the one who approved the decision with the principal."

I silently backed away and tiptoed to the teacher mailboxes next to the staff room to wait. In my box, I found the in-service agenda for Thursday and a note from Jeb. From the formal tone and legible handwriting, I guessed the note had been written by Mrs. Keahi.

The note said:

My secretary informed me of your encounter with the Raven Queen's servants. Please refrain from leaving the school grounds unless accompanied by a powerful Witchkin such as a Celestor like myself or Mr. Thatch until further notice.

J.E.B.

I needed to go to the internet café and print my lessons. It was going to take me forever to remember all the vocabulary for each project and make tests from scratch. If only my phone could get a good internet signal in the Unseen Realm to connect to Google Docs.

As desperate as I was, there was no way I was going anywhere with Thatch, and I didn't know what a Celestor was. Jeb had said he could chaperone. I would ask him.

My roommate was still ranting in the admin offices when I peeked in again, so I made my way to my dorm room to pick up books and then headed to my classroom. The walk down the hall and up the stairs felt like it took forever.

I selected *Lucid Dreams and Subconscious Messages* from the top of the stack. The surprise of a roommate yelling at me had distracted me from writing down my dreams and meditating. I couldn't even remember my dreams now. I would get to the journal tomorrow. Meditating might not be so difficult now that the door was repaired and I didn't think Thatch was going to sneak up on me.

I skimmed the other exercises in the book. Anchoring and being able to tell the difference between reality and a dream seemed pretty important if I was going to avoid Thatch sex dreams. I practiced the observation exercise for a while, but there was only so much one could do while awake. The thickest of the books, *Wards and Protective Charms for Advanced Magecraft*, intimidated me with all the pictures of Celtic runes I couldn't read, and I was lost reading *Elementia Magic Volume II: Thunder, Lightning, and Weather Magic* so I moved on to one of the skinnier books.

My chair was hard, and the sunshine called to me, so I brought the smallest book outside and read it on a bench under an oak tree. The shady tree made me think of my mom—or fairy godmother—and I patted the tree like I would pat an old friend on the back. Oak gave Mom the most strength.

"Pardon me, but you don't strike me as someone with a tree affinity," a man with a hint of an accent said. He might have been Greek or Transylvanian. Immediately I thought of Dracula.

I glanced around. A shirtless man with a tan pushed a wheelbarrow across the lawn toward me. He definitely wasn't a vampire from the way he basked in the vitamin D. A heap of weeds were piled inside the wheelbarrow. He smiled jovially.

"My mom—well, my adoptive mom—has a tree affinity." I shaded my eyes to see him more clearly.

A gap showed between his front teeth as he grinned. Between his dark features, ripped abs, and excess of body hair, he resembled a Greek god.

"Aren't you here a little early?" he asked. "Classes don't start until next week."

"Other teachers are arriving this week too." Though I wished my roommate hadn't.

His mouth made a little *O* and understanding crossed his face. "I'm sorry, I thought you were a—pardon me." He laughed.

My face flushed with warmth. "A student, I know. I get that a lot." That was one of the problems with being young and petite.

He dusted his hands off on his brown pants and extended one to me. "I'm Sam. I tend to put my foot in my mouth. Or hoof, rather."

I stood to take his hand. As he shook mine, I realized the pants I'd thought he wore were fur. I stared for a beat too long. He coughed.

"Oh, you're Satyr Sam," I said. I'd overheard some of the teachers talking about him the night before at dinner.

He sighed in exasperation. "Why can't people just call me Sam?"

"Sorry, I'm new to this school." As if that explained my social awkwardness. "I'm Clarissa Lawrence."

He scratched his chin, studying me. "You look like someone. Wait, don't tell me. Did you have a sibling at our school?"

Dread settled in my gut. "I don't think so."

"Your parents went here?"

"Something like that." I hoped he wouldn't recognize me from the portrait. I didn't need one more person to hate me. "Hey, by any chance do you know who the teacher is with short dark hair? She's my roommate and just arrived this morning, but she didn't introduce herself. She may have been a little . . . distracted."

"Tall and evil-looking?" he asked. "Wears all black, usually in fringed dresses? Likes to kill small animals and possibly children?"

"Um, probably." I didn't know the latter for a fact, but it wouldn't surprise me.

"That hot mess is Vega Bloodmire. She's your roommate?" He whistled and shook his head. "If you can survive her, you can survive anything."

"Right." Wasn't she the one Josie had warned me about?

He cheerily resumed his weeding, leaving me to feel even worse about my roommate situation.

I tried to focus on reading about the history of the school. If I mastered the required reading, maybe I would be able to move on to real magic. I used the same studying techniques I had learned in middle school that helped me all the way through college. I got out my highlighters. Every time I came to a vocab word or definition I thought was important, I used yellow. For dates, I highlighted in pink, and for important names I used green. I read the headings and subheadings, text that was bold, text around pictures, and skimmed the rest. Then I reread what I'd highlighted. Time flew by.

Chapter thirty-two, the second to last chapter, was torn from the book. I hoped I wouldn't be tested on that chapter. It was about that time I wondered if Thatch had meant to give this book to me or loan it to me. The pages were brittle and yellow, the cover leather.

I didn't look forward to going down to the dungeon and asking. Maybe he wouldn't be there, and I could leave a note on his desk.

The dungeon was as dark and creepy as the last time I'd been there. Sconces lit the walls with blue flames that made the walls look even moldier. Water dripped somewhere in the distance. I had to walk through a dank and windowless classroom, down a hallway, and through a torture chamber I'd been told was the detention room, through another torture chamber I'd been told was Thatch's relaxing room—it was Josie who told me, and I didn't know how much of that was a joke—and to his office. A metal torture chair across from his desk shone under a chandelier; the focused lighting reminded me of a spotlight. His desk chair was a comfy cushioned one, modern with padded arm rests and made from a combination of metal, fabric and plastic that felt out of place in a dungeon.

Behind the desk was a closed door that might have been a closet. Thatch's desk was everything Jeb's desk wasn't. Files were stacked neatly in piles with a lesson plan book closed on top. An ink quill rested next to a blotter pad.

Thatch wasn't anywhere in the dungeons. Lucky me. I could leave a note, only there was nothing on his desk to write a note on. I hesitated, not wanting to intrude on his personal space.

"Hello," I called. "Felix Thatch?"

No reply. I pulled open a drawer to see if he had Post-its. Something inside the desk screamed. I closed it quickly and tried another drawer. A hand reached out and grabbed my wrist.

This time *I* screamed. I slapped the hand, but it didn't let me go. I dug my phone out of my pocket. Before I could press it to the hand, it snapped away, and the drawer closed. My phone wasn't even on.

"Give me your Post-it notes, or I'll touch you with the dark arts of electronics," I threatened.

I tried to open the drawer a smidge, hoping it would shove paper out at me, but no such luck. I opened the bottom drawer. This one screamed louder than the first. If I didn't find Post-its soon, I was going to write a note on his blotter pad.

In the bottom drawer, a black book rested on a heap of files. I considered closing the drawer, but I hesitated. Something inside me nudged my hand toward that book. Was it the intuition I usually ignored? Or my trouble-maker gene?

I flipped back the cover. The book whispered, drawing me closer. I couldn't make out the words. Patterns and symbols drawn in ink covered the page. I turned another page, the whisper momentarily ceasing and changing to something that sounded like another language. This drawing featured a serpent covered in scales made of runes. The detail was incredibly intricate. On the next page was a beautiful woman with long dark hair. Scrawling cursive covered her face, obscuring enough of her features I couldn't tell who she was. The whispers of this page sounded more like French to me. Between the next pages of the book was a chunk of yellowing parchment that looked like it had been torn from another book.

At the top it was labelled: "Chapter Thirty-Two." I had found the missing pages from my history book! My intuition had led me here. Unwittingly, I'd used magic.

Apparently, Thatch hadn't wanted me to find this chapter. I opened my book to the appropriate section and placed the pages inside. Immediately the torn section crinkled, and the paper shifted. The parchment knit together before my eyes. The seam where it had been torn healed itself. If only people healed that easily.

I set the book on the desk and reached to close the leather journal where I'd found the missing pages. The ink drawing that had been underneath the parchment caught my eye. The rendering reminded me of the portrait of my mother in the hallway, a witch in a Victorian gown. A snake twisted around her body, the head striking out at a raven. More birds circled the figure. Designs in the background incorporated pentagrams and runic writing.

When I held my hand over the drawing, the paper felt as though it vibrated with electricity. Inhaling, the ink smelled like blackberries and starlight. Magic was at work here, but what it meant, I didn't know.

A deep voice from the doorway made me jump. "Why are you going through my desk?"

I slammed the drawer closed. Thatch stood in the doorway, his lips pressed into a line and his nostrils flaring. I couldn't blame him. I was being a sneaky snoop.

I tried not to act suspicious, but my voice squeaked. "I'm sorry. I wasn't trying to . . . um . . . I was looking for Post-it notes so I could leave you a note."

He withdrew his wand from the pocket of his old-fashioned vest. The tip of it fizzled with blue sparks. That didn't bode well. He strode forward.

"My eggs were burnt this morning," he said.

"Um." I watched his wand with trepidation. "That's unfortunate."

"Aren't you going to ask me why?"

"I don't need to. You're going to tell me." I backed away until I bumped into the wall. "I'm sure it's going to somehow be my fault for being born."

He touched the tip of his wand to each drawer of his desk. The drawers clicked and thudded as though bolts were locking in place. "You need to stay out of the kitchen. It interrupts the brownies."

"This is the second time someone has mentioned brownies, but I haven't seen any set out yet."

His brow furrowed. "Set out?"

"To eat."

"I'm not talking about food. I'm talking about sprites. Household hobs. Brounie or brùnaidh. They aren't meant to be seen. Every time you go into the kitchen and interrupt them, they have to hide." He stepped closer.

I slid along the wall away from Thatch, afraid to turn my back to leave. "I didn't know." I had a lot to learn if I was ever to become a real witch.

"Is that all you have to say?" He loomed closer to me. His wand reminded me of a sparkler on the Fourth of July.

"I'm sorry. If there's anything I can do to make it up to you, let me know." I slipped around the desk, putting that between us. I bumped into the edge with my hip and sent a stack of files and the papers inside to the floor. "Sorry."

He eyed the mess with annoyance. With a flick of his wand, the papers flew back onto the desk, arranging themselves in order. "Your reason for setting foot in my office, uninvited?"

I snatched up my book, brandishing it like a shield. "Can I keep this book? Or do I need to give it back?"

"It's on loan from the school library. Teachers can keep books as long as they need."

Craptacular! A library book. I was in so much trouble. The librarian was going to kill me when she saw the highlighter.

My mouth went dry. "Is this checked out in your name?" I prayed it wasn't.

He leaned across the desk. With one of his long arms, he easily reached across the expanse between us and tore the book from my hands. Gloom settled over my soul. I was going to get in trouble for highlighting *and* stealing back those pages.

He opened the book to page one. His jaw dropped as he stared at the highlighted pages. "You've defaced a limited edition. What kind of black magic is this?"

"It isn't magic. It's called a highlighter. It helps you study the material."

He waved his wand over the page and muttered low enough under his breath that I couldn't understand what he was saying. The spell reminded me of the ones on the pages of his journal. Electricity tingled in the air. My senses grew confused. I tasted Baroque music and smelled midnight.

Yellow, pink, and green ink dribbled off the parchment and rolled onto the floor. He turned the page and waved his wand over it. More ink dribbled out. He turned another page before flipping through more chapters of my highlighting skills and groaned.

I giggled. It's not that I thought it was actually funny. I just tended to giggle when I was nervous.

He shoved the book at me. He pointed at the door with his wand. "Get out. This is a waste of my time. One of your new friends can help you undo what you've done. If you have any."

I ran to my room with the book, wanting to read the missing section before Thatch realized I had appropriated it. Vega was out—to my relief—and I sat at the desk, golden sunlight illuminating the text. The previous chapters of *Womby's: A History of the School* had been filled with a compilation of biographies, articles, and anecdotes written in a journalistic style that matched the eccentric mishmash of architecture of the school. When I saw the heading of the missing chapter featured my biological mother's name, I knew I would not be disappointed.

It was only going to be a matter of time before Thatch figured out what I had done. I intended to finish reading the chapter, even if he stole it away from me. I took out my cell phone and used the camera to photograph each page. I zoomed in to make sure the text was readable and reshot the ones that came out blurry. After I felt satisfied I had my own copy of the book, I put my cell phone away and read the pages.

Chapter Thirty-Two
Principal Alouette Loraline

Unlike many of the headmasters and principals of the school, an air of mystery surrounds the former headmistress, her origins, and her demise. She started off her teaching career as governess to two Witchkin children born into the nobility of the Dragon Court, Yin and Lee. Upon questioning the Yaoguai families, as the Fae are called in Chinese, Prince Lee simply answered, "It's true she was my governess. I have no more to say about her."

Whether she worked for the Dragon Court by coercion or choice is unknown. After ten years of employment in their household, she started her career as a teacher at Womby's Reform School for Wayward Witches, and then left after five years. No information is available about her from that time.

Next, she served as a teacher at Lady of the Lake School for Girls. Former teachers of the school remember Alouette Loraline as being friendly, nurturing, and a hard worker.

Former headmistress, Ethelinda Snow, said of her former employee, "Miss Loraline always arrived early and stayed late to work with students who needed extra help. She devoted hours of her personal time to the betterment of others. She took a special interest in the underprivileged, scholarship students, and those who had been raised in the Morty world who came to the school with fewer advantages in magic than others."

My biological mother didn't sound so bad. She sounded like someone who cared. I wanted to be that kind of teacher.

One of Loraline's former coworkers from her short stint at The Elementia Academy of Arts and Alchemy shared many stories of Loraline coming to the aid of failing students. The most notable was a story provided by Lou Albinka:

"I remember she tutored this one kid every day after school during May and June, helping him with wards and protections spells so he could be safe after graduation. She didn't even teach that class and there she was, studying up on it and trying to show him. The kid didn't care. He skipped tutoring, and she wrote him detentions so he would have to come in to study. I walked in on him cussing her out because she told him he couldn't leave the classroom until he finished his homework.

"I asked her, 'Why do you bother? He doesn't appreciate it.' I didn't think he was going to graduate. But he did. She worked with him so he passed all his classes. And you know what? The Raven Court snatched him up. All that work for nothing, but she continued to do it for other students. She always said some of them would survive, but I thought she was batty."

My heart clenched. My mother had been an idealist who hadn't allowed the system to crush her optimism. Good for her. I would help my students like she had. That meant I needed to learn everything. I needed to study magic, not just to protect myself, but to protect them as well.

I skimmed the following pages for juicy details. I didn't know how long I would be able to get away with reading the chapter. Thatch might burst through the door at any minute and demand the section I'd stolen. I scanned until I found a promising paragraph.

After being rehired as a teacher at Womby's Reform School for Wayward Witches,

Loraline was caught with restricted books on the Lost Court in her dormitory. Her advisor and department head, Jebediah Ebenezer Bumblebub, came to her defense when asked about whether he recognized this as early signs of her turning to the dark side. "You fall off the turnip truck or somethin'? What do you expect from a Celestor? Knowledge is everythin'. Headmasters ain't got no right to be makin' restricted sections for teachers. Those books in her room didn't mean nothin'."

Loraline's thirst for knowledge became more apparent as evidence surfaced that she dabbled in the dark arts. Rumors circulated among students that their teacher used blood magic, pain magic, necromancy, and mind control. She allegedly used the forbidden arts of physics, calculus, genetics, psychology, and computer science.

Such claims were dismissed by administration as unfounded.

I laughed out loud at this. How could psychology be a forbidden science? Or math. Everyone needed math. I could understand computer science since electronics drained Witchkin of magic, but the rest had to be a joke. As for the blood magic and other weirdville stuff, it wasn't like students always told the truth. During my year of student teaching, two students had lied to their parents to get out of detentions. The worst part of it had been that it worked. I wasn't convinced my biological mother was evil yet. Even Jeb had come to her defense.

In her first years at Womby's, Loraline taught alchemy, later moving on to divination and Fae studies. Much of her personal time she devoted to alchemy experiments mixed with the inferior human arts, sometimes with disastrous effects. One of her experiments blew out a wall of the back wing. Numerous attempts were made to repair it, but no magic worked effectively on the stone, and that section of building has thus been left unrepaired. It is theorized the forbidden arts of science and electricity were involved.

Loraline spent an inordinate amount of time in discourse with teachers and students on the Fae Fertility Paradox.

Note to self: look that up later.

Despite these eccentricities, Loraline was well-liked by students and staff. She was considered a good teacher, if not a little zealous in her approach. She quickly moved to the rank of department head and then vice principal after only fifteen years at the school.

Six years later, Loraline became principal. Shortly afterward, students began to disappear. Loraline made complaints to the Witchkin Council and Fae School Board, claiming Fae were at fault. She correlated the increase in graduation rates and resulting decrease in tithes with a rise in abductions while students were off-campus. Such allegations were dismissed, as she had no proof, nor did the council think any house of Fae would be willing to break their own laws and risk the consequences.

As a result of the abductions, Loraline saw fit to hire a Fae staff member to head security, causing parents to question the wisdom of such a move when Fae were supposedly behind the abductions. Several wealthy families withdrew children from the school, which caused further budgeting problems.

Loraline spent more and more time away, supposedly collecting donations from prestigious Fae families. At first she was praised; she inspired patronage from those who had never previously donated to the school. Later, such uncommon abilities in fundraising raised suspicion from the Witchkin community who wondered what Loraline promised in return for such investments.

In her twentieth year as principal, the Queen of the Silver Court accused the principal of being a descendent of the Lost Court. Shortly after, Loraline unleashed an unspeakable evil on the school. Down in the walled-off depths underneath the school dungeon—

I turned the page. The heading at the top said: "Chapter Thirty-Three." No! There had to be more. I rubbed the previous page between my fingers to see if the parchment had stuck together. Why would the section be removed from the book if there hadn't been more to it? Unless Thatch had figured out I'd stolen the section of the book he'd been hiding, and then removed it . . . with magic.

I opened up the photos on my phone. I had no better luck there. The last page I'd photographed was the same as the last one in the book I'd pilfered. Probably Thatch had figured out what I'd done before I'd ever reached my room.

Here's what I knew so far about my mother: She was a Celestor, she was considered evil because she studied topics people didn't like, including math and science, and Thatch didn't want me to know about her.

The bigger question was why. And how was I going to find out?

CHAPTER NINE
Unexpected Gifts

The book in my hands came from the library. That meant I had a means to solve this mystery and find out what Thatch was trying to hide from me. I probably should have been studying how to control my powers, or even getting my lessons ready, but there was only so much time in one day. My most urgent priority was finding out what Thatch had removed from the book.

I wrote down the title and edition on a Post-it and raced to the library to find another copy of the book before Thatch figured out what I was about to do.

The old woman behind the counter reminded me of my high school librarian. She wore a silver bun pulled behind her head. Her high white collar and puff sleeves was reminiscent of Victorian attire. Only instead of a cameo, she wore a little animal skull at the nape of the lacy collar. The morbid brooch told me she didn't believe in preserving all life like Josie did.

Her hat was tall and conical like most witch hats, but a collection of red roses and animal skulls weighed one side so that it flopped down in a way that reminded me of the fancy hat my grandma—my adoptive father's mother—wore to tea parties.

I smiled at her, trying to give off an air of friendliness. "Hi, my name is Clarissa Lawrence. I'm the new teacher here."

From the way she pursed her lips, I could see she already knew who I was.

"I teach arts and crafts," I said.

She didn't tell me her name. She just looked me up and down like she didn't think much of me.

"And you are?" I prompted.

"Gertrude Periwinkle."

"Professor Thatch told me teachers could check out books." He'd implied it anyway. "He gave me a list of books to read to get acquainted with the school. I wondered if I could check out a copy of *Womby's: A History of the School.* Preferably the seventh edition."

She nodded to a large cabinet of drawers on my side of the counter. "Have you tried the card catalog?"

"A card catalog?" I asked dumbly. It wasn't like I hadn't heard of them before, but I'd never used such an archaic method myself.

She sighed in exasperation. "Jeb mentioned you've lived among Morties your entire life and you might be . . . lacking in certain skills."

She walked around the desk and showed me to a wooden cabinet with dozens of drawers. She opened one. I couldn't believe anyone still used these things! But I guessed this was the alternative to a computer database. She shuffled through the cards, explaining how the system worked. It sort of made sense alphabetically and numerically. When she found the card, she waved her wand over it.

"Thirty-four copies," she said. A black X hovered in the air above it. "All copies are currently checked out."

"By who?" I asked. Not that I didn't already know the answer.

"Professor Thatch."

Of course.

"Does this system work for subject as well as title?" I asked. "Do you have any books on the Fae Fertility Paradox?"

She clasped a hand to her heart, her face shocked. "That information is restricted."

"I'm a teacher. Can't I check out restricted books?" Jeb had been quoted as saying he didn't think knowledge should be restricted.

"No, you cannot." Mrs. Periwinkle's eyes narrowed. "The principal is going to hear about this."

"I'm sorry. I don't know what the Fae Fertility Paradox is, so I didn't know it was anything evil, you know, like psychology and mathematics." I gave a nervous laugh. I was soooo not good at acting innocent.

Her mouth twisted into a sneer. "Are you trying to be funny?"

"No, not me. Never funny." I backed away.

I decided not to ask about the books related to blood magic or the Lost Court. Apparently, I'd made another enemy.

I'd also underestimated Thatch's cunning. I would find out what he was hiding from me about my mother, though at this point it looked like the only way I would be able to do that was to break into the restricted section of the library.

Gertrude Periwinkle did not come across as someone I wanted to mess with. Even so, I didn't have a better plan than breaking into the library. The best I could do for the moment was scope out the layout and observe the school's defenses. I returned to the library two more times, peeking in to see if Gertrude Periwinkle was still around. The moment she left, I snuck behind the counter to see if she had any forbidden books under there. All I found were some volumes that needed repairs. I lingered in the door of her office, trying to act casual, as though I were simply going there to ask her a question and was surprised to find the room empty. It was hard to hide my nervousness when I was sweating buckets and my own shadow cast on the wall made me jump.

Mrs. Periwinkle was as organized as Thatch: papers stacked neatly, everything arranged tidily on her desk, and nothing of interest left out. All the enticing books with titles like *Blood Mages of Ancient Times*, *Necromancy for Business and Pleasure*, and one with faded words that looked like it said *How to Serve Man—Not Just a Cookbook* were all stored in a locked glass case. If I had my lockpick kit, I could break in, though I didn't know which book would help me find out anything I wanted to know about the Fae Fertility Paradox, Lost Court, or my mother. And I didn't know if the librarian had cast any spells to protect against larceny.

I scanned the titles in the not-so-restricted shelves in the library. While I perused other potentially helpful volumes, Mrs. Periwinkle returned. She eyed me with a frown but said nothing.

I continued exploring the library, pausing when I found the yearbooks. They weren't anything like the expensive books with glossy color photos most schools produced. These were thin, and the photographs were poor quality with somber, unsmiling students. The photos reminded me of old daguerreotypes. I found the books for the years I would have been in high school, scanning the pages for Derrick Winslow. I didn't find him. Maybe he hadn't gone to Womby's. There were other schools in the Unseen Realm, but I didn't know how to start searching for him.

Derrick had said not to look for him, but that had been in a dream. The real Derrick might want me to look for him. Perhaps if I made friends with the librarian, she would help me do research. Not that I could imagine that going over well if she found out I intended to break into her office and steal forbidden knowledge. I had so much to do this school year: learn magic, find out about my biological mother, and figure out what had happened to Derrick. How was I going to fit in teaching underprivileged Witchkin and keeping them out of trouble into that equation?

I had a jillion lessons to prepare. Eventually I went back to my classroom. My life would have been so much easier if I had a computer and a printer. When I next stepped into my dorm that afternoon, I saw my roomie had decorated. Birds tweeted in a cage that hung from one corner of the ceiling. They sounded cheerful until I listened closer.

"Hey, wartface! Free us at once!" one of the birds sang in a melody that reminded me of Chopin.

Were they talking to me? I didn't have warts. I looked around. I was alone.

"If I let you out, my roommate will be mad at me," I said. Not to mention Vega Bloodmire would probably hex me.

"Fucking bitch," the other bird said in sing-song. "I told you she wasn't going to help us."

I stared, appalled at the bird's language. "Excuse me? Do you think insults and a potty mouth are going to get you any sympathy?"

It was hard to pinpoint what about the room's makeover gave it a homicidal Downton Abbey feel. An old-fashioned cuckoo clock rested on the wall between beds, not so different from the one my grandma had in her house. A small, but well-made rug in an Art Nouveau style had been spread between the door and bed. It took me a moment to realize the flowers and geometric designs formed a giant skull. An Oriental dressing screen stood in the corner to the side of the window and desk. At first I thought the imagery showcased a Japanese cherry tree with red blossoms. Upon closer inspection, I saw the jagged branches impaled small birds and butterflies on spikes. The red appeared to be splatters of their blood. I would have taken Bob Ross's happy little trees any day over this. And I was the one who got to lie next to that screen at night and try to have sweet dreams.

A plant hung from the ceiling in the corner near the desk. When I neared it, the Venus flytrap jaws snapped at me. The desk now had an oil lamp, as did the nightstand, along with a vase of black roses. The room was more practical with a clock, candles in sconces, and some of the other items, but it also had a creepier vibe. The coffin sticking out from under Vega's bed, the gilded frame containing a portrait of a skeleton, and the noose suspended over my bed didn't help the room's ambiance.

On top of one wardrobe my monster roommate had set another potted plant and a marble bust of what looked like herself. Every shelf on the wall she'd filled with books, including the spaces I'd hoped to fill. Someone must have missed her ever-so-important kindergarten lesson when they taught the vital skill of sharing.

I carefully removed the crystal ball from my wardrobe and placed it on hers, as well as the bottles of bright fluids. I cleared the books from the bookshelf on my side of the room and set them on top of the books on her shelf. I removed the noose from the hook on the ceiling and flung it onto her bed. At least she hadn't tried to take up any of the room in my wardrobe. That would have been unforgivable.

I pretty much hated every macabre decoration except for the guillotine next to the desk. That would come in handy for chopping papers. I wished I had one in my classroom.

Considering all the time Vega had put into decorating, one would have thought she'd take a little more care in cleaning up after herself. She'd left her dirty clothes next to the desk. It wasn't just one dress either. It was a huge pile of dresses that smelled like alcohol, cigarettes, and too much perfume. She'd even thrown in a heap of undergarments.

It was the plate of food on the desk that gave me pause. Cookies were stacked next to a sandwich. The note said: *For you. To make up for our last encounter.*

The cookies were gingersnaps and didn't look like they were made from the hearts of children. It was tempting, but I had a suspicion that the same roommate who hung a noose above my bed was unlikely to set out cookies and a sandwich for me. At least not without poisoning it. But, I was hungry, and the food in the cafeteria for teachers sucked.

I carried the plate downstairs to Josie's classroom. "Can you tell if this has been poisoned?"

She laughed like I was joking. "Who is it from?"

"Vega Bloodmire."

"Ah. Say no more."

She waved her wand over it. A hazy lavender aura swirled around the food, making the air smell like the forest. She closed her eyes and muttered under her breath in Japanese. The light faded. "Nope. No poison. And it's all organic and vegan too." She stole a cookie and bit in. "Yum!"

I sat at one of the student desks and set down the plate. "So, what's the deal with Vega? Is she a vampire?"

"She wishes. Why?"

"The coffin. Her pale complexion. She dresses like she's from another era."

"No, I just think she's old. Most Witchkin live a long time, not that it makes us immortal like *yokai*—I mean, Fae—but many of us live longer than average if we don't get ourselves killed by Fae. Or zapped by cold iron and electronics. I heard Jeb is like three hundred."

"What about the coffin?" I bit into half the sandwich. It was a cucumber, avocado, and alfalfa sprout sandwich with a creamy sauce that gave it zip. It was pretty good.

Josie made a face. "Vega is into some kinky stuff. She told me she once did it in a coffin. Gross, huh?"

I shrugged. To each their own. Who was I to judge someone's sex life after almost killing my former boyfriends?

Josie and I chatted away as she prepped her classroom. I offered her another cookie and the other half of the sandwich.

"Do you know what a Celestor is?" I asked. "I want to go into town and access my lesson plans and do some internet research later, but Jeb said I could only leave if I go with Thatch or a Celestor." Plus, I was ready to do some research on forbidden subjects. Mwa-ha-ha!

"Ugh! Thatch? Not that bag of dicks." She made a face. "There's no way I'm going with you if you invite him along. Pro Ro is a Celestor, so he could come with us if we can find him, but he was running errands earlier. We could ask Vega, but I'd rather punch myself in the face than hang out with her. She might be as powerful of a Celestor as Thatch, but she's even more of a bitch than he is."

"But what does that mean? A Celestor? I don't know all the witch lingo yet." *Womby's: A History of the School* had implied my mother was a Celestor.

"It's a category of Witchkin, someone whose affinity allows him or her to excel in clairvoyance, telepathy, apportation, or projection. Usually they use the stars or the sky as a power source. Of course, Thatch would be one. That's why he acts so snooty and superior."

"You're not a Celestor then?"

"No, I'm Amni Plandai. I derive my power from nature, animals mostly, but plants too."

"Oh," I said in disappointment. If only Josie could be my chaperone. She'd kicked Raven Court ass the other day.

"Jeb will be okay if Khaba walks down with us. He's got some seriously powerful mojo of protection. We don't have to worry about the Raven Court with him around." She leaned in confidentially and lowered her voice. "He's Fae."

"Khaba?"

"Dean of discipline. He handles security, wards, and school rules stuff."

The book had mentioned Alouette Loraline had hired a Fae to keep the students safe from . . . other Fae. It did sound suspicious now that I thought about it.

"By the way, don't let him see your phone. He'll turn a blind eye to us going to the internet café if we say we're just getting lunch upstairs, but he'll confiscate your phone if he sees you with it on school grounds." She sighed, and a dreamy look came to her eyes. "I love the big guy, but he can be such a stickler about following rules. All Fae are." She stared off into the distance, smiling.

"No phones it is."

My fairy godmother had told me not to trust Fae. I wondered how Khaba was different than those of the Raven Court. I would have to wait to see if he sucked laughter out of people's faces and lived to drain magic from Witchkin.

CHAPTER TEN
I Dream of Djinn

We agreed to meet at four thirty, outside the front of the school. That gave us plenty of time to walk down to the Lachlan Falls, secretly recharge my phone while I printed my lessons from Goggle Docs, and do research before it got dark. Until that time, I worked on my magical history studies and lesson plans for my first-day activities. I had so much to do.

At four fifteen I made my way out of my room, down the stairs and along the hall to the front lobby. Outside standing in the sunshine, Josie stood next to a man below the front steps of the school. He glanced over his shoulder. I froze on the steps.

An old witch had once told me I would meet a tall, dark, and handsome stranger who would be the love of my life—or something along those stereotypically sappy lines. I didn't believe her soothsaying held any truth to it.

Still, for just a moment, I wanted to imagine this tall, handsome man was my soulmate.

I was in the presence of some godlike being. Magic radiated off him in waves. He was tall, and as I joined Josie, I realized his leopard-print shirt was unbuttoned down to his navel, revealing the amount of time he spent in the gym on his mad gains. He was bald, but young, no older than thirty-five. His face reminded me of the ancient Egyptian pharaoh, Akhenaten with full lips and deep-set eyes. His complexion was the color of sandalwood. He even smelled of amber and frankincense. His fashion sense may have been modern, but he gave off an ancient and powerful air.

He set a hand on his hip and looked me up and down. "So, girl, you're the one I keep hearing about. Daughter of a succubus?"

My eyes went wide. "My mother—Loraline—she was a succubus?"

"It's just a guess. I never asked. That would be rude." He waved his hand in the air with the flamboyance of a professional drag queen. "All I can say is she was a real man-eater." His accent was slight, somewhere in between Middle Eastern and something else. Something older.

I wanted to ask him what he was, but my fairy godmother had told me I wasn't supposed to ask personal questions like that, so I didn't. Breathlessly, I stuck out my hand. "Clarissa Lawrence. Art teacher."

"Dean Khaba. You may call me Khaba. Charmed, I'm sure." He raised an eyebrow, his expression amused. "Everyone keeps saying you look just like Loraline, but I don't see the resemblance. You look far less evil." He sounded disappointed.

"Did you know her well?"

"I met her about thirty years back while I was rocking the Kasbah scene. She used her wish to free me from being a slave to the lamp in exchange for—" He waved his hand at the architectural monstrosity behind me. "—being indentured to the school. Your mother was a sneaky one, equal to any Fae in wit and treachery. I had great respect for her . . . until the end."

Magic rolled off him like a strong perfume. I blinked, trying to concentrate. He'd been a slave to a lamp.

"So, you're djinn?"

Josie punched me in the shoulder. "Clarissa! That is so rude." Josie was small, but she packed a punch. "Don't ask people what kind of Fae they are."

They were going to think my mom hadn't taught me any Witchkin manners, which would have basically been true.

I rubbed my shoulder. It was easier to see through the nimbus of magic around Khaba now that I could only focus on the charley horse in my arm. "Sorry. I forgot. Don't answer."

Khaba cast a disdainful glare at me. "Don't worry, I won't."

Josie slipped an arm around his waist and hugged him. "I keep asking Khaba when he's going to grant my three wishes, but he keeps putting me off."

He grimaced. He patted her on the head as if she were an endearing but annoying dog.

"Shall we?" He extricated himself from her and strutted down the path.

We followed a dirt trail around the back of the school where there was a fountain with cupids and bushes trimmed into the shapes of animals. Our path intersected a thick lawn and took us into the forest that enclosed the school grounds. The sun was uncomfortably warm, and I had to jog to keep up with Khaba's long legs. Even then, Josie and I both lagged behind, affording us a great view of the way he wiggled his butt as he walked.

Josie jogged beside me. "Isn't he gorgeous?" She squealed.

"Well, yes," I admitted.

She giggled. Did she really have no gaydar?

"I know you're talking about me. It better all be flattering," he called over his shoulder.

"Hey, can you walk slower?" I shouted after him.

"If I did, you wouldn't burn as many calories. You'll thank me later."

"Burning calories isn't high on my list of wishes," Josie called after him.

I laughed at their banter. Josie trusted him, and I wanted to have faith in her judgement, but I couldn't help thinking of what the textbook had implied about a Fae having a dubious agenda working at a school. Did Khaba resent being indentured to Womby's, or might he have ulterior motives? Anyone with as much magic rolling off him as he had wasn't one to disregard lightly.

The shade of the trees offered us shelter from the sun. I didn't mind jogging—I had actually intended to go earlier—I only wished I hadn't worn a dress and my striped leggings. Soon Khaba disappeared out of sight. Trees rustled behind us. The black silhouettes of birds fluttered through the branches. I couldn't tell what kind of birds they were.

It was fine, I told myself. I had a qualified chaperone. The Raven Queen's servants weren't going to attack me. Only, Khaba wasn't anywhere in sight.

The bushes near me shook. The forest was part of the school grounds, so we were safe. Even so, I picked up the pace. Khaba waited for us at the end of the forest trail. He watched the black birds circling in the sky over the meadow.

Josie and I emerged from the trees to join him.

Khaba no longer smiled. "Stay close to me while we're off school grounds." He held himself tall and confident as he strode ahead of us.

I glanced up, afraid those birds were representatives from the Raven Court. They might swoop down at any moment.

Lachlan Falls was quaint, everything made from brick and stone, reminding me of an Irish village. The people looked Irish, but at the same time, not quite human. A man with a long pointed nose smoked a pipe on his perch at the top of his horse-drawn wagon, eyeing us with curiosity. Fiddling came from a pub called The Devil's Pint. Clotheslines hung between windows of cobblestone houses. Children in old-fashioned clothes and flat caps played jacks in the alley. It looked more like the set of *Outlander* than the modern era.

I wiped the sweat from my brow. Now that we'd left the comfort of the shady woods, the sun beat down on us. Josie removed her hat and fanned herself.

"Where is Lachlan Falls, exactly?" I asked. "And the school?"

It wasn't the first time in my life I suspected I wasn't in Kansas anymore. Or more accurately, the continental United States.

The moment I'd signed my contract, I'd been whisked to the school by magic to settle details of my acceptance as the school's art teacher. I'd only been at the school for a few hours that day, and I hadn't known where it was.

After being returned to my mom's house in Eugene, Oregon, I'd had a chance to pack my bags and prepare for the school year. I received instructions in the mail for reaching the school the nonmagical way. It was far less pleasant.

I booked a train ticket for Seattle. From there, I'd taken a Greyhound charter bus to the Olympic Peninsula near the Hoh Rain Forest. If I hadn't been lugging two suitcases around with me, I might have explored Forks, Washington, to see if I spotted any landmarks from the *Twilight* movies.

Jeb had met me at the last stop and escorted me along the path into the woods that led to the school. The principal was unexpectedly spry for being an old man, and the walk had winded me more than him.

I was pretty sure there wasn't really a magical school in the Olympic National Park, so somewhere along the lines we must have passed into another world.

Khaba scanned the street and waved us forward. "We're in the Realm of the Unseen, or Unseen Realm, as some call it. On the border of Faerie."

"In Japanese we call it *Yomi-no-kuni*," Josie said. "Although, the direct translation is 'land of the dead' and this isn't actually an underworld with spirits, but there are creatures we call *yokai* and *kami*. It's a place Witchkin and Fae can live together peaceably."

"More or less," Khaba said.

Josie nodded. "The farther into Faerie, it gets dicier."

Our feet crunched over the dirt road. A little girl with corn-silk hair smiled at me from an open doorway. She held a doll that looked like a goblin. I waved to her, and she waved back until a woman yanked her back inside and slammed the door.

"This is why Witchkin have to put up with tithes and all the other Fae crap," Josie said under her breath. "We have to live in the Unseen if we're going to get away from Morties and all their poisons."

It wasn't a huge village. Two women sat knitting in the shade of a cottage's porch, chatting amiably. Gaelic or something close to it accented their words. One looked me up and down and crinkled up her nose as she said something to the other. They glared in an unfriendly way.

I would have liked to go into all the witchy-looking shops like: *Brooms, Magic Carpets and More; Potions Emporium;* and *Diviner's Delights*, but Josie suggested we eat dinner first. At the end of the street we turned down the next road and passed one more row of stone buildings. The building on the corner had a satellite dish. The sign above the front door said: "Happy Hal's Tavern and Internet Café."

Josie glanced over one shoulder and then the other, the gesture furtive. There were a few children in the street, but none appeared particularly interested in us.

Khaba stopped at the door. "I expect you ladies to be done with your fish and chips in an hour. I have some errands to run and then you're coming with me to get groceries from. . . ." His gaze flitted to a man with elf ears poking out of his strawberry-blond hair. The man leaned against the side of one of the buildings. He wore a kilt, but that was all.

"Yummy." Khaba cleared his throat. "Excuse me. Let's make it an hour and a half. I need to take care of some kilty pleasures first. It's about time someone made *my* dreams come true." He winked at me as he said it. "Ta ta for now, ladies."

Josie giggled, "You're so *punny*." She snorted as she laughed, which made me laugh harder.

A bell rang above the door as we entered a candlelit room.

I nudged Josie. "Don't you think it's kind of odd the way he just left us? He's supposed to be chaperoning to make sure the Raven Court doesn't follow us."

Josie put a finger to her lips and lowered her voice. "Khaba can't come in, but the Raven Court can't either with all the electronics that will diminish a Fae's powers. We're perfectly safe."

Maybe she was right. I was still on edge from the last time we'd encountered the Raven Queen's emissaries.

The man behind the counter sat on a stool. He nodded to us. "What'll it be, lasses?"

The red of his hair reminded me of the neon orange on a toy troll dolls' head. His face was wide, and his smile unnervingly mischievous. A man at the bar nursing a pint of ale glanced over his shoulder at us. He looked ordinary except that the hair sticking out from under his cap was made from snowy white feathers.

Josie waved to the red-haired man behind the bar. "I'll have an order of fish and chips and afterward forty-five minutes of internet and electricity recharging."

He arched an eyebrow at me. "And you, lass?"

"The same."

He eyed me suspiciously. "You got gold?"

I looked to Josie uncertainly. "I have cash."

"American denominations," Josie said. "I have coin. Copper and nickel." She shook the loose mauve dress she wore. Metal jangled from her pockets.

"Thirty dollars. Each," he said.

"That's highway robbery!" Josie said. "What happened to your teacher discount?"

"Oi! Bring me gold and I'll charge you less." He took her money and shoved it into a purse that hung from his belt.

I hadn't planned on it being thirty dollars for dinner. I shuffled through my wallet and held up my credit card. "Do you accept credit or debit?"

His eyebrow arched impossibly high. "Plastic! Bleh! Ye aren't from around these parts, are ye?"

I counted out all my cash, knowing it wouldn't be enough. "I only have twenty dollars. I didn't know." I would have dug more cash out of my sock drawer hiding place, but I hadn't wanted to carry all my money with me.

He plucked the bills out of my hand. "First-time discount. Next time, bring me gold." He licked his lips like the word "gold" tasted delicious.

He jumped off his stool and waddled out a door behind the counter. The top of his head came no higher than my waist. Clanking pots and pans echoed from another room.

"What is he?" I whispered.

Josie led me to an empty table. "I don't know. Maybe he's part goblin or leprechaun. Don't ask."

The man at the bar swiveled on his chair and looked us over again. He was the only other patron. I pretended I didn't see him watching.

"How does this place stay open?" I asked Josie.

"Hal closes it most of the summer. But business picks up during the school year. You should see how many kids have internet addictions. This is the busiest place for kids after school and evenings." She smiled. "And teachers. Of course, we aren't supposed to be here. We'd usually have to sneak in through the back door and use a private room, but in the evening after the kids have curfew, we can hang out here."

I didn't know how I was going to be able to survive without magic *and* instant access to the internet.

Josie went on. "Twice last year, Thatch caught me here when he was rounding up students. At least that's what he said he was doing, but I'll bet he was here for the same reasons I was." She laughed.

The man at the bar stool grunted. I glanced at him again. He quickly turned away.

Josie turned to him. "What? Don't act like you aren't staring."

He mumbled something that might have been an apology and exited.

"I don't know what it is about people today." Josie shook her head in consternation. "Usually the townsfolk are friendly. I would swear everyone is acting like they'd never seen staff from the school here before."

I had a feeling I knew what was going on. Like Pro Ro, they noticed my resemblance to Alouette Loraline. And like Thatch, they feared I would fall in her footsteps.

I waited impatiently for the fish and chips. My time for getting lessons ready was dwindling away. Dinner arrived within twenty minutes. The meal was good, better than the school's food, but everything was greasy. I'd probably have indigestion later.

A thought occurred to me. "So, I'm not going to be stuck here forever because I ate Fae food? That fairytale isn't real?" All those obscure bedtime stories my fairy godmother had read to me as a kid hadn't just been for enjoyment. Some of them were true.

"That fairytale is true!" Josie said. "But this isn't Fae food. You'd know if it was. It would make your mouth water and be like mana from the gods." She wiped her fingers on a cloth napkin. "Most of the food here is harvested in the human world. What is grown here in the borderlands still has too much influence from the Morty world to be considered pure enough to be Fae."

"So, I should be careful with what I eat?"

"You don't have to worry at school or at restaurants in towns like Lachlan Falls. But you shouldn't accept food from strangers—especially not from Fae. It's like selling your soul to the devil."

"Right. I will not accept Turkish delight from beautiful women riding sleighs," I said.

Josie looked at me quizzically. I took it she had never read *The Chronicles of Narnia*.

She led me down a set of stairs. With each step that we descended, the change in the air grew more obvious. The hairs on my arms prickled.

"Do you feel that?" I pointed to my arm. It was the kind of electricity one felt before lightning and thunder.

She shrugged. "Maybe you're more sensitive to it than the rest of us. All the more reason for you to stay away from electronics."

The deeper we descended, the more charged the air grew, and the more energized I felt. My skin tingled pleasantly with the promise of a storm. How strange that I'd only been away from Morty civilization for a few days, but already I noticed how electricity affected me.

Sconces lit the walls with a warm orange glow. We must have gone down two floors before we came to internet utopia. Thirty computers lined three rows of the lab. They were more state-of-the-art than the typical school computer lab. The blue light of two computers screens lit the room. Josie plugged her phone charger into the outlet underneath one and logged on to a computer. I followed suit. It all looked so normal and banal, like I was in some internet café in Eugene.

I didn't feel my life force sucking away from me via the electronics and outlets. If electricity was supposed to drain my powers, why did it feel like I'd come home the moment I stepped into the internet café?

I couldn't deny all the times electronics had faltered in my presence. Nor could I deny I was the reason lightning had struck one of my ex-boyfriends. My magic had felt like electricity. I'd blamed everything on sex and arousing thoughts, but there was an electrical component that didn't make sense. Thatch had given me a book on lightning and thunder elementals that I still needed to read. Maybe I would be able to discover how my magic worked with Thatch's help.

Or he might hex me, drain all my powers, and have his revenge.

The sign above the printer listed the cost per page. First I printed out my advanced lessons on perspective and portraits, then the beginning level ones on line, shape, and patterns. As I waited, I opened an incognito window to do my secret research with less risk of raising magical alarms—if they had such things.

I wanted to use this time to discover everything I could that the school didn't want me to know. I looked up blood magic and pain magic. Nothing came up except *Dungeons & Dragons* stuff. I glanced at Josie's screen before I typed in the Fae Fertility Paradox and Lost Court. I gave up after scanning five Google pages of irrelevant headings. The time whittled by and I still had so much to do. I printed more vocabulary lists and worksheets for shading, facial proportions, and one-point perspective.

I checked my email and then used Skype to call my mom's ground line.

My adoptive mom, I corrected myself. My fairy godmother. It felt strange to think of her that way. She picked up on the third ring.

"Hi, Mom, it's me." The connection buzzed with static.

"Clarissa!" she squealed. "I'm so happy to hear from you. I've been so worried. How is everything? Do you have students yet?"

"No, that's next week. I've been getting my classroom ready. I was thinking it would be nice to have my art supplies here and display some of my art. The classroom is pretty barren. Can you mail stuff to me in this, um, dimension?"

"What? What did you say? There's too much static."

Curse Skype for the horrible connection! It was worse than usual. Probably magic interfered with it.

I repeated myself.

"Sure, honey, just email me a list of things you need, and I'll mail it to the school's P.O. box. Send that to me too, okay? Or better yet, why don't I take off work and visit you? I can bring you everything then."

That was just the kind of thing she would do. "That's so sweet, Mom, but school is starting, and I have so much to do. Let's hold off on a visit for a little while."

"Sure, sure."

I hated how sad she sounded. "Also, I'm pretty sure I need some money from my bank account transferred into gold currency."

"Yes, I'd forgotten all about that. It's been a long time since I've been in the Unseen Realm."

I lowered my voice and glanced at Josie again. She wore headphones plugged into the computer and was playing *League of Legends.*

"Also, can you pack my lockpick kit?" I quickly added, "It's for a stairwell that leads to my closet. I need to get in because I don't have a key." I wondered if she would be able to hear the lie in my voice. Josie didn't look up from her computer. I didn't want her to find out I was planning on stealing that book Thatch had removed the important pages from.

"I'll look for it," Mom said.

I lowered my voice just to be safe, afraid how Josie would take it that I had an interest in "restricted" information. "Mom, do you know anything about the Fae Fertility Paradox? It was mentioned in some book I was told to read, but there was no context for it."

Her voice came out all crackling and loud. "What? The Fae what?"

I wished I'd brought my headset with a mic to talk into. I repeated myself.

"What book was that in?" she asked.

"*Womby's: A History of the School.* I wondered what it was."

"This is about Alouette Loraline, isn't it? I don't want you getting into any of the nonsense she was part of. It was some pretty dark stuff, nothing a good girl like you needs to involve herself in."

"Math. Science. Computers. That isn't dark."

She tsked. "Witchkin have different values than we do. You've lived in the Morty Realm your entire life. Some of their rules aren't going to make sense to you. But I hope you can at least understand why blood magic would be wrong by our standards—and theirs. We do not use other people's blood to do harm. We do not use pain magic."

I didn't want to be that kind of witch if that was what Loraline had done to people.

The papercut and the *Guernica* incident in my classroom had been worse than I'd first realized. It had been blood magic, and my fairy godmother would have been so disappointed in me, even if she knew it was an accident.

I glanced at Josie. She tapped away at her keyboard and muttered under her breath. I was pretty sure she was cursing—as in swearing—not incanting a spell.

"I'm not going to get into any blood magic or cult-like stuff," I said. "I just wanted to know what the Fae Fertility Paradox is."

Static filled the silence, sounding like a demonic language. "I've been out of the loop for a long time. I don't know the specifics of the paradox, but I can tell you about Fae fertility. It's common knowledge they can't have children anymore—at least most of them can't. They need Witchkin, but they resent us. They're allergic to just about everything in the human world, but they need humans to have children, which gives them the ability to sire

Witchkin. There's a lot more to it than that, but you don't need to know any more. Let the Fae figure out their own fertility problems."

"But it isn't just a Fae problem. It's why you couldn't have children. It's why you adopted Missy and me."

I hadn't meant to bring up my deceased sister. The words ached in my chest and made my throat tight.

Growling static filled the silence.

"Honey, I've got to go. I have a yoga class at six. Please don't get involved with the Fae. You saw how the Raven Court can be. They'll enslave you and chain you to a bed to pop out babies. And even if you're infertile like I am, they'll chain you up and use you for their own pleasure just because they can. That's what Fae do. They use Witchkin. Promise me you won't get involved, okay?"

"I won't let the Raven Court chain me to a bed to pop out babies," I said dryly.

We said our goodbyes. I kept thinking about electricity and Loraline's experiments. I didn't know how it related to fertility. Could she have discovered the answer to the Fae Fertility Paradox, but someone hadn't wanted her to succeed? Or maybe all of this was wishful thinking because I didn't want to be related to the Wicked Witch of the Pacific Northwest.

I went back to Google Docs and printed out vocabulary lists and warm-up exercises until my time was up and my computer shut down. Josie swore at the computer.

"No!" I said. "I need more time!"

Josie yawned and stretched. "Half an hour depletes our powers so much, that's about all I'd recommend. Today we really pushed it at forty-five minutes. You really should try to cut back. It isn't good to depend on computers."

I didn't feel drained. I felt more alive and ready to teach than ever, and I still had so much to do. How was I going to be able to balance my computer time between what I needed for art lessons and the information I needed to know about my mother's magic?

On the way out of the building, Hal waved. "Gold! Bring gold next time."

"Precious, my precious," Josie said under her breath.

I burst into giggles. She pushed me out the door where we both busted up.

"How does Hal get internet in another dimension?" I asked.

"I don't know." She wiggled her fingers at me. "Magic. Or a generator."

A generator created electricity and relied on diesel. That had nothing to do with fiber optics, telephone lines, or some way to connect to the internet.

Khaba met us outside, promptly at the appointed time. "How was your .

. . meal?" he asked, a knowing smirk on his face.

"Great!" Josie said. Her eyes were droopier than I remembered. "I love me some fish and chips."

"Right." He looked down at us, amused.

Two could play that game. "Have a nice time with your . . . errands?" I asked.

"What can I say? Some like it Scot."

I was pretty sure the accent in Lachlan Falls sounded Irish more than Scottish, but what did I know? The Unseen Realm was on the border of Faerie. Plus, it wouldn't have fit Khaba's puntastic reply.

I winked at him. "Sounds like someone has a kilt complex."

His grin widened, the superiority that had been there moments ago fading. "Kilty as charged."

Josie giggled like a school girl. Khaba patted her on the head. "Come on, ladies. We have one more stop before going back to school. I didn't have time to go on all my errands."

"Gee, I wonder why," I said.

He gave me a playful shove. Where his hand touched my arm, it tingled with magic. Whereas the Raven Court had been as cold as winter, his touch was warm and friendly. I wanted to like Khaba, but I couldn't forget everything I'd experienced thus far regarding the Fae. How did I know he wasn't in cahoots with the Raven Court?

Ye Green Grocery was in the center of the village. From the outside, it resembled the other stone buildings. The interior looked like an apothecary made for hippies, the psychedelic colors of the shop modern in comparison.

"I need to restock my supply of sweets," Khaba said. "It's a matter of life or death, or else I might not make it through the school year."

Josie followed him down a bulk food aisle like a puppy. I wondered if I should tell her it was never going to work out.

I perused the aisles, taking in the array of love potions and teas promising eternal youth.

The old man behind the counter had pointed ears and long silver hair parted down the middle. The print on his tie-dyed shirt said, "Hug a tree. Kiss a fairy. How about starting with me?" He squinted at us and readjusted his Lennon-style sunglasses over his nose.

"Well, I'll be pelted with a rotten goose egg!" His voice came out hoarse and raspy. His accent was less Irish and more British. "Is that Professor Loraline?"

I looked around, realizing he was speaking to me. Ugh. Not another person who was going to hate me for being like my mother.

I ran a hand through my pink hair. "No. Sorry. It just happens I look like her. Tragic coincidence."

He waved me closer. Reluctantly, I approached the counter.

He scratched the stubble on his chin. "Indeed. You must be related. Have any urges to bathe in the blood of children?"

"Um, no." Had my mother done that?

"Have you tortured anyone to death or to the brink of death in a rite of pain magic for the supposed good of all Witchkin kind?"

"No. Did she really do that?"

"So they say." He shrugged. "What about a desire to eat the hearts of your enemies?"

That sounded like a stereotypical witch sort of thing. "I don't even like chicken hearts."

He chuckled. "I hear the hearts of your enemies taste just like chicken, so there probably wouldn't be much difference if one needed a substitute." He removed his glasses. His eyes were vividly blue, brighter than the sky. "Have ever you killed anyone?"

I swallowed. "Not on purpose."

He grunted. "I have just the thing for you."

"I wasn't going to buy anything. I was just looking."

"Nonsense." He waved me after him. He shuffled along with a cane, stopping at the shelf of candies, then continued to the bulk food aisle. "You need my maple pecan granola. It will help keep negativity from clinging to your aura."

I didn't need granola. School food was free, part of the room and board, even if it was blah. Then I saw it. This wasn't ordinary granola. It was balls of crunchy, nuggety goodness. I always loved to snack on the bigger chunks that came out of the cereal box. Maybe a snack for those times when school meals didn't cut it would be nice. It sparkled and shimmered in the light.

"It will cleanse your chakras," he said. "And believe me, you need it."

"Do you take credit?" I asked.

He sighed in exasperation. "If I must. Next time bring gold. Or your firstborn child."

"Ha!" I said. There were plenty of teen mothers I'd met during my internship at high schools who would gladly have paid him in the latter, but he couldn't be serious.

I paid him at the front register. I found out the old man's name was Clarence Greenpine.

The old man squinted at Khaba and Josie in the bulk food aisle over his glasses, lowering his voice so that only I could hear. "Keep your friends close, your enemies closer, and Fae . . . keep them as far from you as possible. You understand me, lass?"

I glanced over my shoulder at Khaba. I didn't know what to say to that. Khaba was Josie's friend, and Josie was my only friend so far. He'd been decent to me. I didn't want to hate him just because everyone else said all

Fae were bad.

"Promise me you'll be careful," Clarence said.

I nodded. That I would do.

Khaba rolled a wooden wheelbarrow full of candies to the front of the store. I'd never seen anyone purchase so many sweets in my life. Clarence rang him up, but Khaba didn't pay with cash or a card.

"Credit?" Clarence raised an eyebrow.

Khaba nodded. "I'll be back later to pay my debts." He glanced at Josie and me. "When I'm alone."

Khaba handed four of his six paper bags to Josie, who made no complaint about carrying the majority of his groceries as we headed out.

Khaba peeked in my paper bag. "Honey, did he bewitch you into buying granola?"

Bewitch me? No, I'd bought it of my own free will, hadn't I? I considered the way it had sparkled enticingly. "Whoa. He tricked me, didn't he? Is that legal?"

Khaba shrugged. I hadn't even realized someone had cast a spell over me. I would need to be careful in this realm.

Josie smirked. "Did he tell you it would cleanse your aura?"

"Um, yeah. Won't it?" I asked.

Khaba waved at the bag. "More like cleanse your colon."

"Did he try to sell you the 'special' granola, the stuff with weed slipped into it?" Josie asked.

My eyes went wide. "No."

Khaba smiled. "Good thing or I'd have to confiscate it from you."

They both laughed harder. I guessed the border of the Unseen Realm was a lot like Oregon and Washington with legalized marijuana if they could slip it into granola.

I filled the rest of my evening with studying and meditation from the dreaming book, and I even squeezed in a thirty-minute jog. The landscaping was beautiful, with beds of flowers along the paths in front of the school and benches placed under shady trees. Hedge sculptures lined one section of the path. A shrub pruned to look like a unicorn was raised up on its back legs. It turned its head and watched as I jogged past. I stared at him in surprise. A topiary merman raised his trident, barring my way.

"You shall not go into the forest," he said sternly.

"Um. . . ." Maybe talking shrubs were normal here. "I wasn't going to," I said. "I was just going to jog around the school."

"Sure, she is," the unicorn shrub said to the merman. "That's what all the students say."

"I'm not a student. I'm a teacher." It was bad enough humans and

Witchkin thought I looked young, but did the hedge animals have to mistake me for being a kid too?

The merman snorted. "Do you have your teacher identification?"

"No." No one had said anything about having a name tag or getting a card printed. This was just one more thing to add to my to-do list.

The merman didn't remove his trident from my path. I jogged back the way I'd come. I now noticed the blackberries barring the way into the forest along the edges. Some of the paths that led into the woods were guarded by stone statues reminiscent of classical Greek art. If I really had wanted to go jogging in the woods—which I didn't want to after my encounters with the Raven Court—I could have used the unguarded path Josie, Khaba, and I had taken earlier around the back of the school. Instead of taking the fork that led to the front of the school toward the Morty Realm, I headed along the path around the back of the school that led toward Lachlan Falls.

I stopped and stretched in the long shadows at the rear. At the end of a long arm of hallway, one of the brick towers was crumbled and in disrepair. This had to be the section of the building chapter thirty-two had mentioned. The place my biological mother had destroyed.

The sun sank lower, an orange circle visible through the tree line. Shadows stretched from the school, the jagged edges of the broken tower resembling claws. I glanced over my shoulder, saw no one in sight, and left the path to jog closer to the ruins. Blackened wood was scattered in with the debris. It didn't look like anything special. I wondered what my biological mother had been trying to do. Had she succeeding in solving the Fae Fertility Paradox? Was that how she'd had me? Was it how she'd died? Something about that must have made Thatch nervous.

I climbed to the top of a heap of rubble, scanning the wreckage, waiting for my mother's mysteries to be revealed. No ghosts appeared. No secrets unfolded before me. Disappointment weighed me down. I wasn't sure what I expected. It was growing too dark to see much in the debris anyway.

My shirt clung to my back with sweat, and I shook it away from my torso as I gazed down at the topiary animals and statues across the grounds. Greenhouses were situated farther behind the school, and a stable lay beyond that.

It seemed like it was time to call it quits for the day and go shower. I didn't know how the school managed to heat water in my Victorian-looking wing with their limitations in technology, but I wasn't about to question a good thing.

As I started climbing down the rubble, movement at the edge of the woods caught my eye. Someone walked along the path toward the trees. I scrambled down the heap of rocks, not wanting to draw attention to myself and for someone to accuse me of being too inquisitive about my mother or summoning dark magic. By the time I reached the bottom and jogged back along the path, I could see the figure's gray suit and black hair.

Thatch.

He carried an armful of books. Another immense stack floated behind him. He glanced over his shoulder in a sneaky sort of way that told me he didn't want to be followed. I dodged behind the rubble, spying on him from the shadows.

Those must have been more of the textbooks he didn't want me reading. All I needed was one. I stuck to the shadows closest to the building, heading in his direction. He took the path toward Lachlan Falls.

Nothing guarded the forest. I didn't understand how the school protected children from leaving. I had seen the boundary of the school grounds outside the woods on the way to Lachlan Falls. Fae could just as easily snatch students after dark if they left on this forest path.

I jogged up to the trees. In the distance I saw a flicker of movement as he walked through the woods. Was it really worth entering the forest and risk accidentally crossing that boundary just for a book? I considered the way Thatch had sneakily looked over his shoulder. He was up to something.

For better or worse, I intended to find out.

The moment I crossed into the gloomy shadows of the path under the immense oak, something snapped at my arm like a rubber band. A long wooden switch lashed out at the back of my legs, hard enough to make my knees buckle.

Now I knew why this path wasn't guarded with statues or hedge animals. The trees stood watch.

I flinched back from another whipping switch.

"Stop it! I'm a teacher!" I shouted.

The trees creaked and groaned like laughter. Their leaves rustled in a shush of whispers, but I didn't speak tree. I couldn't understand what they were saying. I pushed myself up, ready to go back, but a long wooden vine circled around my legs, binding them together. I struggled against the coils and tried to yank myself back toward the school.

"Let me go! I'm not a student." When that tactic didn't work, I tried, "I'm going back to the school now. I promise."

I pointed to the mismatched architecture behind me. Another switch lashed out at my wrist, smarting the skin. Wooden vines coiled around my arms and pinned them to my sides.

A raven circled overhead in the darkening sky. Not a good sign. My heart thundered in my rib cage. The Raven Court wasn't supposed to be able to cross onto school grounds. This part of the forest was still under Womby's protection. Had Thatch called the bird? Maybe he knew I'd followed. What if this had been a trap?

The vines were rough against the bare flesh of my legs and arms. The cords yanked me upward, tipping me upside down. I swayed, suspended in the air about ten feet above the ground. A tree poked at me with a twiggy limb, making me rock back and forth.

It was hard to tell from upside down, but the grooves in the bark of the tree near me reminded me of a face, with deep cracks for eyes and a gaping hole for a mouth. It lifted me closer. The hole stretched wider.

I hoped the trees here weren't carnivorous. The raven cawed, the sound echoing through the silent woods.

I tried the one spell I'd been able to do in the past. "Abra-cadaver! Abra-cadaver!"

Nothing happened. When magic failed, all that remained was the one tactic I had left.

I screamed.

CHAPTER ELEVEN
This Is Why Treebeard and All the Other Ents Lack Wives

My heart pounded so loud it drowned out the creaking laughter of the trees. The raven cawed loudly, and I was certain it was trying to summon emissaries of the Raven Court. My blood rushed to my head, pounding fiercely. Within thirty seconds, I had a headache. It was hard to think of anything else to do, so I kept screaming. Maybe someone would hear.

The tree pushed me away. Or I thought it pushed me away. Then I realized the tree on the other side of the path had yanked me closer. It brought me toward its mouth. The trees played tug of war with me, first one tree trying to eat me and then the other.

I screamed louder.

"Hey, what are you doing?" a man with a Transylvanian accent shouted.

The trees thrust me into their canopy, farther from the school grounds, trying to hide me. Twigs snapped against my face. Their leaves rustled and whispered, sounding like words.

"Help! I'm up here! Help!" I said.

"What have I said about scaring people? Not cool," the man said, his voice familiar. "Put her down. Gently."

The trees spoke again. I tried to make sense of their sounds, but it was too exotic to understand.

"She was telling the truth. She's not a student. This is Miss Lawrence, our new art teacher. That's not a polite way to introduce yourself to a new staff member, now is it?" His accent came out thicker as he raised his voice.

I spotted a pair of shaggy legs and cloven feet. "Sam?" I asked.

"The one and the same. Twiggy, Oaky, are you going to follow directions the first time I ask you? Or am I going to have to rename you Lumber and Firewood?"

The trees thrust me out from the shadows and dropped me on the ground, not at all gently, but at least not on my head. Scratches covered my arms and legs.

Sam stood over me, a silhouette against the blooming orange and crimson of the sky. He extended a hand and helped me up. "What were you doing in the woods? It's getting dark." Just as the first time I'd met him, he wore no clothes, his ripped abs obvious despite the hairiness of his chest. The fur growing over the lower half of his body was thick enough to resemble pants.

"I was jogging. I wasn't going to go into the woods. I just wanted to . . . have a look." I didn't know if I should mention Thatch going into the forest.

The raven swooped lower, landing on a branch.

I leapt back and pointed. "Look, it's the Raven Court. They're here for me. We need to get help."

A gap showed between Sam's front teeth, and his thick black hair flopped back as he laughed. The trees laughed with him, shaking and creaking. "No, that's just Professor Thatch's pet. She's how I knew something was going on over here. I saw her circling, and then I heard you scream. She tends to do that—the circling—before swooping down to peck some little creature's eyes out."

Cheery.

"Not that I think she would have done that to you. Probably not, anyway." Sam waved his arms at the bird. "Get out of here, you little vulture. No eyes for you today."

The oak tree nudged the bird off its limb, and she took off.

"Thatch has a raven as a pet?" I asked. "Isn't that a little odd? Aren't they the Raven Queen's servants or something?"

"That isn't a raven. It's a crow." Sam trampled deeper into the forest and bent down to snap a leaf off a low shrub. His hooves clomped over the hard dirt.

"Let's see the battle wounds," he said, holding out a palm.

I lifted my hands, examining the scratches on my arms. Sam squeezed a comfrey leaf. A drop of milky fluid oozed from the vein in the center. He spread the plant ointment over a red line on my wrist. He tore the leaf and applied more plant goo onto my face. He was a handy guy to have as a friend. Not only did he excel at healing, but he also commanded the respect of the trees.

Sam examined a scratch on my cheek. He smelled green and musky, like earth and plants. His hand was warm on the back of my knee as he applied comfrey leaf to my legs. I was suddenly aware of how close he crouched, the fur of his legs brushing against my calves. A flutter of excitement tickled my core. He stared up at me, a question in his expression. His fingers lingered on my leg. His brow furrowed, and his lips parted.

The scratches he caressed with milky plant fluid were already diminishing. A strange green sensation washed over me, like a thousand flowers blossoming inside me. I had never known healing magic using plants could be this sexy.

"Are you casting a spell over me?" he asked.

"What? No." I was not aroused by a satyr. I wrenched myself backward, nearly stumbling over a tree root. The absence of his touch left me cold and shivering. My stomach ached. Maybe I was aroused a little. It wasn't bestiality if he was half human, right?

He shook himself and stood. "You remind me of someone. What's your affinity?"

"I don't know." Everyone was big on affinities here. It sounded like I was going to have to add that to my to-do list. It was getting pretty long. "I'm still learning about my magic. I was raised in the Morty Realm."

"You're not a tree affinity, but there's something earthy about you. Fertility magic? No, that's not quite right. It reminds me of someone else. . . ." The longer Sam scrutinized me, the more I worried he would figure out who my biological mother was and let the trees eat me.

I cleared my throat, wanting to change the subject. "Thanks for the intervention with the trees," I said.

"No problemo." He coughed. "Twiggy and Oaky here apologize. Don't you?" He pointed a finger of warning at them.

From the way they creaked and groaned they sounded more like they were laughing than apologizing.

"Try not to be too hard on them," he said to me. "They're probably teenagers in tree years."

One of the trees whispered something. Sam held up a finger in stern warning. "Hey! Be polite. There's no need to imply something nasty like that." The apology in Sam's eyes melted as he looked at me again. His expression reflected fear and then horror.

Craptacular. He'd figured it out. Or perhaps the trees had told him.

"You're *her* daughter, aren't you? Shit!" He backed away. "Get out of my woods."

Just what I needed, another enemy.

The moment I turned away to trudge back to the school, one of the trees snapped at me with a twig, making me jump. Sam didn't tell them to behave this time.

I had a feeling I wouldn't be able to escape the school if I wanted to. Not that I had any reason to leave, but nonetheless, the thought unsettled me.

CHAPTER TWELVE
Friendship Is Magic, and Other Things My Little Ponies Taught Me

After my shower and reading in my classroom, I headed for my room at nine. I found my dorm occupied by my new roomie. Vega paced the room, filling the entirety of the space like she owned it. She ranted about the brownies leaving her dirty clothes for her to wash herself. "Of all the nerve, having to clean my own clothes!"

Yep, a real hardship.

"Those ungrateful little hobgoblins!" A string of swear words followed. She kicked at her guillotine, which didn't seem like the smartest move. "I'll skin those little fuckers alive."

I peeled back the covers to my bed, yawning. "What do you mean? Why are they ungrateful?"

"I left the obligatory gratuity." Vega waved a hand at the desk. "They were supposed to do my fucking laundry and clean the room while I was setting up my classroom, but the impy bastards just took the food and left. I even apologized for not bringing something earlier." She swore and continued to rant.

Realization washed over me.

"Oh. So that food on the desk was . . . payment? Is this like a laundry service?" I had wondered how the essentials here worked. My mom hadn't fully prepared me for this world. It had been too long since she'd lived here.

Vega huffed. "Don't call it that. Those fucktards will leave the school if you try to 'pay' them. And most will leave if you thank them. All you can do is apologize or leave presents." She plopped onto her bed and dramatically draped an arm across her forehead. "Good servants are hard to find these days."

I considered setting out some high-fiber granola for the brownies to make up for what I had eaten. I edged closer to my wardrobe where I'd stashed some.

Vega continued to complain. "Fae can be so temperamental. They're all about the rules."

"I don't understand. What rules?" I asked.

"Don't you know anything?"

"Nope."

She huffed dramatically. "Never thank a Fae or else you'll owe him a favor. It's like selling your fucking soul to the devil. I've had more than enough experience with that." She sat up abruptly.

I shrank back, afraid my face was painted with guilt and she knew I was the one who had eaten the food intended for the brownies.

"I know what will make me feel better. Aside from a room to myself." Vega stalked over to the bird cage, flung the door open, and snatched up a bird.

"No! Please! No!" the bird sang.

I watched in horror as she held the songbird up to her overgrown plant. The hinged jaw of the large Venus flytrap opened.

"You aren't going to—" I started.

Vega let the bird go, and the plant snapped it up whole. The bird struggled, one wing flopping violently from the side of the plant's mouth. My heart dropped down to my stomach as I watched the plant consume the little bird.

And people were afraid *I* was evil?

I glanced around the room at the other evidence of my roommate's nefarious intentions. Her bottles of potions lined my wardrobe. The crystal ball was on there again. And that room hog had filled my shelves with her books. Evil.

See if I decided to do her any favors! I was keeping that granola for myself.

The following day I did my homework in order to get a handle on my dream magic. I woke up early and wrote down my dreams, meditated, and read before I met the rest of the teachers at our first official staff meeting. It started off full of gusto with a pep talk from the principal, then turned into hours of boring details that nearly put me to sleep. And we had two days of this. Oh joy.

We sat on hard wooden chairs around a large conference table in the staff room. A banner with the school's crest and team flags covered most of the puke-green wall across from me. A wood stove rested in the corner, topped with a dusty tea kettle. There wasn't even a coffee maker or microwave like most schools, but I guessed that made sense with the Witchkins' aversion to electricity. It certainly didn't have a popcorn machine like Hamlin Middle School, but it would have been a nice perk if they had enchanted one to run on steam power and magic.

Like the previous days I'd been at the school, it was clear I was less than welcome, especially among the older staff members. Jackie Frost, the teacher who taught elemental magic, and Silas Lupi, the anatomy and physiology teacher, eyed me with disdain. Evita Lupi, wife of Silas Lupi, taught a variety of animal magic classes and oversaw Saturday study hall. During the break, Josie introduced me to Evita. She greeted me with tepid enthusiasm.

"You've got to meet Grandmother Bluehorse," Josie said. "She's so warm and friendly. She took me under her wing last year when I didn't know anything or anyone."

She looped her arm through mine and walked me over to an old woman in a gown fringed with green moss and lichen that matched the flora and fauna growing from her green witch hat. She reminded me of Radagast from *Lord of the Rings*, only female. And Native American. And without bird poop dripping down the side of her head.

I held out my hand. "Nice to meet you Grandmo—"

She lifted her nose up at my hand. "Only the children are allowed to call me that. It's *Professor* Bluehorse to you."

Josie's smile faltered. "Um. Sorry. My mistake, Professor."

Jeb waved at Professor Bluehorse and swaggered over. "There you are, Grandmother. I reckon you'd make a fine mentor for Miss Lawrence. She needs somebody to look out for her and—"

Professor Bluehorse cut him off. "You want me to protect the daughter of the witch who killed my husband?"

"Well, when you put it like that, it sounds a bit . . . ahem." Jeb coughed.

My eyes went wide. No wonder she didn't like me. I wondered how many other staff members my mother had wronged.

During our morning team meetings, I sat with Amadea Kutchi, my department head; Sebastian Reade, a quiet middle-aged man who was the foreign language teacher; and Jasper Jang, a bald but youthful man who taught choir, band, and drama.

The first thing that came out of Jasper's mouth was, "Son of a succubus! I don't care what they say, I am not teaching stagecraft. That's what the art teacher is for."

"Hang on to your hobgoblins," Coach Kutchi said. She jerked a thumb at me. "We don't even know if she'll be alive next semester. That's when you're putting on the school play, right?"

"Excuse me," I said. "I can hear you."

The rest of the staff meeting didn't go any smoother.

Teachers were given the afternoon to prepare for their incoming classes. It would have been a smart idea to use the time I had to get ready for classes. Or I could have read the books Thatch had given me. I should have done either. But all I could think about was how the other staff had whispered about me and avoided me like the Ebola virus.

I went to Josie's room to see if she was in to talk. She wasn't. I peeked into the next classroom down the hall to see if she was visiting another teacher. Evita Lupi glanced up from her desk and scowled. She was undoubtedly angry because Jeb had banned Mr. and Mrs. Lupi from sharing a room on campus because he feared conjugal acts might bring out some kind of sex magic from me. I didn't blame him.

I hurried past Mrs. Lupi's room.

Sticking my head through the next door, I found Julian Thistledown leaned over a planner at his desk. Just as the previous times I'd seen him, a nimbus of golden light glowed around him, making him resemble an angel.

He stood the moment he saw me. "May I help you, Miss Lawrence?"

"I was just looking for Josie." I backed away, intimidated by his beauty.

Julian Thistledown may have been extreme eye candy, but that was all he was going to be. Even if Jeb hadn't laid down the law earlier, I was not going to fall for another guy whom I would accidentally electrocute with my magic.

Julian called after me. "How are preparations going? Ready for classes?" He left his desk and came closer. His sandy-blond hair was rakishly tussled, and smears of ink stained his fingers. He gave off a sexy, absentminded professor vibe, someone good-looking, but unaware of it.

I resisted the urge to be sucked in by his good looks. I ventured back into the room, answering his question to be polite. "As ready as I'll ever be."

His room was smaller than mine. The rows of table desks didn't take up as much room as art tables. The back contained bookcases full of textbooks. The walls were decorated with portraits of wizened witches and school crests and colors.

"You seem down. Was it that meeting? I couldn't believe how rude teachers were on your first day." He spoke quickly, energetically, like he'd had too much caffeine. He was comical, the adorable kind of guy I easily fell for. Even when I didn't want to.

I cracked a smile. "It's just frustrating. Everything here is so . . . different than I expected."

He nodded sympathetically. "The adjustment to our realm must be difficult. I wish our staff had made you feel more welcome. It doesn't seem like Thatch is helping much. Isn't he supposed to be your mentor?"

"Thatch!" The bane of my existence. "He was supposed to give me books to read, but he ripped out the pages of the most important sections." I hesitated, not wanting to say more, but Julian's brows were furrowed in concern as he listened. Maybe he did care. I opened up a little bit more. "I want to know what my mother did and why science is considered evil. Thatch keeps thwarting every attempt I make to learn about her." I sat down on a desk.

"That's our Felix Thatch, out to make everyone's life miserable to entertain himself. Did you hear about what he did last year with everyone's prophecy chocolate?" Gold lights glittered around his face. "After all that work Puck did, he switched them!"

I found it hard to focus on his words when I kept thinking about how beautiful he was. I forced myself to look away. "Josie filled me in."

He lowered his voice. "Science isn't evil, by the way. Just dangerous. Fae can't tolerate electricity or cold iron or many synthetic materials, so the evil overlords ban them. They might label those items as 'wicked,' but keep in mind, Witchkin just consider them toxic."

"Like an allergy?" I asked.

"Just so. Many of us Witchkin are sensitive to plastic, blue dye number two, and other human-made chemicals to some degree, but to a lesser degree than Fae."

"That doesn't sound evil. Just practical to stay away from."

He leaned against one of the desks across from me. "You have to understand, we aren't the ones making the rules in this world. Nor do we publish the textbooks. The Fae don't exactly want us to learn about science, or we might learn how to weaken their magic." He waved a hand dismissively. "It's all about Fae privilege and keeping Witchkin down."

He seemed well-versed in this topic. I was glad that I had stayed to talk to him. "Do you think that's why Thatch doesn't want me to know about my mother? So I don't discover something she learned about the Fae? Something that could harm the Raven Court?" Thatch had to be working for the Raven Queen. He had a pet raven, and he acted E-V-I-L.

"The Raven Court? Hardly. I'll let you in on a little secret." He leaned in conspiratorially. "For the last five years Thatch has applied to be the art teacher—for your position. Jeb refuses him every time for lack of experience. Thatch is taking out his anger on you."

"No way. He's not an artist. Is he?" Although, those creepy ink scribbles in that leather-bound book looked to be as much art as magic if they were his. "Why would he want my position?"

"We all joke it's because he wants to finger paint occult symbols on the walls and summon demons like that other art teacher did a few years ago."

Julian disarmed me with his humor. I found myself laughing along with him. He was easy to talk to and friendlier than most of the staff.

His smile faded, and he stared off into the distance as if lost in thought. "Now that I think of it, Thatch was the one who gave Mr. Ife the idea to teach finger painting to students because he wanted to get Ife fired."

"Finger painting? At a high school level?" That was evil. Anyone who did that probably would be the kind of person to summon a demon. I wouldn't be *that* teacher.

"So, what happened to Mr. Ife? Did he get fired?"

"No, the demon got Abebe Ife. Still, that wasn't as bad as what happened to the other art teachers. Agnes Padilla was snatched by Fae. Then there was Jorge Smith, attacked by the students."

I swallowed. "Wait? *All* the art teachers have died?"

"No, not all of them. Lisa Singer wandered out of bed in the middle of the night and mysteriously disappeared." He leaned in closer. "Lisa and I were good friends. She told me she suspected Thatch was up to something nefarious. She kept seeing him send that bird of his into the forest with messages. I told her not to confront him, but she didn't listen." He shook his head sadly.

How could Jeb not see Thatch worked for the Raven Queen?

"You watch out for him," Julian said solemnly. "We don't want the fifth art teacher in six years to go missing."

Holy cow! This job was cursed! I slid into a chair, picking Julian's brain about the school and the previous art teachers' disappearances. I had a suspicion the teachers' deaths somehow were related to Thatch. Had they stumbled upon some secret he wished to keep hidden, or had he truly wanted their job?

"How long have you taught here?" I asked, wondering if he had been around long enough to know anything useful about the school's distant past.

"Five glorious years." It was hard to tell if that was sarcasm or he really enjoyed his job.

In any case, he hadn't been around long enough to meet my friend. Derrick would have graduated before that. Then again, Derrick wouldn't have started a magical education until his senior year. Maybe he stayed on longer.

"Do you remember having any students with wind affinities when you first started?" I asked. "I had a friend, Derrick Winslow, who came here. He has blue hair."

"He doesn't ring a bell, but wind affinities blow through all the time— no pun intended." He chuckled at his own joke.

"Oh." Another dead end. The more I asked around about Derrick, the more pointless the search for him felt. Maybe I wasn't meant to look for him. Fate kept pushing me toward other mysteries.

"What about . . . ?" Did I dare ask the question? So far Julian had been cordial, and I didn't want to ruin that like I had with Satyr Sam. "You're a history teacher, right? So, you know about the school's history? About my biological mother's history?"

He cleared his throat and held himself taller, as if proud of himself. "It happens I know quite a bit about the school. I could fill you in on some of the magical details of the Unseen Realm. There must be a lot you don't know."

I couldn't tell if he was evading the question about my mother. "Is there some reason no one wants to fill me in on what my mother did?"

"Everyone wants to forget about her and the murders." He lowered his voice. "From the way I hear it, no one is exempt for encouraging your mother's proclivities. No one wants to be associated with the dark arts or the crimes she committed. But your presence here makes it impossible for staff to pretend she didn't exist. It's a topic best not gossiped about on school grounds.

"I wasn't here when the incident happened, but enough of it is general knowledge. I'm sure I could satiate your hunger for . . . information." He said it in a teasing, flirtatious way.

My face flushed with warmth. "Sure."

I tried not to let his beguiling smile lure me into more amorous thoughts. He had just hinted at something important: motivations for Thatch. My supposed mentor had to be hiding books from me because he didn't want me to figure out his involvement in Loraline's crimes. I wondered if Julian would object if I told him everything I wanted to know. "Do you have a copy of *Womby's: A History of the School?*"

"I do, but it's a horrible copy. After I took the job here and acquired my materials, I realized it had pages torn out."

Why did that not surprise me? "Chapter thirty-two?"

"Indeed! You must be psychic."

I cleared my throat. "Have you ever heard of . . . the Fae Fertility Paradox?"

He flinched as if startled by the question. "Ahem, no. I don't know anything about that. It isn't part of the curriculum. Perhaps I have a book about it I can loan you. I'll have to see." He chuckled nervously. "But I can fill you in on just about anything else."

From his reaction, I could tell I'd blown it. He probably thought I was a freak now too.

Josie walked by. That was all the excuse I needed to end the awkward conversation. I rose and pointed to the door. "I should catch Josie before she gets away. Maybe we could talk about my mother another time— somewhere off school grounds."

"Yes, of course. It truly has been a pleasure chatting with you." He took my hand in his. The unexpected warmth startled me. "Pardon my forwardness, but would you like to walk down to the pub after dinner? Not as a date, of course. Jeb wouldn't allow it. Just as colleagues." He flashed a dazzling smile, white teeth straight and perfect. "At least until the principal sees the silliness of his new rule and lifts the ban on allowing dating between colleagues this year." His thumb smoothed across the back of my hand. "We could discuss the more . . . taboo subjects you were inquiring about."

My stomach gave a little flutter. Julian Thistledown was handsome, funny, and smart—a history teacher. He was willing to tell me about my mother. He would be a good ally. Perhaps more importantly, he didn't act like I was a pariah. At least not when I didn't put my foot in my mouth.

"I'd like that," I said. "If Jeb lets me. He doesn't want me to leave the school with anyone who isn't a Celestor. Are you a Celestor?" I didn't know what Julian's affinity was, but it would be handy if he used the stars or moon as a power source like Thatch did. I was certain I would prefer Julian as a chaperone.

He straightened his ascot. "We didn't have that team at the school I attended. But in any case, I wouldn't be a Celestor. My affinity is the equivalent of Plandai, or plants." He gave a sheepish smile. "I'm probably not considered strong enough, nor do I have an affinity that would lend itself to the defensive magic of Celestors, nor am I good enough at *everything* like Mr. Thatch to be a suitable chaperone for you. Perhaps Darshan is available to come with us."

"Uh. . . ." Pro Ro seemed like a nice enough guy, but there was something off about him I couldn't put my finger on. Maybe I just didn't like how close he'd stood next to me when I'd been looking at the portrait of my biological mother. Perhaps it was something more. Then again, a witch was supposed to trust her instincts. I struggled to find a logical excuse. "We could, you know, find someone else."

"We can see if Josie and Khaba want to come with us," he suggested.

"Sure. They're great."

"It's a date! I mean, ahem, an undate. I mean, see you later."

We both laughed at his awkwardness.

Julian was cute, and I already found myself liking him. I was glad I hadn't let my first impressions bias me against him, but at the that same time, a hint of guilt tainted my joy. I still loved Derrick. I didn't know what he felt about me after all these years. He might blame me for the tornado, or he might resent me if I grew close to someone else.

Julian lowered his voice. "We can talk about some of those other topics you were inquiring about . . . off school grounds."

The promise of knowledge was the most tempting of forbidden fruits. It had nothing to do with the idea of an "undate." My mood soared as high as a hippie on special granola as I skipped down the hall to find Josie.

In her classroom, a book floated in the air in front of her. She turned a page with her wand, not looking up as she asked, "What's up, buttercup?"

"First, would you see if you could check a book out for me from the library? Mrs. Periwinkle might give you a different answer than she did me."

"Is the librarian hating on you too? What book do you need?"

"*Womby's: A History of the School.*" I launched into the story again. "Thatch gave me a book to read, but he removed some of the pages." I sat on the edge of a student desk. I wanted to confide in her. I wanted to trust she wouldn't think I was a bad person if I told her why. "The thing is . . . I want to know who my mother was. Everyone keeps telling me she was an evil bad-ass. They tell me I'm like her, or I'm going to be like her, or they don't want me to be like her. But I don't know why. I never met her."

She nodded sympathetically. "For sure. Haters gonna hate. Ain'ters gonna ain't. Sounds majorly annoying." The book floating in the air drifted down to the desk.

"Do you know anything about her? Who else did Loraline kill besides Grand—err—Professor Bluehorse's husband?"

"I don't know. I wasn't here. Have you tried talking to the principal?"

"Every time I try, Mrs. Keahi sends me away."

"That sucks balls."

"Julian Thistledown doesn't have a copy of the book that Thatch hasn't already censored. Thatch checked out a class set from the library, or that's what the librarian said if they aren't conspiring to keep me ignorant. Thatch is just . . . such a butthead."

She twirled a lavender streak of hair around a finger, staring off into the distance. "I bet Jeb has one. He has a copy of each textbook teachers use in his bookcase. You can ask him—if Mrs. Keahi ever lets you see him."

Who knew how long that would take? My shoulders deflated. No, I wasn't going to let this get me down. I had plans for the evening. I lifted my chin. "On the plus side, Julian asked if I wanted to go to the pub after dinner."

"Oh, a date," she said with a wink.

"Just as friends."

She smirked. "Right."

"But Julian isn't a Celestor, so I don't think Jeb would consider him powerful enough to 'chaperone' me off campus. I thought I would see if you and Khaba wanted to—"

"A double date!" she squealed. "Yay!" She jumped up and down in happiness. "I'll go ask Khaba." She ran off.

That poor girl. I had no idea how to break it to her Khaba would never be interested in her.

It wasn't a date, I told myself. Still, I put on makeup and wore a green, lacy dress that showed a hint more cleavage than I would wear at work. I was only going out to learn more information.

Julian, Khaba, Josie, and I walked to Lachlan Falls after dinner. From the outside of the Devil's Pint, the pub looked small and run-down, the sign advertising drinks above the door too faded to read except for the word "ale" that had been repainted. The inside was immense, like Mary Poppins' purse, and crowded with people. Men in kilts with cracked skin that reminded me of tree bark laughed loudly from a table by the door. Tall, shaggy beasts that might have been sasquatches mingled with dwarves wearing tartan plaids and pixie-like women in leafy skirts.

I stared in awe at how inhuman people looked. Josie nudged me with an elbow, and I stopped gaping.

The music was somewhere in between Celtic fiddling and rock. Lines of dancers crowded the floor, twirling and kicking as fast as Michael Flatley in *Riverdance*. It was fun to watch, but too loud for conversation. I nursed a beer more out of politeness than enjoyment.

Every time I asked Julian a question about my biological mother's history, he shouted, "What? Speak up."

No way was I going to shout out all the questions I had about Loraline.

Julian tugged me to my feet. "Let's see what you've got, twinkle toes."

I'd never tried traditional ceilidh dancing before. Neither of us were very good at the reels, but it was fun and energetic. It reminded me of country-western line dancing with do-si-dos, twirls, and lines that shifted so each person took turns dancing with multiple partners.

While Julian linked arms with his corner partner, the two-headed woman in a plaid skirt ran her hand over Julian's chest and winked at him. A twinge of jealousy spiked in me before I pushed it down. This wasn't a date. I was here to get information out of him.

Still, part of me wanted it to be a date.

Julian looked from the woman to me with a sheepish smile as he returned to his place in the line across from me. More than a few women batted their eyes at him.

With his good looks and charm, Julian could have had any woman in the room. But he wanted to dance with me. I was flattered. And a little bit intimidated. Jeb had made the non-dating rule for a reason. He knew my past. I didn't want anything bad to happen to Julian.

Josie and Khaba partnered with us in the next dance.

Josie stood next to me clapping in time with the music as she stared at Khaba across from her. "Isn't he the dreamiest man in the room?" she gushed.

"Who? Julian or Khaba?" I asked.

She shoved me playfully in the arm. A cloud of enigma and allure lingered around Khaba. Whether it was his unbuttoned shirt showing off his washboard abs, or the glow of Fae magic, he inspired longing from men and women alike. Still, I was more drawn to Julian's subtle good looks.

I leaned toward her. "I think we're dancing with the hottest men in the—"

Julian linked his arm through mine in a spin. I had missed the cue for my turn, and I laughed now in a whirlwind of delight.

At the end of the song, Khaba shouted to be heard over the clapping. "Now that all eyes in the room are on me, I can sit back and see who offers to buy me a drink."

"I'll buy you a drink," Josie said.

"Aren't you cute? Go ahead. Buy me a drink if you want." Khaba pinched her cheek.

When I next glanced his way, Khaba lounged at our table, talking to a man at the table next to him.

As I danced, a creeping sensation wormed its way down my back. I felt someone watching me. I studied the faces in the room, but no one seemed particularly creepy with all-black eyes and midnight wings.

We finished another dance and Julian placed his hand on the small of my back, leaning in close. "I need another drink. Want anything?"

The gesture was intimate and familiar, probably too familiar, but I didn't mind. I found myself leaning toward him, my hip touching his leg. "I'm fine."

Longing throbbed inside me. Pangs of pain jolted through my core as he parted from me. I couldn't tell if it was my magic or someone else's. I scanned the room again.

On my way back to my seat, I dodged through the crowded tables, keeping to the perimeter where I could more easily maneuver through the loitering people. Even if I wasn't getting any good gossip from Julian as I had originally planned, I was having such a good time, it was hard to stop smiling. I didn't think anything could ruin the pleasure of this moment.

I was wrong.

Alone in the corner sat a figure in a tweed suit, stooped over his notebook. There to ruin the mood was Felix Thatch.

CHAPTER THIRTEEN
Professor Jerk-Face

Thatch looked up from his notebook the moment I attempted to retreat. I bumped into a satyr carrying drinks to a table behind me.

"Watch it!" she shouted.

Some of her ale splashed down the back of my dress. I squealed as the liquid drenched my back. I dodged forward and out of the way, putting me closer to my archnemesis.

Thatch's voice rose above the roar of pub, his usual lack of enthusiasm evident. "Good evening, Miss Lawrence."

"What are you doing here?" I asked. Two seconds later, I realized that probably wasn't the best way to greet my magic teacher.

He crossed his arms and leaned back in his chair. "Contrary to popular belief, I do occasionally leave the dungeon."

I glanced down at his notebook. Gesture drawings filled the page. He'd captured the poses of the dancers in quick, confident lines. So it was true. He was an artist. And a good one from the way he'd grasped such fleeting moments of people in movement with a few simple lines. The energy and body language of a woman reminded me of Josie, though I couldn't put my finger on why.

Maybe he really did want my job. Anyone who could draw like him should be an art teacher. He made my drawings look amateur by comparison.

Thatch followed my gaze and snapped the book closed.

"So, um, you like to draw," I said, lamely. I was so not good at small talk.

His disdainful glare didn't help.

"You could be an art teacher. You're a good artist." I smiled, trying to find common ground that might make it easier to connect.

"I know." He crossed his arms. "But administration feels *anyone* can teach an elective like art. Only someone as brilliant as myself can teach alchemy."

Apparently, they didn't need that person to be humble.

Julian laced his arm through mine. His smile grew strained. "Mr. Thatch," he said.

"Mr. Thistledown." Thatch's eyes narrowed.

"I trust I'm not interrupting anything," Julian said.

"Not at all," I said.

The tension in the air between them was so thick it could only have been cut with a lightsaber.

Julian tugged me toward our table where he set his drink next to mine. "Come on, it's the fairy reel. You don't want to miss this." He cast a venomous glance over his shoulder.

"What was that about?" I asked.

He squeezed me to his side. "I don't like how he looks at you. It's the same way he looked at Agnes Padilla, and now she's dead."

I wanted more details about the previous art teacher. The music started up, drowning out the ability to gossip quietly. I didn't know how Khaba flirted with the good-looking man next to him without shouting. Magic probably. It didn't surprise me his newest beau wore a kilt.

Julian started toward the dance floor, but hesitated, eyeing the drinks on the table. He pushed them back from the edge and then turned to me with a wink. "Call it magic, but I had a premonition our drinks were going to get bumped." He chuckled good-naturedly.

Common sense was more like it, but it was hard not to laugh with him. His good mood was infectious. He escorted me to the dance floor to start the next set. Josie danced with a man with bat wings.

I felt Thatch's eyes on me when we danced, making my skin crawl. I tripped twice as Julian and I promenaded, which would have been embarrassing enough, but knowing someone I didn't like had witnessed it made my humiliation even worse. Julian do-si-doed with his corner partner. I glanced at Thatch. He made no attempt to hide his staring.

When it was my turn with Julian again, I leaned in close. "What do you think about getting out of here after this song and going somewhere quiet where we can talk?"

He nodded his head like an eager puppy. "Sure!"

I spent the rest of the song separated from Julian, dancing with the women in the line.

As the dance ended, Julian stepped toward me, but the crowd filled in between us. Music started up almost immediately, the song slow. Couples partnered up on the dance floor. The next moment I caught sight of Julian, an elderly witch in a pointed hat took hold of his arm, saying something to him I couldn't hear. She was so weathered and stooped she looked like she was a thousand years old. He crouched down to listen. When he glanced at me, his smile was apologetic. He held up his finger to me as if to say he'd be a minute. I thought the old crone meant to talk to him, but instead she took his hand, and they danced in a slow swaying shuffle.

I smiled, touched that he was willing to dance with the elderly woman. The gesture made me like him even more.

I made my way back to my table, avoiding Thatch's area of the room. I passed Khaba where he stood against the wall now, flirting with one of his kilty pleasures. I couldn't see Josie in the crowd. It was only when I made it around a group of especially tall spindly men and women who reminded me of trees that my table came into sight.

Thatch stood next to the table, looming over my drink and staring down into it. His lips moved, though I couldn't hear the words. It looked like he was hexing my drink.

I was probably warier than most people about leaving drinks unattended. Plus, Thatch was the kind of villain anyone would have distrusted. Khaba was the worst chaperone ever.

I shouted to be heard over the music. "What are you doing?"

He straightened. "Nothing."

"You put something in my drink, didn't you?"

"What drink?" He extended his finger toward the cup and toppled it over. I jumped back, but not quick enough. Beer splattered across the front of my dress and down my legs.

"Oops," he said with a smile.

Some people had a bogeyman in their closet. I had Thatch.

The morning after the undate with Julian, I sat at the desk in my classroom, reading the final book Thatch had given me. Mini Post-its color-coded the pages. I would have read in my dorm, but the room was small and there was only room for Vega. Or so she'd told me.

As I finished the last sentence of the last paragraph, the door to the stairwell that led to the closet creaked open. To my horror, Thatch skulked in like a shadow. I nearly jumped out of my striped socks.

I knew the stairs that led past the walk-in closet went somewhere, though I hadn't ventured into the mess of spiderwebs. I prayed there wasn't a secret passage from Thatch's room to mine because that would be one more level of torture I didn't deserve.

The possibility of a secret passage between the dungeon and the art room linked one more detail between him and the past art teachers who had all mysteriously died.

Thatch eyed my Post-it organization with disdain. "Did you finish your required reading?"

His timing was impeccable. How had he known? Had he been spying on me?

"Why did you tip over my drink last night?" I asked.

"Because I enjoy making people miserable. Is that the answer you were looking for?" He said it in his usual snotty way, but there was something else, a defensiveness I hadn't seen a second before.

So long as he was answering questions, I figured I might as well ask another. "You've taught at this school a long time, haven't you? Do you remember my friend, Derrick? The one with blue hair?"

"No." His poker face remained blank.

"Yes, you do." I knew he was lying. He'd met Derrick when we'd been in high school. "He was the one with the wind affinity. He blew away with the tornado. A long time ago, you told me he would be found and brought here. Did he go to Womby's?"

"I can't be troubled to remember every student who went here. In any case, I didn't come here to discuss your past relationships. I wish you to return my books . . . if you haven't defaced them all."

"Tell me about Derrick. Did he graduate from here? I just want to talk to him, to see if he's okay."

"Remember what happened the last time the two of you grew too close?" He arched an eyebrow. I refused to let him make me feel guilty. "You would do better to focus on not killing people than romancing men. You'll only draw out your magic by involving yourself with Derrick again." A sinister smile flashed across his face. "However, if I can't persuade you not to seek him out, I shall help you find him."

I could hear the catch. "Yes?"

"After you allow me to drain your powers and turn you mortal."

"No."

He shrugged. "I had to try."

So did I. "Why won't you really tell me about Derrick?" Frustration welled up inside me, a dam about to burst. "And why don't you want me to know about my biological mother—What are you doing?"

He stacked up the books on my desk and tucked them under one arm. His expression was infuriatingly apathetic.

"I'm not done with those," I said, reaching for them.

He stepped back, out of my arm range. "Yes, you are. I cast a spell that alerted me when you finished, and you have." He tossed the book on lucid dreaming back onto my desk.

Perhaps I still needed that one.

"Okay, I'm done with most of them, but I have questions about—"

"No questions allowed. Now that you're done, this has absolved me of my duties to see to your education."

I walked around the desk, my eyes on that pile of books. I wanted them back. "But you didn't educate me. I want to know what my mother did. I want you to tell me why you've torn the pages from those books and what you're hiding."

He stepped out of my reach, closer to the closet door. "It's none of your business," he said coolly.

The frustration I'd been trying to hold back broke through the dam of self-control I'd constructed. "It is my business! She was my mother. I want to know what she did. What are you hiding?"

He dropped the indifferent monotone, venom lacing his words. "I'm not hiding anything."

I stepped in front of him, blocking his escape. "You don't want me to know something. Something *you* did. What is it? Were you her accomplice? Is that what the other art teachers found out? And it's in those books you snuck into the woods behind the school when—"

"Were you following me?" Fury flashed in his eyes. "You're a nosy, little sneak who should mind her own business."

I caught the warning in his voice. I'd said too much. "No, I was jogging, and I happened to see—"

He shifted the books into one arm and whipped out his wand. It sizzled and fumed, shooting out white-hot sparks. I stumbled back.

"My obligation is fulfilled." He said in an expressionless monotone, as though this was the least interesting conversation in the world. "For every question you ask, I'm going to punish you with a spell that will dull your curiosity and sedate you into complacency."

I sealed my lips closed. More than ever, I loathed him. He thought he could scare me into disinterest? I would wait until my mom sent my lockpick set. Then I would break into his office or the school library at night, and I would find out what he was hiding.

CHAPTER FOURTEEN
An A for Effort

The first day of school started on Tuesday after Labor Day, just like it did for public schools in the Morty Realm.

It wasn't difficult to tell which high school students came from the Morty Realm via the bus stop outside Forks, Washington. Those were the sweaty kids with limp hair who had walked two miles through the forest in the heat. The ones coming from Camp Giggles, the coal mine summer program run by dwarves, sported sooty clothes and a vacant look in their eyes. Those from wealthy families, presumably who had been kicked out of their other schools, wore designer clothes, too much makeup, and Axe body spray. Upon first glance, the group resembled typical teens as they filtered in throughout the day.

While other teachers chaperoned and directed students from the bus stop in the Morty Realm into the woods to the school, I was assigned hall-monitor duty alongside seniors directing traffic outside the girls' dormitory. Five minutes after students arrived, I smelled smoke coming from the student restroom. I ran in, colliding into a girl with long brown hair and pointed ears. I found the toilet paper on fire.

"Hey, come back," I called after the girl. "Did you do this?"

She didn't turn, and I didn't know her name.

I tried to douse the flames with handfuls of water from the sink, but as the fire licked at the wooden walls of the stall, I could see that wasn't going to work. Not knowing what else to do, I removed my cardigan and ran water over the pink sweater in the sink until it was soaked, slapping it over the fire and dousing the flames.

Five minutes later I found Vega in the hallway, yelling at students. She wore what must have passed for flapper casual, only the hem of her skirt was outrageously high for being a school teacher. Upon second glance I decided the skirt wasn't that revealing; she just had a lot of leg to show off at her height.

Vega lifted her nose at the charred cotton dripping in my hands and the soot on my white blouse. "Who are you supposed to be, Cinderella? Stop fucking around and go monitor the hall before one of the students does something dangerous."

Too late for that. I dropped my sweater into a garbage can.

Students changed into school uniforms and assembled downstairs at four p.m. The great hall used as a cafeteria was a large round room. Built into the structure of the stone walls were Stonehenge-like arches with wooden doors under each that led to different wings. The room would have given off the air of a sacred site full of wisdom and learning if it hadn't been for the mustard-yellow paint coated over the arches and avocado-green walls above that. The ceiling tapered upward to a point, like the underside of a giant witch's hat. Colorful banners decorated the walls, clashing with the colors of the seventies-style stained-glass windows made into abstract patterns.

The jarring architectural styles and gaudy colors burned into my retinas. I forced myself to look away before the artist in me grew depressed.

About four hundred students sat in rows on wooden benches facing the head of the room. This would be the smallest school I'd worked at. Some of the differences from normal teenagers were minute, a subtle green tinge to a complexion or leaves growing in a student's hair. Other differences like the horns, tusks, and incisors that stretched beyond the lips were more noticeable. The beauty of some surpassed human supermodels. The impish and exaggerated facial features of others bordered on grotesque.

I knew I wasn't supposed to ask, but I wondered what each one of them was.

I stood in the back of the great hall with Josie next to the main entryway, the two of us framed by one of the Stonehenge-like pillars. Staff members sat dispersed among the students or stood clustered together along the walls, watching the students while the principal addressed the student body. It was the kind of motivational pep talk admin did at every school on the first day.

"I believe in you. I know y'all are hard workers. Y'all are going to do a bang-up job, and you're going to have a hog-killing time of it to boot." Jeb hooked his thumbs into his belt, looking more like a cowboy than ever.

As I gazed out at the sea of students, I wondered how many of them would graduate with the skills they needed to resist the Fae. How many of them would become enslaved? Dread settled like a lump of ice in my belly as the ghosts of students past haunted me with pessimism.

"There's somethin' else I gotta mention." Jeb chewed on the end of his mustache, pausing. His eyes swept over the crowd of students. "This school ain't like a school for Morties. We got rules for a reason, and those rules are to keep you safe. Last year our community suffered from the loss of an excellent staff member. Earlier in the year two students met an untimely end."

He folded his hands before him and ducked his head as if in prayer. The hall was so silent I heard every rustle of clothes. My breath sounded loud in my ears.

He cleared his throat. "It's dreadfully important students remain in their beds at night and don't wander the school grounds. This school has restricted areas for mighty good reasons. Please make the jobs of your teachers easier by following the rules. And please," he added with a smile. "No hexing your teachers this year."

Laughter rolled through the crowd. I didn't think it was funny considering my predecessor had been cursed by students. Everyone here seemed so cavalier about human life—or Witchkin life.

Jeb withdrew his wand, and the crowd shushed. Students looked at each other eagerly. He waved his wand around and created a ball of white fire up on the dais.

Three teachers at the front of the room stepped forward. The teachers lassoed magic from their wands and propelled it toward the white flames at the center of the stage.

I shouldn't have been surprised Thatch was one of these teachers, him being the Celestor team department head and a Merlin-class wizard.

The stream of magic from Thatch's wand came out purple with sparkles of silver and gold, overpowering the other rivers of light. The magic encompassed the ball of white, feeding it and making it shimmer with his flavor of magic. It reminded me of the cosmos and the infiniteness of the galaxy, of the unknown, and the quest for knowledge. It was strange how all these inspirational ideas sprung to mind as I gazed at the artistry of light pouring into the white ball of fire. There was no rational explanation. Except for one.

Magic.

I got giddy just thinking about it. Finally, I was getting to see the good stuff.

Thatch's colors swelled brighter. I smelled starlight and tasted wisps of dreams on my lips. I wanted to hate his magic, but it was so beautiful I couldn't. It was incongruous that such inspiring magic came from a horrible man. Shouldn't his magic have tasted like slug-slime and been baby-poop yellow?

The light from his wand receded but didn't completely diminish. He stepped back as another teacher strode forward.

Shooting in from the side came a stream of liquid orange fire intertwined with blue ice. The light came from the hand of the second teacher in this trinity, Jackie Frost. Unlike Thatch, she didn't use a wand.

Jackie wasn't particularly young or old. She was average in her age, her looks, and her build. Her hair was a medium brown with a typical "mom" haircut: soft waves in the front and spikes in the back. Nothing about her stood out, but as her magic overpowered the sphere, the tips of her short hair paled, growing white and then blue. Her face turned clear like ice, and her clothes looked as though they were made from frost. Flames danced with flurries of snow around the sphere Jeb held. I felt hot and cold at the same time. Wind swirled the elements, and the ball of light swelled. A calming breeze washed over me, and I breathed it in. As the extremes of the hot and cold tempered each other into steam, patches of brown flashed through the fingers of mist. I felt grounded and at one with the earth and the rocks.

Someone sighed near me. To my right, Josie stood with her eyes closed, a smile on her face.

The final magic that spilled into the ball was green and yellow. Trees and vines made of light shot out of Professor Bluehorse's staff. The perfume of spring flowers and pine mixed with the scent of herbs from my mom's garden. The sensation of rose petals as soft as silk brushed across my cheeks. Intermingled in the ecosystem of greenery fluttered butterflies and birds. I was suddenly aware of the grass outside and the trees in the forest beyond. I heard the heartbeats and the breaths of a thousand woodland animals. Far below the stone of the castle, worms and insects burrowed in the cool dirt for safety. Images of animals and plants flashed in the globe.

It was so beautiful and inspiring it made me appreciate the splendor of every living creature . . . even spiders. I wanted to apologize to Josie for every spider I'd killed in my life, but I couldn't tear my eyes from the hypnotic beauty swirling in the ball of light.

My stage illusions were paltry compared to this.

The witches backed away from the sphere. The light from their wands petered out. The orb was a rainbow of colors, mixing and spiraling, crashing like waves inside itself, representing the colors they'd thrown into it. There was red too. What rainbow palette would be complete without it? I hadn't seen them feed the color red into the sphere, but there was blood in living creatures, so it made sense the red might have come from Professor Bluehorse.

Jeb lifted his hands. The sphere rose higher. It had to be as tall as him now. "The light of these three affinities represent the trinity of our sacred sources of magic. When all our teams work together, our rainbow lights the world."

I placed a hand over my heart, touched by the sappy sentiment. This was so much better than a public school.

Jeb rapidly arced his arms downward and the ball crashed down before him. "Yee-haw!" he shouted.

A kaleidoscope of color shot in every direction. I closed my eyes against the explosion of light. A few students shrieked. Others laughed. When the spots had cleared from my eyes, I found some of the students had ducked or raised their arms to cover their faces. Giggles erupted from chagrined students.

A white fire crackled on the dais. The principal stepped around the white flames. They flickered as high as a bonfire.

"I asked three of our staff who each represent one of these affinities to demonstrate their magic so that new students will know what their affinities look like and feel like. Head of our Elementia team is our master of the elements, Professor Jackie Frost. Through rain or shine, snow or blisterin' heat, she helps guide those whose affinity comes from fire, water, wind, and earth. She heads the team that provides the tools needed for careers in minin', magic smithin', pyromancy, and weather sorcery."

She bowed, and the students and staff clapped.

"Heading the department of Amni Plandai is Ethel Bluehorse, though I reckon you know her as Grandmother Bluehorse. She's there for the students who draw strength from animals and plants. She'll help guide students toward careers in dragon and unicorn husbandry, healin', herbology, and other related fields."

The small, hunched-over woman stood and waved. Students cheered. I guessed she was popular with the kids.

"Celestor is the third point of our trinity. This group derives power from the stars, moon, sun, and cosmic energies. These are the students who are strongest in divination, telekinesis, and the most challengin' forms of magic. Celestors often become renowned scholars in secondary forms of magic as well." He offered a sheepish smile. "I, myself, was Celestor when I was in school. Currently Professor Felix Thatch heads this team." The applause was tepid at best. Not even all the teachers clapped. I felt bad for Thatch, even if he was the most annoying person I'd ever met.

Then again, if he hadn't drenched me in beer a few nights before, and then threatened to silence me with magic for seeing too much and asking too many questions, I might have been more willing to show some enthusiasm as well.

"These three affinities dwell in all of us, but each of us are strongest in one area." Jeb lifted his hand and gestured to the school crest hanging on the tapestry above him. The logo that had been quilted on the fabric showed three images arranged in a triangle. At the top was a collection of silver stars on a purple background. To the right was a picture of a fire on top of rocks with raindrops and spirals that were probably supposed to represent fire, earth, wind, and water. To the left was a butterfly made of leaves.

The composition was unbalanced, too much negative space in the lowest section of the design. It looked like something else should have been placed there. A fourth and missing element. Or the designer had simply been a bad artist.

Jeb gestured to the crowd of students. "No matter what your affinity, we aim to prepare y'all with skills for the real world. For you tenderfoots, part of this involves discoverin' who you are. Everythin' y'all do this year will be to support your affinity so you can be the strongest Witchkin you can be. Y'all gotta work with your team to increase your skills in magic and study with other like-minded students. Each team competes against other teams, winnin' points in academics and sports for excellence."

I noticed how he left out fine arts. Administrators always left out achievements in art, drama and music. How disappointing that my students were unlikely to receive any more recognition for their achievements than I had in high school.

Maybe that was some of the bitterness of my chocolate prophecy leaking through.

He pointed to a scoreboard on a wall with the three teams' symbols. "Y'all will earn points for good behavior. Points will be deducted for poor behavior. At the end of the semester, the winnin' team will earn. . . ." He paused for dramatic effect. "a pizza-and-ice-cream party!"

Students cheered. Wow, the power of pizza was greater than I could have imagined. Apparently, it didn't matter whether the teenagers were inner city kids or Witchkin at a special school in another dimension. Some rewards were universal.

"Without further ado, it's the moment y'all have been waitin' for. I'd like to invite freshman and transferrin' students to step into the fire to discover their affinity."

"Oh my God!" I said. Step into the fire? That sounded dangerous.

Other teachers cast dirty looks at me. Josie nudged me. I pressed my lips together, not wanting to embarrass myself further.

Coach Kutchi called the students up in alphabetical order. I wrung my hands in nervousness, as anxious as they were. The first student closed her eyes and stepped into the fire. The white flames turned green as she stepped through.

"Amni Plandai," Coach Kutchi announced. She sniffed the air. "I think I detect a more specific affinity for mint."

The young woman came out of the fire unscathed. She smiled and joined the table with the green-and-yellow banner above it. This was so cool! Someone could make good money using pyromancy to divine majors for college students. I wanted to know what my affinity was.

I wasn't sure of the next student's gender, or what he or she was from the impish features of the face. The student's hair was short and the build androgynous.

The fire flashed orange and blue, and then became white as wind blustered out of the flames.

"Wind, a clear member for Elementia."

Wind, like Derrick.

As the ceremony went on I noticed a pattern. Most of the students were sorted into the Amni Plandai or the Elementia team. Fewer were placed in Celestor.

The magic was beautiful to watch. More than ever I wanted to know what I was.

I looked again to the school crest above Jeb. I couldn't help feeling like something was out of place. There was no red in that rainbow. What would red even represent?

I tugged on Josie's arm. "Let's get closer."

We scooted around the edge of the round room to where Bluehorse, Thatch, and Frost stood. I wondered what would happen if I "accidentally" fell into the fire and discovered my affinity.

With each student that entered the fire, I wished it could be me. By ninety-something, I could barely stand it any longer. I needed to be sorted. If I found out what my affinity was, maybe I would be able to learn to control my powers and have a normal relationship. I wouldn't have to put up with Thatch's half-assed mentoring. Somehow, I had to get myself up on the dais.

Another freshman walked into the fire, a diminutive girl with dark skin. The flames flashed orange and blue and I thought she would be placed in Elementia. Then the fire transitioned to purple and silver.

Students whispered. Teachers turned to each other in confusion. The flames changed again and turned green and yellow. For a moment they settled on red, eliciting gasps from the teachers before changing again.

Grandmother Bluehorse stared with terror in her eyes. Sebastian Reade, the middle-aged foreign language teacher, shuffled back. The team colors flashed in and out of focus as though the affinity couldn't make up its mind. Each time the fire settled on red, people tensed. Something was happening, but I didn't understand what.

"She's a Red," one of the older students whispered on a nearby bench.

"What's a Red?" I shook Josie's arm.

She stared transfixed. "There isn't such a thing as a Red."

The color shifted again.

"Good golly! This is unprecedented," Jeb said.

"What does it mean?" I asked Josie.

She stared, open-mouthed. "This never happened at my high school."

"It's the prophecy!" someone shouted. "The Red will bring our downfall."

Oh great. One more thing I didn't know about. I was at a school with a prophecy. I would have to ask Josie about that later.

Jeb's voice boomed over the murmurs. "Calm yourselves. There's a simple and rational explanation for this."

Yeah, because magic was always rational and simple.

"This must be a student who excels in all these kinds of magic so strongly it's difficult to discover her affinity," he said.

The flames flickered like rainbows again, and a student emerged. The fire returned to white.

The girl's expression was as confused as everyone else's. "I'm sorry. Did I do it wrong?"

I gasped. It was one of my former students from Hamlin Middle School in Skinnersville, Oregon.

CHAPTER FIFTEEN
Out of the Frying Pan

Back when I'd taught my practicum in Skinnersville School District, every day felt like *Lord of the Flies*. And that was just in the staff room to get a cup of coffee.

Twice during my internship at the middle school, Thatch marched in, claiming to be the district psychologist. He came to observe a student with supposed autism, drawing my suspicion when he implied it was Imani Washington. Her talent in art surpassed her peers, and she was academically gifted. She was sociable with others, and she exhibited no traits of learning disabilities that I could see.

Now that I knew Thatch was the equivalent of the school's magical talent scout, it made more sense why he'd been there.

Presumably he'd been there to observe me as well.

Seeing my former student, Imani, at the head of the great hall on the dais, I wondered how many of those unexplained occurrences of classroom magic had been me and how much of it had been her. She stepped back from the sorting fire.

Imani looked around in confusion, her dark eyes frightened. "I'm sorry, sir." She turned to Jeb. "I didn't mean to—to break it."

"I know that student!" I said to Josie excitedly.

She put a finger to her lips and shushed me.

"Don't you worry, darlin'. You didn't do nothin' wrong," Jeb said. "The fire likely needs another moment to decide." He waved her back in.

Imani hesitated before stepping into the fire. Her dark curls danced in the flames, but her clothes remained still. The fire flickered into rainbow mode again, reminding me of Christmas lights in a disco.

I leaned closer to Josie. "What if someone has more than one affinity?"

"We all have more than one. It's like someone who is good at the arts *and* math. This is the equivalent of Gardener's intelligence test so students can focus on the skill that will give them the best chances of survival after graduation."

"So, there aren't any students who tie for houses, and they can't figure out which affinity to choose?" I asked.

The rainbow flicking from Imani grew faster, more erratic. Students squirmed on the benches, turning to talk to each other. Their voices rose in excitement. One of the older teachers sitting in the crowd stood, admonishing them.

"Teams, not houses," Josie said. "I don't know. Well, actually. . . . I know of one student. My grandmother used to tell me a story about the old days. . . ." She lowered her voice even more, making it difficult to hear over the students murmuring. "Water. Earth. Fire. Air. Long ago the four nations lived together in harmony. Then everything changed when the Fire Nation attacked."

I leaned closer. I knew this. She was quoting something familiar, but I couldn't put my finger on it.

Her eyes sparkled with mischief. "Only the Avatar, master of all four elements, could stop them—"

Ugh! I couldn't believe I hadn't caught it from her first words. She was quoting the opening of *Avatar: The Last Airbender.*

I finished for her. "But when the world needed him most, he vanished."

We both giggled, drawing a glare from Mrs. Periwinkle, the librarian, sitting on a bench beside a group of students.

I waited a moment before whispering, "What if a student doesn't have an affinity? Or one that doesn't fit into those three categories?" I glanced again at the school crest with the missing red color.

She shook a head. "If someone doesn't have enough magic, they'd be a Morty and get burnt in the fire."

The strobe light of Imani's affinity flashed with stronger pulses of red that drowned out the other colors. No one had added red, but there it was. I couldn't help feeling that meant something.

Electricity sparked deep in my core. My mouth tasted like blood, and I realized I was biting my cheek. More than ever I felt drawn to the fire. I wanted to discover my affinity. I scooted forward, hypnotized by the flames. The tug of the Raven Court's lullabies had been nothing compared to this. I stepped toward the dais, ready to throw myself into the fire to discover my affinity next.

Thatch stepped in front of me, blocking the fire from view. I halted, uncertain whether he'd intentionally cut me off to thwart me or it was a coincidence. My frustration shifted to curiosity as he drew closer to the stage. All eyes were riveted on Imani, except for mine.

Thatch's back was turned, and I couldn't see what he was doing, but I noticed the gesture of his hand at his side making a pulling motion at her. His fingers sparkled red and then white.

The affinity fire drained of color and turned to white. Some students clapped and cheered. Others looked scared. There were too many voices speaking at once to hear what anyone said.

Jeb beckoned for Imani to exit from the flames. "I reckon white is the unity of all colors." The rest of what he said was lost in the chatter of the students. Thatch and Jeb spoke off to the side. Jackie Frost and Grandmother Bluehorse joined them.

The fire was empty. People were distracted. Now was my moment to find out what I was.

Then I noticed Imani. She hugged herself, looking lost. I waved to her, trying to draw her attention. That frightened look in her eyes changed to surprise as she noticed me.

I dodged around the teachers, inching closer to the dais, torn between throwing myself in the fire and comforting Imani. I reached Imani first. She threw her arms around me.

"Miss Lawrence, I can't believe it!" Her arms shook, and she tried to smile, but I could see the anxiety in her expression.

"It's okay, honey. You're safe here." I rubbed her shoulder consolingly.

She nodded. As I stared out at the rising anarchy of the students, I wasn't so sure my words were true.

Jeb raised his hands and the roar of the students died down. I strained to hear what he said. "Miss Washington, I'm gonna place you in Professor Thatch's team. He'll take care of you real good."

Felix Thatch elbowed me out of the way and walked Imani over to the smallest group of students. That poor girl! She'd have to study with his team, under his guidance. Just like me. Maybe we could study together.

Jeb bellowed over the excited students. "Settle down. We still got seventeen more affinities to get through. Next on the list, Coach Kutchi?"

The teacher sorted through a list of papers, apparently having lost her place in the commotion. The tension in the air was as thick as one of my mom's frozen smoothies. People kept sneaking glances at Imani.

The moment it grew silent again, a loud farting sound ripped through the hall. That broke some of the tension, and students laughed. I wanted to laugh too, but as a teacher I knew I wasn't supposed to.

The rude sound ended when Thatch pulled a dark-haired young man from a table by his ear. The boy's face was almost human, but his pointed nose and chin were exaggerated just enough to make him look like a goblin. He stumbled along at Thatch's side.

"Ten points deducted from Elementia," Thatch said loudly. "And a detention effective immediately." The scoreboard on the wall now showed negative ten points under the four elements symbol.

Josie and I shifted to the side to allow Thatch to pass. The large double doors behind us parted for Thatch as he dragged the boy off.

The entire school stared after them. Thatch turned left toward the stairway to the dungeons. I didn't think the farting noise was detention-worthy. The kids had been nervous after the unexpected pyromancy results. They'd needed something to distract them.

Jeb continued the ceremony with the remaining students, but the kids were restless. The word that kept resurfacing in whispered conversations was "prophecy."

"What is the prophecy?" I asked Josie.

She leaned closer. "I haven't ever looked up the exact words, but the Madam Cleo of the Dark Ages foresaw someone at this school not being sorted into one of the teams, or being a misfit of the affinity fire, or something like that. This Witchkin would become the chosen one who would bring back the lost arts. The dark arts. This would either unify all Fae and Witchkin or lead us into war. You know, the usual hippie-dippy prophecy that every school boasts. My school had their own version. I think it's mostly to keep kids in line and make them conform."

Jeb finished testing the students. Out of one hundred and eight incoming freshmen, only twenty-one were divided into the Celestor team. That meant Thatch had an easier job than the other department heads.

"Transfer students, please step forward," Coach Kutchi shouted.

Seven students came forward.

Josie whispered, "They're from rival schools, probably kicked out for good reasons too. Keep an eye on those kids this year."

Each of them stepped through the fire, revealing their affinity. "This is all for show," Josie said. "They already know what they are. It's just the rest of the school doesn't."

"Can't an affinity change? Why aren't students tested every year?" I asked.

"It can change, especially if a student has two strong affinities, but it takes a lot of work to shift the balance. In all the history of the school, only two people have ever switched affinities."

What did that mean for Imani? If she had two affinities and one was taboo, how would that affect her as a student? What if *I* had two affinities?

Jeb raised his arms for silence. Conversation died away. "Have I missed anyone? Is there *anyone* else who still needs to learn her affinity?" He didn't address Coach Kutchi. He stared out at the audience of students. He scanned the teachers standing at the perimeter. His gaze stopped at me.

A string tugged at my heart. He meant me. I needed to find out who I was, what I was. This was my chance to figure out how my magic worked. I stepped away from the wall.

A hand grabbed my wrist and jerked me back. I stumbled into one of the stone archways, banging my elbow against solid rock. Thatch stood there. I hadn't realized he'd returned.

He bent himself in half to growl into my ear. "He's not talking about you. He's talking about the students."

"But—" I looked to Josie on the other side of me.

She stared with wide eyes. "You don't know your affinity?"

Thatch squeezed my wrist so tightly it hurt. "It will be mayhem in your classroom if the students learn you can't use magic. You can expect anarchy all year, not to mention how it will put your life in danger." He looked to Josie. "Tell her what a foolish idea it would be to show the entire school what a dunce she is at magic."

She chewed on her lip. "I hate to say he's right. . . ."

The principal called out once more. "No one? No one else then?"

I wrenched my wrist free of Thatch's talon-like fingers and rubbed feeling back into my hand. I wanted to find out what I was. If only Thatch had stayed in his detention dungeon. It was more obvious than ever how much he wanted me to fail.

Josie patted my shoulder and offered me a sympathetic smile. The hall was silent again. Someone coughed.

"Very well," Jeb said. "The fire will burn all night in case anyone else wishes to find her affinity." His eyes met mine across the room.

Yes! He did mean me!

Waiting until the students were in their wings was unbearable. An hour after they were supposed to be in bed, I lay in my room, too excited about the prospect of finding out what I was to fall asleep. I listened to the ebb and flow of Vega's breathing, wanting to make sure she didn't catch me. Finally, I struck a match and lit the candle on the nightstand. I stuffed my feet into slippers and wrapped myself in a housecoat.

My cell phone remained under the safety of my pillow. I could have used the flashlight app, but I didn't want to waste the battery. Nor did I want to get caught with it after what Josie had told me about it being considered a weapon. If I was found roaming the school at night, it would look bad enough. Nervousness percolated inside me. I considered what I would say if someone caught me out of bed.

Then I remembered my trump card.

I was a teacher. Forget what students would say! If I saw a student, I would ask what they were doing out of bed. And if Vega or anyone else caught me, what would it matter? The staff all knew I couldn't do magic. It was reasonable I would want to know my affinity.

And yet. . . . I couldn't shake the sense that I was doing something wrong.

Ominous shadows stretched toward me in the darkness. Several times I thought I heard a creak on the stairs above me or thought I saw a shadow shaped like a towering man, but each time it turned out to be my own shadow stretched unnaturally in the candlelight. Trying to find my way to the great hall took me longer than it usually would have, but that was mostly due to pausing at every landing to listen for danger.

Recollections of what had happened to the previous art teachers slithered up my spine, chilling me in the cool night air. I didn't want to be the art teacher who died before the first day because she fell into an indoor moat or got eaten by a dragon.

The doors to the great hall were unlocked. The handle thunked as I opened one to enter the circular hall. I poked my head inside. White flames lit the dais. The glow had dimmed from dinner time, but it still burned. Hopefully the pyromancy would still work.

I padded past the benches and tables that had been set up for dinner. This was the moment I had been waiting for. I hesitated for just a moment at the edge of the flames. Josie had said someone without magic would be burned by the flames.

I was a witch. I had no reason to believe the flames would burn me.

Even so, I held my breath and stepped in. The fire blazed whiter and higher. It was hot and cold at the same time. Tingles danced over my skin, feeling like a tickle more than a burn. A laugh burst out of me. I covered my mouth to stifle the sound before anyone heard me. The white light turned crimson. I stared in wonder.

What did red mean? It wasn't on the banner. People hadn't reacted favorably to the idea of a Red affinity. The color didn't change like Imani's. I didn't smell or taste anything. No breeze came like it had for the wind elementals.

I closed my eyes and tried to use my intuition. I wasn't used to using magic on purpose. I breathed in the smokeless fire. Tingling filled my lungs and more tickles coursed through me. It was hard not to giggle.

The fire caressed my flesh. A sense of well-being and comfort filled me. I tried to relax into the feeling of being red. It was comfortable, natural, but I didn't know what it meant. I hugged my arms around myself, sinking deeper into the cozy sensation. The warmth made me think of my first kiss, Derrick's arms snug around me. Usually the memory of my first love sank me into guilt. That kiss that had been his undoing. It had released a whirlwind of feelings and uncontrolled magic out of both of us. That tornado had swept him away.

Instead of the usual sorrow I felt when I thought of him, arousal flushed my face. That nervous energy in my core changed from a fluttering to a pleasant pulse. I felt wet between my legs. The scent of Old Spice and butterscotch wafted toward me. I could almost feel Derrick on the other side of the flames.

I inhaled deeply and choked on a plume of smoke. That wasn't right.

I opened my eyes to find my pajamas engulfed in flames.

CHAPTER SIXTEEN
Into the Fire

It wasn't often that I found myself in such a predicament as being on fire. I jumped out, screaming. Immediately, I stopped, dropped and rolled.

"Agh! Stupid! No! Darn!" I cursed like a goody-two-shoes version of a sailor as I smacked the flames from my clothes and hair. Or maybe that vibrant glow was my hair. I couldn't tell. My hair was already bright from the hot-pink hair dye.

I abruptly stopped screaming when I realized the flames didn't hurt. I wasn't burned. It was incredible! Not much was left of my pajamas and housecoat, though. The remnants of fabric smoldered in the darkness. The white flames of the fire dimmed behind me and left me in darkness. I didn't know what I had done with my candle.

Leave it to me to have some kind of bad reaction to something over a hundred kids experienced without problem. On the other hand, they hadn't stood in it. They'd walked through. Maybe that's where I had gone wrong. Or maybe the fire didn't like impure thoughts. There were so many rules everyone took for granted that I still didn't know.

Well, at least it was dark. I could slink back up to my room in obscurity, and no one would be the wiser about my mishap or my freakish Red affinity.

I should have known not to jinx myself by counting my blessings too soon.

The moment I started crawling toward the edge of the dais, blue light burst through the door. I hugged my arms around myself and curled my knees up to my chest, afraid I was about to get caught *and* expose myself in my less than modest Cinderella attire.

Julian ran up the aisle between tables. Of course, it would be the hot teacher I liked who would catch me like this. He shot light out of his wand, and the chandelier in the center of the ceiling sparked to life. His jaw dropped when he saw me huddled on the dais. I didn't know who was more mortified. I prayed he couldn't tell I'd been aroused in the affinity fire and that had caused my clothes to burn off.

"Miss Lawrence? Are you quite all right? I heard a scream."

"Yeah, I'm fine." I gave a little wave. "Sorry about that. You can go back to bed."

My sleeve disintegrated into ash. Black soot streaked across the exposed skin of my arms and legs.

He strode forward. "What happened here?"

"Long story."

He removed his cloak. Underneath he wore an old-fashioned nightshirt that fell to his ankles. Not that I should have been one to judge clothes in my lack of attire, but it looked pretty ridiculous. Or at least, it would have on anyone else. The ensemble managed to make him even more attractive.

He kneeled beside me and draped the cloak over my shoulders like a chivalrous knight.

My stomach cramped. Someone's shout in the hall drew my attention. Ugh, of course. Someone else had come to my rescue. Pro Ro stood there, fully dressed. He gaped at us. I hoped he didn't think we were doing anything elicit.

"Miss Lawrence? Is that you?" he asked.

"Yeah. Unfortunately."

He strode forward. The cramping in my core increased. The stabbing pain reminded me of PMS. This had happened the last times Pro Ro had been present. I'd thought it was Thatch's presence and my nerves, but now I wasn't so sure. I tugged the cape more modestly around myself. It was bad enough one teacher at the school had to see me nearly naked, but two?

"What in all the stars happened?" Pro Ro eyed the black ashes around me.

I shrugged. "I guess a half-cotton, half-polyester blend is a bad fashion choice for the affinity fire."

"Why would you step into the affinity fire?" Pro Ro asked.

"I wanted to find out my affinity," I said with a sheepish laugh.

My humiliation was complete when I spied Thatch under an archway. He shook his head at me in disgust. He'd caught me half-naked, but at least he didn't know my affinity.

"Do you know what your affinity is now?" Julian asked.

I hesitated. People hadn't reacted positively when they'd suspected Imani's affinity had been red. There was no way I could tell the truth.

"I thought you were Amni Plandai, some kind of fertility sprite," Pro Ro said. "Wasn't that why Jeb prohibited dating amongst staff?"

"Indeed, probably an Amni Plandai." Thatch strode forward. "Isn't it time everyone moved along? It's past teacher curfew."

My stomach continued to churn. Thatch had been the one to tell me not to go into the fire in the first place. He knew what I was. Or he suspected. But he'd just covered for me.

I intended to find out why.

Vega's cuckoo clock awakened me at the butt crack of dawn. Instead of a pleasant bird coming out and cuckooing six times, it screamed six times. I was so tired from my late-night excursion and shower, I probably wouldn't have opened my eyes if it hadn't been for the macabre alarm clock. As it was, I shot up and stared at the wall in horror as the clock finished its repetitions.

So that was what Vega had meant about setting her alarm.

Vega pushed herself out of bed. "I call dibs on the bathroom."

Her morning breath was like death as it rolled out of her mouth. Three feet between beds was not enough distance. I didn't want to imagine what the stench would be like any closer to her. I flopped back into bed and turned toward the window. I slid my phone out from under my pillow and checked to see if it truly was six. It was. I shoved my phone back under. A few seconds later the shutters flew open and bright morning light filtered in.

I wrote in my dream journal like I was supposed to and meditated on what I wanted to dream about next. I still didn't have any more control over what I dreamed about than I had before trying the exercises in the book.

Probably, I shouldn't have meditated under the cozy warmth of the blankets because I fell back asleep. I might not have gotten up on time if it hadn't been for Vega opening the door and slamming it.

She waved at the air, making a face. "Fucking-A. It smells like death warmed over in here. Try a breath mint."

I arrived in my classroom forty-five minutes before first period. The other teachers in the school had homeroom first period, except for me—and three out of four department heads.

Nervous energy percolated inside me. I didn't feel like a real teacher. This would be my first time teaching in my own classroom without a supervising teacher—aside from those times during my internship I'd been left unattended as a student teacher. Each of those times something bad had happened. I prayed I wouldn't accidentally turn the students into frogs.

I wrote my name on the board and looked over my lesson plans for the day. The names on the list had changed since the last time I'd looked— Josie had assured me that was normal. My beginning class had thirty-five, mostly sophomores, but quite a few freshmen as well. The other classes were smaller. At least I could look forward to a fifth-period prep.

Thoughts about my Red affinity kept storming through the fortress of my teacher zone. No one else had a Red affinity. Maybe that had something to do with the prophecy Josie had told me about. From the student and staff's reactions toward Imani, I already knew being different wasn't going to be an advantage.

I should have spent the morning making a seating chart and readying additional supplies. Instead, I spent an hour and a half in the library trying to covertly research the Red affinity while evading Mrs. Periwinkle. I still hadn't gotten a handle on the card catalogue, and I couldn't find anything useful. Just before first period ended, I dashed up to my classroom to hurriedly staple my syllabi and sort papers I intended to hand out.

I needed to figure out my affinity, learn how to use magic, spy on Thatch to see what he was hiding from me about my mother, learn where Derrick was, *and* teach art. I already felt frazzled trying to do everything.

A chime went off at nine thirty when first-period homeroom ended. I didn't know how students were going to make it to my room with a fifteen-minute passing time. I couldn't get across the twisted maze of passages that fast, and some of them had classes outside in the greenhouses. Then again, some of the students might be able to use magic, whereas I couldn't.

Sleepy-eyed students trudged in around nine forty. I smiled and welcomed them. A few mumbled half-hearted greetings back. Students filled in the seats at the back of the horseshoe of tables first, then as more shuffled in, they took the seats closer to me. After half of them had come in, I remembered the seating chart, but looking at their sullen faces, I lost my nerve.

The teenagers ranged in size, like in any class, but many were smaller than the average teenager. For the first time since teaching my practicum at the middle school, I wasn't the shortest person in the room.

On the opposite end of the spectrum, some were taller than professional basketball players, and as bulky as football players, with muscles that rolled like rocks under their skin. Yeah, I was a little intimidated.

A boy with a pig snout instead of a nose came in telling a story to a student with fur sprouting out of his face. "And I was like, bro, that is fucking—"

"Excuse me. This is a classroom," I said. "Please refrain from profanity."

"Dude, are you the teacher?" the pig-snout boy asked. "I thought you were a student."

So much for thinking I resembled an adult. Already we were off to a rough start. I tried not to let my frustration show.

A bell went off at nine forty-five.

I called roll. I marked three students absent. By the time I reached the end of the list, two students strolled in. A short goblin-faced boy with dark hair took a seat in the back. He looked like the kid Thatch had hauled off the day before for making the farting noise during the assembly. A pretty girl with long brown hair walked up to an occupied seat beside her friend. I might have been wrong, but I suspected she had been behind the toilet-paper-fire incident.

She leered at the student sitting beside her friend. "You're in my seat."

The other teen quickly vacated it. Already I knew who I was going to have trouble with.

"Balthasar Llewelyn?" I asked.

"The one and the same," the goblin-like student said.

"Hailey Achilles?"

The girl lifted her chin. I took that as a yes. She was more human in aspect than her friend, though her ears were long and pointed. Her eyes burned a fiery orange. I put stars next to their names on the list so I would remember to ask Josie about them later.

I tried to squash my nervousness with a smile as I gazed out at the class. "My name is Miss Lawrence. I'm here to teach you art. Who likes art?"

A few timid hands went up.

"Great! I'm so excited to teach you drawing. I have a syllabus for you so you know the expectations and procedures." I retrieved the stack from my desk and passed out the papers.

"How tall are you?" one of the students asked.

Not this again. I thought I would at least be spared this humiliation at such a diverse school with varied heights.

"How old are you? You look like you could be a student," someone else said.

My forced smile hurt my cheeks. "Where I come from, those aren't considered polite questions." I finished passing out the syllabus.

I went over the expectations and procedures on the paper. The two students who had come in late talked to each other, not listening to anything I said.

I raised my voice to be heard. When that didn't work, I said, "Excuse me. I need you to be quiet."

That worked for about thirty seconds before they continued, louder than before. Finally, I just stopped talking and stared at them.

Balthasar laughed. "Last year we would soooo have gotten away with it if that stupid, fart-breath teacher hadn't caught us."

"I literally could have busted a gut when I saw the expression on his face. Literally," Hailey said.

Students turned to look at her, annoyance crossing their faces.

"Where do you think Bumble-ass is keeping the answer keys this year?"

Balthasar asked.

"Shut up!" someone in the class said.

"What's your problem?" Balthasar's voice came out slithery and wet as he looked around. His eyes came to rest on me.

Irritation swelled inside me, the pressure cooker of frustration threatening to explode. I crossed my arms. "It's difficult to shout over you. Please refrain from talking while I'm talking."

Hailey lifted her chin. "What are you going to do about it?" A blaze of orange sparked in her eyes. More than ever I was certain she'd started that fire in the girl's restroom.

"What team are you?" I asked.

"Can't you tell?" Her nostrils flared.

I couldn't tell if she was sniffing the air or she was angry. Probably smelling my fear.

She glanced away as if thinking. "Amni."

I knew a lie when I saw it. She wasn't Amni Plandai. There was nothing plant-like or animal-like about her. I had a feeling she wasn't Celestor either.

I slowly said each word, watching her reaction. "Ten points . . . from . . . Elementia."

One of the kids in the class howled. "So not fair!"

A few students snickered, their amusement cut short when Hailey turned to glare at them. "Like I care."

I continued reading the syllabus. I made it another half page before the whispering and giggling in the corner started. I looked up. "I will give you plenty of free time to talk as we do art, but right now I need you to listen and read along."

"Reading is stupid. This is boring," one of the students shouted.

"Why haven't you just glued people's mouths closed yet like Miss Bloodmire does?" one of the students asked.

There was a spell for that? That did seem like something Vega would do.

"Where's your wand?" someone asked.

I could have said my wand was up my sleeve, but I had short sleeves, so it was obvious it wasn't. Plus, I didn't have a wand to take out and threaten them with. I used the classic approach passed down from one teacher to the next since the beginning of time: avoidance. "Why do I have to use a wand? Professor Bluehorse uses a staff. So does the principal."

"They're old school."

"Maybe she's like the coach." They gave each other knowing looks.

Yes! Classic misdirection. Changing the subject was working.

"What does that mean?" I asked. "What does the coach use?"

A girl sitting at the front of the horseshoe raised her hand. "Coach Kutchi says wands are offensive phallic weapons from the old days of patriarchy. Plus, if you want to be good at sports, you need to keep your hands free of pointed objects that might accidentally stab you in the eye."

"That's a pretty good point," I said. "No pun intended."

"Do you play pegasus polo?" someone asked.

"That's not why she doesn't have a wand," said a soft, squeaky voice in the center of the class. "I heard she isn't even Witchkin. She's a Morty." The student was huge, reminding me of a tree with the cracked bark of his skin.

I lifted my chin and tried to say with confidence. "I am a witch."

"Prove it," the pig-snout boy said.

A bead of sweat rolled down my forehead.

One of the kids in the front row opened a book and started reading.

"Hey, put that away," I said. "We're still going over the syllabus."

One of the students in the back of the horseshoe carved his name into the desk with his wand.

"Stop that!" I said.

Hailey Achilles stood up. "If you're a real witch, stop me." She walked along the perimeter of the horseshoe toward the door.

I thought she meant to leave. Maybe I was a bad teacher for thinking it, but I didn't care if she left. One less troublemaker.

My gaze fell on her moving lips. She said something I couldn't hear. The air smelled like rotten eggs and cinnamon, a putrid mix. She held up her wand.

"No," I said firmly. "Ten points from—"

Light exploded from her wand. I flew through the air, my back slamming into a wall and my head following. All the air whooshed out of me. Spots danced before my eyes. I couldn't tell if the shimmer in the air was magic or a concussion.

It was bad enough when public-school students cursed and called you all manner of rude names, but in a magical school, curses could be dangerous.

"Recess!" one of the students yelled in triumph.

"Class is out early. Woohoo!"

I sucked in a breath. My classroom was upside down and everyone was on the ceiling. I blinked. The tables and chairs were twenty feet up, on the high ceiling of the room. Students ran out the door, their bodies defying gravity. One student sat in the front row reading his book.

Another student cowered under his table. He peeked out at me. It was about then I realized I was the one who defied gravity, not them. I was stuck to the ceiling.

I didn't move a muscle, afraid any change would make me fall twenty feet to the floor and bust my neck.

"Help," I whispered.

CHAPTER SEVENTEEN
Did You Rub My Lamp?

I forced myself to remain calm. Panicking wasn't going to get me down from the ceiling. I needed another teacher. Maybe Josie or Jeb could help me.

"Hey!" I called out to the student reading his book, who had ignored the entire scene around him. He continued reading. I shouted louder. "Go get the principal. I need help."

Still no response. Maybe he was deaf.

There was a child hiding underneath one of the tables. I tried to get him to run to another teacher, but he didn't move. Since my students weren't willing to assist me, I shouted for help until my throat was hoarse.

It felt like I'd been glued to the ceiling forever, though the now functioning clock on the wall showed it had only been fifteen minutes.

It was about then that Thatch marched through my door, wand in hand. "I demand to know why you released your class an hour early. Students are running wild on the school grounds." He looked around the room.

I should have been happy to see another teacher who could help get me down. But not Thatch. I considered my options and chose not to answer, because, let's face it, Thatch was scary even when he wasn't angry. Plus, he was armed with a wand.

Thatch pointed to the student too absorbed in reading his book to notice someone had even entered the room. "You. Where is your teacher?"

The kid didn't look up. Thatch grabbed the kid's book and snapped it closed. "Where is Miss Lawrence?"

The kid glanced around the empty classroom. "Oh. Uh. . . ? Is it lunch time?"

Thatch shoved the book at the student. He rounded on the child still under the desk. The boy was shaking. Poor little guy. I didn't want Thatch to be a jerk to some innocent kid who hadn't done anything to anyone.

"Up here," I whispered.

Thatch whirled, looked to my desk, and then to the closet.

I cleared my throat. The kid under the desk pointed to the ceiling.

Hands on his hips, Thatch looked up. His eyes met mine. "What are you doing up there?"

"Do you think I want to be up here? The students cursed me."

"That isn't a curse. It isn't even a minor hex. It's a charm."

Like I cared what it was. "So . . . um," I tried to find the words to ask him to help me down, but my pride tied my tongue into a pretzel.

Any other decent human being would have offered to help me, but not Felix Thatch. He raised an eyebrow, as if waiting for me to grovel.

I stomped down my ego, my words coming out in a rush. "Would you please get me down?"

He muttered under his breath and circled his wand above his head. Purple light soaked into me, pelting my skin like rain. My legs and arms became unstuck from the ceiling first. It sounded like Velcro being torn away, but it didn't hurt. The rest of my body ripped away all at once. I plummeted toward the floor. I screamed and covered my face with my arms. Abruptly, the freefall stopped short of the wooden boards.

My heart thundered in my chest. I slowly pivoted in midair so that my body was upright. Thatch used his wand like a remote control, lowering me toward the floor. Dizziness washed over me, and I wobbled off balance. I tried to right myself, but my feet weren't planted on the ground yet.

"Stay still," Thatch said through clenched teeth.

I tried, but vertigo set in. I flailed out in an uncoordinated attempt not to fall over, but as my feet met the ground, I stumbled into a table, tripped, and fell flat on my face.

As I pushed myself up, I found Thatch covering his eyes with his hand, groaning. Apparently, I didn't need him or his magic to make me look like an idiot.

"What happened here?" he demanded. If he were a doctor, his bedside manner would probably kill the patients. "Well?"

Being snapped at after being attacked by my students was the last thing I needed. I couldn't take any more stress. I shook so hard, I could barely fumble in my pocket for my key to the closet. He stalked after me as I rushed for the door and unlocked it.

My voice came out in a croaking whisper. "Excuse me, I need a moment." I darted through the door and slammed it closed before the waterworks started.

Thatch said something from the other side of the door, but I couldn't understand him. The stairs leading to the dungeon were dark and probably covered in a thousand years of rat droppings and spider carcasses, but I didn't care. I plopped myself down in front of the open door to the supply closet and wept.

It looked like there was a reason for all that salt on my prophecy chocolate bar.

I hadn't even made it through the first period of the day. My students thought I was a joke. The staff hated me. My affinity was red, and no one else was red. I was the worst teacher ever. I should never have come here. I hadn't even learned how to use magic yet, and I didn't know if I would at this rate.

I hid and felt sorry for myself until no more tears came.

When I emerged from the stairwell, I peeked into my classroom. It was empty. What a relief. I needed to move on from this bad start and make myself presentable for my next class. If this had been like a normal art room with a sink for clean up, I would have splashed water on my face to get rid of the crust of tears. I didn't trust the bucket of water in the broken sink to be clean, so I slunk to the nearest girl's bathroom, which was all the way down the tower on the main floor, and washed up there. I scraped the cobwebs out of my hair and made myself presentable again.

I would master my magic, I promised myself. Next period would be better. I chanted mantras of optimism to myself all the way back to my room.

I should have prepped for my next class, but I needed to learn how to use magic and pronto. I skipped lunch and read a book Julian had given me on Fae history. Red affinities were mentioned, but nothing useful, like: *This is how you shoot lasers out of your eyes at bad students.*

There was an interesting chapter on a lost court that had been destroyed, but the text didn't say if they were related to a specific affinity or not. As far as I could tell, a Witchkin's affinity wasn't necessarily related to specific Fae courts. The section of book I'd stolen from Thatch had also mentioned something my mother had been interested in called the Lost Court.

A short while later, someone cleared his throat in the doorway. I glanced up.

Khaba leaned there, looking elegant and sleek. His gold shirt was unbuttoned down to his navel, showing off his pectoral cleavage and the top of a six-pack. I didn't know how he got away dressing like that on a school campus, but I wasn't going to be the one to complain. He was so yummy I could see why Josie obsessed over him.

He glided forward, as smooth as a jaguar. "The principal asked me to check on you."

I stood. "Right. Thanks."

He opened his arms and gestured for me to come closer. Tentatively I stepped forward, still not certain I trusted a Fae.

He embraced me in a bear hug. "Oh honey, you poor thing! No one deserves to be attacked on her first day."

I relaxed into the comfort of his arms. A hug must have been the balm my soul needed. I leaned my cheek against his sculpted muscles and tried not to drool on him.

He released me and patted my shoulder. "All things being considered, you got off easy. Pro Ro's class broke all the crystal balls playing dodgeball in his classroom last period. What a mess that was for the brownies to clean up. He's going to have to leave out something really nice for them." He went on to tell me some of the other deeds students had done in their other classes, making me laugh at his animated retellings.

"Let's see your class lists," he said.

I handed them over.

He scanned the first class. "Ah, I see you figured out who the biggest troublemakers are going to be." He placed a star next to another name. "Watch out for this one. She's a Celestor and very smart, but lacking in the ethics department, if you know what I mean." He made notes on my other class lists. "Ben O'Sullivan is a transfer student. Already he's gotten himself two detentions today. He's in your seventh period."

I nodded, grateful he was willing to alert me.

"Now here's the thing about these students." Khaba ran a hand over his bald head. "If you can connect with them and get them to like you or respect you, you can convince them to do just about anything. But a lot of them come from rough backgrounds. They've been abused, enslaved, or coerced into using magic for their guardians' gain."

As much of a pain in the butt as these kids had been so far, I could see why they might not react well to a new teacher. From all the stories I had heard about Fae using Witchkin, I could only imagine how difficult these kids' lives had been. I wish I knew how to be that cool teacher who knew how to relate to students. These students had no respect for me. I didn't know how I was going to be able to face them again.

Khaba sandwiched one of my hands between his own, earnestly gazing into my eyes as he spoke. "Trust doesn't come naturally to them. The other half of the population are spoiled brats who have had everything handed to them on a silver platter—and I mean that literally. These are kids who need us to ground them in reality. That sense of entitlement isn't going to get them far when dealing with Fae who would sooner drain them of their magic than be impressed with wealth."

I nodded with understanding. This wasn't so different from what I'd learned student teaching. It was just that these students had weapons, and I didn't. They had wands and magic.

"Now, I don't do this often, but . . . I'll grant you a wish." Khaba took a seat in my chair.

Khaba wasn't at all like what I'd first expected. He wasn't an evil Fae with ulterior motives—at least not that I could see. Perhaps my mother had selected him for the position as dean because he was a valuable asset and he truly cared about the school. Then again, he was Fae. Julian's words came back to me. This was the Unseen Realm. There were rules.

"Is there a . . . price for this?" I asked.

"Of course there is. If I'm going to do this, I need you to rub my lamp." He removed his shirt and tossed it on my desk with the practiced manner of a male stripper. He was ripped like an Egyptian god. His eyebrows lifted expectantly.

His words sank in. I was still having a hard time concentrating while gazing at his rock-hard biceps. "When you say, rub your lamp, um . . . is that a euphemism?" He was so hot, I wouldn't have minded—except that I wasn't supposed to risk exploding untamed sex magic on the school.

He laughed. "Honey, I don't swing that way. But I do need a good shoulder massage now and then." He leaned back and kicked his feet onto my desk.

Besides this looking unprofessional, I didn't want anyone to assume I was pursuing a relationship with another staff member and risk my job. I glanced at the door. "What if someone comes in?"

He snorted. "As if half the school hasn't seen me without a shirt at one time or another." He pointed to his back. "The sooner you get started, the sooner I can grant your wishes."

Wishes. As in plural. "I get more than one?"

"Three *small* wishes."

I darted behind him. Between his shoulder blades he sported a tattoo of a golden lamp. I rubbed it.

He giggled, "That tickles. Harder. Rub like you want those wishes. That's it. A little to the left. Higher."

I wasn't actually rubbing the lamp at all. I was giving him a shoulder massage. I tried not to think about how attractive he was. His skin shimmered like bronze. I forced myself to focus on kneading his muscles. His powerful, chiseled muscles. My stomach flip-flopped. Magic inside me fluttered. I pushed away thoughts of how hot he was. Sexy thoughts always got me in trouble. I did not want to electrocute someone trying to help me, nor did I wish to make another enemy.

His muscles were as dense as boulders. My hands ached after only a minute. That helped ground me in reality.

"What is your first wish?" Khaba's voice came out a satisfied purr. "And don't try to ask for something major like world peace. My limitations are within this school and confined to the short term."

Hope lifted my spirit. I could ask for information about my Red affinity. Whether I should, was another matter. Khaba seemed nice enough, but what if he saw me as bad because of it? What if he only offered to grant my wishes because he wanted to find out information about me? The kind of wish someone made revealed their darkest desires.

"I wish for an easy first day of school." Immediately I regretted my wish. "No, I mean, I want to be able to do magic." That was more important.

"Sorry, that isn't the way it works. You've already stated the wish."

It was fine, I told myself. I still had two more wishes.

He pointed to his back. "Your wish is my command . . . so long as you keep up that massage, honey." He snapped his fingers. He gestured to his right pants pocket. "Ask me if that's a jar of sweets in my pocket or I'm just happy to see you."

There was definitely a sizable bulge in his pocket I hadn't noticed a moment before.

"Um. I assume that's a jar of candy," I said.

"Not candy. Sweets." He pulled out a clear glass jar filled with multicolored candies. It started off as a reasonable quart size but expanded to a gallon jug. The glass thunked and candy rattled as he set it on the table. On the front was a label that said, "Sweets."

He tapped the lid. "Try one."

I popped the lid open and selected a yellow candy. The moment I set it on my tongue I tasted lemons and sunshine. Warmth and happiness radiated from my mouth and into my chest. The dark clouds of my day evaporated. I felt like a new person. I giggled and hugged the jar.

"I'm going to leave this jar with you today and today only. If at any time you need this to recharge—or you have a student who needs a little pick-me-up—you can use the sweets to help you manage about an hour's worth of time a little easier. Now, I want to point out a little goes a long way, and you can't use this all the time or else you're going to become dependent and go through withdrawals. Make sure you bring me the jar during the staff meeting after school." He pointed to his back. "Over here if you want two more wishes."

I set down the jar and dug into the knots of his muscles with gusto. The lamp had migrated to the left. I focused my efforts onto that shoulder blade.

"Wow, I feel great!" I said. My mood had improved one hundred percent. "This is better than coffee. Next wish. Okay, boy, let's see. . . ." My mouth worked faster than my mind. "I want magic—and lots of it. I don't want students to ever glue me to the ceiling again. I want to be a powerful witch—the most powerful witch ever. Like my mother—but not evil. Can you do that? Or is that too big?" So much for not revealing my deepest, darkest secrets. My mouth had run away from me.

"Instant magic? That would take a lot of rubbing. No offense, honey, but I don't want to take off *all* my clothes." His smile was amused.

Heat flushed my face.

"In any case, that request isn't officially school business. My wish granting is limited by the duties and boundaries of the school. Might I suggest something related to your classes or students?"

My mind was already racing to my next problem. "What am I going to do tomorrow? How will I manage those kids? Rotating A/B schedule, right? Today one, three, five, and seven. Plus, homeroom—of course, I don't have homeroom—but I'm just saying. Tomorrow two, four, six, and eight. Who do we appreciate? You!" I couldn't stop talking and had to clamp my hands over my mouth to shut up.

"I'll stop in tomorrow morning with the jar again. That can be wish number two. But you have to say what you want in the form of a wish. And you need to keep rubbing." He pointed to his back.

I kneaded my thumbs into his shoulder boulders. The lamp had drifted downward when I hadn't been looking.

"I wish for tomorrow to be a happy, easy day. Yay!" My enthusiasm bubbled over, making me sound like a motivational speaker on crack. "Wish number three. I wish for art supplies for the students. A closet full of art supplies. Or the administration to give me money for art supplies. Or I'd settle for a superpower so I could steal art supplies."

He barked out a laugh. "That's a pretty big wish. I'd have an easier time moving mountains than increasing your budget. And you're going to have to work on your superpowers on your own. Dig a little deeper in my muscles, and I'll see what I can come up with."

"Okay, new wish. Different wish. School business. Here it is: I want Thatch to be nice to me. I mean, I *wish* for Thatch to be nice to me." Even for a day. I did have to see him in the dungeon later.

Khaba was silent. I leaned over his shoulder to take in his grimace.

"No matter how much you rub my lamp, that's magically impossible. Let's go back to art supplies. What exactly do you need?"

Seventh period was a beginning-level class, mostly made up of freshmen. A few sophomores and juniors were mixed in. I didn't know if I'd have enough sweets for all my classes, but this one was going to need it; I had numerous experiences dealing with ninth graders during student teaching to know what fourteen-year-old monsters were capable of. I greeted each student with a smile and a piece of candy as they entered the room.

"Miss Lawrence!" one girl squealed. Imani ran up to me and threw her arms around me. "I'm so glad I have you as my teacher this year again."

I was so surprised by the hug, I nearly dropped the jar of candy.

"Imani! I'm glad to see you too. I didn't know you were Witchkin until, well, yesterday." I patted her shoulder. She was one of my favorite students, and that wasn't just the sweets talking. There was one familiar face I knew from my other life, and I was glad it was her.

"I didn't know I was a witch either," she said. "And I didn't know you were a witch. But there was that weird day in health class. You know, the day with the bananas."

She meant the day I'd been subbing for a sex-education class. I'd never taken sex ed in high school, but I was pretty sure it didn't normally involve the bananas coming to life to sing and dance about reproduction as students tried to put condoms on them.

She lowered her voice to a whisper. "Do you think that magic was mine or yours?"

"I don't know." I held out the jar of candy. "Do you have Mr. Thatch's class?"

She giggled. "Yeah, first and fourth period. He's scary, isn't he?" She selected a pink candy.

I lowered my voice. "I recommend you save that candy for his class period."

She eyed the candy and glanced back at the happy, complacent students who had come in before her. She nodded with understanding. "Got it."

She chose a seat in the front of the U of desks. "Miss Lawrence is my old art teacher," she whispered to another student near her. "This is going to be my favorite class."

With the aid of Mr. Khaba's sweets, the last class of the day went smoothly. I only needed the candy once during the period to recharge. I went over the syllabus, gave students an art pretest, and awarded points for good behavior. I wouldn't see them again for two days. That meant I would have two days to figure out what to do with the third-period class from hell. I wasn't going to have the jar of sweets with me then.

On the other hand, Khaba hadn't said I couldn't keep a few sweets for emergency purposes. I wrapped a handful in a tissue and placed them in the top drawer of my desk.

By the time school let out at three thirty, I was exhausted. I had an hour before the four thirty staff meeting.

There was only so much time in a day. As much as I wanted to know about Derrick's disappearance, my mother's investigations into the Fae Fertility Paradox, and whether Thatch had murdered the former art teachers—for their positions or because they'd stumbled upon something he didn't want them to know—I had more pressing matters to focus on.

I needed to survive teaching. That meant I needed to learn magic.

I went to the staff meeting after school in the conference room, scanning the faces of the old witches, wondering who might make a better teacher than Thatch. Grandmother Bluehorse was loved by the students and known for her wisdom, but the disdain on her face when she glanced at me wasn't exactly welcoming. My own department wouldn't even look at me. Already, teachers had made it clear they wanted nothing to do with me. I could ask Josie, though she wasn't considered a powerful witch.

Julian's sky-blue eyes met mine from across the table. He smiled. My heart fluttered. I could ask him.

Waiting until after the meeting finished was torture. I followed Julian to the front courtyard where he had a shift watching students as one of his duties. I glanced around, making certain Thatch wasn't around.

Julian waved to me, joy brightening his face.

I got to the point. "Can you teach me protection spells from students?"

He nodded solemnly. "Tough first day?"

"You could say that."

He wandered over to a bench and sat. "Wards are difficult to learn. They're the hardest form of magic. Did you know Miss Bloodmire teaches the warding classes?"

No wonder so many students disappeared with Vega as the teacher for their most important class.

"If you want to learn magic, we should start with something simple and work our way up to wards," he suggested.

"Oh. Yeah, I guess that's a good idea. I was just hoping to learn to protect myself sooner." I tried not to let my disappointment show.

"How about this? I'll construct a few extra wards around you, just something small to bounce student curses off you. The problem with these kind of wards is they don't last long. I'd have to renew it in a couple of days."

"That sounds like a lot of work," I said. "For you, I mean."

He winked. "I don't mind if you're willing to put up with spending time with me."

After his duty was over, he escorted me back to his classroom and performed a spell. It took half an hour of sitting still in a chair as he muttered incantations. At first, I didn't feel any different, but slowly pressure built around me. Magic fluttered in my belly, nudging my abdomen like it wanted to escape. Even through my closed eyes I kept seeing red, and my mouth tasted like cherries and strawberries. I felt hungry and thirsty and full of yearning like I'd never experienced before. My arms and legs wanted to move, to run and do cartwheels, but I suspected I was supposed to sit still and meditate.

That nervous energy shifted like it had in the affinity fire. My skin hummed with electricity. Molten desire burned through me so intensely I unbuttoned the top two buttons of my blouse. I wanted to collapse into his arms and kiss him. I let myself sink into that fantasy, imagining the taste of his lips on mine.

When he was finished, the air around him shimmered more intensely than ever. He was so beautiful. Green magic of the forest pulsed through him. He eased into the chair behind his desk.

My restless leg syndrome faded, and I was left with languid muscles. Thinking was an effort through the fogginess of my brain. I slouched back in my chair, smiling back at Julian. It felt as though all my inhibitions had been removed.

I dreamily blurted, "Have you ever heard of a Red affinity?"

He bit his lip. "That's a dangerous question. Why do you ask?" He glanced out the doorway.

Vega passed, looking especially grouchy as she eyed me in Julian's room.

"No reason," I said quickly. Why did everything I wanted to know about have to be dangerous? My drowsy bloom of fatigue faded as the carelessness of what I'd asked crashed me back into reality. I hoped Vega hadn't heard me.

"I think I have a book on it somewhere." He stretched his neck and yawned. "That ward was exhausting. I hope you don't mind, but magic lessons are going to have to wait."

If he was as fatigued as I'd felt, I didn't blame him. It was for the best, anyway. I needed to leave before I blurted out every single secret thought in my head. If that's what his magic did to me I was going to have to be more careful.

He took my hand in his. Lightning jolted through my core, and I withdrew my hand, afraid I was about to explode. The heel of someone's shoe squeaked out the door.

Was it a coincidence Pro Ro happened to walk by?

The following day, with the influence of mood-altering candy, I had a fresh start with classes two, four, six and eight—the B day. I was back to the joys of another A day after that, periods one, three, five, and seven. I didn't have the entire jar of candy, but I was armed with extra wards. Even so, my palms sweated, and I had trouble keeping my smile tacked in place. Khaba sat in on my class to ensure my day started out on the right foot. The first student handed me a note, eyes cast on the floor, downtrodden. The next student handed me a note, and the next one did too. The papers were apology letters!

"Mr. Thatch made us write them in detention," a student complained.

It looked like my apology notes were written in blood. Well, that was kind of sweet in a creepy way. It was the thought that counted. On the other hand, I wasn't sure Thatch had intervened with the students on my behalf because he wasn't completely evil, or because he just liked to punish the kids and make their lives miserable.

The first week was a battle even with sweets and extra wards. The second week wasn't much better. Partly that was because I spent my weekend planning a curriculum around a lack of art supplies. Khaba did bring me five reams of low quality computer paper he'd scrounged up, two boxes of golf pencils, and a giant tub of crayons. He also carried in a box of recycled paper from the office, one side covered with memos or discarded worksheets, the other side blank.

"I'll drop off recycled paper once a week from the administration wing," Khaba said.

It wasn't exactly the art materials I'd wished for, but it was something. I now considered I should have asked for information as my third wish. Not about my affinity—that was too dangerous, but I could have asked him about my mother or Derrick. Or what was up with Thatch.

Then again, that paper did come in handy. Too bad the students made paper airplanes out of them. That was sort of art.

I counted the days that passed without another major incident. I hadn't accidentally killed anyone at the school or blown anything up. Julian's wards seemed to help.

On Friday of week three, I woke to the usual cuckoo clock's screams. Blinking, I found Vega, clad in her all-black nightie, retrieving her towel and shower bag from her wardrobe. She magicked the shutters open with a wave of her hand. The gray ebb of dawn illuminated the room. Even though she had just risen, her short bob was immaculate. She lacked my usual bedhead or groggy appearance.

Her lack of calling dibs on the bathroom made me sit up. She crouched down and picked up a note that had been slid under the door.

She sighed dramatically. "Homeroom is canceled. We have an emergency staff meeting at eight. I wonder who died this time."

CHAPTER EIGHTEEN
Teaching to the Test

Since I didn't have a homeroom, I usually could take more time getting to my classroom in the morning than the other teachers. The day of the staff meeting, I had to cut out my meditation, compete for the bathroom with four other female teachers, eat breakfast, and get to the meeting on time. I made it to the staff room at seven fifty-nine. Everyone looked at me when I walked in like it was my fault the meeting had been called.

Josie waved, and I sat next to her. Vega slouched against the back of her chair on my other side, managing to exude elegance even though she barely looked awake.

Jeb fidgeted with the curls of his silver mustache. "I hain't called y'all to this emergency meetin' for nothin'. I'm afeared someone broke into my office last night. Mr. Khaba, will you appraise the staff of the situation?"

Khaba gestured to the chalkboard on the wall. It was hard to tear my gaze from his far too-tight hot-pink pants. The blank green slate wavered behind him. A diagram of Jeb's office appeared in chalk. "Protective wards to keep students out are set here at the front door, at these windows, and at this back door." He pointed. "In addition to my wards, Jeb boobytraps his desk, along the bookcase, and in various places where he keeps potions and items that might endanger the students. We utilize a variety of spells that use different affinities. That way, even if a student breaks through our fire spell because he or she excels at fire magic, the student still will fail at an ice spell, a venomous-animal spell and so on."

All this was easy enough to follow, but I had a feeling there was something more to the reason we'd been called in. Perhaps someone had gotten hurt from that venomous-animal spell.

Khaba tapped the drawing of the principal's office. "I have ascertained the break-in occurred sometime between one and two a.m. while my security staff was patrolling other parts of the building."

"Or sleeping on duty," Vega muttered under her breath.

Khaba's eyes narrowed. "The guard on duty happened to be patrolling the teacher wing at the time of the break-in."

"Ugh. Watching us in our sleep, then." She snorted.

"As far as we can tell, nothing of value was stolen. Possibly a book from the glass case."

A book? A book on the forbidden arts? Or something only Thatch didn't want people to know about?

"The only item definitely stolen was a bottle of whiskey that was left on the desk, but that may have been mistaken as a gift by a brownie and be unconnected to this incident," Khaba said. "We are checking Principal Bumblebub's list of inventory to confirm nothing more was stolen. Either the culprits didn't find what they were looking for, or they were scared off when my security guard returned to the West Tower."

"Why have we canceled homeroom for this?" Jasper Jang rubbed at his bald head, his expression confused. From the way he projected his voice, I could see why he was a theatre and music teacher. "Students break in, vandalize, and steal all the time. Remember last year when Rex Danu urinated all over my prop room?"

"Thank the gods he graduated," someone whispered. "I bet the Fae snatched him up and swallowed him whole."

I glanced around the table, wondering who would say such a horrible thing about a student.

"This is the principal's office we're talking about. Of course we should be concerned." Professor Bluehorse pointed a gnarled, arthritic finger at Jasper. "Show some respect to your elders."

Khaba smoothed his fingers over the lapel of his leopard-print shirt. He'd actually buttoned four of the buttons today. "This is the first time a student's magic didn't set off my alarms. The door was unlocked with a key, not with magic. The wards at the door didn't react, nor did the others I'd set in place around the room. They acted as though an administrator was there, not an intruder. But our surveillance using the magic mirror and crystal balls shows no one. We can see the glass being smashed and items thrown to the ground, but we can't see who did it."

"So they had invisibility charms," Coach Kutchi fished something out of the pocket of her tracksuit. A steaming mug of coffee appeared in her hand, the fragrance of mocha and caffeine wafting toward me. "I see it all the time on the field. Kids try to be sneaky and sabotage the other team."

"That alone wouldn't work," Jeb said. "As Mr. Khaba stated, they managed to bamboozle our wards and make a big bag of nails of my office."

Pro Ro raised his hand. "As professor of divination and soothsaying, I would like to help with the investigation."

Khaba nodded. "We'll take all the assistance we can get."

Julian waved his hand. He flashed a smile that showed off such straight white teeth it would have made his dentist proud. "As professor of History of Magic—"

Thatch coughed loudly. "Because a history lesson is going to help them investigate who did this."

Julian sat back in his chair, his expression hurt.

Khaba went on. "If Principal Bumblebub's door hadn't been left wide open, we wouldn't have known until this morning. My security guard took one look at the shattered glass panels of the bookcase and woke me. Clearly this is sophisticated magic."

There must have been something I was missing. I didn't see how using a key and smashing a bookcase was magic.

"I suggest we give the entire school Saturday detention," Vega said. "Just until the guilty party comes forward and confesses."

Jackie Frost crossed her arms. "Are you volunteering to give up your Saturday to do this, Miss Bloodmire?"

"I have someone else more . . . persuasive in mind for the job." Vega eyed Thatch with a smile. It was unlikely he could punish all students in his detention.

Jeb frowned. "Other ideas?"

Pro Ro cleared his throat. "This isn't necessarily advanced magic. The culprit may have simply had a key. That isn't sophisticated; it's theft. He or she used brute force, again an inelegant solution. Invisibility cloaks and temporary transparency spells are a dime a dozen."

I was glad I wasn't the only one who saw this as a nonmagical occurrence. This person didn't even need the key to the office. He or she might have used a skeleton key or a lockpick kit like the one I had at home.

Jeb chewed on his mustache, thinking it over. "That means it's someone who don't think like a Witchkin. A new student coming in fresh from the Morty Realm for sure. Someone who ain't got no magic under his belt yet. You can hang your hat on that."

"Detentions to all freshman, then," Vega said.

Khaba raised a finger to stop her. "This person still had enough power to not set off alarms past the entrance. Most fourteen-year-olds haven't enough skill, nor enough raw talent. This child is different."

Teachers exchanged glances with each other. I could tell what they were thinking. A freshman. Someone different. They thought it was Imani. But she was a sweet kid. She wouldn't break into his office. She had no reason to steal alcohol, books, or anything else.

"What's the name of that new girl? Imani Jefferson? Washington?"

someone said.

"The one with the rainbow affinity?" Silas Lupi's voice rose.

"No one has a rainbow affinity," Thatch said adamantly. "She is Celestor."

There had been a lot of red flashing in the rainbow fire. I had a feeling she was red like me. Dread settled like a lump in my gut as the teachers continued to murmur about Imani.

Josie nudged me. "Only the avatar, master of all four elements. . . ."

I didn't laugh. An innocent girl was about to get blamed. This felt like a witch hunt.

Thatch cracked his knuckles, his grin sinister. "I would like to volunteer my persuasive skills in questioning the child."

That was the tipping point. I would not allow Thatch to touch her and torture her in the dungeon. I stood up. "It wasn't her. I know her. It wasn't."

"You *know?*" Thatch raised an eyebrow. "Would you care to enlighten us on your method of divination?"

That was just like him to come up with a snarky response. "She used to be my student at Hamlin Middle School. I can vouch for her character."

Thatch leaned back in his chair, ever the picture of nonchalance. "I would still prefer to question her myself and come to the same conclusion."

Jeb waved a hand at me, indicating I should sit. I did so, frustrated I didn't have greater sway here.

Jeb went on. "This is exactly why I hide those dang answer keys to the exams in the vault under the school, behind multiple locked doors, and guard the doors with dangerous creatures—Or I will after they arrive next week, anyway."

I raised my hand. "Why don't you just let the students steal the answer key and then change the answers on the test? Then you could see who stole it when they take the test."

The teachers busted up laughing. Apparently, I'd said the wrong thing. Yet again.

"Bless your heart, Miss Lawrence. Your naïveté is so endearing." Jeb doubled over and wiped his eyes.

Professor Bluehorse smoothed her hand over the moss and lichen growing on her staff. "We don't make the exams students need to take each semester. Our Fae elected schoolboard does. Every school takes the same tests."

I stared in open-mouthed horror. "So everything we teach is to the test?" Ugh! This was just as bad as public schools with standardized tests. Only, in the real world—the Morty world—it wasn't Fae who decided who got funding based on test scores or anything else, it was the government. This system didn't seem much better.

Jackie Frost pointed an accusing finger at me. "*You* don't teach to any test. You just teach arts and crafts. Only core classes have required exams we have to grade."

"It isn't like elective teachers don't give tests," Coach Kutchi said.

The meeting descended into squabbling over priorities of subject area content. Why had I ever thought the education system in another dimension would be any different than it was at home? Jeb sat in his chair, leaning his forehead into his hands. His eyes were dark with lack of sleep and his frame fatigued. He didn't stop the teachers from arguing amongst themselves. He closed his eyes and appeared to doze off.

Mr. Khaba cut through the commotion. "Do you not understand the seriousness of this? This isn't about a simple act of vandalism. If a student can get into Principal Bumblebub's office, they can get the answer keys under the school. They can get into . . . other places under the school."

"Like the crypt?" Vega said, her face paling.

She *would* care more about the dead than the living.

Jeb sat up at the mention of his name. "Hear, hear, Mr. Khaba. Well said. We can't have this interfering with our sleep and causing backdoor trots."

I tried to figure out what the principal was talking about.

Khaba's brow furrowed. He repeated himself more slowly. "Any student who is clever enough, skilled enough, and resourceful enough to open up secret vaults under the school to retrieve answer keys, can also unleash the forbidden magic Loraline stored there." He looked out across the table of staff. "Do you all want an unspeakable evil set free and wreaking havoc at this school?"

I shrank back as people glared openly at me. I supposed they thought the rotten apple didn't fall far from the maternal tree.

"It would be unthinkable." Thatch crossed his arms. "Worse than a free djinn."

Jeb tugged at his beard. "Is that sarcasm, Felix? This ain't no laughing matter."

Why didn't they just store the stupid answer keys off campus or somewhere not next to the vaults of unspeakable horrors? Duh. I considered saying something to that effect, but I didn't want the entire staff to laugh at my "endearing naïveté" again. I would ask Josie instead later.

I had a more pressing question anyway. "It seems like there's a lot of student mischief and dark energies and forbidden magic going on at our school. But I don't know how to protect myself from black magic," I said. "How am I supposed to teach students when they're hexing me?"

Jeb stroked his snowy white beard. "Yep, I smell what you're steppin' in. You need someone to teach you advanced magic and pronto. Volunteers?" His gaze roved over the teachers.

Vega crossed her arms and looked away. The older teachers glared at the principal defiantly. Josie bit her lip. Tentatively she raised her hand. "I can teach simple charms and herbal magic."

Thatch snorted. "You? The human studies teacher? Please. What are you going to teach her? The best place to buy granola and how to sneak into the back door of Happy Hal's without students seeing you?"

Her face paled. "No! I don't—I mean, we don't—I'm a good role model for students."

My loathing for Thatch twisted in my chest. What was his problem? The first chance I got, I wanted to speak with Jeb about Thatch's animosity.

Julian raised his hand. "I happen to be an expert at protection spells. I used to be the wards and magical self-defense teacher at my old school." He winked at me. "I can teach you a thing or two about using a wand."

Vega nudged me with her elbow. "In case you're too dense to realize it, that's a euphemism."

My face flushed with heat. The truth was, I wouldn't mind getting better acquainted with his . . . wand. So far he had been the nicest person to me on staff besides Khaba and Josie. I would have even considered dating him if a relationship with a coworker was allowed.

And if I wasn't afraid of the storm of magic brewing inside me.

Julian continued, "Miss Lawrence doesn't have a wand, I notice. She needs a mentor to get her started."

"Witchkin don't need to rely on a phallic object to harness their energies," Jackie Frost said.

Coach Kutchi nodded in agreement. "It was a tradition started by the male institution of warlocks centuries ago meant to exclude women."

I tried not to laugh. I knew who the two feminists on staff were.

"What? What was that?" Jeb squinted at the teachers before his gaze fell on Thatch.

Thatch cleared his throat. "Might I suggest Coach Kutchi? She's a formidable defense teacher, and Miss Lawrence is unlikely to encounter any . . . roving wands with the coach's teaching methods." He glanced at Julian.

Julian shook his head, his eyebrows knitting together. "What? No! That's a horrible thing to imply."

"Hmm. Yes, clever idea." The principal grinned broadly.

Professor Kutchi crossed her arms. "As if I need one more thing on my plate."

This was almost as bad as being picked last for dodgeball. I didn't want to be a burden to anyone.

Jeb went on. "Thank you kindly for volunteering, Professor Thatch. I can't think of a more suitable teacher."

I shook my head, trying to catch Jeb's eye. I did not want Thatch as a teacher again.

Thatch tilted his head to the side. "Excuse me, sir, but I believe you misunderstood my suggestion. Professor Kutchi would be the obvious choice as instructor for Miss Lawrence's education. She's her department head."

"I reckon so. Her education will be safe in your hands. Thank you kindly."

Thatch raised his voice. "I said, 'Professor Kutchi should teach her.' Or any of the female teachers. It would be inappropriate for a male teacher to work so intimately with Miss Lawrence. Especially after your decree that relationships among staff be forbidden. We wouldn't want Miss Lawrence to have another . . . accident." He quirked an eyebrow at me.

My face burned with shame.

"Yep, I wholeheartedly agree. There's no beatin' the devil around the stump on this one. You're the best candidate. I've got no worries about your professionalism."

Thatch's face turned red. A few of the teachers snickered.

I nudged Josie. "What is up with Jeb? Is he under the influence of some kind of spell?"

She shook her head and whispered, "He probably forgot to recharge his hearing spell again, and he's not a very good lip-reader."

Thatch and Jeb exchanged a few more words which I missed as I whispered to Josie.

Thatch burst out, "Merlin's balls! I don't want to teach her." He rose and stormed out, his long dark hair billowing behind him like liquid shadows. The gray tweed of his suit twisted and spun into smoke that dissipated into the air.

That was one way to make a dramatic exit. It was vaguely reminiscent of the Raven Court. Not a good sign considering they were supposed to be the ultimate evil and he was my teacher. Still, the spiraling remnants of his spell were impressive.

"Whoa," I said. "Someone doesn't like being volun-told."

Vega's perfectly groomed eyebrows came together. "Volun-told? That sounds like a spell I would like to learn."

I shrugged. "It has about the same amount of power as a minor hex."

The meeting finished half an hour before third period started. Jeb was out the door first, the other teachers sluggishly exiting the staff room. I pushed my way through those ahead of me, gaining a dirty look as I accidentally elbowed Silas Lupi. From the way his mouth drew back from his pointed teeth and his yellow eyes shot daggers at me, I knew I hadn't endeared myself to the other teacher.

I ran out the hall and up the stairs after the principle. "Headmaster

Bumblebub, wait!"

He continued his slow shuffle up the steps. I remembered what Josie had said about his hearing. I kept running, shouting to be heard as I repeated myself.

He paused, using his staff to lean on as he turned around. "Please, call me Jeb. And if you must, I'd rather you call me Principal Bumblebub, not Headmaster. Headmaster is such a prissy, Yankee title, ain't it?"

I panted, out of breath. "I've been trying to schedule an appointment with you. Has Mrs. Keahi told you?"

"Told me what?"

"That I wanted to see you." Seeing his blank expression, I went on. "I've been hoping you would educate me on some of the mysteries surrounding my mother and why everyone hates her." Particularly Thatch.

"Ah." He continued climbing the stairs. "Mr. Thatch said he gave you a kit and caboodle of reading material. Was it . . . inadequate?"

I walked along beside him. "It would have been fine, I guess, but he ripped pages out so I couldn't read about my mother."

"That's as interestin' as all get-out." He tugged on his beard. "Suppose that's his pride. He don't want one more person to know he was ever capable of failure."

I placed my hand on the sleeve of his gray robe. "Please don't make him my teacher. He's so nasty to me."

"I'm gonna let you in on a lil' secret. He's all hat and no cattle. He gave up one of his preps so you could have an extra period to study magic. It was his suggestion. Did you know that, darlin'?"

I shook my head, not sure whether I believed this or if it was another instance of being volun-told. I remembered the day Josie and I had examined the schedules. We'd assumed Thatch's lack of a free homeroom had been why he'd been in a bad mood. More likely he was always in a bad mood.

Jeb waved a hand airily toward the dungeon. "Thatch has come to me several times, insistin' I train you myself. When it comes to your education, he's worse than a cat in a room full of rockers. He ain't fixin' to be your teacher, not after his history with your mother, whereas I think he'd do a bang-up job on account of it. He knows the temptations of black magic like nobody's business. He'll be more invested you ain't goin' down the same path she did."

Ah, so Jeb's incompetent deafness had been a ruse.

"But he's not the best teacher for the job. He's so. . . ." I didn't know where to begin. Dare I say the word out loud? *Evil.* It was unlikely he would agree. "Mean."

"There's a mighty good reason for his prickly nature. He don't want others to see him as weak and vulnerable after what happened twenty years ago. Twenty-two years ago." He tucked his thumbs under his belt. The buckle was a giant silver unicorn encased in a square. "He don't permit himself friends, nor does he trust his peers after the way he was betrayed. Last year I thought with Miss Kimura befriendin' him, or tryin' to anyway, he might grow sweet on her."

Josie had tried to be friends with him? Their feud was deeper than the houses of Stark and Lannister from *A Song of Ice and Fire*. It was hard to imagine them ever being on friendly terms.

"As you're mighty keen in observin', he's got some issues to work through. You bein' here at the school, well, it's my hope he'll learn to forgive your mother for what she did, and your presence will be cathartic for him. Sooner or later he'll to come to realize you ain't her." He cupped my cheek in his hand in a grandfatherly way. "I told you life here would be more difficult than getting a devil to pray in church. It'll take time before people see you as an individual."

"What did Loraline do to him?"

He patted my head. "It isn't my place to say. He'll tell you when he's ready."

I wondered when that would be.

CHAPTER NINETEEN
Unjust Accusations

The thing I wanted to do most was warn Imani Washington that Thatch might interrogate her, but there was no time. I only had a few minutes to get from the administration wing to my classroom before third period. I raced through the twisting corridors and unlocked the door for the students waiting in the stairwell. Apparently, news traveled fast. Students murmured about the break-in as I ushered them inside.

It was an A day. That meant I had Balthasar Llewelyn and Hailey Achilles. Hopefully they wouldn't try to stick me to the ceiling today. They sauntered in two minutes late, taking seats in the back as I took attendance from the stool at the front of the room.

"I'm the chosen one," Hailey said to her friend. "The prophecy is about me, not her."

"That Imani *mutt* just wants attention."

I looked up at that. The kids' eyes went wide around them. From their reactions, I could tell "mutt" meant something rude relating to half-breeds.

"Mutt?" I hopped off my stool and went over. "Did you just say 'mutt' in my classroom?"

Students whispered and nudged each other. "The teacher just said a bad word."

Ugh. Now I was going to be the potty-mouth teacher who said racial slurs. I blazed on, pointing a finger at Hailey. "We do not use derogatory language in my class. Is that clear? And I will not allow you to talk that way about other students in my classes. Ten points from Elementia."

Later I was going to ask Josie what "mutt" meant.

I finished taking attendance. Before we started our lesson, I read an article about Joan Miro, asking students to take notes as I read. I asked questions afterward, and we looked at his art. As I went around to check off work, I realized most of the students had written down every single word I'd said. Or tried to. I didn't know how they could read what they'd written.

"When I read an article or you read from a book, do you know how to take notes? Have you ever had a teacher show you?" I asked.

No one raised a hand.

"Five points to the first person who can tell me," I said. Still no one answered. "Have you learned summarizing in your history classes?"

"We used to do it at my old middle school," a human-looking boy said. "But I haven't done it for a long time."

No wonder these kids did so poorly in school. They needed literacy strategies. I could help them with that, and if I was lucky, connect with them in the process.

I lowered my voice to a whisper. "Do you want me to teach you how to cheat on your homework?" I could barely contain my excitement. This was going to get them on my side!

"Cheat?"

Students looked around at each other confused. This was exactly what my sixth-grade teacher had told me and how she had sparked my interest in learning study skills. "You don't actually have to read an entire book to get good grades. You only need to find the important sections. Do you want me to show you how?"

"Yeah, I want to know how to cheat!" Maya Briggs shouted.

For the next hour, we used art history as a vehicle for learning how to take notes and find the most important information in a text. I walked through the aisles, smiling at how excited the students were that they thought they were getting away with something. It felt like my first breakthrough with this class.

Hailey had one sentence written on her paper. Sort of. It was illegible, and a lot of letters were backward.

She crumpled it up when she saw me standing there. "This is stupid. This is an art class, not a writing class."

"Art history and criticism are part of art. You don't have to do the written work." I shrugged, using my best poker face. "You just won't get points for what you don't do."

"Well, I'm not doing it." She threw the paper in the trashcan and walked out the door.

I ran to the doorway. "If you leave, I'm assigning a detention."

"Don't care."

"With Thatch." I didn't know if I actually could do that, but it was worth a try.

She hesitated on the steps, actually considering it. "Still don't care."

One of the students whispered. "This is one of the only classes she doesn't skip."

Until today, apparently. My biological mother hadn't given up on her students, and I didn't want to be the teacher that would either. But so far, Hailey was the biggest pain-in-the-butt student in all my classes.

Ten minutes later, Josie came in. She must have been on her prep. She adjusted her pointed hat and surveyed the students taking notes. "What is your class doing? This isn't art." From the way she lifted an eyebrow, one might have thought she was the art police.

I beckoned her over to the far side of the room and into the back stairwell that led to the closet. The kids were in sight, but we had some privacy so I could tell her my diabolical plan to help students learn better.

"Absolutely nefarious," she agreed. "You'll have to give me tips for my students later."

"Hailey Achilles left class," I said. "I'd have thought this tactic would appeal to her of all students. I told them it was *cheating*. Wasn't she one of the ones who tried to steal answer keys last year?" That's what she had claimed when I'd overheard her anyway. I didn't know why the staff hadn't considered her as a suspect for the break-in. Or for murdering teachers.

"That was her. She skipped my class all last year. I'm not surprised she walked out today. She's constantly in detention. Next year she'll be one of our 'super' seniors." She wiped her black-rimmed glasses on the front of her green-and-purple tunic-style dress. "Listen, do you think it's really a good idea to tell them it's 'cheating?' I mean, think about it, do you want them to tell the other teachers you taught them to cheat on tests? Especially after Jeb's office was broken into, supposedly for tests." She eyed me the same way a high school teacher might eye a suspicious teenager.

"What? I thought they'd broken in for the alcohol." Or a book. Could Thatch have been the culprit? He was supposed to be extremely skilled at spells.

She pulled me deeper into the closet, closing the door. "It was you, wasn't it?" Josie pointed accusingly at me. "You broke into Jeb's office, didn't you?"

"Me? No way! Why would you think I broke into his office?"

She raised an eyebrow. "Because I told you he had that book you wanted, and there was a book stolen from his office."

"I don't have the kind of magic that would do that."

She crossed her arms, unconvinced.

I peeked out the door. The students worked in pairs, too busy chatting to care what the adults were saying. I whispered, "I haven't done magic on purpose before."

"Whatev. Just be careful." She pushed past me and left.

Great. Now my only friend thought I was a thief and a liar.

Because I had a lunch duty and didn't see Imani during that time, I wasn't able to warn her about Thatch's interrogation. I peeked into Thatch's classroom during my fifth-period prep, thinking I could talk to him instead. His students were the image of complacency. Every student had his or her head down as they wrote an essay. I wondered if they ever used any of the cauldrons, vials, and chemistry-looking equipment stored on the back counter and in the glass cupboards.

Thatch sat at his desk, writing in a leather-bound journal. Perhaps it was the same one I'd seen in his desk earlier with his satanic art.

The black raven sat perched in a domed cage in the corner. It squawked and a student looked up.

A freshman from one of my classes nudged his friend. "Look, it's Miss Lawrence!"

"No talking," Thatch said. He continued writing in his book.

I put my finger to my lips so the students wouldn't get in trouble for speaking. A couple waved, and I waved back.

I tiptoed to the front of the room. "I was wondering if you had a moment to talk about a student."

Thatch snapped his book closed. "I'm in the middle of teaching right now."

I glanced at the students silently writing. Right. Teaching.

I mouthed the words. "It's about Imani Washington."

"You may return during my prep, seventh period."

"I have class." He probably knew it too. "How about after school?"

"I'm busy torturing small animals and possibly children at that time." His smile was amused. I couldn't tell if he was joking or not. "You may return at four thirty."

My prep period oozed by with the speed of molasses on a cold day. I couldn't remember what period Imani had Thatch. When I saw her seventh period, I took her aside, into the closet. I kept the door ajar so I could see into my classroom and keep an eye on the students working on their line assignment.

"Imani, I need to talk to you about something serious." I took a deep breath. "But I don't even know where to begin."

Her face crumpled. "It's about that break-in, isn't it? Everyone thinks I did it, don't they?"

"Not everyone." I hesitated. Now my suspicion rose too. "How'd you know that's what I was going to ask you about?"

"Mr. Khaba called me into his office. Everyone's talking about it." Her eyes filled with tears. "But you know I didn't do it, right?"

"I believe you, honey." I patted her shoulder.

"You have no idea how much it means to me." She threw her arms around me and buried her face against my shoulder. "I hate how everyone looks at me. Everyone's so mean here."

"Tell me about it." I handed her a clean tissue from my pocket.

Beyond the closet door one of the students drew on his classmate's art with a quill. The other student shoved him away. Any minute now I was going to have to intervene.

Imani sniffled. "I was different at home and I'm different here. At home my family was afraid of me because I could make things happen. I was magic, a witch. At school, black kids said I wasn't black enough. White kids said I wasn't white enough." Her voice came out high and muffled against my shoulder. "Here, some of them think I'm not magic enough. They say I'm a freak because of the affinity-fire test. I don't know the most basic rules of Witchkin etiquette and keep asking dumb questions. I still don't understand how magic works. And I made enemies on my first day because I asked someone what he was." She blew her nose on the tissue, holding it up like she didn't know what to do with it.

I took it from her and shoved it into my pocket. I handed her another. She didn't deserve to be treated like a pariah. No one did.

I said, "I've made a few of those same mistakes too." And a few enemies.

"You did?" She pulled away. "So the rumor is true? You don't know this stuff either?" She dried her eyes.

"Yeah, it's hard being the least magical teacher."

"I heard about what your third-period class did." She grimaced. "That must have been brutal."

"So you understand why I'm concerned. I don't want people taking things out on you because you're new. You were the only one who reacted differently in the affinity fire so people assume things—even if they shouldn't. I don't want this to create more negative attention." I swallowed. "At the staff meeting today, Mr. Thatch offered to, um, question you." That sounded a little less scary than torture. I didn't want to alarm her. We could build up to the severity of the situation. "I wanted to warn you. I don't know what else I can do. Maybe you can ask to have another teacher present." I felt so powerless. "Maybe Mr. Khaba?" Thatch wouldn't dare to do anything cruel with Khaba present.

She waved me off. "Mr. Thatch already talked to me. We're cool. He asked me about my meeting with Dean Khaba and when I told him, he asked, 'Did you do it?' I said, 'No,' and then he asked me how I was liking my fun class. That's art." She shrugged. "Mr. Thatch isn't as bad as I first thought he was. He only punishes the bad kids in the detention dungeon.

He loaned me books to read to help me get caught up so I'd know how to fit in better."

"That's nice. . . ." For real? It sounded like he'd given her something more useful than what he'd given me. "Did it help?"

"Well, not yet. It's a lot of reading, and they give loads of homework here. I'm only on the first book, but he said there's no rush." She shrugged. "He lets me read in his room after school."

Hmm. That didn't sound like the Felix Thatch I knew. What was he up to? Did he suspect her Red affinity? Perhaps he intended to do something to her. "Maybe you should hang out with people your own age during your breaks. You should study with friends." Not alone with some creepy older man.

She bit her lip. "I don't have any friends."

"Yet." I squeezed her shoulder. "You will. Maybe if you study in the library, you'll meet other kids your age."

Someone screamed in my classroom, "Take that, penis breath!" Light flashed, and I ran back into the classroom, the conversation with Imani coming to a premature end.

After school I found Thatch's classroom empty. Two students were strung up in the dungeon, sobbing and screaming. I ducked my head down and passed them. They whimpered and called out to me. I hurried past, guilty and conflicted about Thatch's method of discipline.

I didn't feel quite as guilty as I rounded the corner to Thatch's office and their cries stopped.

"Man, I am so bored," one of them said.

"This is so lame. I didn't even punch Jeremy that hard. It wasn't like I broke his nose."

"Yeah, but it was bleeding."

Thatch sat at his desk. I wondered if Imani had convinced him of her innocence or he had pretended to believe her—pretended to be nice to her—so that he could better keep an eye on her. He shoved the book he was reading into the lowest desk drawer. No screams went off. He removed a package from the second drawer and placed it on the table. The air smelled vaguely of chocolate.

He folded his hands in front of him. "Sit."

I sat in my torture chair, trying to avoid the rusty bolts sticking up along the perimeter. I got right to the point. "Imani didn't break into the principal's office. She had no reason to steal something. And she's smart enough she doesn't need an answer key."

"I know." The candlelight in the room cast his face in flickering shadows, making it difficult to read the expression on his face.

"You do?"

He tossed his glossy black hair over his shoulders. His beautiful mane was his most redeeming feature. "I've been a teacher for over forty years. With experience, one develops an uncanny ability to know when one is being lied to."

"Whoa, how old are you?" He didn't look a day over thirty-five. Maybe forty if he aged well, but he had to be using some kind of wrinkle-free glamour.

"That is none of your concern. The point is, I didn't need to question her."

"I thought. . . ." I swallowed. I had feared he might torture her into a false confession. Or pretend to be nice so she might confess and then he'd punish her.

"You thought *what*? That I would torture an innocent student for the pleasure of it?"

"Well, that is what you led the staff to believe." A shrill scream punctuated the air, coming from the dungeon beyond.

"Have you ever given the idea of hell much thought?" He leaned back in his chair, staring at the ceiling. The lazy tilt of his head, the relaxed slouch in his chair, and the way he half closed his eyes reminded me of a satisfied cat after it had feasted on a mouse. "Have you ever considered where the devil must have begun?"

I had no idea where he was going with this.

"What is the job of a school teacher other than to police and punish students? I have become detention master in this miserable job. I perform the necessary evils because everyone else thinks they are too clean and pure to do so themselves." He sighed overdramatically.

"Um. . . ."

"Just as the devil, I only punish those who . . . deserve it." His lips twitched as he said the word "deserve," as though it brought him amusement.

That hint of emotion whispered of his humanity. I could almost believe he had a nice person inside him, waiting to burst free. With the light flickering across his face and the smile softening the harsh line of his lips, it reminded me of how beautiful he was. Not just his hair, but his face, his smile, the smoky slate of his eyes.

I wet my lips, forcing myself to look away from the perfection of his features. "Is that how you see yourself? As the devil?"

He ignored the question. "I had no reason to punish Imani Washington." He leaned forward. "The principal's reasoning is flawed. He and Khaba assumed it was one of the students." His lips curled into a smug smirk.

"You don't think it was one of the students?" Did he know I suspected him?

He snorted. "This came in the mail for you." He pushed the package across the desk. The box was one of the standard flat-rate sizes from the post office. "It was accidentally placed in my mailbox in the office. Your box is overflowing with papers. I suggest you clean it out so that little mix-ups like this don't happen in the future."

The packing tape had already been cut and the contents looked as though they had been rifled through. My mom had sent me a few of the things I had asked for and a few things I hadn't. She'd sent me some postcards of art from the Friday Art Walk in town, two boxes of colored pencils, three pairs of cotton panties—clean underwear was just the kind of thing my mom would worry about—and a note. I shoved the panties under the colored pencils, my embarrassment turning to anger. The big jerk had gone through my package?

Probably he'd read the note from my mom as well. It said:

Clarissa,

I'll go through some of your other boxes next weekend, but I wanted to send you your lockpick kit so you could get into your closet. I miss you. Hugs and kisses.

Mom

Thatch folded his hand on the desk. The implication sank in. I was so busted.

CHAPTER TWENTY
A Deal with the Devil

This looked bad.

I'd stuck my neck out claiming I knew the break-in hadn't been done by the student in question. Thatch hadn't thought Imani had been the one to break into the principal's office. He thought it was an adult. Me.

The lockpick box was small. Now that I looked more closely, I could see it peeking out from under the colored pencils. Craptacular.

"I didn't break into Jeb's office," I said quickly.

He leaned back in his chair, a satisfied smirk on his face. "You had the motivation. You wanted a taste of his forbidden knowledge."

"I wanted to know about my biological mother, yes. That didn't mean I was going to break into the principal's office."

"No, but you planned on breaking into *my* office? Into the library? Haven't you ever heard curiosity killed the cat?"

And the former art teachers.

I stared at the meager contents of my box. It had been a pretty stupid idea.

This was the kind of thing that could get a teacher fired from a school, especially a teacher whose mother had already established her criminal history and plenty of prejudice for her future generations.

I had a bad feeling about what he was going to do to me now. "Are you going to chain me up in the dungeon?"

"Only if you haven't done your homework."

I stared at him uncomprehendingly. Was he saying what I thought he was? Hope blossomed inside me. "Are you going to teach me magic?"

"That depends on you. I am willing to make a bargain with you."

I thought back to all his references to being like the devil. "I'm not going to agree to let you drain me."

"I didn't think you would." His lips curled upward in amusement. "If you would be so kind as to allow me to continue. . . . I will teach you magic *if* you promise to start behaving as a professional and cease your endless inquiries about my personal life."

He meant about him and my mother. Him and the missing books. All the secrets he'd been trying to keep from me. Did that mean I was close to discovering something? This was the ultimate temptation. What was more important, learning magic or learning if he had been my mother's accomplice? Magic or figuring out if he had killed the other art teachers?

"Well?" he asked.

I wouldn't survive teaching the school year without magic.

"I want you to teach me," I said.

He waved his wand at the stack of books on his desk. One slid out of the middle of the pile and levitated in front of me. "Your first task is to read, *Magical Etiquette for Dunces*." The way he looked me up and down told me who the dunce in the room was.

The volume fell, and I had to dive out of the chair to catch it on top of the box I was already holding. The book was about as thick as an unabridged dictionary.

"More reading?" I asked.

He flicked his wand at the stack and another floated toward me and then another. "Next you shall read, *Runes for Defensive Magic* and then *The History of Magic*, volumes one, two and three."

I struggled to hold the heavy tomes. "What about practical magic? How will I actually learn to ward off the kids' spells?" I didn't want to get turned into a Jackson Pollock painting like the last teacher.

"After you've completed your required reading, we shall discuss the practical application of wards and shield charms."

"This isn't teaching me. You're just handing me books again. I need to learn how to protect myself in case someone tries to hex me onto a ceiling again."

"Continue with your meditations and lucid-dreaming exercises. I will ensure your classroom is properly warded against hexes, curses and malicious charms."

"But—"

He stood. "And I forbid you to allow Julian Thistledown to construct half-assed wards that will interfere with my superior magic."

I didn't know how he knew. "If I want Julian's wards—"

"If I am to teach you, I expect you to follow my instructions." A malicious smile curled his lips upward. "And if you want someone else to teach you, you may take your complaints to Jeb. That is, if Mrs. Keahi is willing to schedule an appointment for you."

If he thought assigning reading was *teaching* and keeping up his end of the bargain, then I would find my own covert way to inquire about him and his past to spite him. Like in old stories about making pacts with the devil, I would have to be sly and outwit him. I would be as shrewd as my biological mother.

I shuffled the books around to hold them better and placed the box on top. Inches away from my nose, the aroma of chocolate became even stronger. One of the items caught my eye.

"Why is there an empty Ziploc bag?" Almost empty. There were brown crumbs and flakes of coconut. I yanked it open. It smelled like pecans, coconut and chocolate. My mom's earthquake brownies? Where were they?

He coughed. "As I said before, I thought the box was intended for me. Your mother should have put her note at the top of the box instead of the bottom."

It was one thing to go through my box. Quite another to eat my brownies! That was unforgivable. Fuming, I left.

As I stomped down the hall, it occurred to me, Thatch hadn't actually been nasty with me. I'd gotten off easy. Maybe it had been my mom's brownies. Her cooking was more mood-altering than Prozac and Khaba's sweets combined. I should have taken advantage of that. I could have asked him questions and asked him for the colored pencils he hadn't been willing to give me earlier in the year.

When I got to my room, I realized there weren't any actual tools in the lockpick kit. That meant Thatch had them. He could have used the kit to break into Jeb's office. Was this why he hadn't pressed the matter of me being the culprit? More than ever I wanted to know what he was keeping secret.

CHAPTER TWENTY-ONE
The Dungeon Master's Rules

After school the next day, I went to Julian's classroom and told him about Thatch's mandate. "He said if he's going to be my teacher, he won't allow anyone to cast wards on me. You included."

Julian set aside his lesson plans. "Is he teaching you then?"

"If only. He gave me a truckload of books to read." I sat in one of the student desks, admiring the way sunlight glistened in his hair and made his skin glow. "The only practical exercises I'm doing are basic, trying to figure out the difference between reality and dreaming while I'm asleep."

"Don't let Thatch discourage you. You'll get there." He bit his lip. "I could help you with some simple spells. Are you free right now? I can show you plant magic."

Thatch had forbidden Julian from casting protecting spells on me. He hadn't said anything about Julian teaching me. I needed to learn magic. I would take what I could get, even if I had to learn in secret.

"That would be great!" I could barely contain my excitement.

He removed a potted plant from his desk and set it on the student desk where I sat. Though there were no flowers on the green shrubby bush, I recognized it as an oleander from the days I had helped my mom grow plants in the garden.

Julian seated himself in a chair next to me. "I'm going to show you how to make flowers bloom. This is a simple trick even beginners can do easily."

He touched his wand to a stem. The air shimmered green and smelled fresh like spring. A sprig shot out and turned into a bud. The flower opened and blossomed so that a single pink star stood out amongst the viridian leaves.

"I push my will into my affinity and then take a thread of that and visualize it flowing up my arm, into my hand, and out my wand. It's important to keep your intention firmly fixed in your mind."

"I don't have a wand."

"You don't need one at this stage for simple magic, but it will help focus the energies to a concentrated point of exit as you become more advanced." He lifted my hand and placed it near a different stem, walking me through the process.

My belly fluttered at his touch. I tried to ignore the excited anticipation inside me. A balloon of energy swelled up just under my diaphragm, making it difficult to breathe.

"That's right. I can feel it," Julian said. "We just have to draw some of that magic out of you." He made a motion with his hand in front of me as though he was scooping a handful of water out of a well.

I whimpered at the shock of energy jolting through me. It felt as though his hand was inside me, caressing my organs. The sensation shifted from pleasure to pain. My stomach twisted. Julian released me and jumped back. Magic crackled out my hand, blue light flashing. I fell out of my chair and turned away from the flare of heat. The burnt perfume of lightning lingered in the air.

"Well, that was odd." Julian coughed. "That shouldn't have happened with me here to help you."

It wouldn't be the first time I'd proven myself to be a freak.

I blinked, still seeing spots of dancing light. As those cleared, I gasped. The entire plant was a blackened crisp. Julian waved the smoke away. Shakily, I clambered back into my chair.

I stared in horror at what I had done. "I'm so sorry. I didn't mean to destroy your plant."

"It's all right. Accidents happen." He used his wand to cast a spell. The smoke traveled in a cloud to the open window.

I shook my head, tears filling my eyes. "You don't understand. I can't have any accidents." Thatch had said he would drain me if I had any more accidents. This was just the kind of excuse he was looking for to show Jeb why I was a menace. And I was. If I had used magic while students had been around, one of them might have gotten hurt.

"We all have accidents when we're starting out. All of us." He placed an arm around my shoulder. "I'll bring the plant to the greenhouse. Grandmother Bluehorse might be able to do something for it."

I touched a finger to one of the blackened leaves. It crumbled into ash. Charred shapes that might have been flowers littered the shrub, though it was difficult to tell now that everything was barbequed.

"I killed it."

"It's just . . . sleeping."

We both burst into laughter. I blinked away the tears that had been

148

threatening to overflow. He wasn't quite as adamant as Josie with her Amni Plandai affinity. She'd insisted all life was valuable. Maybe plants didn't count.

He patted my shoulder. "Feel better?"

I nodded. I might have failed my first lesson, but I was pretty lucky I had such a patient teacher. Thatch wouldn't have used humor or encouraged me with such understanding and patience.

"Plant magic doesn't come naturally to you, which means you must not be Amni Plandai," Julian said. "Do you know your affinity?"

I bit my lip. He had asked me before at the affinity fire. I wanted to confide in him, but I feared his reaction.

I shook my head. "Does that mean I can't work with plants if I'm not Amni Plandai?"

"Anyone can learn other affinities. It just takes more work to learn outside your natural talents—especially if your power is weak. Some Witchkin haven't enough magic to protect themselves from Fae. I suspect that isn't the case with you."

Not if I could blow up a plant.

"Perhaps we should experiment with animals and the elements to see if we can draw out your affinity and discover your strengths."

"I would rather not experiment with animals and accidentally blow them up." Already my mind was imagining poor little puppies splattered across my classroom. The walls would be painted red with blood, and surely that would give away my affinity. Jeb would see me as evil. They would say I was just like my mother.

Though the section of book I had found in Thatch's desk had said Alouette Loraline was a Celestor, not a Red affinity. Maybe that made me even worse than she was.

"Nothing living, of course." Julian tapped his chiseled jaw. "Perhaps some potion ingredients like 'hair of dog' or 'wing of moth.' Next time I'll bring some leaves and we'll start a little smaller. Maybe it would help if we found you a wand."

I nodded. "I would like a wand." I would feel like a real witch if I had one.

His face was close to mine, his lips inches away. He stared into my eyes. Energy spiraled around inside me, twisting and turning. Desire spiked in me. I leaned into him.

He was going to kiss me. Did I want him to kiss me? I liked him, but I didn't know him well. I wasn't supposed to be dating, because I couldn't control my magic. My fairy godmother had once told me she thought I intensified other people's magic, which might have explained the plant.

Yet all those reasons faded away into oblivion the moment he lifted my chin and touched his lips to mine.

The kiss was the most magical part of my magic lesson. It felt like a storybook moment that restored harmony to a fairytale kingdom. I could have drunk him in and forgotten about the mandate that I wasn't to date if the sensation of a knife twisting in my belly hadn't grounded me in reality. Another reminder my affinity wasn't going to allow me to lead a normal sex life.

I stumbled back from him, gasping at the pain.

His expression turned to confusion. "I'm sorry," he said. "Perhaps that was too forward."

The lightning raging inside me made it difficult to speak.

"I-I can't do this," I said and left.

For days, I kicked myself for how stupid I'd been to stumble away without further explanation. I daydreamed about that brief kiss, wanting more. How was it possible some hottie who looked like a fashion model was interested in me? It was a little too good to be true.

Of course it was too good to be true.

Even if my affinity hadn't wanted to kill me every time I kissed a man, I wasn't allowed to date. Jeb had forbidden me from romantic relationships. I would not date Julian, I told myself. I wanted to keep my job.

Over the next two weeks, I struggled to keep up with my reading, creating new lesson plans that implemented study skills and literacy strategies, and grading an endless supply of papers. I went on another "undate" with Julian. We took a stroll in the woods behind the school, looking for a stick that would make a suitable wand so I might focus my powers.

The more time I spent with Julian, the more I liked him. He gave me something to look forward to each day.

Yet, there was this hesitancy inside me, a fear I would mess it all up. I couldn't stop thinking about all the weird things that had happened to my ex-boyfriends. Maybe it would be different if I had a Witchkin boyfriend.

Then I remembered the plant. I did not want to electrocute Julian. Or anyone else.

Julian didn't bring up the kiss or try to kiss me while we were on the outing looking for a wand. I worried he might think I disliked him.

The moment I started to broach the subject, my evil roommate showed up and flirted with Julian. Only weeks before, Vega had said there was no one at our school worth dating. He tolerated her presence with polite professionalism, all the while sneaking embarrassed glances at me.

I didn't even get a wand out of the excursion.

Julian found excuses to visit my room during the day while he had his prep. He talked to the kids about their art, and he gave helpful suggestions to students. It was nice to have a friend.

After Julian left one morning, one of the boys complained, "Ugh, History of Magic is the most boring class in the world."

"No way. Nothing is boring when I get to see Mr. Thistledown teach. He is hot!" one of the girls giggled.

I couldn't disagree. The boys groaned and rolled their eyes.

After school, Julian brought me cookies and used spells to hang up more art posters and a couple framed drawings of my art in my classroom that my mom had sent me in my most recent box.

It would have felt like a date as Julian and I sat in my classroom, eating cookies and talking about our next excursion to look for a wand if Felix Thatch hadn't slithered out of my closet, frown on his face. "My my, I didn't think the room could get any more sappy and insipid. Then Mr. Thistledown graced us with his presence."

Thatch always knew the exact moment to make my life the most miserable.

On Friday, I carried two of the books Thatch had given me down to the dungeon to return them during the lunch break. I had hoped to give the dusty tomes back to him in the cafeteria, but no such luck. Stepping into his lair wasn't exactly the highlight of my day. My stomach fluttered in nervousness. I peeked into the classroom.

Imani sat at a desk in the back, reading a book and eating a sandwich. Thatch corrected papers at his desk.

"Hey, kiddo, what are you doing here?" I whispered.

Imani leapt to her feet and hugged me. "Miss Lawrence!" She wasn't chained up like kids were in after-school detention, so that was a plus. Still, I didn't like her spending time alone with him. It wasn't healthy for her to grow attached to someone so dangerous.

I patted her shoulder.

"Mr. Thatch lets me eat lunch in here." She lowered her voice. "As long as I don't talk to him while he's at his desk working."

He didn't look up from the papers he was correcting. "Stop hugging Miss Lawrence. There will be no public displays of affection in this room."

She rolled her eyes. "He's in a crabby mood today."

Only today? How about this decade?

I placed the books on the least cluttered corner of his desk and slowly backed away, hoping he wouldn't offer further comment.

"Where do you think you're going?" he asked.

I froze.

"We have matters of education to discuss." He waved a hand at Imani. "Lunch break is almost over. Leave us so we can discuss what a wicked child you are."

She made a face at him.

"Don't say that about Imani! She's a nice young lady," I said.

"Define nice. Look at her reading quietly over there. Such a troublemaker." He didn't smile as he said it, but from the twinkle in his eyes, he appeared to be . . . teasing?

She laughed and brought him the book. "Thanks, Mr. Thatch." She reached into her bookbag and set a red apple on his desk.

He eyed it dubiously. "Is it poisoned?"

"No!"

"Pity. You could have used the potion you learned in class. We could have tested it on one of the teachers." He looked me up and down. "Volunteers?"

She laughed and threw her arms around him and hugged him, pinning his arms to his sides. My eyes widened in surprise. I stepped forward, ready to pry her off him.

He squirmed back. "No hugging allowed."

She ran off, laughing like a sprite. She was so buoyant and happy. I only wished she had friends to share her enthusiasm with instead of grumpy old men. I thought of myself at her age and how lonely I had been until I'd met my best friend, Derrick. And how lonely I'd been again after the tornado had stolen him away.

I hoped nothing bad was going to happen to Julian, like a tornado.

Thatch leaned his elbows on his desk and sagged forward. "I keep telling her not to hug teachers. It will put them in an awkward position and give some adults the wrong idea."

"Some kids are just affectionate." I shrugged. "I used to hug my teachers a lot when I was in elementary school."

"She isn't in elementary school. She is a teenager. Unscrupulous men will take advantage of her affinity and use it against her. Fae especially, but Witchkin as well." He eyed me pityingly. "Like they do with you."

"What? No." He didn't know anything about me.

"Like your . . . boyfriend does."

A jolt of trepidation shot through me. I crossed my arms. "I'm not allowed to date, remember? I don't have a boyfriend." I was screwed if he thought Julian and I were dating. It would be just the excuse he was looking for to get me fired.

"Of course you don't. Tell me, have you ever visited Julian Thistledown's classroom?"

"No."

He snorted. "Perhaps you should. If you witnessed his incompetence as a teacher, you might not find him so alluring—"

That was the final straw. Julian was a great teacher—he was kind and patient in our lessons. Thatch was a grouchy young-old man. "Do you *ever* have anything nice to say about anyone?"

He drummed his fingers against the wooden surface of his desk. "I don't *hate* Dean Khaba. Mrs. Keahi baked cookies for me once when I was ill, so I suppose I don't mind her either. Vega Bloodmire is a competent teacher. Our librarian, Miss Periwinkle, is brilliant and has the most attractive . . . mind I've ever met. I suppose I could go on if I had to, but it might be a stretch. Is that enough for you?"

Of course he would compliment my evil roomie and all the mean people at the school. I rolled my eyes. "What did you want to talk to me about? You said we needed to discuss my education."

"Have you finished your reading?"

"I have one more book. Please don't give me any more books to read. I need to learn how to do magic. It's around me every day. I can feel it building up inside me. Any day now I'm sure it's going to explode out of me in a tornado or a lightning storm or something."

His eyes narrowed. "He's kissed you, hasn't he?"

My face drained of warmth.

"No. Who? No." I tried not to sound guilty, but from his disdain painted across his face, I could tell he knew the truth.

CHAPTER TWENTY-TWO
K-I-S-S-I-N-G

Thatch glowered at me, the accusation hanging in the air between us like a noose.

Yes, I had kissed Julian. And it was none of Thatch's business.

Mostly. I supposed other teachers had a right to know if my magic was going to explode their school.

When Julian had kissed me, the cramps in my belly had intensified like I was experiencing miniature jolts of electricity in my ovaries. At first I had only felt these stabbing pains when Pro Ro had been around. By the sixth week of school, weaving magic with Julian, sitting next to Mr. Sebastian Reade at lunch, or being near any adult Witchkin male for a prolonged amount of time brought stabbing pain in my core.

Except for Thatch. Yuck. His resting bitch face was enough to make me puke in my mouth. Plus, Pro Ro had said Thatch had some kind of relationship with my mother. Double yuck.

Thatch crossed his arms, waiting.

I cleared my throat. "I don't know what you're talking about."

"Do you know why the headmaster discouraged dating for *every* staff member?" His eyes narrowed. "Because of you. Because of *your* history. One wanton act and you're going to bring a cyclone down on this school. If I tell the principal what you've done, he'll know he can't trust you. He'll see how arrogant and selfish you are, and know he was wrong to allow you to come here."

I loathed Thatch even more that he was right. I was being selfish by allowing myself to fall for a guy when my feelings for him might draw out my magic.

"Please, don't tell Jeb. I love it here. I want to learn to use magic and—"

"Then stop sneaking around like a teenager. Learn some self-control." He snarled out the words.

I stumbled back.

He straightened his cravat. "I expect you to finish the last book by Saturday. You need to block out a two-hour period of time Saturday afternoon so we can discuss your reading. If you have satisfied my standards of excellence, then I will teach you how to . . . not explode people accidentally."

So he wasn't going to tell the principal? Like all nice things that happened in my life, it was too good to be true.

Never had I simultaneously dreaded and eagerly anticipated a Saturday more. Tomorrow, I was going to learn magic. I hated postponing my Saturday plans with Julian, but he was understanding. I had to disappoint Josie as well. She was less understanding.

My dorm room was empty in the evening. Vega hadn't told me where she had gone. I was just glad to have the room to myself so that I could read in solitude. Before bed, I practiced meditating using the exercises from the lucid-dreaming book.

The meditation came to a halt when a snap and sharp pain in my right side drew my attention. I pulled out my phone from my pocket. The plastic frame was so hot I had to drop it on the blankets. Maybe it had drained me of power. Electricity was supposed to be a Witchkin's weakness. I shoved it under my pillow and tried to get back to my visualization, but I felt too fidgety. My legs didn't want to stay still. It had to be anxiety.

I decided to leave my phone in my room during my lesson. I didn't want it to interfere with my magic. The idea of being parted with it made me even more nervous. My phone was my only protection against Fae. Not that I expected the Raven Court to suddenly show up in Thatch's dungeon. On the other hand, I didn't entirely trust Thatch.

At noon on Saturday, I trudged down to the dungeon. Thatch stood in the back of his classroom, leaned over the counter of lab supplies. He was dressed as impeccably as he would be on a workday in one of his tweed suits with a cravat tied around the high collar of his shirt. Light crackled from his wand as he zapped the black surface of the counter. I peered around him to find he was erasing graffiti carved into the wood.

The words, "is a faggot" slowly disappeared under the erasing spell he used.

"I finished reading the last book," I said. "I'm ready to learn magic."

"Unlikely."

I didn't know if he meant I wasn't ready to learn, or he didn't think I had read all the books. "I can prove it. Ask me anything from the books."

He finished erasing the graffiti, at last looking up. "Very well." He smiled, his eyes sinister. "A little test, shall we?"

He spun on his heel, his perfect hair billowing behind him. I followed him down the hall to his office. Students must have behaved moderately well this week since no one was chained to the walls in the dungeon.

I paused at the entrance of his office. His black bird perched on a ledge inside the wire cage. The bird tilted its head to the side, watching me with interest.

"Why do you have a raven in here?" I asked.

He seated himself in his cushiony desk chair. "She is a crow, not a raven. She's my pet. Witchkin have familiars."

More likely the bird was his messenger to the Raven Court. Too bad Vega and her bird-eating plant couldn't get their talons on his supposed pet.

He waved a hand at the metal chair in front of his desk. The rusty metal bolted together wasn't the most inviting. Just looking at it, I had a bad feeling someone had died in it.

I tried to find a comfortable way to sit, but the lack of ergonomics alone served as a torture device. I kept my hands in my lap, suspecting restraints might clamp down around my wrists the moment I set my hands on the armrests.

I eyed his cushy chair enviously.

"What year was the school founded?" he asked.

"Womby's Reform School for Wayward Witches was founded in 1811 by Wilbur Womby who bought the grounds after the previous school went bankrupt. The word 'reform' was dropped from the name in the nineteen seventies to be more inclusive of students from lower economic groups and at-risk youth." I crossed my legs and smoothed my sweaty palms against my black skirt. This wasn't so bad.

He frowned. He tapped his trimmed nails against the desk as if trying to think of something that might stump me. "What was the original school built on this location?"

"That's a trick question. No one knows what the original school was. Previous to Womby's was Merlin's Academy for Boys, Nineve's Academy for Girls, The Green Man's Monastery—though it sounds like there wasn't much celibacy practiced by those monks—"

He held up his hand. "Enough. Next question. Magical theory." He shifted, and I had a feeling I had said something that either offended him or made him uncomfortable. Maybe it had just surprised him that I knew the answer.

He leapt from book to book with his questions, asking me about protective runes used for wards, Fae history, and magical ethics. It felt pretty good that my study habits had helped me retain names and dates. Already I could see myself beating Hermione Granger's test scores in my fantasies.

His scowl deepened with every question I answered correctly. "Tell me what you *inferred* about the system of Fae courts."

Crap-a-tooey. This was critical-thinking skills. I considered what I learned. "The Fae are organized by region and family. They go by names like the Lotus Court, Lily Court, Verde Court, Silver Court, and so on. There are thirteen major families—"

"Wrong," he said. "There used to be thirteen families. But the Fae and Witchkin joined together to destroy the . . . *wickedest* of those courts."

"Let me finish." I cleared my throat. "There are thirteen major families worth mentioning. One is now extinct, which has been renamed the Lost Court, though books don't say the original name. There are a number of minor families who keep to themselves or are so scattered—"

He enunciated each word in his crisp British accent. "I asked you to use deductive reasoning. What have you *gleaned* from the text about the Lost . . . Red Court?"

The Lost *Red* Court? The book hadn't called it that, but the words felt right, like my soul knew the name even though I had never heard of it before. Already I was deducing like mad.

There had been a Red Court and my affinity looked red in the fire. Not that I was about to share that with him. Then again, his reaction the night of the affinity fire had suggested he'd known and didn't want anyone else to know. "It sounds like Witchkin and Fae don't agree on many subjects, so it's a big deal they came together to fight for a common cause to get rid of the Lost Court." This new knowledge made more sense. They'd wanted to kill all Reds. That book with the missing pages had said my mother was a Celestor, but someone had accused her of being a descendent of the Lost Court, which meant someone had accused her of being a Red.

The prophecy Josie had mentioned was about someone who brought back the lost arts. The lost *red* arts?

He drummed his fingers, his expression neutral.

I stuck to the facts from the books he knew I had read. "Witchkin thought the Lost Court was wicked because—"

"Only Fae-published books call it the Lost Court. And the school board only approves Fae-published books. Witchkin call it the Lost Red Court or the Red Court. At least, those who have heard of it do."

"Ah." No wonder it had been so hard to look up. "The Reds produced heirs through black magic that harmed others, not through procreation. They took life to create life." I couldn't help wondering if that was how my biological mother had made me. No one had told me exactly why she was so bad, other than she killed and tortured people. Maybe that should have been enough.

"That's what Fae-published textbooks tell us."

Was he implying that wasn't the case? "I can get how Witchkin would object to that." Josie's anti-spider-killing obsession came to mind. "But Fae have no problem with killing people. I can't figure out why they didn't like the Red Court."

"Envy. Resentment."

"The book didn't say they were more powerful, just that they could do different magic." My fairy godmother had said the Fae had a fertility problem. "I guess the thing the Red Court could do is they were able to carry on their line, while the other pureblood Fae have been declining in birthrate. This has something to do with the Fae Fertility Paradox?"

The volume of his voice rose. "Where did you hear about that?"

I swallowed. I couldn't admit it had been in the section of the book I wasn't supposed to have. "My fairy godmother."

He shook his head, his lips pressing into a line. "Why must we respond to authority with respect and deference?"

I selected my words carefully. "According to the book, *Magical Theory*, one's elders, teachers, and leaders are to be our masters who will protect us and aid us. In return for our loyalty and devotion to a particular institution or Fae court, we are granted protection from humans and other Fae." It was difficult to keep the bitterness from my voice.

He raised an eyebrow. "You disagree?"

His snotty tone and pissy mood needled its way under my skin. "I'm American. We abolished slavery in the 1860s. The ideas in *Magical Theory* are archaic, feudal, and make me think back to a time when one man owned another. Or maybe it's just a monarchy thing. We have a president, not a king or queen, and the common people get a vote in things because we have a democracy."

He grimaced. "And so we come to politics. Another matter we would do well to avoid, considering your outspoken opinions of the Unseen Realm."

I tried to shrug off my rising irritation. "I've read your required reading. Did I pass your test?" I wrung the hem of my rainbow polka-dot sweater in my hands. "I need to learn real magic. Reading isn't going to protect me from students velcroing me to the ceiling and Fae trying to snatch me. If you aren't going to keep up your end of the deal, why should I?"

"You still haven't mastered the art of . . . manners. Is it because you are American that you are so direct and uncouth?"

I tried to suppress the rising annoyance in me. "Hey, you don't have to take it upon yourself to teach me manners. Jeb just wants you to teach me protection spells."

"Touché." A flicker of a smile touched his lips. It was so brief I wasn't sure if it had been my imagination. "Magic is an ancient craft with strict and precise rituals that require complete discipline and adherence to its rules. I have a suspicion you will not be able to master the methods of protection I must teach you because of your 'Americanisms.' You harbor an unwillingness to part with your modern ideals that have served you so well in your other life, but will inhibit the learning of magic."

"I'm willing to try."

"I am not asking you to *try*. You must dedicate yourself to the single goal of succeeding until you master the technique." He leaned forward, his eyes focusing on mine.

His intensity unnerved me. I smiled in the hope of lightening the mood. "As Yoda said, 'Do or do not. There is no try.'"

His dark eyebrows furrowed. "Who is this Yoda?"

I tried not to laugh. "It's a Morty reference. He's a teacher."

Thatch snorted. "In any case, you need to be able to trust your instructor, to follow directions immediately and without question, or else you are liable to get hurt. Are you capable of doing that?"

I nodded, eager to begin.

He picked up his wand. "Lean back in the chair and close your eyes."

"Is this a meditation?"

"No speaking. We'll see if you have, indeed, been doing your homework and are able to tell the difference between dreams and reality."

I had a feeling this was my real test. I sat back and closed my eyes.

"Place your hands on the arms of the chair," he said.

Reluctantly I did so.

His chair creaked. Fabric rustled beside me. "Relax your muscles." He tapped my shoulders with something stiff and pointy, I assumed his wand.

I wiggled my shoulders and released the tension I held there. He tapped each of my forearms, which made me realize I wasn't relaxed if I squeezed the metal armrests. I opened and closed my hands a few times, took in a deep breath, and exhaled.

He poked me in the stomach. "And these muscles. Am I going to have to tell you every part of your body that you're clenching?"

"Probably."

"Hush. I didn't say you could speak."

I opened my mouth.

"That was a rhetorical question." He tapped me just above the knee, a smidge harder than was necessary. My quads were tense, and I breathed in again and released the tension.

"Focus on your core." He poked me two inches below my navel, where the cramps usually started when I had sexy thoughts.

I held my breath, anxious about where else he might poke his phallic magic stick. His shoes shuffled against the floor, and his chair creaked again. I breathed a sigh of relief.

"Imagine a sphere of energy inside you. This is your power source, where your affinity dwells. Visualize a shield in front of your center, guarding you from outside forces and protecting others from you." The deep monotone of his voice lulled me into a sleepy state. "Imagine the tension in your muscles melting away. Forget about this body as you sink deeper and deeper into relaxation."

Feathers fluttered. The bird in its cage shifted and settled. I tried to ignore it. Thatch spoke on, continuing with the visualization.

A tickle across my wrists drew my attention. A weight pressed down on my arms. Something cold and rough slithered across my skin. I fought the urge to look. I tried to move my arms, but I couldn't. In my mind I saw the snake from my mother's portrait coiling around my arm. Panic rose up in me. I was becoming my mother.

I didn't know which idea was scarier—that I was evil, or he was using snake bondage on me. I screamed and opened my eyes.

I didn't see serpents, but I could still feel the scales scraping against my skin. My stomach flip-flopped. I tried to move, but my arms were too heavy.

"Calm yourself," Thatch said in his usual monotone. "Your mind manifests an illusion based on your fears. The key is to shield yourself."

The moment the sensation of snake restraints faded, I leapt to my feet. "Whoa, hold the mayo, dude! You didn't say anything about snakes or restraints." I didn't even think I had been afraid of snakes, but I sure as heck was now.

Thatch nodded to the torture chair. "Sit."

I eyed the chair warily.

His steepled fingers pressed together with so much pressure his knuckles were white. "You are used to being coddled in your other life among Morties. Your fairy godmother tried to shield you from every evil, but that isn't going to help you in this world."

Mom had tried to protect me from everything—including myself. Ignorance hadn't been bliss. Grudgingly I took a seat.

Thatch went on. "Magic can be a life or death situation, and that is what I prepare my students for. You need to think fast on your feet, comply instead of complain, and be ready for anything."

I crossed my arms. "I'm not asking to be coddled. I just want some communication." I wasn't trying to sound whiney, but my voice grew high-pitched in agitation. "You could have warned me you were going to restrain me with invisible snakes. In fact, you could have told me *anything*. I still don't know what this training entails."

"I have no control over what terrors your mind comes up with." His jaw clenched. "This chair will help draw out your deepest fears so that you can learn to ignore any stimulus that would set off your energies. Everything you experience is an illusion created by the chair in combination with your subconscious mind. If you have been doing the exercises in the book I gave you, you should be able to tell the difference between reality and illusions, which will make it easier for you to shield yourself. Is that enough *communication* for you?"

I nodded.

"If I am to teach you magical self-defense, you will need to master your body. You will learn to keep your magic shielded no matter what anyone throws at you."

My magic. My affinity? He didn't say it, but I suspected he meant so no one would find out what I was. I should have been grateful he wasn't willing to tell everyone what I was, but it only made me more suspicious of his motivations.

"Close your eyes," he said.

I did so. I didn't like this, but I didn't see what other choice I had if I was to learn to protect myself.

The melody of his voice calmed me as he walked me through a visualization of my body relaxing. I could see the red swirling ball of light inside my core more quickly and clearly this time.

"As your emotional state rises, the energy inside you will grow. It will control you and make you a slave to your affinity if you do not succeed in controlling it. You must minimize the size and intensity of your energy. Do not allow external distractions to diminish your hold on yourself."

I wanted to ask if he meant external—as in real things—or the subconscious things my mind was supposedly making up when I sat in the chair, but I wasn't supposed to talk. Something tickled against my cheek and whispered down my neck. Pressure weighed across my shoulder and then pressed against my arm. Rough scales raked over the bare flesh of my arm. The snake coiled around my elbow, fastening me to the chair. My heart sped up.

Another serpent slithered up my leg, a tongue flicking out of its mouth as it smelled the sliver of flesh between my striped knee socks and skirt. A long rope of pressure slid over my lap. The snake coiled up around my other arm. My eyes remained closed, but I could see the snakes, green pythons. They glided over my body, in constant motion. One slipped up my neck and around my throat. I held my breath, afraid it was about to cut off my air supply.

This wasn't real, I told myself.

"Protect yourself," he said.

Right, that was what I was supposed to be doing.

I focused my attention on the growing ball of red. Lightning crackled inside me. I soothed it and focused on smooshing the light down. It was a lot like centering and pulling the walls of a clay cone on a pottery wheel. Calming art thoughts filled me. That was better.

Perhaps it was the thought of art that caused my subconscious to resurrect Derrick. He stood before me with his blue hair wafting in the breeze. He wore his Matrix-like trench coat and mismatched clothes. I wanted to reach up and touch the stubble on his chin, but I couldn't move my arms. He leaned closer and his lips pressed against my mouth, his hunger ravenous. I leaned in, tasting him, wanting him more than ever.

The red energy inside me swelled. Warmth flooded through me.

"You aren't following the directions," Thatch said. "Ignore the distractions your mind creates."

Got it. Ignore. I focused on the ball of energy again and imagined it growing smaller. The snakes tore at my clothes with their fangs, yanking the fabric apart. Shreds fell away. I didn't see Derrick, but I felt his hands on my naked shoulders. He swept my hair aside and kissed my neck. He cupped my breasts. One moment it was him and then next it was Julian. I wasn't certain who I wanted.

Someone said my name, but the voice came from a distance.

My affinity swelled. Desire filled me. Heat flushed my face.

A loud bang snapped my attention away from the meditation. I blinked. Thatch stood behind his desk, a book in his hands that he had apparently slammed on the desk.

His face was livid with anger. "What are you doing? I told you to master your body, not to give in to it. Do you understand what risk you take not being able to control yourself?"

"Yes. I might hurt someone or myself." I stared down at my lap. My clothes were intact. No one else was there. The illusion was gone.

"Or worse yet, you might allow someone to use your magic against you." The anguish in his eyes was as palpable as a knife slicing through flesh.

He looked so forlorn and lost. Finally, it came together in my mind. My mother definitely wasn't a Celestor. Without a doubt, I knew she was a Red. "That's what Alouette Loraline did to you."

All that meanness inside him made more sense. This is why Jeb wanted Thatch to teach me. It was hard to hate Thatch when I felt bad for him. In his crabby, resentful way, he was trying to help me so no one would do the same to me.

A muscle in his jaw ticked. "We agreed that if I was to teach you, you wouldn't ask impertinent questions."

"I'm sorry," I said.

Not just sorry for resurrecting his demons, but sorry I was related to someone who had hurt him. I suspected I understood his motivation for agreeing to teach me.

"Stop looking at me like that," he snapped. "Focus on the problem at hand. You aren't in control. You can't tell the difference between your own desires and someone else's. Haven't you noticed how your mind says one thing and your body says another?"

I shifted against the hard metal of the chair and hugged my arms around myself. "I've been told that on occasion."

"But you still doubt it." He came around the desk. He sat on the edge across from me, a tad bit closer than I was comfortable with. "Give me your hand."

I hesitated. I didn't like him. I didn't completely trust him. But if I was to learn, I was supposed to obey the dungeon master. I extended my hand. His fingers were as chilled as icicles as he took mine.

The corners of his lips curled upward, though his eyes remained unsmiling. "Tell me, what do you feel toward me right now?"

Besides annoyed, creeped out, and intimidated? I wasn't sure which of those it was most appropriate to admit. I doubted he wanted to hear pity either.

"You detest me," he said coolly without emotion. "You find me to be despicable. Is that correct?"

I didn't answer. I didn't want to insult him.

His grin grew broader even as his eyes narrowed. He stroked a thumb against my palm. His touch was whisper soft. My body burned against his cold, warmth flooding to the flesh he caressed. He massaged my skin in slow sensuous strokes. Electricity jolted up my spine. I was uncomfortably aware of my panties and how much I wanted to remove them.

My breath caught in my throat as pleasant tingles raced up my arm. This was just like Oregon Country Fair all over again. He'd tried to drain me then. The past grew distant in a haze of inconsequential details I no longer cared about. I only could think about the present.

"Are you going to drain me?" I asked.

"Would you be able to stop me if I was?" he asked.

I tried to draw back my hand, but he didn't release me. Admittedly, I didn't try very hard. I didn't want him to let go. His touch made me melt.

"If one were planning on draining you, he or she would need you at your most vulnerable. When you lose control of your affinity like this, you are too weak to stop anyone from hurting you." His voice came out as a soft purr as he stroked my hand. "Pray, what do you think of me now. Do you still detest me?"

I laughed. He was so funny. I'd never detested him. I stared into the stormy depths of his eyes and felt like I could sink below the steely surface. I leaned closer.

"Do you get it yet?" he asked. "Do you understand your affinity?"

My brain felt foggy. It was hard to focus on his words when he was so beautiful. Not just his hair, but the angular line of his jaw, his high cheekbones, and aquiline nose. He was a sexy off-limits professor. I was the student with a crush on her teacher. I sighed.

"Do you understand what I could do with this knowledge?" he asked. "What *anyone* could do to you? The Raven Queen won't need to force you to go with her if she discovers this. She'll seduce you into her service. Is that what you want?"

I nodded dumbly. I liked listening to the music of his voice.

"You're an idiot." He scowled. "Fortunately, I know the antidote." His grip tightened on my wrist. The ice of his fingers dug into my skin, jolting me back to reality. The pleasantness that had been there moments before was replaced by fear. Pain grounded me, reminding me how vulnerable I was. I had almost agreed to allow him to drain me.

I pulled back harder, in earnest this time. "Let go. You're hurting me."

"Indeed, that's the point. Are you still too stupid to understand?" Regret and sorrow built in the storm clouds of his eyes, drowning out the venom of his words. He released my wrist. "Go away and come back after you've formed a hypothesis. And for Fae's sake, don't share it with any of the staff or students."

For once I had no problem following Thatch's advice. Already I knew I had to keep my Red affinity secret. If someone learned what I was and could control me through touch, that meant I was even more of a danger to myself and others than I'd realized.

CHAPTER TWENTY-THREE
Walkabout

Sunday afternoon I went on a walk with Julian in the forest with the intention of finding a magic wand. As soon as the school was out of sight, he tucked my hand into the crook of his arm. It felt nice being close to someone. Immediately I was aware of the red ball of energy inside me. I pushed it down and imagined it getting smaller. I shielded myself, determined to protect myself and others.

Discreetly, I removed my hand from his arm.

Thatch's lesson was still fresh in my mind. I was still creeped out by what Thatch had done, how he had made me want him. I tried not to hear the song "Hot for Teacher" in my brain or allow fleeting fantasies of his lips on mine to creep back into my awareness. It made my lucid-dreaming exercises of imagining only what I wanted to dream about even more challenging.

As if the whole thing hadn't been freaky enough, I kept thinking about Pro Ro's innuendo that Thatch might have been my mother's lover. I was not going to let anyone seduce me with magic or my affinity again, least of all someone who might be my father for all I knew.

Julian's hand brushed against mine, sending fluttering feelings up my arm and into my core. It was difficult to concentrate with the way the light glowed on his skin. He was so beautiful I wanted to paint him.

"I've set up a little picnic for us next to the stream. I hope you like chocolate-covered strawberries and champagne." He played with a strand of my pink hair. "I know I like strawberries."

I had purposefully dyed my strawberry-blonde hair pink after years of listening to such comments. I rolled my eyes and flipped a handful of hair in his face, laughing as he jerked back. He poked me in the side and chased after me.

The trees along the path shifted into ancient growth, some so wide they rivaled those I'd seen in Redwood National Park of Northern California. Curtains of moss hung from trees, wafting in the breeze. The trail wove up and over lush hills that overlooked green canyons. I had always loved hiking and had seen pictures of the Hoh Rainforest years before, but this transcended the beauty of the Pacific Northwest. Pink-and-yellow lights flitted through the trees. I couldn't tell if they were butterflies catching the sunlight or fairies.

Motion caught my attention to the right. Two centaurs, a bare-breasted woman and a child, watched us from the canyon below. Warily, they backed away. Knobby little creatures that blended in with the texture of tree bark peeked at us from around clusters of ferns and patches of flowers. It was enchanting. I wished I had brought my sketchbook.

There were multiple forks in the paths. I couldn't keep track of where we were with the sun directly overhead and the twists in the trail. Fortunately, Julian strode forward confidently and purposefully toward our destination.

He leaned down to examine a fallen piece of wood and handed it to me. "How's this for a wand?"

In his hand it looked small, but I wore size five shoes, and my hands were as proportionally small. It felt like gripping a sausage. "I think Coach Kutchi would accuse me of succumbing to the patriarchy of phallic wands."

"You're horrible!" He laughed so hard he leaned over, grabbing his sides. "We'll keep looking."

A short while later he found a smaller stick. This one was only the length of my hand and too skinny to be considered more than a twig. I shook my head. "This is like Goldilocks and the three wands."

He arched an eyebrow. "If that's how it works, the next stick you get your hand around will be just right."

"Please say that's not a euphemism."

"Certainly not. You simply have a dirty mind."

We must have walked for an hour before my feet grew tired. I sat down on a fallen tree beside the path to rest. I hadn't packed hiking shoes, just my jogging shoes. The soles were caked with wet earth, and the traction wasn't as good as it had been when we'd first started out. I used a thick twig to gouge some of the mud from the bottom. I held up the stick. Maybe it could be my wand.

It broke as I gouged more mud off my heel. So much for my supposed wand.

Julian tugged the remainder out of my hand and tossed it into the foliage. "Just a little farther."

"Are we still on school grounds?" I asked as Julian guided me on. "The principal said I'm not allowed to leave Womby's property without a Celestor as escort. Where is this picnic?"

"It's just over the next hill. We're still on the school grounds."

A bird cawed overhead. I jumped up, startled to see a black silhouette against the azure sky.

Julian watched the bird fly off. "It's a crow, not a raven," he said.

"How can you tell?"

"I have an affinity with nature. I can tell the difference."

The sight of the bird didn't make me feel any easier. Josie had once told me the school was surrounded by miles of woodland in all directions and warded against Fae courts. I didn't know where that border ended. Even if that bird wasn't an emissary of the Raven Court, that didn't mean it couldn't be Thatch's evil bird looking for an opportunity to peck my eyes out.

Julian led me to the path. "I promise we're close."

A raindrop plopped on my nose.

Laughter came from up ahead. Julian's brows drew together in concern, and he quickened his pace. A minute later we stumbled upon the intended picnic. Three satyrs were sprawled out in the small clearing, devouring food from a basket.

"Son of a witch!" Julian swore under his breath. "That's our picnic."

"You snooze, you lose, dude," the hairiest satyr said.

One guzzled down the bottle of champagne and belched loudly. Another wrapped the checkered picnic blanket around himself. Chocolate was smeared all over his mouth.

Julian kicked at a rock. "I should have used my broom and flown us here. It would have been faster." His shoulders sagged in defeat.

Raindrops tapped against the canopy of leaves overhead, an occasional plop bursting through and dropping on my head.

"Why don't we just go into town and have lunch?" I asked.

His smile returned. "Good idea. I'm fortunate you're such a good sport about this."

The bright sunshine above hid behind clouds. The shadows darkened.

A cold drop of water splattered onto my nose. Another fell on my ear. The leaves above us pitter-pattered with the increasing staccato sound.

I ran to the overhang of an evergreen as buckets of water poured through the trees. It was a little drier close to the tree, but not by much.

Julian shouted over the rain to be heard. "Back along the path." He pointed. "There was a big tree with a hollowed base."

We ran along the trail, slipping into each other in the mud. My pink curtain of hair plastered itself to my skull and fell into my eyes. So much for spending all that time trying to look nice. The giant tree was a few feet off the path. We took shelter in the hollow, squishing together to fit inside. The compartment reminded me of all the times I had imagined what it would be like to be a storybook fairy living in a tree house.

I swiped at the spiderwebs and tried not to imagine all the other things that might be living in the tree. A knot in the wood poked painfully into my side. Between that and the cold, the pleasure I'd felt only moments before leaked away. All warmth had left me with the frigidness of the rain. I shivered against Julian.

He hugged me to his side. "We need to get you out of these wet clothes and warm you up before you catch a cold."

"You don't catch a cold from rain." I smoothed a hand over the worn wood interior.

"Yes, you do. Rain carries horrible curses and magical maladies." He touched my nose with the tip of his finger playfully.

He removed his wand from his sleeve. The words he incanted tasted like pine needles and clay. A swirl of green left his wand and brightened the hollow of the tree as he waved a hand over my clothes.

I expected a warming spell. Instead, my jeans and T-shirt disappeared in a poof. I was left huddling in my panties and bra. I shivered even more. "Julian, that isn't funny! Bring my clothes back."

His eyes went wide. "I'm so sorry! That was an accident. I swear." He squirmed next to me, bumping into me as he removed his arms from the sleeves of his jacket. "Here, take my coat." He wrapped it around my shoulders.

I shrugged into it, giving him the evil eye the entire time. Water beaded up on the long sleeve, but it rolled off. The rain hadn't soaked the fabric.

"I was trying to do a waterproof spell, but something went haywire. It must be something about our magics negating each other." Julian grimaced, his face flushing in the glow of his wand's light. "Are you warm enough? I could try a warming spell, but I'm afraid to try it at the moment."

I tucked my knees more closely to my chest to keep in the heat. "I'm fine."

My magic used to interact strangely with Derrick's too, hence the tornado that had carried him away. Learning to control my magic seemed more important than ever. I didn't want to give Julian a heart attack or lightning to strike him.

The pelting of the rain slowed. Sun peeked through the trees, though it still sprinkled.

Everything about today had gone wrong. I didn't have a wand, I was hungry, and now nearly naked and cold. I huddled against the tree as far away from Julian as I could, annoyed he'd magicked away my clothes, even if it was an accident. More than that, I was mad at myself for agreeing to go out with him, despite Thatch's advice that I should learn to control my magic before I dated men.

I crossed my arms over my chest, attempting for modesty. "I want you to bring my clothes back."

"Oh, um, sure." He swallowed. "I'll try."

He waved his wand over me. Fabric whispered across my skin. It didn't feel like my jeans and shirt. I looked down to find myself in a white cotton dress. I removed his coat and handed it to him. The dress came with puff sleeves. A sock was stuck to my chest with static. I peeled it off.

"You look lovely, by the way. Like an angel." Julian's brow furrowed. "But those aren't your clothes, are they?"

"No," I said with about as much enthusiasm as Eeyore. I flicked the sock at him. The dress was pretty, at least.

"Clarissa, don't be mad at me. Please." He draped an arm around my shoulder. "I'll try for your clothes again in a couple minutes after I recharge. Do you forgive me?"

His green eyes were so forlorn I felt bad for him. "Yes, I forgive you, if you can forgive me for being crabby. Let's just go back to the school." I climbed out of the hollow and stood under the driest section of the tree. I didn't care if it was still raining. I wanted to get to my room and into a warm set of my own clothes.

Julian scrambled out after me. "Good idea." He took my hand and pressed his lips to my knuckles. "I really am sorry about your clothes."

He smoothed his hand over mine, stroking my skin as he stared into my eyes. My affinity stirred inside my core. Warmth flooded my veins. Electricity prickled over my skin. Pleasant throbbing rose up in me again, making me drunk on his touch. I gasped at the way he aroused me.

Thunder rumbled in the distance.

I leaned against Julian, hypnotized by the desire rising inside me. I might have given in to the yearning if Thatch's words hadn't been so recent in my head. Did I know the difference between my own desire and someone else's?

Through the fog of lust clouding my mind, fears of my own magic drifted away. Vaguely, a half thought about the Fae Fertility Paradox and the Red affinity wormed into my consciousness, only to drift away again.

The only thing keeping me from wrapping my arms around Julian and kissing him was Julian. He held me away from him, his hands pinning my arms to my sides as he studied me. "Clarissa, stop. Are you *trying* to use magic on me?"

Magic tingled under my skin. The hairs on the back of my arm rose. I smelled ozone in the air. Lightning would be coming soon. I tried to make myself pull away, but it was painful to do so. The ball of energy inside me grew larger. It pressed against my diaphragm, making it difficult to breathe. My insides throbbed. Sharp contractions of pain lanced up my pelvis.

Not a good sign.

I wrenched myself away, stumbling back over a root. I caught a branch to keep from slipping into the mud.

Julian leaned against a tree, his expression confused. "Clarissa, what did you just do to me?"

I shook my head. I didn't want this to be like with Satyr Sam when he'd accused me of casting a spell on him. I didn't want to be like my mother using Thatch. Before I could get out a word, a booming voice called out to us.

"What are you doing with this fair maiden?"

I turned. Dappled brown horses stood in the meadow where the picnic had been. The three satyrs were gone, but the basket, blanket, and remains of food still lay in the grass. Two brown-gray horses loped closer. I didn't see any riders. As they approached, I saw they weren't horses, but unicorns. My breath caught in my throat.

Yes! I'd always known unicorns were real. They were beautiful, but not at all what I had imagined unicorns would look like. For one, their fur wasn't white. Most of their horns were the pale bone hue of deer antlers rather than gold. Another was black like a bull's horn. They reminded me of wild mustangs. There were about a dozen in their herd.

"Feral unicorns!" Julian whispered. "Don't make any sudden moves." He slowly reached for my hand and tugged me behind him.

A sable-and-ochre unicorn with an ivory horn stomped closer. His voice was stern. "I asked a question. What are you doing?"

Julian tried to answer, but another unicorn interrupted in a deep rumbling voice. "What have we here?"

One of the unicorns nudged his head against another's shoulder. "A student and a teacher by the looks of it."

"I'm not a student," I said.

"Sure you aren't, honey."

Not this again.

One nudged at the picnic basket in the clearing with a hoof. He neighed. "Look at all that litter they left. Humans. Typical."

"That wasn't us. That was the satyrs," Julian said quickly. "We were about to be on our way when you came upon us."

The unicorn snorted. His nostrils flared. "I smell a lie. Or a liar. Or both."

"Someone is going to pay for this mess," one of them said.

I spoke quickly, filling in the details. "We were planning on having a picnic, but we found the satyrs eating our food. Then there was a rainstorm."

A dappled brown unicorn snuffled the basket and sneezed.

My apprehension faded as more unicorns trampled closer, bringing with them a sense of security and calm that wrapped around me like a blanket and made me feel safe. My eyes were riveted by the beads of water rolling off the stallion's rippling back muscles. I still couldn't believe what I was seeing. Unicorns!

The one with the black horn stomped forward. He was sleek and elegant. The sun peeked from behind clouds and sparkled like diamonds on the raindrops clinging to his tail and wild mane. He lowered his head, his posture inviting. He edged closer. His long black eyelashes blinked—or winked—as he watched me. He was beautiful. I reached out a hand to pet him.

"Don't," Julian whispered. He slapped my hand away.

The black-horned unicorn growled—something I didn't know an equestrian species could do—and slashed his horn at Julian. We both jumped back from the unicorn, though in the opposite direction from each other.

The unicorn stomped between us. The remaining herd in the clearing sniffed and hoofed the ground. The unicorns circled around Julian and me but kept us separated. I dodged back from one, only to stumble into another.

Julian shoved one away. "Get back. I command you. You're trespassing on school property. Principal Bumblebub will fine you for this."

One of the unicorns snorted. "We aren't on school property anymore, pegasus breath."

"That's right. Do you know what the fine is for hexing a unicorn? We're on the endangered species list, you shag-haired, donkule fornicator," a brown one said.

My eyes went wide at their turn of phrase. I suspected they were swearing in unicorn.

A gray unicorn kicked his brother. "Hey, you're in the presence of a maiden, mule monger. Watch your filthy mouth."

The flank of one brushed my shoulder, and I stepped back. I stumbled into the black unicorn. He nuzzled his face against my neck. "Mmm, you smell nice."

Another unicorn snuffled at my hand. I petted his nose. His rough tongue raked against my fingers. "She tastes like sunshine and gumdrops."

Did horses even eat gumdrops? Did unicorns?

He brushed against me, nudging his head under my hand to be petted. He snuffled my hair and face. I squirmed back, giggling.

"She smells like a virgin."

My delight soured into mortification. This wasn't exactly high on the list of news I liked to advertise about myself.

Another nuzzled my neck and licked my ear. "She tastes like a virgin."

I wiped the unicorn saliva away and backed up. Hadn't a Witchkin once told me unicorns in the Unseen Realm liked the taste of human blood?

Another unicorn tried to cuddle me. I squirmed back.

"Like a virgin." One of them started to sing the Madonna song. I didn't even know how they could have known eighties music considering they were allergic to electronics. Maybe they hung out with my bad students.

The way they wove around reminded me of sharks. Warily, I edged away.

Julian stood there with his wand out, looking absolutely helpless.

"Stop crowding me." I used my firm teacher tone. "I don't like this." I shoved at one that brushed against my shoulder.

I was surprised when they obediently backed off and gave me more room. They continued circling but gave me a wider berth. No one tried to nuzzle me.

"Sorry," one said. He kicked another unicorn still singing Madonna. "Knock it off. You're making her uncomfortable."

"Guys, behave." The black unicorn nodded to me. "I can see the purity of your heart." He lifted his head to eye Julian. "And the depravity of his."

"Depravity?" Julian's face turned red. "Listen here, I will not take such insults, you horny mustangs." Sparks flared out of his wand.

One of them snickered. "Hey, if you're trying to say I'm hung like a horse, well, yeah. Thanks, pegasus breath."

Julian made an arc of light in the air with his wand. One of them knocked it from his hand with a horn. Julian yelped and staggered back as a unicorn pushed him away. Another unicorn placed himself between Julian and me. We were even farther from each other now.

My heart pounded in fear for him as they poked at him.

The nearest unicorn sniffed the air. "He smells like sex and lollipops. A suspicious combination."

"He smells like the Verde Court to me. Remember the Green Man's Monastery back in the day?"

"I say we stomp him with our hooves."

"No!" Julian and I said at the same time.

"Does Jeb know you've wandered this far into the forest?" the black-horned unicorn asked.

"Principal Bumblebub," one of them corrected. "Show some respect for the senile old hinny."

"I don't know," I said. "I'm sorry if we've trespassed into your . . . um, territory."

"Isn't she a sweetie? Listen to those manners," one unicorn said to another.

"I don't suppose you'd be willing to give us directions back to the school?" I said. "If you can, we'll be on our way."

"Better than that, we can give you a ride."

"Really?" I'd always wanted to ride on a unicorn. I was still undecided about this herd, though.

"Ride me!" said one.

"No!" said another. "Me! Me!"

Julian nudged his way around the beasts, trying to make his way closer.

"Sweetie, you can ride me all night long."

"Um. . . ." I didn't know how to respond to that. Never in my imagination had I pictured unicorns being so . . . dirty. These unicorns were definitely from the wrong side of the tracks—err—forest. I probably didn't want to ride a unicorn after all.

A gray unicorn kicked the black unicorn. "Shut up, chimera butt. This is a classy young maiden. You're going to keep your horn—and everything else—to yourself. What's our motto, stallions?"

"Consent, a hundred percent," the herd neighed.

Well, that was nice. Better than some humans.

I backed away, still uncertain. The ring of beasts followed me, constantly moving, keeping a wall of bodies between me and Julian. A crow landed on a branch above Julian's head, white bird droppings splattering on the ground beside him. He leapt back, cursing.

I wanted to go back to the school, the sooner the better.

I wet my lips, trying to come up with an answer. "I've never ridden a horse. Or even a broom like the kids at school. The equestrian class at Womby's covers pegasus and kelpie training and riding, but I had a Morty education. I probably wouldn't be any good at riding. I'd be more comfortable walking, but we'd welcome an escort." My gaze flickered to the crow.

"They teach unicorn riding at your school, but those aren't real unicorns at Womby's," a dappled unicorn said. "They're domesticated and inbred to the point of being mentally handicapped. All because Witchkin value the color of a unicorn's hide more than anything else."

"White unicorn privilege," one of the tan ones said.

Across from me, Julian rolled his eyes.

A gray unicorn said, "They don't even talk."

"And they can't do magic. Has a domesticated unicorn ever done this?" The one to my left stomped his foot. His body turned purple. His tail faded from brown to green.

Awe distracted me from any apprehension I'd been feeling. He looked like Magestica, what I'd renamed my favorite My Little Pony from when I'd been twelve. I'd only stopped playing with her because my older sister, Missy, had teased me and asked, "Aren't you a little too old for playing with Barbies and toy animals?"

I was saved the heartache of dwelling on my deceased sister's words—or our relationship—by the unicorns' next magic trick.

"I can do way better glamour than that." The next unicorn shook out

SARINA DORIE

his mane, and it turned bright blue with glitter in it. "Ride me back to the school. Look how pretty I am."

"No," Julian said. "We aren't riding anyone!"

"Please, ride me," another begged. "I'll behave. You can wash my mouth out with soap if I swear." He changed his mane to silver, and his body transformed into a kaleidoscope of blue, green and purple tie-dye patterns. I imagined the hippie owner of Ye Green Grocery would like his style.

"Yeah? Well, look what I can do!" One of the unicorns passed gas loudly. A rainbow poured out of his behind before evaporating into the air.

I didn't want to admit it, but it was impressive.

"Not in front of the maiden! What is it with you, Clyde?"

They continued showing off their glamour, competing like peacocks for me. I oohed and aahed at their palette of colors as they pranced. It was the most wonderful sight I'd ever gazed upon. The icing on the cake was when the gray one, Bart, changed his body to all black and his mane and tale into a rainbow.

I stroked his tail, entranced by the shifting threads of color. He flicked it at me, and I laughed as glitter sparkled in the air. Giddy delight filled me. I felt like I was six years old, and I'd just been given the best birthday present in the world. I had always wanted to ride horseback. This would be magical.

"Do you promise you'll take us straight back to the school?" I asked.

"What? No, you can't be serious," Julian said. "We are not riding a gang of feral unicorns back to the school. We need to set good examples for the students. Unicorns are dangerous." He stepped toward me, but a unicorn bumped him with his rump and blocked him every time he tried to get around the animal.

"Who will Julian get to ride?" I asked.

One shook his head. "Him? No freakin' way."

Another snorted. "We've already told you, he's depraved."

"I am not! I just find you attractive," Julian said to me. "They don't know the difference."

"Pervert," a unicorn muttered none-too-quietly.

"Why do you keep saying that?" I asked.

Bart neighed. "Well, for one thing, he's not a virgin."

Did they say that about all nonvirgins?

One of the unicorns tossed his sparkly mane. They were fantastical. I giggled. This moment was so surreal. "What if I promise to vouch for his behavior? Will you take both of us back to the school then?"

"I don't know. The herd needs to talk about this."

They trampled into the clearing, whispering. Fluttering feathers drew my attention. Instinctively I twitched away from the sound. The crow tilted his head and watched us, the intelligence in his eyes unnerving me further.

Julian dove forward and grabbed me by the arm. "Come on. Let's slip off before they notice." He tugged me back toward the path.

I ground my heels into the dirt. "No. I want to ride a unicorn."

"Have you completely lost your senses? You haven't even ridden a domesticated animal before. Do you think you'll do well with these? Plus, they're macho, chauvinist womanizers, this lot."

I wrenched my arm away. "They're sweet."

"You're just impressed with their glamour. I can turn a domesticated horse into rainbows and sparkles if that's what you want, but don't trust these blokes."

The unicorns turned back. "We've drawn straws. Jo Jo will take him."

The tie-dye unicorn said, "But he needs to clean up his trash first."

I waved my hand at the picnic mess. "That's right. Don't be a litterbug."

Julian gave me a withering look. He trudged over to the picnic basket and stuffed the remnants of food inside.

The crow cawed, startling me. My heart quickened. I watched the bird out of the corner of my eye, expecting it to change into someone from the Raven Court at any moment. If that happened, I was jumping on a unicorn's back, with or without Julian.

A red, yellow, and orange stallion bowed his head down. "Tell us who you choose as your devoted steed, milady."

I pointed to the rainbow unicorn. "Bart."

The others grumbled and stomped their hooves. Bart was a tall horse, and I was the shortest teacher on staff. His back was almost as high as my head. I had no idea how I was going to get up.

"I'm sorry," I said. "I'm going to have to hold onto your mane to pull myself up."

"That's fine. I like having my mane pulled."

I ignored the comment. I heaved myself up. One of them nudged me under my bottom to lift me higher. As soon as I was situated, Bart clomped around the clearing, allowing me to get a feel for riding. He gave me pointers on how to lean, to wrap my legs around him, and to move my hips in rhythm with his motion. As sexual as his instructions sounded, he refrained from dirty jokes.

"Good girl!" one said.

"You're getting it!"

Their chaste encouragement astonished me after their previous euphemisms. I found myself relaxing around them and enjoying myself.

I squealed in delight. "This is what it's like to ride a unicorn?" I was so lucky. This had to be the caramel in my prophecy chocolate.

"Okay, I'm done cleaning up the litter," Julian said behind me.

The unicorns chuckled. I had heard enough students' mischievous laughter to know when they were about to play a prank.

I started, "No, do not even think—"

My ride reared up and charged across the meadow. Julian called after us. My heart galloped in fear, about as fast as the other unicorns trampling after us. Maybe I should have listened to Julian when he'd said they were up to no good.

It was too late now.

CHAPTER TWENTY-FOUR
Alice and the Looking Glass

"Wait!" Julian called.

"No!" I said. My protest turned into a scream as I flattened myself against Bart's neck and held on for dear life.

Bart's feet dug into the soft earth of the forest floor. I clung to his mane as he cantered in the lead. It was either hold on, or let go and fall, which would probably involve being trampled or impaled. Bart leapt over fallen tree trunks and wove around trees. I ducked as he raced under a low bough, shrieking as leaves whacked me in the face.

"Be gentle with her, Bart. It's her first time," one of the other unicorns called.

"Shut up, donkule butt."

After about five minutes, they slowed. I was panting, and my arms shook from clinging so tightly to his mane.

My voice came out in as a quaking squeak. "That wasn't very nice."

"Milady, we were doing you a favor," Bart said. "If we hadn't intervened, that pegasus fornicator would have balled—"

"Ahem, language. You are in the presence of a lady," one of them said.

"He would have behaved in an ungentlemanly manner."

"That wasn't his fault," I said. I didn't want to explain to them the sexual depravity had all been my own—my magic that I couldn't yet control. "Take me back to Julian this instant."

They eyed each other, something silent passing between them.

"Ask us to take you somewhere else," Bart said.

"Take me back to the school."

"As you wish, milady."

I'd heard that when some women ride horses it is a deep, spiritual

177

experience—and the friction gives them an orgasm. Not me. I chafed and got blisters.

I was famished, and the ride to the school took forever. Partly that was because the unicorns insisted they needed to stop at the stream for a water break. And then they needed to show me their vocal talents, which consisted of singing eighties love ballads. Those unicorns weren't bad, they just wanted attention. Not so different from my students.

I thought about Hailey Achilles and Balthasar Llewelyn, my worst students. Did they act out because they wanted attention?

I didn't think twice about sitting on Bart's back as he led the herd of unicorns onto school grounds. Probably I should have given it more thought. Charging up to the school caused quite a commotion. Satyr Sam dropped his gardening shears and ran off, waving his arms. Students loitering outside screamed and ran away. Witchkin flocked to the windows.

Bart wanted to let me off at the front doors of the school, but I could already see we had trampled beds of flowers and caused an uproar. I insisted he let me off on the lawn by the topiary animals. I slid off, every muscle in my back and legs aching.

Bart bowed his head. "If you ever are in need while traveling in the forest, just call upon us, the Singing Stallions."

"I thought we were the Sarcastic Stallions," Jo Jo said.

"No, last week you said we were going to be the Sexy Stallions."

"Shut up, pegasus breath."

The unicorns continued to bicker as they departed. I waved goodbye to them. Apparently, not everyone could claim to have ridden a unicorn. Students ran up to me, peppering me with questions.

Chase Othello pushed back a handful of her neon purple hair. "What were you doing riding wild unicorns?"

Maya Briggs elbowed someone out of the way to ask. "Was it scary?"

"Did you tame them?" Hailey Achilles ran up to me. "Does this mean you're a virgin? I hear they prefer virgins."

"That's none of your business," I said. I sounded like Thatch.

"Are you going to join the equestrian team?"

Coach Kutchi came swooping down on her broom a few seconds later. Professor Bluehorse arrived in a swirl of green mist that smelled like spearmint and cooking herbs.

Coach Kutchi looked me up and down. "I didn't know you were a unicorn rider."

I smoothed a hand through my windswept hair and tore out a twig. "I didn't know either until today." I hoped that wasn't saying something unusual about my affinity.

"That was reckless and dangerous. Think what kind of poor example you're setting for these impressionable young minds." Professor Bluehorse waved her mossy staff toward the growing swarm of students.

"What are you wearing?" Coach Kutchi asked. "That attire is hardly professional."

I looked down at the white dress. It was pretty grimy. Also, a black bra and panties under a white dress was probably a little more Madonna-esque than was appropriate at school. I needed to get up to my room and change before Jeb saw me and fired me.

Coach Kutchi continued to bluster. I waited until she took a breath to interject, "Don't you want to know *why* I was riding the unicorns? They tricked me—"

"I don't want to hear your excuses," Coach Kutchi yelled. "You're lucky the principal doesn't reprimand you for inviting intruders onto campus!"

Grandmother Bluehorse shook her head at me in disgust. "We're lucky no one was impaled by those horns."

As soon as the two teachers were done chewing me out and left, the students began their questions again.

"Will you teach me how to call unicorns?" Maggie Greenwood, one of my sophomores asked.

"How did you tame them?" another girl asked.

"Tell us all about it!"

"Maybe later," I said. "I need to change."

I trudged all the way back into the school, my legs as wobbly as jelly. I was exhausted. And hungry. I knew I was supposed to stay out of the kitchen, but I didn't think I would make it to the teacher's dormitory for my stash of granola. I snuck in, grabbed a muffin, and ran out.

In the hallway, I passed a polished suit of armor and did a doubletake at my reflection. My pink hair was puffy and wild like a fire sprite. Between the volume of my hair and the white nightgown, I looked like I'd come out of an eighties commercial for tampons.

I munched on the blueberry muffin, making my way down the hall and up the stairs toward the teacher wing. I nearly choked when I heard the arctic chill in Thatch's voice from around the corner.

"Tell me the truth, you insolent nincompoop, or I will dismember you myself," Thatch growled.

I froze, afraid I had been caught by Thatch and was about to get in real trouble now.

He went on. "Is it really such a coincidence that you were dating Agnes Padilla and *friends* with Lisa Singer, and they both ended up dead?"

Confused, I realized he wasn't talking to me. I tiptoed closer to the corner.

Someone managed to get out a raspy response. "I wasn't dating Jorge or Abebe. Are you going to blame me for their deaths too? I have it on good authority, they found you with blood on your hands when Lisa's body was found by—"

"You're lying about what happened to Miss Lawrence today." Thatch's voice held an edge of warning.

It dawned on me who Thatch spoke with now. Julian hadn't told me he'd dated one of the former art teachers. No wonder he hated Thatch if he thought the alchemy teacher was behind their deaths.

Julian's voice came out a raspy hiss. "You're lying about that book. I know it was you who broke into Jeb's—" He choked.

No way! That was what I had suspected too.

I peeked around the corner. Without touching him, Thatch lifted Julian in a Darth Vader choke hold against the wall. Julian's feet dangled above the ground, kicking frantically as he clawed at his neck.

Whoa, hello dark lord.

"Stop!" I said, rushing forward.

Thatch turned to me. He lowered his hand, and Julian fell to the ground. Julian stumbled to his knees and coughed.

Thatch's eyes roved up and down my attire before settling on the remainder of muffin I'd squished in my panic. "I see someone is alive and well enough to be pillaging from the kitchen again."

I hid the muffin behind my back.

"Clarissa! You're all right!" Julian panted, doubled over with his hands on his knees. "Thank goodness. I was so worried."

Thatch eyed Julian disdainfully. "How fortunate for you." He inclined his head in a curt bow to me before slipping off into the shadows.

From what I'd just witnessed, I was further from understanding Thatch's motivations than ever.

Khaba rounded the corner, whistling cheerfully. He eyed me with interest. "Wow, love the wild woman look. It would be perfect for riding unicorns. Did you know your mother tamed feral unicorns?"

I shrank under his scrutiny. Julian coughed. Just one more thing that made me like my mother.

"By the way, we've got another box of recycling for you to pick up in the office if you need more art paper. No magic lamp rubbing necessary," Khaba said. "But you'd better get that recycling before Miss Bloodmire does. She claims she needs scratch paper."

As much as I didn't want Vega to get that paper, I hesitated. "Maybe I should change first. Jeb or Mrs. Keahi might think I look unprofessional." I waved a hand at my attire.

"Have you seen what I wear, darling?" Khaba laughed. "In any case, Mrs. Keahi is on holiday this weekend, and Jeb won't be back until dinner."

I excused myself and ran off. The box of recycling was on Jeb's desk. When I was coming out of the office, Balthasar Llewelyn was walking by in the hallway.

He jumped back. "Holy shit! Is this what teachers wear on weekends?"

"Only when she rides unicorns, dummy," a girl I didn't know said.

During dinner, wild unicorns were all my students wanted to talk about. After dinner, Vega endlessly complained about someone getting the recycling before her. I tried not to smile.

Now that we were seven and a half weeks into the school year, just over a week away from the end of first quarter, I'd gotten used to waking at the butt crack of dawn. I went to bed every night by ten and got up each morning at six.

In the days that followed my wild ride with the unicorns, I was stiff and ached. At night, I tossed and turned, unable to get comfortable. I had just managed to fall asleep when someone pounded on my door at midnight.

"See who died," Vega said, rolling over in her sleep.

I stumbled out of bed in the dark, stubbed my toe on the foot of her bed, and flung the door open.

"Miss Lawrence, Miss Bloodmire, you've got to come. Quick," Julian said, his words coming out in a rush. My sleepy brain could hardly decipher what he was saying. "It's the students. Some of them have left their beds. They've gone under the school to look for the answer keys."

"Does the principal know?" I asked.

"I couldn't find him in his private quarters, nor Mr. Khaba. Besides that, two of the students are young ladies. I thought it would be best to fetch you both to see to the girls. Miss Bloodmire?"

Vega lifted her hand and flashed the bird at him.

I threw a robe on over my pajamas and stepped into my slippers.

"Hurry. I found a secret passage they used." He grabbed my hand and led me down the hallway.

I'd just gotten used to the twists and turns of the passages during daylight hours. At night with the curtains drawn and the only lights coming from an occasional sconce, I lost my sense of direction. We raced down the stairs. At the ground level floor, Julian lifted a tapestry of a knight battling a dragon on the wall. Under the textile, he revealed a dark passage. I ducked under. He held up his wand and lit the way.

"Be careful," he said. "It's rumored there are boobytraps in some of the secret passageways."

"Who are the students?" I asked.

"Hailey Achilles and Balthasar Llewelyn. There was another student with them, but I couldn't tell who."

"How did you find out about their plan?"

"Stealth." He pulled something out from underneath his cloak. It looked like a wad of plastic wrap until he shook it out and it disappeared from sight. I couldn't figure out what he was doing, lifting one arm in the air and then the other. His arms disappeared, then his head, and then his torso. His head appeared again, discombobulated from his chest. He reached behind him, and his head was gone again.

"The hoodie of invisibility."

"Hmm," I said. His legs were still visible. "Are you sure about this? Maybe they knew you were there, and it was just a joke they were playing on you."

"I heard them plotting in the corridor outside the girl's dormitory. They didn't see me. I made sure of it."

My brain was groggy with lack of sleep, but not so sleepy I couldn't grasp his words. Blame it on the unicorns for putting the suspicion of potential depravity in my mind. "Wait, what were you doing at midnight outside the girl's dorm?"

He lowered his voice. "I wasn't at the girl's dorm initially. I was in the dungeon, spying on Thatch. He's been acting suspicious. While I was spying, I heard students, and I followed Balthasar to the girl's dorm."

Julian had accused Thatch of breaking into Jeb's office—and possibly he had done so using my lockpick kit.

"Did you discover anything interesting about Thatch?" I asked.

A shriek down the hallway drew my attention. We both took off running toward the voice. It occurred to me that if we came face to face with some kind of savage beast that wanted to bite our faces off, I wasn't armed with much. I hadn't even grabbed my cell phone.

Julian tugged on my sleeve. I couldn't see him with his invisibility hoodie other than his wand raised in the air illuminating the path. He ran faster than me, and I struggled to keep up. My slippers flopped noisily against the stone. I wished I had an invisibility hoodie. And longer legs.

"If we can catch the students who stole the answer keys, we'll be heroes," Julian said. "No one will ever turn away my help because I'm a mere *history* teacher."

Oh boy. This went back to his rivalry with Thatch. It was hard to say who hated him more, Josie or Julian.

Julian's light rounded a bend, and I followed a second behind him. I tripped over an uneven stone and collided into a set of armor. Stone grated against stone, as though a door made of bricks was opening. The metal armor clanked and loudly echoed, but it didn't fall over.

Unlike myself.

I climbed to my feet. The hallway was dark and silent. The air was cold. I didn't see wand light anymore.

"Julian?" I called.

No answer came.

I glanced behind me. It was dark. A slight glow came from around the corner up ahead. A line of light shone from under a large wavering rectangle. I smoothed my hand over the surface. It felt like fabric. Another tapestry? I didn't see the light from Julian's wand down the hall, so that must have meant he'd gone under without me, though I didn't understand why. I shifted the tapestry aside, following the glow of light from up ahead.

"Julian?" I whispered more quietly, not wanting to draw attention to myself in case this was the part of the school where corpses from centuries past were about to stalk me down the hallway.

The only sound was my labored breath.

The moldy hallway up ahead brightened, blue light shining in from what looked like windows. Smooth polished panels in the wall shimmered like quicksilver. On the other side of the first glass was someone's bedroom, a figure curled up in the bed. From the peace pipe decorating the wall and the leather moccasins on the floor next to the window, I guessed this was Professor Bluehorse's room. Her windowsill was open, moonlight spilling across the jagged edge of the plants in the window box. They kind of looked like strawberry plants. Only the leaves were longer and narrower. I squinted. Maybe that was marijuana.

The room was cast in a bluish light that reminded me of a computer screen lighting a dim room. I touched the surface, the window rippling like water. It felt cold and tingly, and my fingers passed through. My hand turned pale silver in the light.

I backed away and went to the next one. From the guillotine in the corner next to the desk and the vacant birdcage hanging from the ceiling, I recognized this as my room. Vega lay asleep in her bed. The perspective of the room came from the spot where the full-length mirror stood against the wall. The shape and size of the window was the same oval of the mirror. Everything was blue through the mirror, the true color of the room diffused by the light of this spying enchantment.

Vega didn't stir as I watched her. A shiver stole down my spine at the idea anyone could spy on us this easily without getting caught. I remembered that time I'd been meditating at night and had thought I'd seen movement by the mirror. Surely, someone had been watching me. How many times since then had I looked in the mirror and not thought anything of it? What was this place, a spying hallway?

Mirror, mirror on the wall. . . .

More window mirrors lined the wall like those I'd seen so far. Most were ovals like my room's, but some were rectangular. A child-sized ladder dangled from a small square that was level with my face, showing a view of the boy's dorm. A young lady sat on one of the boy's beds. They were making out in the dark.

I didn't know who those students were, but I was going to report them to the dean of discipline. After I found my way out of here. Though, maybe it would be a little suspicious if I said I'd been spying on them in the boy's dorm.

A few feet further down the passage I stopped when I saw Jeb in his office. He sat in an easy chair in the corner, a tumbler of amber fluid in his hand. Khaba lounged on the settee, feet kicked up on the table. Julian had said the principal hadn't been in his bedroom. I could only guess he must have been in his office and not heard Julian's knocking. Khaba's voice was muffled, but I could mostly understand what he was saying.

I should have just walked through the mirror and told them about the students out of bed, stealing answer keys and making out, but I hesitated. I wondered if I was going to get in trouble for performing magic if I walked through a mirror. I was banned from magic.

"It has to be him," Khaba said. "All the evidence suggests it. He's the only one who's been here long enough. Last year, the year before, and the year before that. These accidents are not coincidences. Someone has been murdering staff members for years and trying to sabotage our school. I think that person figured out Jorge Smith was snooping around on your behalf and killed him."

Jeb shook his head. "It ain't Felix Thatch who's behind this. He's loyal to the school and our mission. Why do you reckon he would play turncoat now?"

Guilt seized me that I was eavesdropping. Then again, this was good material. If someone had dirt on Thatch, I wanted to be the first to know.

"That's what I'm saying. This isn't anything new. You've let your pity for him get in the way of your judgement," Khaba said. "I can only hope I'm incorrect." He swished the ice around in his tumbler. "If you're wrong about him, and he's still working as an agent for the Raven Court, that puts all our students and staff at risk. Especially Miss Lawrence."

I sucked in a breath and forced myself to breathe slowly, quietly, not to draw attention to myself. Could it be that Thatch still worked for the Raven Queen? I held my breath, afraid I might reveal myself.

Jeb looked up. "Lord have mercy! I smell what you're steppin' in. You don't think he's going to kidnap her and skedaddle over to the Raven Court, do you?"

"It's a possibility. More likely, he'll teach her dark arts and resurrect the demon her mother summoned all those years ago."

"Khaba, darlin', you hush up. Thatch weren't never involved in none of that. He was a victim of a heinous crime. Loraline used him and his magic and left him for dead. It took him years to recover. He's lucky she didn't completely drain him and turn him into a Morty for good."

My eyes widened. That's what my biological mother had done? She'd summoned a demon and used Thatch's magic to do so? He must have suspected I might let someone do the same to me. Or feared I would fall in her footsteps and use others, hence the reason he had wanted to drain me.

Khaba walked across the room and poured himself another drink, his back to me. "No, she didn't completely drain him. She didn't kill him. That's why I'm suspicious."

"You're in a cantankerous mood tonight. Why do you got to be like this?" Jeb set his drink down. "Come over here, and make an old man's wishes come true."

I covered my mouth, stifling a gasp. He couldn't be implying what I thought he was.

Khaba tsked. "I know how you are with your wishes. They're going to take a lot of . . . friction." He unbuttoned his shirt, facing Jeb. The lamp that had been inked between his shoulder blades was no longer there. He cleared his throat. "What do you know? My lamp seems to have migrated south today."

Khaba unfastened his belt. I rushed away before I could get an eyeful of Brokeback Hogwarts. Khaba, I had always known about, but Jeb? He was gay? Not that there was anything wrong with that, but who would have thought?

I couldn't help feeling a little miffed too. After all that business about not releasing sexual energies around the school for *my* benefit, making all the other teachers resent me, these two hypocrites were getting it on in Jeb's office! I couldn't even confront them about it without admitting I knew because I'd been eavesdropping. Nor could I interrupt and tell them about the students out of bed until I found a way out so I could knock on the door to his office.

At least Mrs. Keahi wouldn't be guarding it for once. I didn't doubt Jeb and Khaba would both be in foul moods when I did interrupt them, though.

Then again, if I caught the students myself and brought them to Jeb, I suspected the principal would forgive me for interrupting. Or better yet, if I caught the students and reasoned with them about the folly of their plans, I could make them see stealing answer keys wasn't the way and that they should return it voluntarily. They might pass the test the Fae Council mandated they take by using the answer key, but they still wouldn't have the skills they needed to survive in the real world.

They needed to study magic. I could help them. I would be the good witch my mother had once been before she'd turned bad.

I looked through more mirrors, finding an empty room I suspected to be Julian's from the portrait of himself hanging on the wall. I wondered if someone special had given it to him like the former art teacher he'd been close to. Julian wasn't in his room, but I hadn't expected he would be. I still didn't know where he'd gone off to.

Josie was asleep in her room.

Another room held a canopy bed with burgundy curtains. No one slept there. On the walls were tasteful art of eighteenth century landscapes that reminded me of Rembrandt's use of light and shadow. I peered closer at the oil paintings. The sheep in the meadow looked peaceful enough, but the dragon setting fire to the village in the background was a little morbid. As for the other painting of dappled unicorns running free in a forest goring a knight, well, that one was pretty dark too. A large unfinished painting leaned in the corner next to a trunk. In the painting, a skeleton reclined on a brocade couch. Thatch was the only other artist I knew of at the school, so I guessed it might have been his.

Everyone's room seemed to be visible from this hallway, which was weird because all the staff rooms were spaced so far from each other and on different floors. I came to a mirror showing Thatch next.

He stood in the middle of a marble bathroom with Grecian columns behind him. His eyes were closed, and he muttered under his breath too quietly to hear through the barrier. He held his arm over a stone sink. Blood dripped from a razorblade. A thin stream trickled down his wrist.

Emo much? Why didn't it surprise me he was a cutter?

On the other hand, maybe he wasn't a cutter, and this was magic. It looked like blood magic or pain magic, not that I knew exactly what that was from the vague descriptions in books. It's not like they explained how one did it. I just knew it was forbidden. He was as much of a hypocrite as the principal.

The next room held Pro Ro sitting in a circle of candles on a hardwood floor. He was awake too. I swear, Vega and I had to be the earliest to go to bed around this place. A skylight of stars shone over Pro Ro's head as he chanted. I couldn't tell what language he spoke. In the center of the circle where he sat, symbols had been written in chalk.

Speckles of light danced across his tunic, making him look like he was made of stars. I didn't want to stare or invade his privacy, but I couldn't tear my eyes away from the bewitching flickers dancing over him. He muttered under his breath, the light growing brighter.

He held a piece of paper in his hand, lifted it up to the heavens, touched it to his lips, lifted it again, and set it down before him. The paper was a photo of a woman with blonde hair. It took me a minute to recognize who smiled at the camera.

It was a photo of me.

CHAPTER TWENTY-FIVE
Brownie Points

Pro Ro continued chanting. The candle flames in his room changed from gold to blue. I stood on tiptoe and craned my neck, trying to see the photo better. It couldn't be me. Why would he have a photo of me?

Yet, there I was. The photo was a couple years old, one I recognized from my mom's house when I'd bleached my hair. A halo of light circled the photo. I felt light-headed. Was this a spell? I focused on the sphere of energy inside me. The red light of my affinity felt like it was diminishing. Was that good or bad? Thatch had seemed to think it was good, but he'd also implied it was bad if someone else controlled my magic. What was Pro Ro doing?

"What be ye doing here?" a scratchy little voice asked.

I whirled, seeing no one.

"Down here, lass."

I looked down to find myself staring at a knobby little creature with legs and arms that reminded me of sticks. The naked man carried a wicker basket on his back, overflowing with clothes.

"Excuse me," I said. "I don't believe I've made your acquaintance. I'm—"

"Room 201, ladies size four, bra size 32 B, striped socks, no thongs. Granola and muffin gifter. I ken who ye be." His accent was Scottish or perhaps Welsh, only there was something that reminded me of an older American dialect as well. Perhaps it was a Fae accent.

"Huh?" I asked, not understanding half of what he said.

He muttered another inventory of my clothes sizes and attire. From the wicker basket, it looked like he had some of my clothes inside it.

"Are you a brownie?" I asked.

He squinted at me. "What's wrong with ye? Donnae ye never see a brùnaidh afore, lass?"

Another naked creature lurched out of one of the windows, carrying a sack over his shoulder. This one looked me up and down. "Bogie bollocks! It be that one again."

"Pardon me," I said. "I'm looking for Julian Thistledown. Have you seen him? We got separated. He thought some students had made their way into one of the secret passages, looking for answer keys to their exams."

The brownie threw down his sack. "Have nae seen no students down here. Donnae you ken, this hall be off-limits to Witchkin's and their prying eyes?" From the way he looked me up and down, I took it he meant it was off-limits to teachers as well.

The first one with the basket dragged it past me. "Saw a trio of those nasty bootlickers earlier, I did. Down a different passage. Thank Nimue they dinnae find their way down here and muck up our cleaning schedule. Unlike a certain lass."

I fidgeted with the ties of my robe. "If you can show me where they went, I can get out of your way."

The first brownie harrumphed. "Ye human folk always be demanding something, ye are."

"Why donnae ye leave out some special granola for us next time?" the other brownie or brùnaidh said. "Ye ken what I mean, lass? Clarence Greenpine's 'special' mix from Ye Green Grocery, eh?"

"Are you talking about the one that has marijuana in it?" I asked. That was what Khaba and Josie had implied. "Are you sure I can bring that on school grounds?"

"Aye." He knocked on the wall. A door that hadn't been there before materialized. It was about three feet tall. He opened it. "This will get you out of our way. Take the path to the right, and for Nimue's sake, donnae go through any doors like they did. Use the tapestries to exit."

"What do you mean, 'like they did?' Who is 'they?' The students? Or Julian?"

The brownies didn't answer. They dragged their baskets along the hall. Already I doubted my plan for showing Jeb what a valuable staff member I was would work.

I crouched through the door and took the fork to the right like they'd instructed. The next exit was a normal sized door in the wall. It was wooden with a metal latch. I tried to peek through the keyhole, but I didn't see anything beyond. A short distance down the hall was a tapestry of swirling designs. I peeked around it. Beyond looked like one of the school corridors with a candle lit in a sconce. It was quiet.

I walked a few paces back to the door. The brownies had said not to take the door. But someone had taken the door. Students? What if I opened the door and I released an unspeakable evil upon the school like my mother had?

I walked back to the tapestry, about to duck under when I heard a muffled giggle. It definitely came from behind the door. My students had to be there. I ran back and flung the door open. No one was in sight, but the hallway beyond looked normal enough. I tentatively walked through. The door closed behind me, sealing me in darkness.

I groped around for the handle, wanting to open the door again and shed more light on the place I was stepping into before I tripped down a stairwell or fell into some monster's feed trough. The handle was gone. The door had disappeared. In its place was the uneven texture of a stone wall.

Fan-freakin'-tabulous. Now I was stuck.

A faint light glowed from up ahead. I groped along the wall and tripped over a suit of armor's foot. The metal dinged in the quiet.

"Someone's coming," a voice whispered. "Hurry, before we get caught."

I tiptoed toward the voice, my arms out in front of myself like a zombie. I groped my way around a corner. Three shadows ran down the hallway away from me, a dim light radiating from someone's wand.

I ran now too, having just enough light to see by.

They whispered in that way teenagers often did in my class, thinking they were being quiet, though I could actually hear them across the room.

"I think we lost him," one said.

"Teacher or student?"

"Can't tell."

He? I loved how they assumed their pursuer was male. Like a female teacher wasn't perfectly capable of going out in the middle of the night chasing them. Of course, their other female teachers were probably far wiser than I was. Vega had gone back to sleep. No one else had gone off with Julian, unarmed and gotten herself lost. Maybe it did seem like a macho guy thing to do.

I needed a plan. If I had known how to get back to the student dormitory, I would have waited for the students to return and apprehended them there. Or pounded on the principal's office until someone answered. I was more concerned I had no idea where I was or how to get back. My best option was to keep following them.

I was lost, but it wasn't like I was in any danger. Those brownies had warned me not to go through the door, but obviously they had been punking me. There wasn't any danger ahead. If there had been, the students would have gotten into it by now.

The students stopped at the end of the hallway. One of the students must have had an invisibility Snuggie because a sliver of neon pink shirt was visible as well as a pair of feet and a floating head. The other two students wore all black so I couldn't actually see much of them. Shadows writhed in front of them. At first I thought it was the light of their wands making shadows dance, but as I neared, I heard the hissing.

"Oh shit!" I recognized Hailey Achilles' voice.

"Son of a succubus!" I knew that curse from hearing it in my third period class. Balthasar Llewelyn.

The shadows in front of them rose, something immense and sinewy.

"You shall not pass," a wet inhuman chorus of voices hissed, unified in one song.

The words were so epic fantasy I would have died of laughter, except that the thing kept getting bigger. I had a feeling those kids, *my* kids, had no idea what they were facing. Neither did I.

"Return the way you came," the voices said. "This is your last warning."

Any rational, sane person would have done whatever that thing asked. But my students weren't the brightest bulbs in the pack, so I had no faith they would do the right thing.

"Run!" I yelled.

I ran forward to grab them and yank them back, but one of them shouted a magic word that sounded like gobbledygook. An explosion of light shot out of his wand. Energy hit me in a wave, and I fell back. The spell illuminated the creature before them. It was a six-headed snake, a hydra.

It lunged and snapped, the kids dodging and rolling with the agility of Cirque du Soleil acrobats. I dove back into the shadows. More fireballs were thrown at the creature. It batted the fire right back at the kids, flames exploding on the stone floor. Hailey slashed out with her wand like a sword. One of the heads fell.

Even I knew that was a bad move, and I wasn't from this world. I had read Greek literature in college. Out of the cut stump, two more grew.

The echo of something metal being struck dinged in the air. The hydra fell over, plopping loudly onto the floor and writhing. The students ran past, opening another door and slamming it behind them. I didn't want to follow them. I considered going back to Jeb's office and interrupting his tryst. I could wake one of the teachers from the hall of mirrors. Except, I couldn't go back. The hallway didn't lead anywhere useful. Or if it did, I didn't know where I might end up.

I had no way out but forward.

I edged closer, toward the door. The hydra flopped around in a puddle. Molten wads of fire clung to the ceiling and the walls. Enough light shone on the creature that I could see it better. It was smaller now, fairly limp, and about the size of half a dozen garter snakes. Cold, wet water soaked my slippers. I stood in the middle of an immense puddle. Now that I looked more closely I could see water gushed out of a bucket that had tipped over. It wasn't a normal amount of water, more like a lake being dredged.

Couldn't anything be normal in this world?

The hydra moaned pathetically. A couple of the serpents slapped the floor, splattering the water. I placed my hand on the door. It moaned again.

"Help. Please," it wailed in its chorus of voices.

Crap. The pitiful sight tugged at my heartstrings. How could I just leave it?

I turned back to the hydra, hoping my kindness wasn't going to bite me in the ass later. "All right, little guy. I'll see what I can do."

I crouched down and heaved the upturned bucket back into place. It was heavy with the creature half in and half out of it. Snakes were not my pets of choice, and I wasn't keen on touching them, especially after my weird magic lesson with Thatch. I tried to coil the snake bodies in the bucket as gently as I could while keeping my hands away from the heads. I removed my house coat and sopped up the water, wringing it out in the bucket over the hydra.

"More water. Please, so thirsty." One lifted its head and brushed against my hand.

I jerked back, falling on my butt in the wet puddle. I mopped up more water and wrung it out. I couldn't see how deep the water went in the bucket, but it didn't look very full.

"You have saved us. We owe you a boon," the hydra said in its slithery chorus.

"A favor or a wish?" I asked, thinking of Khaba. All the wishes I'd witnessed from him so far hadn't been magic.

"A wish." They coiled around themselves, looking as though they were fighting for the water at the bottom of the bucket.

I could ask them to help me become a powerful witch. I could get information from them about the Red affinity or the Fae Fertility Paradox. They could give me the missing chapter I had wanted to read. There were so many things I could wish for.

On the other hand, genies in stories were always being used for their magic. Khaba had implied Loraline had tricked him into agreeing to becoming the djinn of the school with her 'selfless' wish. I didn't want to be greedy and selfish like she'd become, but I had so many things I needed.

The serpents pushed at each other, trying to get at the water in the bottom of the bucket. They whimpered, sounding like newborn kittens. I couldn't leave them like that.

"Can I wish for all the water to be returned to your bucket?" I asked.

"Why would you wish for that?"

"It doesn't look like there's enough in there. Would that help you?"

"Yesssssss."

"Okay, then. That's my wish."

The level of the water in the bucket rose. A unified sigh came from the serpents. One brushed its head against my wrist. I stood, my dripping housecoat still in hand.

"Such a silly wish," one serpent said to another. "I would have wished for those students to be locked inside metal cages with spikes."

I started toward the door, but I hesitated when I heard the hydra's next words.

"If I was her, I would have wished to know more about the curse someone cast on her."

"Or asked for it to be lifted," another serpent said.

"What curse?" I asked. In my dream, Derrick also had mentioned a curse. Did this have something to do with what I'd seen Pro Ro doing?

"Nothing, dear. Our obligation to you is fulfilled."

I scooted toward them again. "How can I break the curse?"

"You need a protective ward for that. A protective rune."

"Where can I find a protective rune?"

They gave a collective shrug. "You could start by looking in a book."

Ugh! As if I wanted to do more reading. Then again . . . maybe I didn't have to. Thatch had made me read a book on runes. I had skimmed a chapter on protective spells. Maybe there was something in the book that could help me.

"Thank you!" I said. Maybe I hadn't completely lost my wish in the process of giving it away.

"A parting word, before our obligation is fulfilled," they said. "Don't follow those students into that room. Any harm that should befall them is their own doing. Let it not be yours as well."

I bit my lip, staring at the door. "Those are my students. I have to try to help them."

They tsked in unified exasperation. They didn't try to bite me as I passed. I opened the door.

"Don't say we didn't warn you," they said.

I stepped through the door, hoping for the best, expecting the worst.

CHAPTER TWENTY-SIX
My Night with Rembrandt and Friends

The room was so bright I had to blink several times before my eyes adjusted. It was daylight. My first thought was that I had spent all night chasing those damned kids, and now I was going to miss breakfast and morning classes. As I stood there just past the threshold, I realized the sun was too high for it to be morning.

I didn't close the door this time. I wanted a way out in case I was walking into a boobytrap.

I stood in a forest. These trees weren't the Sitka spruces and western hemlocks of the Hoh rainforest, nor the maples or alders near the school covered with curtains of hanging moss and ferns. This forest was drier, denser. There was no trail.

Something about it wasn't quite right. The colors were a little too bright and unreal to have actually come from nature. Silence rang in my ears, the quiet unsettling. No birds flew in the sky. Chipmunks and wildlife remained absent.

My slippers squished over slick pine needles and dead leaves. If this was a portal to another world, or another time, I was probably going to be stuck here forever.

I could hear the other teachers talking about it now. "Fifth art teacher in a row. We knew it was only a matter of time. Stupidity was the downfall of this one."

Maybe I could ask for directions from the hydra. First, I had to get out of here. I turned back to the door. I had purposefully left it open for a reason.

Wouldn't you know it? The door slammed closed.

Damn it! Now what?

My footprints had made blurred blobs of color on the ground. I stared at the muddy earth perplexed. I touched a finger to the moss of a tree. My finger came away coated with a glob of yellow green. It smelled like oil paint. The more closely I stared at the tree, the more unreal the tree looked. For one thing, the lighting wasn't right. The shadows on the tree should have been on the same side as the cast shadow, but it wasn't. I didn't have time to ponder the impossibility of the physical properties of light and shadow, though.

"Did you hear that?" Balthasar whispered.

Hailey groaned. "Someone followed us."

I stepped toward the voices.

"Hex him!"

"You will do no such thing," I shouted.

A white light shot out from behind the trees and blasted into a branch above my head. I dove out of the way and rolled onto the leaf-covered floor. Dead leaves and pine needles stuck to me in greasy globs. Footsteps trampled away.

"I am your teacher. You will stop right now and go back to bed!" I called after them.

No one stopped. I scrambled to my feet, running from tree to tree in cover from spells. My feet slipped over the wet earth.

Without warning, the forest changed, and I stood in a meadow of sheep. In the distance a dragon breathed fire at a village. The sheep were frozen in place. I'd seen this scene before. It was a painting on the wall in one of the rooms. A spell came crashing in from the side, hitting a lamb in front of me. It exploded in a shower of white globs, most of which landed on me. I ducked lower, hidden behind more sheep and wiped the paint out of my eyes. My nightgown looked like an impressionist painting.

A teen with red hair and freckles pointed in my direction. "Get her! Curse her!"

I ducked lower, trying to see where the others might be around the sheep legs.

"That's a teacher!" Hailey said. "They'll kick us out if we kill her."

"So? Do you want to get caught?" Balthasar asked.

"It's not like she has any magic or anything she can use against us." The red-headed boy looked like Ben O'Sullivan, another one of my trouble-maker students.

I considered yelling at them again, but I wasn't sure what I could say that would make them fear me enough to convince them to listen.

I don't know the exact minute I went from being the adult in control to being the prey hunted by predatory little monsters. Probably the first day of school. In any case, I found myself crawling behind the sheep to get to the other side of the painting to escape. Another sheep exploded next to me.

I tried to use my stern teacher voice. "Stop it right now. If you don't go back to your dorm willingly, I'm going to give you detention for a month. With Professor Thatch."

I crawled the rest of the way through the flock and raced across the space between the sheep and the crumbling cottage at the edge of the painting. For a blink of an eye the world went dark, and I staggered. I found myself in a room with a skeleton reclined on a brocade settee. One arm was painted with muscle and sinew, but it looked incomplete. Pencil lines remained in some sections around the bones. I ran behind the macabre figure and kept running. Something exploded behind me. Only half the skeleton remained. The rest was scattered in a pile of blobs on the floor.

"No hexing teachers. A hundred points from Elementia and Amni Plandai," I said.

The next setting I found myself in didn't squish under my feet like the other ones had. It was dim and cluttered. I dodged behind a piece of furniture covered in a sheet. The disorder reminded me of the storage room on the bottom of Jeb's tower, but we had a lot of rooms filled with forgotten junk at the school.

A single sconce on the wall cast the room in flickering light and shadows perfect for hiding from students. On the other side of a looming box someone muttered under his breath.

Light glowed above me. A chandelier lit with candles flickered to life. Not so great for hiding.

"I command you to stop at once!" an authoritative male voice said.

It was Julian. I didn't see where he came from, but he was here.

"Fuck," one of the students said.

Finally, I was safe. Or I would be soon.

I didn't want to risk getting hexed in student-teacher the crossfire, so I ducked. My slippers left a trail of mucky colors in my wake. Not wanting to give myself away, I crouched down and hurriedly peeled my slippers and socks off. I squatted behind a table covered in crates and kept my head down. What I would have given for an invisibility hoodie about then. Two figures dressed in all black ran past. I tiptoed around an antique lamp. I could see the exit now. Hailey Achilles stood in front of it, yanking on the handle. It rattled but didn't open. She whirled back and held her wand in a defensive posture.

I still didn't see Julian. Maybe there was another way out, and I could run and get help. I sank down and edged behind a broken desk chair. I would have kept going, but my skin prickled like I was being watched. I turned.

A rectangular box that rivaled the size of refrigerator stood behind me. The looming shape was covered in a sheet. I pinched the corner between my fingers, trying to conceal myself under the sheet without leaving evidence that I had touched it. Underneath was an ornate mahogany wardrobe carved with intricate reliefs of fire, water, wind, and earth. It should have been dark underneath the thick cloth, but one of the doors was ajar. Light sparkled inside and danced like a prism.

Hushed voices approached.

I opened the door wider and stepped onto the wooden ledge. The floor glittered with stars. I stared down in wonder as I stepped into the cosmos. Or more literally, fell into the cosmos.

All right Narnia, here I come, I thought.

CHAPTER TWENTY-SEVEN
This Isn't Narnia

I'd always wanted to crawl into a wardrobe and be transported to another world. I'd stepped into Weirdville tonight with secret passages, monsters, and voyeuristic snapshots of staff I could have done without. You would think that maybe just once the universe might have said, "Hey, hasn't this lady experienced enough? Maybe we should cut her some slack."

That would imply the universe was fair and kind.

My feet met air, and I fell. I flailed my arms, scrabbling for anything I could grab onto. I knocked a wooden hanger from the rack which bumped me on the head. My hand struck something warm and relatively soft. I clasped onto a fistful of fabric with one hand and the rack where the hanger had hung with my other hand.

A vicelike grip closed around my bicep. An arm circled around my back. Someone—Julian?—hoisted me up. My kicking feet struck wood and then someone's leg. He grunted, and I stopped kicking. My breath came in gasps, and my heart thudded in my ears. I struggled for footing, until I found purchase on what felt like a narrow wooden ledge.

"Hey, did you hear that?" Balthasar whispered from outside. "Over here. We need to get her and erase her memories before she tells everyone what we did."

Those little brats! If untrained Witchkin—like them—tried erasing anyone's memories and it went wrong, that person might end up a vegetable.

"What about the other teacher?" Ben asked.

The arms around me held me close. My heart hammered in my chest so hard I was certain Julian could feel it with the way he crushed me to him. I fought to control my breathing, to not give myself away. I buried my face against his chest, muffling my gasps for air. I clung to his jacket as firmly as I could despite the oil paint coating my hands.

"Julian?" I whispered. "What happened? How did we get separated in the hallway?"

He let go with one hand and pressed a finger to my lips.

I forced myself to breathe slowly, to calm myself. I tried to look up, but it was too dark to see. His fingers tangled through my hair and held my head against his chest. His jacket was rough against my cheek. I closed my eyes, listening to the soothing calm of his heartbeat. For the first time all night I felt safe.

The voices of the students faded away. The shimmer of stars below my feet changed. I tilted my head down slowly to look. I didn't want to lose my balance.

Below, the scene was no longer the night's sky, but an angle looking down on a landscape. It was the meadow of fluffy sheep. Well, most of them were fluffy. Some looked burnt.

The landscape flickered to the forest painting. After that came the hydra in the hallway, each serpent head dancing above the bucket as it guarded the door. The images were going backward in time to every place I had been that night.

I tried to look up again, but I couldn't with the way Julian's fingers laced through my hair. He didn't smell like herbs as he usually did. He smelled like oil paint. On the other hand, that was probably me. It occurred to me Julian had never held me this tightly. He'd kissed me and placed an arm around me, but I couldn't recall an embrace so cozy and natural. This was uncharacteristically platonic.

It crossed my mind this might not be Julian. But I'd heard his voice. And if it wasn't Julian, who else could it be? I tried to shift my weight, but he held me firmly.

Footsteps neared the wardrobe. I held my breath. The sheet rustled.

His protective embrace disappeared. He shoved me away from himself. I fell for real this time. I screamed. The air rushed around me. My feet slammed into something soft, and my butt followed. I fell onto my back. The cushion underneath me collapsed a second later. The wind was knocked out of me.

A woman shouted, but my ears rang too loudly to make out her words. The golden glow of an oil lamp flickered to life. Vega sat up in her bed, staring at me open-mouthed. I'd fallen into bed and broken it.

"What the fuck is your problem?" she asked. "And what is that you've gotten all over yourself? Mud?"

"If only."

I insisted Vega accompany me to Jeb's private quarters. She was her usual, crabby self about it and took forever wrapping a black silk kimono around her slender figure. By the time we'd found him, and I'd blurted out the situation, it became apparent he already knew. The librarian stood there in her nightgown, wisps of her silver hair escaping from an old-fashioned bonnet. Ludomil Sokoloff stood in a nightshirt.

Mrs. Keahi burst in a moment later. I soon found most of the staff was awake and running around the school in a state of emergency.

Jasper Jang ran into the room a moment later. "They've caught the little buggers!"

The herd of us traveled downstairs to the storage room. Julian had apprehended the three students with the help of Pro Ro, Professor Bluehorse, and Jackie Frost. Thatch showed up during the commotion and hauled the students off to the dungeon.

I wanted to tell Jeb what I'd seen—specifically about Pro Ro casting a spell on me and students trying to hex me—but Khaba butted in, taking him aside. Pro Ro spoke to him next.

Jeb paced back and forth, ranting. "The dang answer keys are missin'. They took them for sure, and they ain't tellin' us where they are. What are we gonna to do?"

Khaba shrugged. "They obviously hid them somewhere. Thatch will get it out of them."

Vega studied the nonexistent dirt under her nails. "I wonder who admin will be forced to fire first after the school gets fined?" She arched an eyebrow at me.

Not only had I failed to stop the students from trying to hex me, but I had been too busy running for my life to reason with them about how pointless stealing an answer key was. My job was the first on the chopping block. Defeat weighed heavy on my shoulders.

Josie came over and found me standing next to Vega. She looked me up and down. "What's in your hair?"

I shook my head. I was too exhausted to tell her the full story.

Jeb snapped his fingers at Vega. "Miss Bloodmire, you and Khaba check the wards in my office, and see how they got the answer keys. Coach Kutchi, Jackie Frost, go to the dungeon and talk to students in your houses. You can assist Mr. Thatch with the questioning. Pro Ro, Sebastian Reade, get to the astronomy tower, and see if you can see the answers in the stars. Someone find the Lupis. They're good trackers."

I tried to wave Jeb down, but he continued barking out orders. He pointed to me. "Miss Lawrence, darlin', go to my office and pour me a double shot of whiskey. I'm going to need it."

All the staff were grouchy at breakfast from lack of sleep. I probably had managed to get in three hours after the commotion died down. It made for a bad day of teaching.

In the morning, I found three apology notes written in blood on my desk from Hailey Achilles, Balthasar Llewelyn and Ben O'Sullivan. Mostly Ben's note consisted of complaining that Thatch chained them up in the dungeon, and they would be there again during lunch and after school for detention.

I didn't feel bad for them.

There was a time and a place for everything. I waited a day before going to the principal about what I'd seen with Pro Ro. He wasn't in, so I left a note. When he burst into my classroom while I was in the middle of teaching the next day, I thought he was there to see me.

He looked around with wild eyes. "Where is it?"

"Where's what?" I asked.

He sprayed spittle out of his mouth. His eyes were bloodshot, and baggy skin sagged underneath. "The dang answer keys. Where are you hiding them?"

The students stared with wide eyes. Teenagers moved back from him. Jeb's hat was askew, and his plaid shirt buttoned crookedly. He did look a bit unkempt.

"I don't have the answer keys," I said. "Why would you think I had them?"

Jeb whirled. Khaba rushed in after him. He whispered, "I asked you not to get excited and not to rush to conclusions. I didn't say Miss Lawrence had stolen them. My magic indicated she would find them."

I would find them?

He snared Jeb by the elbow and tugged him toward the door. He flashed an apologetic smile. "Sorry for the interruption. Please, don't let this interfere with your teaching."

I stepped out the door after them. "Did you read my note? I was wondering if you had time to talk about something important."

"Is it about the answer keys?" Jeb asked.

"No, but—"

"The only thing you should be worrin' about is the answer keys." Jeb jabbed a finger at me. "Do you know how much that fine is going to be? If you want a job next quarter, you better start lookin'."

I backed away, startled at his vehemence.

Khaba sighed in exasperation. "No pressure."

Jeb continued down the stairs, shouting loud enough I could hear him as he descended. "Where's Pro Ro? I need more divination."

"Teaching class, I expect, since he's a teacher," Khaba said. "Perhaps we should wait until his prep period this time."

"What's the point in having a divination teacher if he ain't gonna tell us where those answer keys are?"

"Just a little reminder, Pro Ro doesn't specialize in dowsing or searching for lost objects."

"Well, it's not like *you've* been good for anything."

To my disappointment, Jeb was too busy to meet with me the following morning or afternoon. When he wasn't off-campus trying to drum up money for the school's inevitable fine, he was meeting with committees regarding the answer key situation.

We had until the end of the quarter to come up with the answer keys. The end of the quarter was a week and a half away. If we didn't locate it, the test administrators would have to make another test. Making a test cost time and money. That money had to come from somewhere, hence the fine from the Fae run school board.

Considering what I knew of this world, I suspected the Fae wanted us to fail.

My future as a teacher/magical pupil at the school looked pretty abysmal. If only I'd had magic, I could have stopped the students and saved the day. As it was, I didn't even know if I could protect myself from that curse.

I checked out a copy of *Wards and Protective Charms for Advanced Magecraft* in the library and found a protective rune used to divert magic from one's enemies. The spell said to write the rune somewhere on my body with ground up coal and virgin's blood. I followed the directions and chanted the magic words as I drew on my arm with a stick of charcoal, but I still felt stabbing pains when I saw Pro Ro in the hallway. Possibly this was because the charcoal had smudged onto the inside of my sleeve and rubbed away. I used a Sharpie next, but that only lasted a day. Next I tried pricking my finger because I was still a virgin. That didn't work either.

There had to be a better way to protect myself. I just didn't know how yet.

After shopping for special granola for the brownies, Josie and I sat in Happy Hal's on a Saturday. My mood was glum as I poured my heart out over a glass of cheap wine I didn't even like. Khaba was off on an "errand." I had a feeling his errand was in the form of his latest kilt complex.

"How am I ever going to master my magic if I leave here?" I asked.

Josie patted my shoulder. "They might keep you on as an unpaid intern. It would give you a lot of spare time to study."

"Have they ever done that before?"

"Well, no. Not that I know of anyway."

My spirits sank lower.

Some guy with a long, wart-covered nose edged past the table. I scooted my chair in so he could get by.

"Excuse me," he said. His hand brushed against my shoulder. My belly cramped worse than a major case of PMS. I shrank away from him, curling over myself protectively until the spasm passed.

Josie's gaze flickered to my arm where she'd drawn the rune the day before, trying to do the spell for me to see if she could get it to work. "No luck with that protective ward yet?"

"No." I lifted up my sleeve. At least this one hadn't rubbed off.

"I hate to say it, but maybe you should ask Vega for help." Josie leaned closer. "She teaches wards and protective spells. She'll probably ask for your firstborn child or something, but it might be worth it, you know?"

"How is it possible I can be cursed? Khaba couldn't detect it. Do you think the hydra was just messing with me?"

"I don't know. Khaba's powerful, but his magic has limitations."

I longed to speak with Jeb, but he hadn't answered any of the notes I'd left him. Mrs. Keahi said he was away on business again. I didn't know if she gave him my messages. She rolled her eyes when I told her it was a matter of life or death.

I'd also made sure to stay away from Pro Ro as much as possible. Since I hadn't been able to speak with Jeb about what I'd seen, Khaba had said he would discuss the matter with him as soon as Jeb returned. A lot of good that did. I had been waiting days for the principal to do something.

"You know what we need?" Josie said. "We should have a girl's day out."

I shrugged, unable to get my mind off my uncertain future.

Josie nudged me. "We could go to a spa and get massages and facials. It will be relaxing and help reduce our stress."

All things being considered, I didn't want anyone to touch me. Not after Thatch had proven his point about how susceptible I was to pleasant sensations. I suspected it wouldn't take much for magic to explode out of me with a massage. If anything, I needed the exact opposite of sensual touch. Pain would help ground me, like when Thatch had squeezed my arm in his office.

"Or if you don't want to go to a spa, how about a movie in the Morty Realm? Something away from all this." She nodded to the café of goblinesque patrons.

The movies, at least, wouldn't bring out my magic. If only there was something I could do that was the exact opposite of feeling nice—like going to the dentist and having cavities drilled without anesthesia, or falling down and spraining an ankle, or getting a tattoo.

The revelation solidified in my mind. I knew what I had to do to ground myself.

"We could get tattoos." Neurons flashed in my brain, dazzling me with my own brilliance. I could solve two problems at once. A tattoo would be painful. The needless pricked the skin and could draw the rune with a virgin's blood—my blood.

Josie frowned. "I don't want a tattoo. They're supposed to hurt like crazy."

I wasn't ready to be dissuaded. "What if I get the rune tattooed on me? Wouldn't it be more powerful if it was permanent?"

A spider scuttled across the table, up Josie's fingers tapping against the wood, and over her sleeve to the corner where it crawled up the wall.

"It's possible," she said. "I've heard of people carving wards into their flesh, though I've never done it. Are you sure you want something that permanent?"

"I can make it pretty. I'm an artist. I was sketching the other day, and I made a little doodle that I thought would be a good tattoo. I'll blend them together."

She eyed me skeptically. "A spa would be more fun."

I tried another tactic. "Sometimes I hear about people getting tattoos as rites of passage: graduating college, having a child, or achieving some goal. I've never celebrated becoming a teacher. This would be perfect."

Josie scrunched up her face, still not convinced.

"We can go to the movies afterward."

"Yeah, okay." She drained the last of her wine. "Khaba can't stay away from the school for more than a couple hours. I don't know if he does movies or there's too much technology and electronics. I'll ask if he'll come with us. The principal won't mind." She winked at me. "Khaba always manages to get Jeb behind his schemes."

I tried not to laugh, remembering the clandestine romance I'd stumbled upon. "I'll bet he does." He knew how to kiss up to the principal.

Outside Happy Hal's we found Khaba speaking with Julian and a red-haired man with elf ears. Julian's eyes met mine, and his grin widened. It was hard to look at him without thinking about kissing his perfect lips.

I waved, uncertain. He and I hadn't spoken much since the unicorns, the one exception being the night the students had stolen the answer keys. I still didn't know what had happened that night and how we'd gotten separated.

On the way back to school, Khaba and Josie walked ahead of Julian and me. Our feet crunched over autumn leaves almost drowning out Khaba's whispers to Josie.

"I don't understand it, but when I use my djinn magic to see the present, the truth is hazy. The future is uncertain. When I ask if the answer keys were stolen, the answer is 'no.' When I ask if the students have them, the answer is 'no.' Oddly, the signs keep pointing to Miss Lawrence, but what role she has in finding them is unclear. A strong magic is interfering with mine. Something Fae."

Josie glanced over her shoulder at me. "A curse? Like the one Pro Ro might have cast on her?"

Julian leaned closer to me. "What are they talking about? Why would Pro Ro cast a spell on you?"

"I don't know." I had a feeling that curse, the reason they couldn't see the missing answer keys, and my affinity problems were all related.

Julian linked his arm through mine. My belly cramped. I didn't want to hurt his feelings, but I didn't want to lead him on either. Until my magical maladies were solved, I wasn't going to have a boyfriend. I pretended I had a rock in my shoe and drew my arm away from his. Separating myself from his warmth was torture.

Sunlight peeked through the golden canopy and flickered onto his cheery face. He was more handsome than usual in this light, his features too smooth and perfect to be real. He reminded me of a Neo-classical painting.

"I've been hoping I might catch you alone," I said. "But there was so much chaos this week and everyone is still going on about the missing answer keys."

He stopped, and his eyebrows rose expectantly. "I've been hoping to speak with you as well. How did we get separated? One minute you were behind me, and then next you were gone."

"I was about to ask you the same question." It appeared he didn't have any more answers than I did. "What about the hallway of spy windows? Have you looked at me through the mirrors?"

"What mirrors and windows do you mean?" His brow crinkled in confusion.

"After we got separated, there was that hallway of mirrors."

He shook his head. "I didn't see any hallway."

"What about that moment in the wardrobe?" I didn't even know what I wanted to say or ask. "It was different. Nice. It wasn't like the other times you've touched me that my magic wanted to overwhelm me." If Pro Ro had cast a spell on me, theoretically he might be draining me, which would deplete my extra magic and change how my body reacted in relation to men. Or the adrenalin in that moment could have done something to my affinity.

"The wardrobe?" he asked.

"Yeah, when you saved me from falling into the portal and were hugging me to your chest." I closed my eyes, remembering the comfort of his arms. It had been exactly what I'd needed. "I can't stop thinking about it." For the last three days I'd been fantasizing about that hug. Not in a sexual way. I simply found contentment in the way my affinity hadn't gone all haywire for once.

He stared in confusion. "Err. . . ."

My confidence faltered. "That was you, wasn't it?"

"Yes, of course, it was." He smoothed a hand over my hair. "I just don't know what it was that was any different."

I hesitated, wondering if I was moving into dangerous territory. "I'll show you." I glanced at Josie and Khaba making their way farther down the path. I tugged Julian behind a tree that would shield us from view.

"Oh, um. . . ." he laughed, sounding nervous. He glanced around as if afraid of being caught.

I pressed Julian up against a fir tree and folded his arms over me in an approximation of the way they'd held me that night. I pressed my body to his. I leaned my cheek against his vest and placed my hands on his chest. He stood still. It was nice, but not the same.

For one thing, we weren't coated in oil paint.

"I think your spine might have been more rigid," I said.

He straightened. "Was this what I did?" He sounded eager, like a puppy who would do anything for a treat.

It didn't change. I squirmed a little more to the right. That still wasn't it.

"It's close," I said. All the mechanics were the same, but I didn't feel the comfortable security he'd given me that night.

He held me for a moment like that. His hand slid up my spine, and his fingers grazed my neck just above my collar. A spike of white-hot energy shot through my core, tearing through me, before subsiding. I gasped at the pain of it.

"Clarissa!" Josie called. "Where are you?"

I waved my hand from behind the tree. I drew away from Julian and stepped out.

Khaba placed a hand on his hip and wagged a finger at me in mock scolding. "Hurry up, slow pokes." From the way he winked, I wondered if that was a pun.

I ran to catch up with my friends.

Khaba raised his eyebrow. "Running errands of your own?"

"Jolly good errands," Julian said, out of breath.

I doubted my 'errand' was anything near as wonderful as Khaba's had been earlier. As we walked back, Khaba agreed to chaperone Josie and me into the Morty Realm—but he wouldn't be able to stay on account of all the toxic substances that would drain his magic. My good mood was cut short when something purple flashed through the trees. Pro Ro skulked in the shadows, reminding me of Professor Quirrell from Harry Potter. He remained far enough back I almost didn't see him.

Suspicious much?

CHAPTER TWENTY-EIGHT
The Master of Pain

I could hardly contain my excitement for going out with Josie to get my protective ward. Early Sunday morning Josie and I sat on the steps out front of the school waiting for Khaba. He was five minutes late. Josie wore a loose bohemian dress that made her look like an earthy witch, even without her hat. I wore a lacy black skirt I'd bought at the thrift store years before and a vintage blouse with puff sleeves. I figured I'd be on some kind of massage table or special chair so I'd worn a pair of knee-length bloomers my mom had sewn for me. The pink bloomers matched my knee high, striped socks. I felt our ensembles were worthy of witches disguising themselves as Morty hipsters.

"So let's see it?" Josie asked.

I showed her my sketch of five yellow stars outlined in purple, placed around a purple rune. I bit my lip, eager to see what she thought. She wound the lavender strand of hair around her finger, her head tilted to the side.

"Well?" I asked.

"What's your affinity? You've never said. Are you Celestor?"

"No. Why do you ask?" I said quickly. If there was anyone I felt like I could trust, it was her, but Thatch had told me not to talk about my affinity.

"It looks a lot like the affinity symbol for Celestors. You know, the stars. And you included purple, which is also their team color."

"Is that bad?" The stars were yellow, not a the silver of the Celestor crest.

"No, it's just odd. I mean, if you're Amni Plandai, it's kind of weird you would want a tattoo that represents a different affinity. It would make more sense if you were getting a flower or a plant."

"Oh." I didn't think I'd ever told her I was Amni Plandai. I wondered why she assumed that. Maybe I just didn't seem like an Elementia. Or maybe it was Jeb's implication I couldn't be around fertility magic and sex after my past magical catastrophes. There was no way to ask without revealing I wasn't Amni Plandai.

"Don't get me wrong. It's your body. Do what you want with it. I'm not judging you."

"I am," said Thatch's cool monotone from behind me.

I jumped to my feet. I shoved my drawing into my purse. Thatch's bird perched on his shoulder. Up close, I could see it was twice the size of a normal crow. My eyes flickered to the bird and back to Josie. Did she find it suspicious that Thatch happened to have a pet bird that was closely related to a raven, as in the Raven Court?

"For once, Miss Kimura is right," Thatch said. "That isn't your affinity. Nor are you able to harness the power of the celestial bodies such as the sun, moon or stars as a secondary affinity because you haven't learned how to do so. Celestors are naturally talented at wards, divination, and the higher arts. Like myself."

I liked my design, and I was even more determined to have it tattooed now that he'd disapproved. I crossed my arms, defiant as a teenager. "Maybe I intend to get flowers and snowflakes tattooed on me at a later date to represent the other teams." What was it about him that brought out the obstinate nature in me?

He snorted. "I'll believe it when I see it."

"What is that supposed to mean?"

"You've never gotten a tattoo before. We'll see if you're up for that level of pain." He lifted his bird from his shoulder and nudged it into the air. It took off, circling overhead. White bird poop splattered three inches to my right. Lovely. I dodged back.

Josie crinkled up her nose in disgust. "Is there some reason you crawled out of your hole in the dungeon? Or was it just to harass us?"

"Harass? You wound me, Miss Kimura." He placed a hand over his heart, his eyes full of mock hurt. "Mr. Khaba is occupied with a student detention." A wicked smile twitched his lips. "I volunteered to chaperone you in his stead."

I seriously doubted he would volunteer. Or if he did, he had a reason. Maybe it was just to annoy me. I considered not getting the rune at all.

Josie shook her head. "We'll see if someone else is available."

"Maybe Coach Kutchi," Thatch said. "Oh, wait. She has practice with Womby's promising equestrian athletes. Pity."

"Julian could escort us." When I imagined his handsome face, a wistful smile tugged at my lips.

"But he isn't powerful enough to escort you and keep you safe from the

Raven Court, is he?" Thatch stroked his chin. "In any case, he's afraid of electricity and the Morty Realm."

My shoulders sagged in disappointment. I'd looked forward to getting this tattoo. Not only was it something I could do to protect myself from being cursed, but it truly represented my rite of passage into the world of magic. Josie patted my back consolingly.

Thatch grinned. "Face it ladies, you are stuck with me."

Josie pointed a finger in his face. "You can't bully us into agreeing to this. We'll just stay here."

"It makes no different to me if you remain here," he said. "I have papers to correct."

Thatch was a Celestor, which meant he was good at wards, and my tattoo was a ward meant to protect me. Even if he was Mr. Grumpy Face, he was the most obvious choice.

"Will you help me activate the ward?" I asked.

He ran a hand through his luscious locks of hair. His expression was pensive, cautious. Maybe it was the lighting, but he looked younger today. He was handsome when he wasn't scowling.

"I could," he said at last.

I looked to Josie imploringly. "I really want to get off the school grounds for a little while. Come on. It won't be so bad. I'll pay for lunch."

A devilish grin spread across Thatch's lips. "How kind of you to offer, Miss Lawrence. I accept."

Thatch opened his arms around us in a move that must have come from Count Chocula. "Let us be on our way."

Inky swirls twisted around us, whipping my hair in my face and ruffling my clothes. I grabbed onto Josie and shrieked—or tried to anyway. The breath was sucked out of me. As suddenly as the cyclone of weirdness had come, it stopped.

Thatch leaned against a concrete pillar covered in graffiti, watching us from a near distance. The white noise of traffic swished by above, blending in with the staccato of rain. We appeared to be under an overpass. It should have come as no surprise that a good hidey hole for someone to appear by magic would smell like urine and be littered with beer bottles.

I skirted around metal cans. Skyscrapers rose beyond our refuge.

Josie rubbed her arms as if she was wiping away slime. "Ugh! Why did you have to do that teleportation spell? We were going to walk through the forest and take the bus into Forks."

Now I would never get a chance to see a close-up of the Podunk town where Edward and Bella had lived in the *Twilight* novels. Thatch probably enjoyed thwarting our adventures.

"Come now. Do you really think they have a tattoo parlor, let alone one open on a Sunday?" Thatch drawled. "Besides, Miss Kimura, I thought you used to like it when I used my transportation spell." He said it in that cloying way of his that was pretend nice.

Josie clenched her fists, glaring at him. "No, I never liked that spell." She had to be over a foot shorter than him, but she was formidable.

"I think the words you once used were, 'It makes me tingle down to my toes.'" He raised an eyebrow.

"Shut up." Her face flushed redder.

Jeb had said Josie and Thatch had once been friends—or at least Josie had tried to befriend him. Obviously, any amiability that once had blossomed between them had wilted.

Thatch escorted us out of the refuge and into the rain. Water rolled right off his jacket. It didn't touch his immaculate windswept hair. A lone black crow watched us from the overhang of a restaurant sign. I hoped it was a crow, not a raven and not his bird, but it was hard to tell. I ducked my chin down and hurried past.

We followed Thatch along a strip of storefront shops mingled between coffeeshops on a busy street. From the steep hills, people dressed in alternative clothes, and the homeless man smoking weed on the corner, I suspected we were in Seattle. My suspicions were confirmed when I caught sight of the Space Needle beyond glass skyscrapers. I stepped under an awning to avoid the drizzle.

"I know where we are," Josie said. "I used to live close to here."

A neon sign of a tattoo parlor indicated they were open. Thatch pushed his way in, letting the door slam in our faces. He was as far from West Coast nice as one could be.

I held the door open for Josie as we entered.

Thatch spoke to the tattooed and pierced receptionist. "We would like to see Hammer."

The woman ran a hand across her silver-and-green striped mohawk. "He's busy with a client. Sofia is available, and Tyrone can see you in half an hour."

"Tell Hammer that Felix Thatch is here for his . . . " He lifted his sleeve and glanced at his bare wrist. "noon appointment. So sorry I'm running a few minutes late." He grimaced and waved a hand at Josie and me. "It's like herding cats."

I shook my head at him. He was unbelievable. Even when he was being halfway nice he was a jerk.

The receptionist checked the calendar, and her eyes widened. "Oh, I'm sorry. You are on the calendar, but he's seeing someone else. Let me go tell him."

"Yes, do that, and be sure to mention my name."

The last glass cases were filled with the most intricate designs. Some reminded me of Pacific island art, others reminded me of Indian henna.

The level of artistry and the macabre element interwoven into each design suggested the same artist. Something about them reminded me of Thatch's sketchbook.

I was drawn to the swirling patterns of Celtic knotwork mixed with barbed wire. I wasn't a barbed wire fan, but I could appreciate the detail.

I pointed to a tattoo with symbols encased inside pentagrams. "Are these runes?"

Josie came closer.

"Yeah. It says, 'I am . . . pain.' Huh, weird. This one says, 'I give you my pain.' Here's one that says, 'I master my pain.' This one is, 'Pain is my master.' The grammar is better than what you'd usually find for a dead language studied by Morties." She glanced at Thatch who stood farther down the wall, examining a cartoon design of the Tasmanian Devil. "But if this is a shop frequented by Witchkin, it makes sense it would cater to our kind."

I kept my voice low, not wanting Morties or Thatch to hear. "Do you think these are some kind of pain magic?" It wouldn't surprise me if Thatch frequented a parlor run by warlocks who dabbled in the dark arts.

Josie shrugged. "I don't know. I've never studied it. Pain magic is banned."

She walked farther down the wall gallery, clucking her tongue when she came to the other panels of cartoons and more generic designs. She pointed to one in Japanese. She frowned at it. "Not everything here is translated as well as the runes. This one says, 'I eat television.' Some idiot probably has that tattooed on his arm." She snickered at another. "This says 'excrement breath.'"

We both broke into giggles.

The mohawk receptionist returned to the room. "Hammer says he'll see you now."

Hammer was a scrawny guy with fire engine red hair sticking out from his beanie. Tattoos covered his arms and neck, and he had the most enormous bull-like nose ring I'd ever seen.

"Sorry about that, man," he said to Thatch. "I must have looked at the wrong day. Let me tidy up and set out clean equipment for you." He bustled around the room, ignoring us.

A woman's yelling echoed from the front. "What do you mean he isn't going to finish my tattoo? I can't have a tattoo of the word 'ass' on my arm. He needs to finish it."

Thatch sat in a chair in the corner, his expression serene.

I whispered, "You did something magically to make him see us, didn't you?"

Thatch smiled by way of answer.

The artist busily wrapped up the materials that were laid out and placed them in Ziploc bags before discarding them. He wiped down the table with disinfectant that smelled like bleach. He had to throw away a lot of materials because of us.

I leaned in closer to Thatch so Hammer wouldn't hear. "You can't do that to humans. It will get them in a lot of trouble. He might lose his license."

Josie shook her head at Thatch and turned away in disgust.

"The correct term is Morties," Thatch said.

Hammer laid out new canisters of ink. He nodded to Thatch. "Did you bring me one of your designs?"

I looked to Thatch, curious about his relationship with the artist. I didn't know he had any tattoos, but then he always wore long sleeves and an ascot or cravat and high collared shirts. Maybe he was like the Japanese yakuza with tattoos hidden under his clothes. After spying on him through the mirror and seeing him use the forbidden arts of blood magic, it made sense he might have a "I am the master of pain" tattoo somewhere on his body.

He might have even designed those tattoos on the walls.

Thatch waved a hand at me. "My . . . colleague brought hers. You'll find it less sophisticated than what I've brought you in the past."

I glared at Thatch, not appreciating the slight to my artwork. I stepped forward to present Hammer with my drawing and removed my striped stocking to show where I wanted it on my ankle.

Thatch rolled his eyes. "Must you get a tattoo on one of the most sensitive spots on your body?"

I ignored him.

Hammer tapped the design. "This should take two hours at the most. The design is big enough it's going to wrap around your ankle and extend a few inches higher. Is that what you want? I can shrink your design on the copy machine." Hammer's septum piercing bounced against his upper lip as he talked.

Before I could answer, Thatch did so for me. "She'll want it reduced in size. Two hours will be . . . a trial for her. It will probably take her three."

Ire spiked through me. Thatch could boss me around about my education, but he didn't get a say in this. "No. I want it this size."

Thatch shook his head at me. "You aren't going to be able to tolerate the pain."

"How would you know?"

Annoyance flickered across his features. He turned away.

"Sure thing," Hammer said. "Just hop up on the table, and I'll make a photocopy of this to work from."

Whenever I'd walked past tattoo parlors, they'd been filled with comfortable looking chairs and cushioned beds that reminded me of massage tables. This table was stainless steel.

As I lay down, I felt like a cadaver at the morgue. It was unnerving. Maybe that's why Thatch liked this place.

From the front pocket of his old fashioned vest, he withdrew a small, black notebook. It expanded before my eyes. He withdrew a small feather from between the pages, pulled on the tip of it, and it burst into a full-sized quill. He hunched over, scribbling in the book. Ink marked the page as he wrote, though he didn't dip his quill in a jar. An artist like myself could use a self-inking quill. Not that I expected he'd give me one.

Josie scooted her seat farther away from him. She retrieved her phone from her pocket.

"Must you do that so close to me?" Thatch asked. "It's bad enough I have to sit here under fluorescent lights, surrounded by machinery that drains my power, but I have to put up with your little machine of death as well?"

She stared at the screen. "You insisted on chaperoning. Deal with it."

"I hear fluorescents are supposed to drain our auras," said Hammer coming back into the room. "But it's the boss-man's choice of bulbs, not mine. I just rent the space." He got out little containers of ink that reminded me of a paint by number set.

"You ever got any ink done before?" Hammer asked me.

"No. This is a first."

"She'll need that moisturizer you use," Thatch said. "What do you call it? Vase line?"

"Vaseline? For sure. I wouldn't tattoo my worst enemy without it. I mean, unless they have an allergy like you do, bro."

What normal person didn't know the word Vaseline? Thatch came across as an absolute dunce from another dimension. Which he sort of was.

The machine buzzed to life. Hammer set the needle to my skin. I flinched and cried out in surprise.

Hammer stopped. "You okay?"

I nodded. "You just startled me."

To my relief, Thatch left the room. I didn't have to worry about him using his magic on me while I was on the table. If he was the kind of person who would switch everyone's prophecy chocolate as some kind of joke, he might also hypnotize the tattoo artist into giving me a tattoo of something horrible because he didn't like my star design.

The needle burned against my flesh. I clenched my fists. If Thatch switched out my tattoo design, it would probably be in another language like Japanese, and say something bad like 'penis breath.' No, that probably wouldn't be the worst tattoo he could think of. It would be the word "yolo" but written in letters made of penises like one of my former middle school students once had drawn on his arm.

I recalled my lucid-dreaming techniques. I wasn't supposed to think of my fears before bed, only the things I wanted to manifest. What if magic was like that too and I caused Hammer to draw a penis yolo on me? I forced myself to think of happy thoughts.

Hammer stopped and reinked his needle. I exhaled, not realizing I'd been holding my breath. The needle surged into my skin, and the sensation jolted up my leg. The vibration rattled all the way through my body up to my head, making my skull bounce against the metal of the table. I was going to have a headache by the time we were done.

"Relax. You have to breathe," Hammer said.

I closed my eyes. Every muscle in my body bunched. The tremor of the machine punctuated my nerves and shot through me. Tears slid down my cheek, and I sniffled.

"Oh honey!" Josie tucked her phone away. "Are you sure you want to do this?"

"Rite of passage," I said through clenched teeth. "Protection."

She scooted her chair over next to the table and held my hand. "I'm not much good at counteracting pain. Not without a book in front of me telling me what to chant, but I'll give it a go."

I glanced at Hammer who reinked his needle again. Josie spoke boldly considering a Morty was in the room. He didn't react. Either he was in the zone or he got a lot of Witchkin in here.

The pain stole my breath away as he resumed. Where her hand held mine, warmth radiated into me. A bubble of numbness traveled up my arm, down my side and into my leg. The anesthesia charm blocked the pain. I sighed in relief.

She smiled. "It's working?"

"Yes."

She closed her eyes, her brow crinkling in concentration. I knew when Hammer pressed the needle to my flesh because I could hear it. After about half an hour, the pain seeped back into my skin. Burning flashed up my leg. I squeezed Josie's hand harder as pain bit into me again.

"Need a break?" Hammer asked. "Cuz I could use one." He did look a little haggard.

"Sure," I panted.

He left the room. I stretched.

Josie's eyes looked bruised. The healthy color in her cheeks had turned ashen.

"Jo?" I asked.

"This is making me majorly tired." She reached into her pocket and pressed a button on her cell phone. "That will help some. I don't want to waste my batteries." She winked when she said it like it was a joke.

Hammer returned a few minutes later, smelling of cigarette smoke. He rolled his shoulders a couple times and sat in his chair again. He yawned, looking sleepy. Two seconds later he resumed his tattoo torture.

Josie closed her eyes again and took several slow breaths. She placed her hand on my kneecap. Warmth spread over my skin. Her spell worked for a few minutes before wearing off. I gritted my teeth.

"Miss Kimura? Are you unwell?" Thatch asked from the doorway.

I hadn't realized he'd returned.

Josie's pupils were dilated unnaturally large, swallowing the brown of her irises. The skin around her eyes was purple against the bone white of her skin. I was in so much pain I could barely focus on her.

Thatch leaned over her. His voice lacked his usual snarkiness. "Josephine?" There was actual concern in his eyes.

He shook my shoulder. "Stop it. You're hurting her."

I wasn't the one doing magic, Josie was. Even so, I could see I'd done something wrong. Josie looked sick, and it was somehow my fault.

He placed a hand under her elbow and helped her to her feet. She must have been out of it because she didn't object.

"You're coming outside with me. There's a park with plenty of trees a block from here. You can recharge your affinity there."

She turned to look over her shoulder. "What about—"

He guided her out the door. "You need to take care of you right now, not worry about others."

"We can't leave Clarissa alone. We're her chaperones."

Their voices grew muffled as they walked down the hall. It was just me, Hammer, and my pain. It did cross my mind this could be a trap. Thatch might have volunteered to be my chaperone because he wanted to find a way to separate Josie from me. He might call the Raven Court here to abduct me. Jeb and Khaba had been discussing Thatch only nights before. I trusted Khaba's judgement. If he was suspicious, I should be too.

Of course, I should have thought of this before deciding I wanted to leave the school grounds with Thatch.

I sucked in a breath as another lance of fire flared in my ankle. After a few more minutes of this, Thatch returned alone. He untucked his wand from his breast pocket and waved it between him and the tattoo artist. The air rippled in a line across the room, separating the artist away from us. The view to Hammer's side of the room reminded me of looking up at the surface of water from below. Our side of the room shimmered blue-green.

Thatch ran a hand through his glossy hair. "Do you realize what you did?"

"No."

"You have used one of the forbidden arts of pain magic on her."

"Forbidden? But—" The intense heat flaring through up my ankle stole my voice.

"Josephine Kimura is an Amni Plandai and not a very strong one at that." He spoke, but it was difficult to understand him with the way the needle stole my concentration. "Are you even listening? Pay attention." He poked me in the shoulder with his wand.

I clenched my teeth, forcing myself to hear his words. Thatch curled his hand around my leg, just above my ankle. I went rigid, expecting his fingers to turn into talons and gouge into my flesh, but they didn't. The pain stayed in my ankle, not moving past his hand. The sharpness was still fierce, but not as intense.

"It takes Miss Kimura hours to recharge after deep spell work, and her powers are mediocre without herbs, ritual, and elaborate incantations—which she hasn't the inclination to memorize." Thatch said. "She was only hired as a Morty studies teacher because of her academic strengths and her experience living in the Morty Realm. You completely overpowered her paltry nature affinity."

"She offered." I swallowed the lump in my throat. "She didn't say it would make her sick."

"Miss Kimura doesn't know what you are." He lifted his chin. "You should have stopped when you saw the effect you had on her. This is the kind of selfish, uncontrolled magic that gave your mother her reputation. It's exactly what people expect from you and the very reason you need a chaperone strong enough and smart enough to recognize what you're doing. If I hadn't walked in on you, you might have killed your friend." He sucked in a breath and exhaled slowly, as if he might be struggling to keep his anger in check. "Like you killed your sister."

My heart clenched. "I didn't—"

He cut me off with a swift swipe of his hand. "Don't lie to me. I'm the one who documented every incident of accidental magic you ever committed. I was the one who cleaned up your every mess, hoping Jeb would never find you and adopt you into our school."

I remembered his not-so-random school visits from when I'd been a teenager. I'd even known he hadn't wanted me to come to Womby's as a student, but I'd never realized why. I hadn't known about affinities and that I was a Red affinity. Even now I didn't fully understand what that meant.

His stormy eyes were cool and unforgiving. "I ensured the safety of the students at Womby's by keeping you away. If I hadn't hidden you from the Raven Court, they would have used you. I could have drained you as a child, but I didn't. Now I'm stuck chaperoning an accidental murderess."

Years of guilt and misery bubbled up inside me. I hadn't meant for anything bad to happen to Missy. My sister had been troubled since Baba Nata, the witch at the fair, had prophesized she would die because of me. Missy had lashed out and told me she hated me. I kept clinging to the hope that things could return to the way they had been and we would be best friends again.

Until the night Missy tried to kill me with her magic.

Later the same night, Derrick and I had kissed for the first time. If our magics hadn't reacted and exploded during that kiss, the storm would never have torn the house apart. The tornado wouldn't have stolen Derrick away, and the house wouldn't have fallen on my sister. I hated Missy, but I never wanted her to die.

Disgust twisted Thatch's face into a grimace.

The grief I'd been holding inside me tightened in my chest. I covered my face with my hands. "I don't mean to hurt people. I wasn't trying to—" The needle stole by breath again. At least the pain remained localized in my ankle.

"There will be no more accidents. From this point on you will be purposeful and aware when you use your magic." He plopped himself in the chair next to the table. "You need to control your powers before they control you."

The moment he released my leg, pain surged up my calf, over my thigh and into my core. The ragged edges of broken memories raked through me. I screamed, releasing years of anguish. Pain shattered my façade of command and made me face the turmoil clinging to my heart. All the self-hatred at my inability to rein in my magic rushed out of me in a whoosh of breath. My body twitched and convulsed as my sorrow and guilt over Missy and Derrick purged itself in another scream.

I was vaguely aware of my foot kicking the tattoo artist.

"Whoa!" Hammer scooted back from the table. "If you need a break, just tell me." His voice was muffled, through a wall of water, but I could understand him. He blinked a couple times and stifled a yawn.

Thatch flicked his hand at the rippling wall. A small hole opened in the boundary. "Give her a moment. I'll make sure she stays still."

I didn't like the sound of that. I drew my knees to my chest. "I've changed my mind. I don't need a tattoo." The catharsis of pain left me limp with exhaustion. I rested my head on my knees.

Hammer shrugged. "I'm taking a cigarette break." He cast a disgusted look at Thatch and walked out of the room. He probably thought I was a major wimp.

And he was right.

"Feeling . . . better?" Thatch asked with a knowing smirk.

"Maybe."

I peeked at my tattoo. My skin was swollen and pink. Five stars and the rune were outlined in pale pink. Only one was outlined in purple.

"What? Why aren't they all purple?" I asked.

"Hammer is a true artist. He outlines with water before filling in the color. It's called a blood line."

"Is that what most tattoo artists do?"

216

"No. They transfer their designs using sticker tattoo sheets or stencils to create guidelines. Tracing is for amateurs."

No way! Tracing was for someone who wanted to save time *and* get it right.

All that work. All that pain. I had sat there through it and made my friend sick, and I hadn't even gotten a freakin' ward out of it?

"This is what we call a teachable moment," Thatch said. "I can't imagine a better way for you to gain control over your body and energy than through pain."

I could imagine better ways. Through rainbows and sunshine. Not that I knew if my magic could be controlled that way. It just sounded nicer.

Thatch removed his tweed jacket and folded it up. As he did so it took shape, looking more like a pillow in a gray silk case. He handed it to me. Reluctantly I took it. I turned it over, trying to figure out what to do with it.

"It's for your head. I expect full concentration with no distractions."

I set it on the table.

"Lie down. Now."

Anger flushed to my face. "I'm not some kid you can order around."

He pointed at me sternly, not making me feel any more grown up and adultlike. "Do you want to kill Miss Kimura? Do you want to suck away the life force of your students? How about an addiction to other people's magic? Perhaps you should go knocking at the door of the Raven Queen and ask her for tips on sucking out souls as well?" The stormy gray of his eyes burned as he spoke the words.

I hated the idea I was capable of hurting others. I hated that I had done so and not just once. I wondered if Josie would ever speak with me again. Maybe she thought I was like my mother too.

I eyed the uninviting length of stainless steel table. "You aren't going to do anything to me?"

"Use some common sense." He lifted an imperious eyebrow. A smile tugged at his lips. "If I was, do you actually think I would admit it?"

In my nervousness, I snorted out a laugh.

Reluctantly, I laid down on the table. I shifted the pillow underneath my head.

"Close your eyes and visualize your body." He walked me through the meditation. It was the same meditation he'd used in his office.

His voice was hypnotic. The monotone lulled me into a calm trance. I felt myself sinking into black water. He tasted like the bitterest of dark chocolates, all sweetness absent. It made me think about my prophecy chocolate.

He poked me in the arm. I opened my eyes to see his wand jabbing into my flesh. "Focus on your energies, not mine."

"Sorry."

Hammer entered the room, a trail of cigarette smoke following him. He clapped his hands together and rubbed them like an excited kid. "Let's get this show on the road." He walked through the waterline as though he didn't even feel it and sat in his seat again.

Thatch placed a hand on my ankle. "I am going to channel your pain so you don't harm the Morty." He remained in his seat. "If you are able to successfully overcome your body's pain threshold, I will gradually decrease the pain flow into myself and allow you to contain it."

"So you're going to take the pain? Like Josie?"

Hammer readied his tools. Any moment now I expected another onslaught of torture.

Thatch grunted. "Not at all like Miss Kimura. I am accustomed to pain. Unlike a simple Amni Plandai with only one affinity, I have mastered many affinities. My studies of the healing arts will enable me to transmute energies into more palatable forms of magic. This will be child's play for a Merlin-class Celestor such as myself."

My concern for his welfare evaporated as his arrogance surfaced. "Got it. Pain is my master. I am lord of the pain," I said, thinking of the quotes in the tattoos in the waiting room.

"Don't be flippant with me." He jabbed me in the ribs with his wand.

I pushed his wand away. "Don't do that."

"Master your body, and you won't feel anything. Unless you desire to."

Thatch adjusted his hand on top of my leg, a few inches higher than my ankle. The other he placed under my knee, giving it a slight bend. As Hammer commenced working, the vibrations continued to rattle through me, but the pain was absent.

"Your body is completely intolerant of pain," Thatch said.

"Duh."

"For you, it's worse than it is for one with an Amni Plandai affinity like Miss Kimura. What you must understand is that pain is simply fuel that can be transformed into other energies. You have two options. You can transform it into something your body is capable of digesting, or you can purposefully send it out. We'll try the latter method first."

I nodded. This was what I had always wanted, to learn practical magic rather than theoretical ideas from books. I wondered what had made him change his mind about teaching me.

Thatch leaned closer to me, his face inches from mine. "Close your eyes and focus on flowing the energy out your body and into my hands."

I stiffened seeing him so close. He was near enough he could have closed the distance and kissed me. Which would have been weird, considering I didn't like him. His only positive quality was his hair.

And he had a deep voice with a nice accent. And sometimes I thought I saw a glimmer of something aesthetically pleasing in the features of his face.

Also, he'd been nice enough to give me a pillow. That didn't mean I was attracted to him. Just because he'd showed me my affinity in his office and I'd felt aroused once. . . .

"Close your eyes," he repeated. His voice was low, a hint of threat lacing each syllable.

I closed my eyes. I bit my lip and then forced myself to stop. For the briefest moment, I wondered what his lips would feel like pressed against mine. I pushed the thought away. He was evil. Why did nasty thoughts like a yolo made from penises and kissing Thatch pop into my head at unexpected times?

I made myself visualize the pain flowing into his hands. We tried that for several minutes. It didn't feel any different from what I'd done with Josie, though I hadn't realized what I'd been doing. As Hammer filled in the color of the tattoo, time slipped by more quickly.

"Now, instead of the pain traveling out of your body, imagine the heat of that pain cooling as it travels into your body. See it going into your core and changing into light." Thatch walked me through the steps.

Hammer said something, but his voice was muffled.

Thatch withdrew his hands. "Pardon me?"

Hammer's voice grew louder, clearer. "I think it would be easier to get the last stars wrapping around the back of her leg if she turned onto her stomach."

Since the table was against the wall, I had to flip over and turn around. My muscles ached like I'd run a mile and dehydrated myself in the process. Hammer rolled his chair and art cart to the other side. I tried to find a comfortable position lying face down. The metal was unyielding and hurt my ribs and breasts. It wasn't exactly comfortable on my hips either. My tailbone ached from lying flat for so long. This stainless-steel bed of torture sucked.

Thatch tugged at the pillow and stretched it, lengthening it before handing it back.

I placed it under my chest and adjusted it to keep my hips from digging into the table. I rested my face against it. "Thank you."

He smiled. It was a small smile, but unmistakable. He looked so much less stern without his resting bitch face. I wondered how much of his unfriendliness simply came from his lack of expression.

I swept a hand over the back of my skirt and smoothed it down before settling against the pillow. The silk of the pillow reminded me of rose petals. I smoothed my cheek against the fabric, enjoying the sensation against my face. The pillow smelled like a chilly winter night staring at the stars. I wouldn't have thought starlight had a smell, but it had to be a synesthesia of magic. His Celestor affinity confused my senses. There was something there underneath that perfume. I inhaled crisp air and dusty books.

"Are you focusing?" he asked.

"Yes," I said. It wasn't a complete lie. I was focusing on something, just not on what I was supposed to be. I visualized my Red affinity swirling inside my core.

Thatch placed one hand underneath my leg, a few inches higher than my ankle. The other he placed on the back of my knee. It felt intimate, more so than before. His hands were cool against the heat of my flesh.

As the vibration of the tattoo needle fluttered up my leg, I imagined the energies changing. More of it shifted from flowing into Thatch. It flooded into me, but what I fed myself was no longer pain. I could see the energy clearly in my mind, changing colors and temperature. It tasted like spring meadows and wildflowers. I smelled sunshine and happy bunnies bounding through tall grasses. The tastes of color and the music of the magic confused my mind, but I didn't want to resist that confusion. I sank into it. My muscles relaxed. I snuggled my face into the pillow.

My awareness of what was happening inside me flared to a new level as Thatch shifted his hold on my leg. His thumb smoothed against the sensitive skin behind my knee. The pleasure that tickled up my leg and touched my core startled me. I flinched and might have kicked the tattoo machine out of Hammer's hand if Thatch hadn't been holding my leg so firmly.

"Sorry," I said.

He tilted his head to the side, studying me. "Don't allow your attention to stray." His voice was more puzzled than stern.

I nodded.

Usually he was pale like the moon, and maybe that was a Celestor quality, or maybe it was from spending so much time in the windowless bowels of the school, but his cheeks were now rosy and flushed. He looked healthy and less vampire-like.

Maybe he hadn't intended to arouse me with his thumb. I certainly hadn't intended to be aroused by him. My affinity seemed to always lead me astray. His gaze flickered to my leg. He removed the hand from behind my knee and lowered the hem of my skirt. It must have shifted when I'd flinched.

A cough from the door drew my attention. Josie stood there, still looking ashen, but her face wasn't quite as drawn as before. She eyed Thatch suspiciously.

"Hi, Josie. How are you feeling?" I asked.

"Fine." Her eyes cut over to Thatch and back to my face. Her eyebrows shot upward in a question.

It was difficult to make my mouth work and keep visualizing the pain changing into butterflies while going into my happy place. Some of my control slipped and the sharpness of the needle bit into my flesh.

"It's okay," I said through clenched teeth. "Mr. Thatch is teaching me how to control—" I was about to say "pain," but he interrupted me.

"How to heal," he said firmly. He gave me a pointed look before turning his head back to her. "And you, Miss Kimura, are distracting my pupil." He flicked a hand at my purse. It flew off the chair and launched into Josie's hands. He threw it at her with enough force that she stumbled back.

I glanced at Hammer. He worked away without looking up. I couldn't tell if he was under a spell or just really into his art. I'd been in the art zone before too.

"Hammer is almost done," Thatch said. "Miss Lawrence promised us lunch, and you need to feed. Get us something to eat, preferably organic." He lifted his nose up in the air, his usual snobby self. "That's more for your sake, not mine."

She tucked my purse under her arm and strode closer to me. "Are you okay, hon?" She stroked my hair.

"I am. Really." I tried to smile, but the unpleasant prickle against my ankle made it difficult. Thatch swept a hand in the air over my calf and let out a long exhale. The bite decreased, and I could concentrate again.

"I did promise you lunch for your troubles," I said. "Get anything you want. Dessert too. Whatever will make you feel . . . better." She didn't act angry, like she thought I was Jerky McJerkface for stealing her energy. It was more than I deserved.

Hands on her hips, she turned to Thatch. "Behave. Or I'll bite your head off."

"It wouldn't surprise me if you were capable of such a deed."

She spun and left.

He wet his lips, the gesture nervous. "Have a care not to speak so openly about pain. One might presume you have an affinity for it."

"Are we healing or using pain magic?"

"Both. As I said before, it's forbidden, as are any of the dark arts that use the body, whether one's own body or someone else's. Pain magic, blood magic, necrophilia-mancy, it's all the same to people."

Necrophilia? Yuck. None of those were my affinity, thank goodness. At least I didn't think so. I had a suspicion he dwelled on the dark side of the Red affinity, whereas mine was less sadomasochistic.

I saw the school crest in my mind, an unbalanced isosceles triangle. It would make so much more sense if the empty space was filled with something. Something red.

"Blood magic," I said. "That's what's missing from the school crest. The Lost Red affinity." Was that what I'd seen Thatch doing in the bathroom when I'd spied on him through the mirror? Now he was teaching me pain magic that he wanted me to call healing. Those times I touched people and had weird electrical reactions, was this all related? A rose by any other name was still blood magic? "The Lost Red Court."

"Indeed. This is your first lesson in your affinity, though it's illegal to teach it, learn it, or speak of it. Now, focus on the problem at hand." He removed his hands from my leg, and the vibration of the needle started up and touched my ankle again.

I willed myself not to flinch. The pain clapped through my body like a thunderstorm. Red flashed behind my eyes. No, I was not going to have an affinity for pain and blood. I wasn't going to be evil like my mother.

He placed a hand on my shoulder, drawing my attention. The pain wicked away. "We'll begin again." He returned a hand to my leg. "I'll stop siphoning more slowly this time, but you must actively participate or else the pain will return. I'm not going to stop it again if you lose focus."

"Got it." I nodded.

There was no motivator like pain. I went back to my happy place and imagined the energies running through my body. Red pain faded into butterflies fluttering through wildflowers. More of the transformed pain went into me and less into him. I couldn't even feel Thatch's hands on me anymore.

After about ten minutes of this meditation, it became easier to focus. I sank deeper inside myself, the world disappearing. Wind and icy mountain stream water washed up my knee, tingling over my hips and into my core. Cold fingers of water smoothed up my leg, stopping just before my panties.

Cold fingers. His cold fingers? Goosebumps rose on my skin. He caressed my thigh.

My eyelids shot open, and I twisted to look at him. "Hey!" I shouted. "I did not give you permission to—"

Thatch sat in a chair, but his hands weren't on me anymore. He held his notebook on his lap, the quill poised over a page. A blot of ink dripped onto the words he'd been writing. His brow furrowed in confusion. He looked from me to Hammer, his eyes narrowing in suspicion as he eyed the artist. For once the venom in his expression wasn't directed at me. He thought Hammer had done something . . . inappropriate? So it hadn't been Thatch sliding a hand suggestively up my leg?

I looked away, embarrassed how quickly I'd jumped to that conclusion.

"Did you say something?" Hammer asked through the filter of our wall.

I shook my head. "Um, sorry, false alarm."

Thatch pursed his lips. He returned his attention to his journal. He didn't help me block the intensity of the needle as Hammer started up again. My muscles instantly went rigid with fire. I could block the sensation of pain and change it if I was ready for it, but I couldn't do it if I was already experiencing it.

"I'm not helping you anymore. You're on your own," Thatch reminded me.

"I know," I said through clenched teeth.

Only when Hammer paused to change the needle head was I able to steady myself with a few breaths and ready myself by imagining the channels opening inside me.

Deer prancing in a sunny meadow flashed before my eyes. The magic tasted serene and whimsical. I could handle this. Cold fingers stroked behind my knee and under my skirt. This was all in my head, like the torture chair. I kept imagining the spring meadow flavor of the energy. The hand massaged my behind in soft circles, making my breath catch in my throat.

Magic gushed into my core like a river overflowing after a heavy storm. The drumming of the tattoo vibrated up my legs and ground my pelvis against the table. The bunnies in the field were all grown up now and rutting like, well, rabbits. A green man made of plants stood in the meadow, his arms opened to me in welcome. Breeding animals surrounded him. I couldn't get the energy to go back to innocent butterflies and wildflowers. A chilled finger slid against my inner thigh.

My breath caught in my throat. The air tasted sharp, wrong, like ozone. Not good.

I couldn't focus on controlling the prick of needles. The pain should have returned. It didn't. Instead, the needles felt good. Warmth surged like a tidal wave into my core. It was every pleasant flavor all at once: ice cream with hot fudge sauce, petrichor, piano music accompanying punk rock poetry, a man's musk, the flavor of naked skin, lasagna, and wet wood overwhelming me in a crashing tsunami.

Currents of pleasure pulsed inside me. A tide of energy stroked me between the legs. A ragged breath of wind brushed against my ear. Or was it a man's breath? My insides clenched. I ground my pelvis against the table. Magic swelled in my core. White light burst from inside me. I moaned.

I hugged the pillow tighter. A heartbeat thudded under my cheek. I nuzzled against his chest. His fragrance shifted from wild forest virility to dusty books and oil paint. I was warm and content. So this was what it was like. An orgasm. A magical orgasm. I giggled into the pillow—chest? I was groggy, and my senses were confused.

The thud drew my attention. Thatch sat several feet away, his chair pushed back from the table. His book was on the linoleum tile. He clenched his quill, but the spine had broken in his fist. Hammer had fallen out of his chair. His needle machine was on the floor. The lamp next to the table was dark. The florescent lights overhead flickered.

Thatch's face flushed red. "Merlin's balls! What did you just do?" His voice came out a breathy wheeze.

Only now that the sensation faded did I question how this had happened. Tornadoes and electrical storms were my modus operandi, not a trip to orgasm town. Thatch's hands had been on his book. He hadn't touched me. He must have used magic. The way he'd looked at Hammer before had to be a ruse so I wouldn't know it had been him. That was the only explanation.

I sat up, hugging the pillow to me more tightly. "What do you mean? What did *you* do?"

Hammer apologized profusely. The sound barrier was gone, and his voice came out loud and clear. "Shit, man. Sorry about that. I don't know what the hell just happened. Electrical failure maybe. Fuck." He tapped the foot pedal for his instrument of torture, but nothing happened other than a clicking noise. He tried the lamp. Nothing. "Fuck. I'll check the fuse box. Fuck, fuck, fuck!" He hurried from the room, swearing some more.

Thatch's face was now purple. A vein throbbed in his forehead. It looked like he was struggling to breathe.

He lowered his gaze. "Let go," he choked out.

I stared at him, confused.

He staggered closer. I leaned back as he stretched a hand toward me. My heart pounded against my ribcage—or maybe it was the pillow's heart. It was so warm. Hard and soft at the same time, like a muscular chest. Yes, there was a heartbeat inside the pillow. I pushed it away from myself, even more confused.

He yanked the pillow out of my arms. Immediately, the unnatural flush to his face faded.

He gasped and coughed, leaning against the table. "Was that supposed to be a joke?"

"Um. . . ?" I didn't know whether to feel embarrassed or angry. I didn't understand what had happened. Had I somehow stolen his heartbeat or stuffed his heart in that pillow? That was freakin' creepy. And then there was the weird tattoo orgasm.

"What did you do to me?" I asked.

He smacked me on the side of the head with the pillow before shaking it out. "That wasn't me. It was all you."

The fluffy shape unfolded into fabric. He shoved his arms into the sleeves of the jacket. He leaned against the wall, glaring at me. I bit my lip. I still didn't know what to think. The lamp next to the metal bed came back on. The tattoo machine rattled on the table. Thatch leaned down and flicked it off. Hammer returned a second later.

"I just have part of a star left," Hammer said. "And the interior of that symbol."

I tilted my leg so I could see it better. The rune was only outlined in purple. Four out of five purple stars were inked yellow inside. The tattoo was incomplete, like my training. Unlike my unrelenting desire to master magic, I could live without one star inked.

"I'm ready to pay," I said.

Thatch turned his nose up at me. "A wise decision. One of your few."

Hammer looked from me to Thatch. His shoulders deflated. "The fuse box has never done that before. I'm so sorry. It won't happen again, man."

"Don't trouble yourself over it." Thatch waved a hand at me. "She simply can't take the pain."

Hammer looked to me. "I only have fifteen minutes left. Twenty-five tops. I don't like to leave a customer unsatisfied."

"Believe me, she is *quite* satisfied," Thatch said coolly.

Not only had the tattoo outing ended poorly, but I'd never gotten Thatch to activate the ward. I considered going to the dungeon to ask for his assistance, but I wasn't ready to face him after what had happened.

In the parlor, I had thought he'd tricked me into letting him use magic on me. But he had said it all had been mine. If that was true, I'd accused him of doing something magically licentious. He had a right to be angry with me. The appropriate thing to do would have been to apologize, but I didn't even know where to begin.

I'm sorry I'm attracted to you and didn't realize it and lost control.

No, that wasn't likely to go over well.

I'm sorry I accused you of using sexy-time magic on me when it was actually me using it on you.

Or:

I'm sorry I put your heart in a pillow and squeezed it. By the way, did you ever give my mother a magical orgasm? And just to be clear, are you my father? Because if that's the case, I'm even sorrier, and I want to make sure you know I'm not into incest.

I wasn't ready for that conversation yet. I was relieved Thatch chose not to join the staff in the cafeteria for dinner that night. Julian also was absent, which was disappointing. I would have liked to sit close to him and bask in his sunshine. It ate me up inside there was no one I could talk to about what had happened. If there was one person I thought I could trust, it would be him.

I sat with Josie at the student table, eating with the kids. I was wary when Pro Ro joined us. He rubbed the bottom of his turban in a nervous gesture. I expected the rune on my tattoo to flare up in pain and warn me an enemy was near, but nothing happened. Probably this attested to the pointlessness of having gotten the tattoo done in the first place.

"What are you doing at the kiddie table?" I asked, trying not to sound suspicious.

"Just wanting to spend more time with the students. No different from you." He made a show of talking to the students, but his gaze flickered back to me.

Even Josie noticed. "Something wrong, Darshan?"

His smile faltered. He glanced at me again.

"Whoa!" one of the girls said. "Is that your real name? Darshan?"

He inclined his head. "My given name, yes."

"What's your first name, Miss Kimura?" the girl asked.

Pro Ro looked to me. "How are you feeling, Miss Lawrence? Has anything been . . . troubling you of late?"

"Troubling me?" Like a spell he'd cast on me? I thought back to the orgasmic tattoo experience earlier. I'd never experienced that kind of magic before. Could it be the rune had reacted to his curse and broken it?

"As you know, I teach divination." He cleared his throat. "There are times I have been known to see things."

"Did you have a vision?" a freshman boy asked.

Pro Ro turned back to the students. "Yes, Jeremy. I saw you passing your Morty Studies mid-term—after studying." He smiled and teased them, indulging them by answering questions.

I excused myself from dinner early. Pro Ro followed me with his gaze, his eyes intense as I traveled down the hallway. I didn't know much about the practical nature of spell work. I didn't know what I'd witnessed him doing to me magically or why. The extent of my abilities to protect myself were what Thatch had taught me. So far I could block pain. Sort of.

When I'd seen Pro Ro the other night, I was sure he'd been performing a spell on me. Today at the tattoo parlor I would have sworn I had felt icy fingers on me. I had thought it was Thatch, but his reaction had told me it wasn't him. I should have swallowed my pride, apologized, and told him about Pro Ro and the photo, how he kept watching me, and that I had cramps while he was near.

I recalled what Thatch had told me. If I didn't get a handle on my powers, someone might gain control over me and use me. I couldn't tell the difference between my own desire and someone else's.

My affinity was so out of whack I couldn't even kiss Julian. I still couldn't have a normal love life. Those sharp pains in my stomach had started that first night at the teacher dinner when I'd met Pro Ro. Was this all a coincidence? Or was it tied together? He might be using me for my affinity like Alouette Loraline had used Thatch.

Only, I didn't have cramps tonight when I'd seen him. Maybe all that energy inside me that had been building up had been released. I might have broken my curse with a magical orgasm. I was willing to buy into any excuse to avoid discussing what had happened with Thatch.

I stopped in the hallway, realizing my feet led me up to Julian's classroom. I smiled, thinking of him and the way his eyes lit up when he saw me. He wasn't in his room when I arrived. I made my way back to the downstairs hallway. A tapestry of a centaur wafted against the wall. I peeled it back and peeked underneath. The wall was solid stone bricks.

The hall of mirror portals the brownies used had been behind a tapestry of a dragon and a knight battling.

If I found the right tapestry, I could spy on Pro Ro. I could discover what he was doing. He might be using a forbidden magic. I walked the length of the main corridor and then moved onto the second level. At the bottom of the stairwell that led to the dormitories, I found the dragon tapestry. I peeked behind my shoulder. No one was in the hallway. I lifted the edge.

There was my passage.

CHAPTER TWENTY-NINE
The Witching Hour

I snuck out of bed at ten thirty to venture back downstairs. The last time I'd witnessed Pro Ro cast a spell it had been midnight. I didn't know if that was the usual witching hour for him, nor did I want to wait that long and miss my opportunity.

This time I brought my cell phone in my housecoat pocket just in case I ran into problems and needed to throw it in Pro Ro's face.

Not that I knew if it would work like it had on a Fae. Josie seemed to handle electronics moderately well. For all Thatch's complaints earlier that day, he had handled being around electronics without any problem. I ended up using my phone on the flashlight setting after I ducked under the tapestry. After a few twists and turns, I tripped on an uneven stone sticking out of the floor just before the suit of armor. Fortunately, I didn't collide into anything this time. I rounded the corner, expecting to find the next tapestry, but there was nothing.

That was strange. I found my way back to the exit and started again. I came to the armor, rounded the corner, but there was no tapestry with a secret passage. What had I done differently that night? I examined the stone where I had tripped and tried to wiggle it. That didn't do anything. I inspected the armor next. One of the arms shifted when I pushed. The air wavered, and the sound of stone grating on stone echoed in the corridor. A faint glow came from around the corner.

Rounding the bend again, I found the tapestry. Blue light shimmered around the edges. Peeking underneath, I saw the mirror hallway.

I passed other rooms along the way, averting my eyes and only glancing up to make sure I hadn't passed Pro Ro's room. I wasn't there to watch my friends undress or give in to voyeuristic fantasies. I just wanted to see if I could figure out if Pro Ro was casting spells on me. The hydra had told me I was cursed. Dream-Derrick had told me I was cursed. I intended to find out who was doing this to me.

Pro Ro sat in a circle of candles. His turban looked as red as blood in the dim light. I was certain it had been purple earlier. A crystal ball was set in a stand before him. His eyes were half-slit, focusing on the crystal. I shifted from foot to foot, waiting for something to happen. I grew tired of standing and sat. Every time his lips moved—which wasn't often—I leaned in closer.

Still, nothing happened. He didn't have any locks of pink hair he used in his spell or have any photos of me.

It was past my bedtime, which is probably why I found myself drifting off. I sat up, blinking my eyes open. Pro Ro still chanted. I stood up again and paced to keep myself awake. I considered going to Julian's window. I longed to see him and talk to him about my day, about Pro Ro, about anything.

A couple feet down the hall, I came to the window to Thatch's room. I hesitated, knowing I shouldn't have looked. It was intrusive to do so, but I couldn't help myself. He was painting.

I'd never seen him without a cravat and a high-collared shirt, layers that concealed him from neck to wrist. His frockcoat and tweed jacket were tossed onto a neatly made bed with a burgundy curtain pulled back from the posts. When he turned to the side to retrieve paint out of an open trunk, I saw the white sleeves of his shirt were rolled up to his elbow, exposing white lines etched into his fair skin. I couldn't make out whether these were scars or some kind of discoloration. His vest—it was actually an old-fashioned waistcoat—was unbuttoned. He'd tied his hair up into a manbun on top of his head. It was unexpectedly cute to see him so dressed down.

The expression on his face was tranquil, something I rarely saw from him. I'd never noticed how handsome his face was when it wasn't pulled into a sneer. It was strange to see him so casual and relaxed. It made me feel guiltier that I spied on him.

He squeezed alizarin crimson out of a tube onto his palette and mixed it with burnt umber and yellow ochre. As he shifted, I got a better view of the large canvas on the easel in front of him. I recognized the painting as the unfinished skeleton I'd seen the other night when I'd glanced at this room, though the canvas had been stashed in a corner then. I'd later walked into the painting.

Thatch shifted and blocked most of the painting from view, but what I could see around his body looked as though he'd managed to repair the damage the students had done. He spat into his paint and stirred it in with a palette knife. I'd never seen anyone do that before.

I moved back to Pro Ro's room, but nothing was happening yet. My thoughts kept wandering to Thatch. He had wanted my job as an art teacher. He was a true artist. How badly did he still want my job? I didn't want to think he'd be the kind of person to kill the former art teachers for their position, but who else had the motivation? Could it be that he'd cursed me, not Pro Ro?

The idea of that made my stomach sick, and I didn't know why. It wasn't like we were close.

My feet took me back to him. He dabbed red sinew over a section of bone. It was a semi-transparent glaze. The bone was still visible through the layer of muscle. It was fascinating to watch. Even without skin on the body or all the muscle in place, he'd captured the lazy posture of the woman he painted. I could see why he thought my rune and stars tattoo was so insipid and simple. I envied his artistic mastery.

He turned again to the side, his wand in his hand. He sliced into the flesh on the back of his hand, scarlet droplets beading up. He dipped his paintbrush in his blood. I didn't know if this was for the sake of color and art—or magic.

Blood magic?

He'd said that was forbidden. Would he kill me if he knew I'd witnessed this?

I wished he didn't hate me so much. It would have been nice to have a friend at the school I could make art with. I leaned as close to the mirror as I could, soaking in his every brush stroke. My nose accidentally touched the mirror and it rippled.

His spine stiffened. He turned, scanning the room. His resting bitch face was back in place.

"Who's there?" he demanded. His voice sounded muffled like the sound barrier spell he had cast in the tattoo shop.

His gaze settled on the mirror. I stepped back.

Oh no! Sir Grouch-a-lot was about to catch me.

I wanted to run, but I stood rooted to the spot. Maybe it was magic. Maybe instincts turned me into a deer in headlights.

He touched a hand to the mirror, level with my face. He was close enough I could now see the pale lines on his skin weren't scars, but intricate Celtic knotwork intermingled with runes. It was his artwork but tattooed with white lines that made it look as though his skin was covered with lace.

His palm pressed flat against the glass. He stared at the mirror, his gaze searching, but not seeing.

His voice came out soft, sad. "Alouette?" There was such hope in his eyes as he said my mother's name it broke my heart.

I wanted to hug him and confess it was just me. I leaned closer. He was only inches away.

He closed his eyes and slouched forward, his forehead resting against the mirror. His hand slid down the silvery surface, smudging it with a crimson streak from his fingers. Sorrow weighed down his shoulders.

I got it now. He'd been mad I'd lost control earlier. Mad I was like my mother. I had used his magic.

More than anything, he was mad I wasn't her.

My chest tightened. I bit my lip, considering touching him. I could reach through the portal. How would he react to that?

His fingers twitched. He moved his palm lower. The red smear over the surface looked like a rune. I was too busy watching his hand to notice anything else. After another few seconds I realized his lips were moving, though I heard no sound. He stared intently into the mirror, not staring at me exactly. He must have been staring at his reflection.

The cell phone in my pocket warmed against my hip. I took it out, about to press the power button. His hand moved, following the direction of my phone as I lifted it and lowered it. Weirdville.

The phone flew out of my hand, hit the mirror surface with a wet plop and landed in Thatch's palm. He tilted his head to the side, staring at it perplexed.

He wasn't supposed to be able to do that. He'd told Josie earlier her cell phone drained his power. Witchkin couldn't use magic on electronics.

He frowned and looked up into the mirror. He wasn't actually looking at me, but he had that expression on his face, the one he wore when he was talking to me. I slowly backed away, glancing hurriedly at Pro Ro's room. It was now dark. I had failed to catch Pro Ro, and I'd lost my phone.

I no longer had any weapon to protect myself from Fae.

All night I worried about Thatch having my phone. What if he went through my photos and found the section of book I'd stolen from his desk and photographed? I'd be in even more trouble. What if the Raven Queen came for me and I had nothing to throw at her?

I kept thinking about Thatch's pain magic and Pro Ro's spell over me, feeling more uneasy as I failed to understand what it all meant.

All day Monday I was grumpy from lack of sleep and anxious over what Thatch might do. After school, I sat at my desk grading art projects students had drawn on recycled paper, my eyes drooping closed. I didn't realize anyone was there until I heard the thud on my desk. I sat up. Thatch sat on the edge, looming over me. He had moved as silently as a ghost.

Before me was my cell phone. I snatched it up and hugged it to my chest.

He pointed a finger at me. "I don't know what kind of magic you're playing with, but you will never spy on me again."

"It was an accident?" I sounded about as lame as one of my students with an excuse for why her homework wasn't done.

He pointed to the phone. "Mr. Khaba will confiscate that if he finds you with it. You might want to hide it."

That was it? He wasn't going to chain me to the dungeon wall or yell at me for invading his privacy? From the wicked way he smiled, I wondered if he'd told Khaba I had an electronic device in my possession for the pleasure of letting Khaba bust me.

I shoved the phone into my sweater pocket and ran all the way back to my dorm. I hid it under my pillow, then thought better of it and turned it on. It didn't work. I popped the back of the phone open and found the battery was missing.

Ugh! That jerk! Where was I supposed to get one of those in the Unseen Realm?

Jeb had been at school for a brief amount of time, but he'd been too busy to see anyone before he'd left. Rumor had it he was looking in Lachlan Falls for the answer keys.

Right. I'm sure the students had time to stash them all the way across the forest and then get back to the school before they'd been apprehended. Still, I could understand he was following any leads that came in. A week remained before he had to come up with those answer keys. It was that or pay the fine.

Needless to say, Jeb didn't have time to talk to little ol' me. I suppose I should have been more understanding—I was the one who would be cut first at the school. But it was hard to think about my job when all I could focus on was whether Pro Ro had hexed me. Did Pro Ro know that I was a Red affinity? Why had he put some kind of curse on me?

To make matters worse, Pro Ro peeked in my classroom twice in the same day, which was majorly weird since he'd never done that before. I longed for Julian to wrap his arms around me and hug me, but he wasn't in his classroom after school.

Because I was a glutton for punishment, I went back to the hall of mirrors. I specifically stayed away from Thatch's room this time. Mostly. I glanced in on the way to Pro Ro's mirror to see if he was done with his macabre painting. His room was dark and the painting was stashed in the corner. Whether he was in his bed, sleeping or elsewhere, I couldn't tell. The curtains of his canopy bed were draped in shadows.

I continued to Pro Ro's mirror. He sat on the floor again, chanting. This time he'd thrown down bones on the floor. I'd heard of that method of divination. The goblet of red fluid next to him didn't look so promising. I wondered whose blood was he drinking. Was this also blood magic?

I sat down on the floor in front of his mirror, waiting for a puff of smoke or a vision to appear. Or for pain to stab into my belly. I took out my cell phone from my pocket. It wouldn't be much good until I went back into the Morty world to get a new battery.

I could only imagine how that conversation with Khaba was going to go. *Would you please chaperone me to get a new cell phone battery? Pretty please?*

Maybe I could get one on the black market if there was a black market in the Unseen Realm. I could use Amazon at Happy Hal's, but I would have to use the school's P.O. box. If my purchase was "accidentally" placed in Thatch's box, I would be out another battery. Maybe Julian would be my knight in shining armor and buy one for me. A guilty smile curled to my lips.

While Pro Ro meditated across from me, I lamented my lack of cell phone. I could have taken photos of Pro Ro for evidence if I'd been able to use it.

I stared at the phone, willing it to work. The plastic was warm in my hand. It pulsed as if it had its own heartbeat. Or perhaps that was just my own.

The battery was just energy. Thatch had told me pain was energy. I could turn magic into energy and energy into magic. I wondered if I could use magic to make a cell phone work. It probably was really hard to do or else Witchkin wouldn't have such trouble with electronics.

I didn't have anything better to do as I waited for Pro Ro to do something impressive. I tried the pain visualization Thatch had taught me, but instead of pain, I sent my energy into the cell phone. After half an hour of effort, the screen lit up!

The case heated up and the stench of burning plastic stung my nostrils. I dropped my phone onto my lap and quickly pushed it onto the floor. The screen went blank. I suspected I had given it too many volts. I tried again, focusing on regulating the energy into a lighter stream. I was able to open the old photos in my camera app. None of my photos had been tampered with.

Beat that, Thatch! *I can do anything you can do better*, I sang to myself. Not literally, but I was getting there.

Pro Ro was still at it with his meditation, giving me the opportunity for evidence. Not that he was doing anything sketchy at the moment other than the goblet of possible blood. Purple half-moons sagged under his eyes. He looked tired.

I raised the phone and snapped a photo. The flash went off. He blinked and glanced around. Oh, shoot! Had the flash passed through the mirror?

I hurried off to bed, afraid he might be powerful enough to suck my phone—or me—through the mirror like Thatch had. I would have to return for more photos another night when he didn't suspect anyone was watching.

I sat alone at my desk before school the following morning. Students wouldn't be coming in for another hour and a half since I didn't have a homeroom. I held my palms a foot apart as I concentrated on making an arc of electricity crackle between them. Pink-and-purple energy shot from one hand to another, reminding me of a plasma ball. Only those were in glass, which might have made it safer.

My department head, Coach Kutchi rushed into my classroom. I hurriedly hid my hands, afraid I'd been caught. I wasn't supposed to be using magic, but now that I had figured it out, I didn't want to stop.

"I need you during homeroom and your prep period today," she said.

"Um." I tried to think of something a normal, not-guilty person would say.

"You're covering for Professor Thatch for two periods. Miss Bloodmire and Mr. Lupi have got his other periods."

"What do you mean? Where is Thatch?"

"*Professor* Thatch," she emphasized. "He's away on business in the Morty Realm. Someone reported an unidentified magical phenomenon at a school. Probably some Witchkin kid who slipped through the cracks. I'm just surprised this is the first one this year. Last year he was away a lot."

Considering I had caused some of those incidents, that was no surprise.

It was actually a noble thing he did, performing this extra duty to help children avoid being captured by Fae. Had circumstances been different, and he hadn't decided he hated me before he'd first laid eyes on me, I wondered if we might have become friends. We were both artists, and I admired his magical competence and classroom management skills. His hair was gorgeous and his British accent seductive. If he didn't scowl at me with such loathing in his eyes—if just once he treated me nicely—I probably would have fallen in love with him on the spot.

I scooped up my papers and dragged myself down to the dungeon. Thatch's homeroom was a group of sleepy students who mostly read. I supposed I should have made the napping students work, but they were quiet, and I didn't care what they did so long as they weren't disruptive. I was so sleepy myself I would have liked to nap.

Twenty minutes in, Khaba dragged Hailey Achilles through the door. Lucky me. Khaba nodded to me.

After gluing me to the ceiling and trying to hex me inside impressionist paintings, Hailey wasn't exactly on my list of favorite students. The most recent apology letter written in blood that Thatch had made Hailey, Balthasar, and Ben write hadn't quite cut it. Still, I had a job to do.

"Good morning," I said to her in the cheeriest voice I could muster. "What homework did you bring to work on?"

She trudged to a seat in the back. "I got nothing."

I walked over to her. "I understand you have a test in your Morty Studies class today. Did you bring your textbook to study?"

She stared at me, aghast. "How'd you know about the test?"

Because teachers talk to each other. Duh. I waggled my fingers at her. "Magic."

That got half of a chuckle out of her, at least. "You going to magic me a book or something? Cuz I lost mine."

Bobby Travis, one of the students from my class, nodded to the back of the classroom. I went to the counter and opened the cupboards. Most were full of alchemy and potion textbooks. The last cupboard held an assortment of textbooks from various classes.

"Which volume of Morty History is it?" I asked.

"First year," someone snickered. "Freshman level."

"How many times has she taken that class?" someone whispered, none-too-quietly.

"Shut up!" Hailey stood up, drawing her wand.

I didn't even know why they let her keep that thing.

"Put it away," I said firmly.

Hailey tucked her wand away. I set the book on her desk with a thud of finality.

"Chapter six?" I asked, guessing.

"Seven and eight," Hailey said, glumly.

I opened the book. There weren't any pictures like in my high school textbooks. I skimmed the first couple lines. Their unit covered ancient China and Japan. "Here's a little trick I learned a long time ago." In fourth grade, but I wasn't going to tell her that. "As you read, make a list of words you don't know. After ten minutes or so, call me over, and we can go over the vocabulary together."

As I seated myself at Thatch's desk, I noted with surprise that Hailey actually followed directions. I managed to grade ten papers from my class and resisted the urge to open any of the drawers of Thatch's desk before she called me over.

"What is this?" She pointed to the first word on her list.

Deciphering her handwriting was a challenge. "Government?"

"Oh, yeah, I know what that is." She pointed to the next one.

"Establishment," I said.

She pointed to more words. It wasn't so much that she didn't understand the meanings, she just couldn't read the words. Together we went back into the text, and I helped her when we came to those words. I asked her a few questions to check her understanding of the material.

"When you have homeroom with Mr. Thatch, we could see if you could come to my classroom instead. I could help you read the next chapter in your history book," I offered.

She leaned back in her chair and groaned. "This is worse than a detention with Thatch or Khaba."

"It's work, I know, but you're doing great."

We made it halfway through a chapter before the bell rang. Students leapt out of their seats for the door.

Hailey shoved the book back at me and grabbed her bag. I went to Thatch's desk and stacked up my ungraded papers.

Hailey paused in the doorway. "Why are you doing this?"

"What do you mean?"

"Trying to *help* me." She said it like it was a bad word.

I lifted my chin. "I'm your teacher. I want you to do well."

"Yeah, but me and Balthasar, we tried to hex you. Ben tried to curse you. You must hate us."

"I can only hope that someday you'll feel true remorse for your behavior."

She rolled her eyes. "I do feel bad. I have lunch and afterschool detention for a month. Plus, Coach won't let me play on the pegasus polo team until I cough up the stupid answer keys."

Not exactly the kind of remorse a teacher hoped for.

"Are you going to?" I asked.

"No, I can't."

"Can't or won't?"

She rolled her eyes and threw up her hands in exasperation in typical teenage fashion.

"Let me know if you change your mind," I called after her. "You can always come to me if you want to talk."

Not that I thought I was going to be able to convince her to tell me where the answer keys were hidden when Khaba and Thatch couldn't, but I had tried. After all, I did want to be employed next semester.

CHAPTER THIRTY
Morty Magic

I was the first teacher to arrive in the cafeteria on Wednesday. I ladled soup into my bowl and selected two slices of French bread before sitting down with the students. I was lucky Jackie Frost arrived next because two boys I didn't know broke out into a fight.

The volume in the cafeteria grew to a roar as students excitedly yelled helpful things like, "Fight! Fight! Fight!"

Jackie rushed toward them. An amorphous ball of murky liquid grew above their heads and then slid between them, spraying out and forcing them apart.

Vega, usually the picture of unhurried grace, came running in from the hallway. What wasn't soaking into the kids' clothes was now a giant puddle on the floor in the middle of the cafeteria. I grabbed a stack of napkins from the staff table and mopped up the puddle, trying to be helpful. Jackie hauled off one kid, and Vega grabbed the other. I was alone in the cafeteria with the students.

The chaos still hadn't settled down, and it wasn't even full of students yet. More teenagers rushed in to see what had happened.

I sat at a table where I could keep my eye on the room. The air was dry, and I kept blinking to moisten my eyes. My goblet of water was now empty. One of the kids complained the soup no longer had any broth. I could guess where Jackie's liquid had come from, and why it had looked so murky.

A student seated next to me bit into a slice of garlic bread, spraying breadcrumbs onto my plate. Too late I realized I had seated myself next to Ben O'Sullivan. There was no way I was going to eat my lunch now that his germcrumbs were on it.

He threw the slice down on the table. "This is stale."

"So what?" another kid said. "We get way worse at the gnome camps."

About half the kids were trying to gnaw through the bread. A few of the older students at other tables closed their eyes and tapped their wands against the mounds of sliced bread on the table. Maybe there was a rehydration spell.

"This sucks balls!" Hailey said.

"Watch your language." I pointed to the other table where teenagers were casting spells. "You could do what they're doing."

"Dude, that is such a good idea! We can use magic! You're a genius, Miss Lawrence," one of the kids said in excitement.

Ben crunched into another slice of bread, spraying the food I wasn't going to eat with more crumbs. Someone across from him waved a wand over the bread on the table and set it on fire. Students leapt back off their benches. The high-pitched shrill of teenage girls screaming almost deafened me.

I could see it was going to be one of those days that everything went wrong. I grabbed my plate of food, overturned it on the flames, and smacked the fire into submission. Ben was the only student who still sat on the bench. His face was red, and he was coughing. Even the teenagers across the table had vacated.

"Miss Lawrence!" a teenager shrieked. She pointed at Ben.

Ben's hands were wrapped around his throat, the universal sign of choking. He was still coughing, trying to clear the food from his throat, but failing. His freckled face was nearly as red as his hair.

Fan-freakin'-tastic.

"Can you breathe?" I asked.

He didn't respond.

"Does anyone have water?" I asked. "Give him a drink of water."

"There isn't any. Miss Frost used it for her spell."

I waved my hand at the kitchen. "Someone, get him water from the kitchen."

"We aren't allowed in the kitchen."

"For the freakin' love of God! It's an emergency. Just go in." I pointed to a girl standing there with wide eyes. She ran off.

I shook one kid by his shirt. "Go get a teacher."

"You are a teacher!"

A teacher who could actually use magic, I meant.

I waved to Josie and called her name. She stood on the other side of the cafeteria, but she didn't see me over the commotion of students on her side of the room still riled up by the fight.

Balthasar raised his wand, pointing it at his friend.

"No more spells!" I shouted. "Do you want him to go up in flames too?"

One of the older kids rushed over with a spell book. "This book has a great charm for wind."

I tore the book out of his hands and threw it on the floor. "Don't use magic unless you know how to use it." Those could have been wise words intended for myself as well.

"Get a wind Elementia!" someone said.

Someone whacked Ben hard on the back.

That was the moment the magic of this world became second to the teacher training I'd received. When I'd taken First Aid while student teaching, the nurse had said everyone always wants to hit a choking person on the back. Sometimes that worked, sometimes it lodged food lower down the windpipe.

I grabbed the kid's arm. "No, don't do that. You'll only make it wor—"

Ben stopped coughing.

The young man who had smacked Ben made a snotty face at me. "See. He isn't choking anymore."

Ben's face had gone from red to purple. The food had been lodged lower. He swayed on the bench. I pushed him upright.

"Help me hold him up." When no one moved, I pointed to two students. Each grabbed one of his arms. I circled my arms around his waist and felt for his navel. I grabbed onto my wrist and moved my fist higher, where I guessed the bottom of his diaphragm was. I dug my fist in.

I performed the Heimlich maneuver, yanking him off the bench as I did so. He nearly toppled onto me, and I pushed him back onto the bench.

"Hold him still," I told the two hanging onto his arms.

"Oh no! What's she doing! It's sex magic," one of the kids said.

Hailey punched the other girl in the arm. "No, it isn't, you moron. It's CPR."

Not exactly, but this wasn't the moment to correct her.

"I did it! I have water!" a girl cried, trying to shove a pitcher at me.

"Can't you see? She's busy," someone said. "Ugh, why are you such a reject?"

I was too focused to respond to the girl or the kid with the attitude.

I struggled with three more abdominal thrusts. Students screamed too close to my ear. My instincts told me to punch them in the face to get them to shut up. Fortunately, I managed to ignore them. After the fifth thrust, a chunk of bread came flying out of Ben's mouth, landing on the table. He coughed, the sound wet and phlegmy.

I tore the water from the girl's hands, sloshing it on myself and Ben as I handed it to him. He gulped it down, stopped to cough, and kept drinking.

"What kind of magic was that?" someone asked.

I pushed a handful of pink hair out of my face. "It's called the Heimlich

Maneuver." I sat down on the floor in the middle of everything, the rush of adrenaline fading.

Hailey elbowed Ben. When he said nothing, she selected a fork from her table and stabbed Ben in the thigh.

He dropped the pitcher and screamed. "What the fuck was that for?"

"Say thank you," she said through clenched teeth.

"Thanks," he said, glancing over his shoulder at me.

He said it almost too quietly to hear. I wouldn't have noticed, except that I realized the kids were actually quiet. Everyone stared at me. Josie crouched at my side, her hand on my shoulder. Professor Bluehorse stood next to Ben.

It was eerily silent. I wondered if I'd gone deaf.

A lone set of hands clapping startled me, and I turned. Imani stood on one of the benches at a table nearby. "Go, Miss Lawrence! You rock!"

The girl next to her clapped. "You just saved that douchebag's life!"

I tried not to laugh.

More students started clapping and cheering. For the rest of the day kids gave me high-fives in the hallway. Julian congratulated me, and even Vega offered me a tight smile. Magic or no magic, the kids had finally accepted me. And maybe the teachers too.

CHAPTER THIRTY-ONE
Unexpected Romances

Pro Ro stood in the hallway outside the cafeteria after dinner. Tonight's turban was a pale blue that matched his flowing robes. Josie and I were discussing Hailey's test score as we came out of the great hall.

Josie was talking so animated with her hands she nearly knocked her mauve witch hat off her head. "This is the highest F she's ever gotten! Usually she just gets two points for writing her name on her paper, and she doesn't always get that because she forgets to write her last name. This was fifty-six percent. It's a record!"

I pretended I didn't see Pro Ro and kept walking. "Aren't there any parents or volunteers who might be able to privately tutor—"

"Ahem," Pro Ro said.

We turned.

"Good evening." I continued walking, unsettled by the intensity in his eyes.

"Miss Lawrence, might I have a word with you?"

"Sure." I grabbed Josie's arm to keep her at my side.

She staggered back. She plastered an obviously fake smile on her face.

Pro Ro chewed on his lower lip. "Alone?" He looked to Josie.

I held her arm even tighter. "Josie and I are going upstairs together. Teacher planning stuff. What's up?"

"Never mind." He turned away and trudged down the hall.

"Creepo," Josie said. "You have got to get an appointment with the principal tomorrow. Don't take no for an answer from Mrs. Keahi. Just walk past her and go in. This is too important."

"That isn't going to help if Jeb isn't at school." He was always off campus for meetings.

I thought of the hall of mirrors. I could probably get in to see Jeb after-hours that way. He might be mad I'd invaded his privacy, but this was more important.

A gentle tap came at my door at eight forty-five as Vega and I were getting ready for bed. My roommate was at her wardrobe, setting out her clothes for the following day. She flicked her hand at me to get the door.

My heart fluttered with hope that it might be Julian. I would have done anything for an excuse to spend time alone with him. It didn't have to be touching—it was better not to be—but just to be in his presence was enough. Almost.

I opened the door, all joy fading. Students were the last visitors I expected. Hailey Achilles held an auburn-haired boy in an arm lock. It was Ben O'Sullivan.

"Um," I said.

"Students aren't allowed up here!" Vega yelled from behind me. "This is the teacher wing."

"It's important," Hailey insisted, eyes on me. "You said I could come and see you any time."

"Ow. Ow. Ow. Let up," Ben said, his arm still twisted behind him.

"What's going on?" I stepped out into the hall and closed the door behind me. "Hailey, why are you twisting his arm like that?"

She shook him. "Tell her."

"Let me go!"

She released him, but she kept one hand on his scrawny neck.

"I'm sorry I tried to hex you a couple weeks ago, and I wanted to thank you more sincerely for saving my life today."

"You're welcome." I had made a bigger impression on the kids than I'd realized.

Hailey nudged him.

"As token of my appreciation, I would like to thank you properly." Ben sighed dejectedly. "I've come to offer you a reward for your services."

I crossed my arms. "What do you mean?"

"He has to grant you a wish because you saved his life. That's how it works for Fae—and those descended from them." Hailey mouthed the word, "Leprechaun."

"Really? I can ask for anything." Delight tickled me.

"I'm only half Fae," Ben said. "I'm limited by my magical abilities. All I have to do is enough to pay my debts."

I crossed my arms. "Right. 'A Lannister always pays his debts' syndrome."

"Huh?" Ben gave me a puzzled look.

There were a lot of things I could ask for as a wish, but I didn't know the skill level of his magical abilities. Even a selfless wish was difficult, considering I could have asked him to behave, to study, or to stay out of trouble. Those weren't magical, of course. Nor did I know if he actually knew how to do any of those. Then again, I'd seen how inept my students were at magic. Maybe I didn't want a magic wish.

In any case, I wasn't going to waste this wish on magic candy or a bucket of hydra water like I had with my last wishes. I needed to think about this and weigh my options. I wanted something that would save my job and the school.

I leaned against the doorway. "Do you know what's going to happen to me at the end of the semester?" Possibly sooner.

He shrugged. "I don't know. Most art teachers don't last that long."

"They might not have enough money to rehire me for next semester. Do you know why?"

"Cuz our school sucks."

I had to give him that. "Art is always the first subject to get cut. Our budget is already stretched thin, maybe too thin to keep me as it is. But the school is facing a fine because someone stole the answer keys to the exams."

He looked to Hailey. "We don't got the answer keys. Everyone thinks that's why we were out of bed."

"If it wasn't to cheat on a test, why were you out?" I asked.

They exchanged glances with each other.

I asked, "Well? You weren't hunting Pokémon, were you?"

Hailey snorted. If she knew what Pokémon and CPR was, she must have been raised in the Morty Realm.

"We were searching for the Ruby of Wisdom," Hailey said.

"Don't tell her!" Ben said.

"It's way better than a stupid answer key. Legend has it that the person who possesses it can master any magical skill. But for centuries it has been lost under the school. The last person rumored to have searched for it was one of the former headmistresses."

"Right." She meant my mother. I returned to the problem at hand. "Professor Thistledown said he heard you talking about the answer key the night you were apprehended."

"No way!" Ben said.

Hailey rolled her eyes. "He's such a tool."

I held up a finger in warning. "I don't want to hear you talk about teachers at this school so disrespectfully."

Ben tried to sneak away, but Hailey grabbed him by the collar and yanked him back. "It would be easy to pass his class if I wanted to," she said.

I doubted that considering her study habits. "Well, maybe you should want to."

She snorted. "You just don't get it, do you?"

"I get that you can't read. I'm willing to help you with that."

"What?" Ben laughed.

Perhaps I shouldn't have said that in front of Ben. Hailey was now going to lose face and behave even worse.

She punched the wall, snarling like a wild cat. "That isn't what I mean." She shook out her fist and shoved Ben away from my door. "Come on, dork breath, let's go. We aren't narcs."

"What are you talking about?" I asked.

They trudged away.

"Great," Ben said. "She didn't use up her wish. That means I still owe her. I hate you."

"Shut up!" she said.

"You, shut up!"

When I opened the door, Vega stumbled back.

I crossed my arms. "Were you listening?"

"No." She made her way over to her bed. "By the way, the next time you're given a wish on a silver platter, you should really consider a charm that will make you taller. Or to make your hair less pink."

"I like pink."

Five minutes later when the lights were out, and we both were lying in bed, she said, "Or to get rid of your freckles."

Ten minutes later she said, "Or to make fish and chips carb-free and fat-free."

Now that I had figured out how to run my cell phone on magically powered electricity, I could use it as a flashlight again. I waited until Vega was asleep before I went to see if Jeb was in his office, in his room, or any of the rooms for that matter. Thatch's mirror was dark red, a slight glow showing through. Probably he'd covered it with a curtain.

Pro Ro was chanting as usual. His turban looked as red as blood again. He sat cross-legged, his hands cupped before him. A fire burned in his palms. Nothing was overly suspicious at first glance. Then I noticed he had a lock of pink hair he burned in the fire. My hair. My core tingled.

I snapped a photo and ran. More than ever, I was certain he had a nefarious plan for me. I wanted to talk to a friend. I wanted to see Julian.

I walked by the other mirrors, considering going to Jeb. My feet took me to Julian's mirror instead. I was drawn to him like a magnet. He was always so nice to me, such a good listener, and so patient. I would have taken him as a teacher over Thatch any day.

When I caught sight of Julian sitting up in bed, I halted. My feet rooted to the floor as shock seized me. He was naked. A teenage girl sat straddled on his lap, also naked.

No, no, no! This couldn't be real. But it was.

My Prince Charming was screwing a student.

CHAPTER THIRTY-TWO
My Future Ex-Boyfriend

I stared, too horrified to move. Hailey's complaint about how to get good grades in Julian's classes finally clicked.

Julian kissed the young woman, his hands roving up and down her back. She was blonde, but I couldn't see who she was. Dinner rebelled against me and roiled in my belly.

That poor girl. She'd been seduced—or worse—coerced by a teacher. I wanted to know who this girl was. She needed counseling.

I needed counseling. How could he do this to me? I thought he'd loved me.

Thatch's reluctance to allow Julian to teach me made sense. Had Thatch known Julian was a womanizer? How could he have turned a blind eye to such unprofessional behavior with students? I tripped back, bumping into a basket of laundry that hadn't been there a moment ago.

I fell on my butt and toppled the contents of the basket onto the floor.

"Oi! Watch it!" the brownie said.

I pointed to Julian and the teenager. "He's sleeping with a student."

"Doesnae look like much sleeping is getting done in there, lass." The little creature threw the laundry back into the basket.

Another spindly creature laughed, dragging a basket of his own down the hallway. "Definitely nae sleeping."

"Don't you care?" I asked. "It's unethical. It's unprofessional. Isn't it illegal? She's a minor."

The brownie kept dragging his basket. "That be some kind of slang? If it is, he's the one using a pickaxe, if you ken my meaning."

"She doesnae look like a dwarf or gnome much to me," the other said.

"A minor, as in underage," I said. "She's a student. He's a teacher."

"None of our business what Morties or Witchkin do."

My vision blurred with tears of frustration. I didn't want to look again, let alone take a photo of what they were doing, but I was afraid if I didn't, no one would believe me. I took a few snapshots and then turned off my phone. Hopefully I wouldn't be accused of keeping child pornography on my phone later.

I didn't know what to do or who to talk to. I doubted Vega would do anything. If Khaba had been in his room, I might have confided in him, but he wasn't. Thatch was out of the question. He'd just tell me I was a dumbass, I shouldn't have been dating a colleague in the first place, and this was what I deserved. From his archaic classroom management methods, I doubted he cared about the student involved.

I trudged down the hall of mirrors. I hesitated at Josie's portal. She lay asleep in a canopy bed. I hated to wake her, but I needed someone to talk to. I jumped through the mirror, tripping on the frame, and stumbled into the foot of her bed.

Josie sat up. "Who's there?"

"It's me. Clarissa."

She touched her wand to an oil lamp. Her hair was in a ponytail and her pajamas were pale pink with skulls on them. Apparently, I wasn't the only one who shopped in the kid's department. She blinked the sleep from her eyes.

"I didn't know where else to go." I flung myself at her and burst into sobs.

She stroked my hair. "What's wrong? Is it Pro Ro? Thatch? Has someone cursed you?"

People who might be trying to kill me felt inconsequential at the moment. "No! It's Julian. I just saw him. He was with a student—in bed with a student."

"What? No way!" Her eyes went wide. "You need to start at the beginning."

She tucked me under the covers and sat beside me while I told her what I'd been doing. She scrolled through the images on my phone. I had to hold onto my phone, so it wouldn't stop working once I broke contact with the device.

She covered her mouth the moment she saw the photo of Julian with the girl. "What a scumbag!" She stopped scrolling when she got to the pics of Pro Ro. "Okay, that's a little creepy too."

I sobbed against her shoulder until no more tears came. "I don't know what to do."

"First, you need to email yourself these pictures. If your phone is confiscated by Khaba, someone else needs to have proof of this. Text them to me, too."

"I don't have service here."

"Email yourself from Happy Hal's tomorrow." She slid out of bed. "First, we're going to see Jeb, and we aren't taking no for an answer." She wrapped herself in a housecoat and then added a violet cape over that. "We're going to tell him and Khaba everything you've seen, but we're going to keep the cell phone out of sight. Unless they ask for proof, we don't need to say you were breaking school rules and using an electronic device. Got it?"

I crawled out of bed and stood beside her. She linked her arm through mine, and we went to the principal's quarters. He didn't answer our knocks, no surprise, it being close to midnight by now.

"Show me the other way," she said. "The way you came to me in my room through the mirrors."

I didn't want to see Julian again, but I led her to the hallway anyway.

We passed a group of brownies dragging laundry baskets in the hallway of mirrors. One raised a fist at me and shook it. "What ye be going bringing more bootlickers into our workspace? Ye ken this isnae a funhouse. Stay outta our passage, and donnae bring no more human folk this way, you hear?"

Josie didn't even acknowledge them. She headed straight toward the windows of silvery light. Teachers were asleep in their rooms. Pro Ro had gone to bed.

I kept my eyes down when we came to Julian's room. It was dark now. I could see him in his bed, asleep. I couldn't tell if anyone else was there with him, though in truth, I didn't try to look very hard. Josie crossed her arms, staring into his room.

Khaba was still absent from his quarters. Jeb's parlor was empty, as was his office. His bedroom was too dark to tell if he slept in there or not.

"Come on," Josie said. "Like it or not, here we come."

We strode through the looking glass like Alice in her adventures. It must have been the thought of Lewis Carroll that made me think of pedophiles anew.

The room was darker than it had been through the mirror. Josie walked over to a lamp and tapped it with her wand. The bed was empty.

The furnishings were tasteful, a medieval mahogany bed with matching dressers, wardrobe, and nightstand carved with the same intricate pattern of flowers. Compared to the clutter of his office, this room was sparsely furnished, looking like it belonged to a completely different man.

"None of his wards are going off. That is so bizarre," Josie said.

I shrugged. "I guess it makes sense. This is how the brownies get around. If an alarm rang every time they cleaned up, it would be going off every night."

Josie opened the door and strode into his sitting room. "That must be how the kids broke into his office at the beginning of the year. And probably how they stole the answer keys."

I wasn't so sure about either of those theories. I didn't think the students had stolen the answer keys. Someone had. According to Khaba, I was the one who would find them. No pressure.

I followed Josie through the principal's private rooms, down a set of stairs, and to Jeb's messy office. She sat at his table and lifted a quill from its stand. "Shall I write him the note or would you like to?" she asked.

"You do it," I said.

I paged through a stack of files on his desk, wondering if Jeb might have simply lost the answer keys in the mess of his office. If I found them, he'd be pleased with me. He wouldn't dare fire the teacher who saved the school.

Khaba threw open the door a moment later, dressed in a long leopard-print muumuu that might have been a nightgown. His jaw dropped, and he looked from me to Josie.

"How'd you know we were here?" she asked.

"You triggered the alarms." He straightened. "The more important question is *how* did you get in?"

I hadn't heard any alarms go off. Maybe they were silent. I didn't want to have to show him the mirrors and endure being sidetracked. I got to the point. "We need to speak with Jeb. It's important."

"We were leaving a note for Jeb," Josie said. "Where is he?"

"Off campus, probably getting raked over the coals for losing the answer key. You know this isn't going to look good for you." Khaba tilted his head to the side, studying me. "Jeb's already gotten it in his head Miss Lawrence is somehow behind the missing answer keys. I'm going to have to report that you broke into his office."

I was going to get in trouble for doing the right thing?

Josie nudged me. "Tell him why we're here."

I started the story again.

When I returned to my room, I didn't get much sleep. I tossed and turned most of the night. I used my cell phone flashlight to check the time on Vega's clock on the wall. It was close to three, and I was still awake. The only thing that would have relieved my stress was slicing things in the guillotine.

I wanted to slice more than paper right now.

But it wasn't fair to my roommate, bitch queen as she was, to wake her up with chopping noises just because I was miserable.

Eventually I did fall asleep. I dreamed I walked through a shimmery blue world. For the first time since practicing the exercises from the book on lucid dreaming, I was aware of myself. I knew this wasn't my normal waking life.

At the same time, the dream had a surreal, otherworldly quality that made me suspect this was more magic than the subconscious at work.

The entire school looked like it was submerged underwater, like when Thatch had cast the spell in the tattoo shop. It must have been passing time between classes in the dream, because the halls were full of students. Yet, no one saw me. I glided up the steps and across the corridor as if I were a ghost.

The everyday shrieks and shouts of the students were muffled. I floated down to the boy's wing and up to the teacher's rooms on the level above. I didn't even know how I knew where the boy's dormitories were. I'd never been there. But that was the thing about dreams. Everything made a lot more sense when you dreamed them.

Soundlessly I floated through a door. Pro Ro sat on the floor in a circle of candles. They dripped into puddles of wax, as though he'd been chanting for hours. Tarot cards were laid out along with a dead chicken.

He stabbed a pink-haired voodoo doll with pins. Blood dripped out from the center of the doll. He chanted in some kind of satanic tongue. A fire flared up in front of him. Out of the smoke, a demon uncurled itself. The demon happened to look a lot like Julian, only with horns and covered in soot. The demon danced, and Pro Ro laughed.

Pro Ro unwound the dark blue turban on his head. I became more aware of my body, of the sharpness in my abdomen stabbing me like knives. My affinity grew and then shrank. The red light inside me fluttered uncontrollably, and I found myself panting and sweating from the lances of fire.

The blue strips of fabric around Pro Ro's temples fell away. His head turned around like in *The Exorcist*, and on the top of his crown was Alouette Loraline's face.

Everyone was always telling me how much I resembled my biological mother; it would have been logical to question how I knew it was her and not me. Her hair was darker, for one, but that might have just been a trick of the light. It had to be the glowing red eyes and the teeth filed to sharp points—both of which I lacked. Her mouth twisted into a wicked grin, and she bit the head off the pink-haired doll. Blood spurted from the doll's neck.

I woke up screaming.

"Six o'clock already?" Vega asked. "That can't be right."

I sat up, panting and frantic with fear.

Vega tapped the oil lamp with her wand, and the room was lit in golden light. She looked at the clock on the wall. She sighed in disgust, turned the light out, and fell back asleep. I laid down, but I couldn't rest. This was just my subconscious mind playing tricks on me because of all the things I'd seen the night before. Plus, the turban thing was so *Harry Potter and the Sorcerer's Stone*, it couldn't be real.

I wanted to believe it was all a figment of my imagination, but my intuition told me it was more than that.

CHAPTER THIRTY-THREE
Try This One Weird Trick That Worked for J.K. Rowling

I was on edge all Thursday morning. Between Pro Ro's curse and Julian's underaged womanizing, I could barely focus on classes. I wondered about that girl who had been in his room. I didn't know her name. My worries flickered back to Pro Ro. What motivation would he have for cursing me?

During third period, Thatch emerged from the stairwell that led to my closet, skulking into my classroom like a shadow. He must have used the passage from the dungeon, but he remained free of spiderwebs. His hair was as immaculate as ever.

Never mind I was in the middle of helping a student with shading, Thatch interrupted. "Headmaster Bumblebub wants me to inform teachers there's yet another emergency meeting after school. Three forty-five. Staff room. You know the drill."

I glared at him.

"What's with you?" He looked me up and down. "You look like death warmed over. And I don't mean that in a good way."

If we'd been alone I would have chewed him out. Why hadn't he told me Julian had been sleeping with students? Why did he let him get away with it? He should have told Jeb. I hated him.

He lifted his hands, in a gesture of feigned innocence. "Don't shoot the messenger."

I crossed my arms.

"Aren't you at all curious what the meeting is going to be about?" he asked.

"No." If it wasn't because we needed a new history teacher, I didn't care.

"I want to know!" one of the students said.

Thatch leaned closer, his tone conspiratorial. "The missing answer keys."

Maybe. That note I had left for Jeb had explained enough to warrant an emergency staff meeting.

Students gasped. "Did they find the answer keys?"

"We'll find out, won't we?" The smirk on his mouth faded as he looked to me. "One would think someone in your position would be more . . . interested in the outcome of today's meeting. The quarter ends tomorrow. If we don't find the answer keys by then. . . ." He raised an eyebrow. "Let's just say, the dark arts and crafts are always the first to be cut."

Students shrieked and cried behind him. "Not art! They can't cut art! It's my only fun class."

Thatch shrugged, a malicious smile on his face.

"Get out." I pointed to my closet.

He straightened. "I was only jesting. They *probably* aren't cutting your position."

"Miss Lawrence is in a bad mood today," one of the students whispered.

"I am not!" I shouted.

Ophelia Maker, a pixie-ish girl whispered, "Maybe it's her time of the month, like that werebear teacher we used to have."

Thatch shook his head at the student. "I highly suggest you close your mouth before your teacher does it for you. I hear Miss Lawrence is highly formidable when it comes to the magical Heimlich maneuver."

I didn't answer. I gave three detentions that day. Obviously, it wasn't my best day.

One day. I had one day before my job might end. I wanted to care, but I was numb inside. Whenever I thought of Julian and what I'd seen, I wondered if I wanted to work at a school where everyone turned their heads the other way every time a teacher behaved with such gross misconduct. No wonder Loraline had gotten away with so much. They were negligent at this school.

My fairy godmother had been right about the rules to this world. The Unseen Realm wasn't a fair place. They didn't value human life here. I would never fit in or agree to the way things were.

After school was over, I trudged up the stairs toward the staff meeting.

Pro Ro caught me in the corridor on the way. "Miss Lawrence, you must come with me. I need to speak with you alone."

I glanced at his blue turban, experiencing déjà vu. My mother was not under there. Nor was anyone else. Even so, everything in my body told me to run from him.

"We have a meeting in three seconds," I said.

He grabbed my wrist. "This is more important. It's about you and Julian

Thistledown. I had a vision."

His touch sent a spasm through my core. I wrenched my arm away. "Oh really? Well, I'm guessing you saw me breaking up with him." I thought better of that statement and quickly added, "Not that we were ever dating." I started up the stairs to the next level where the staff meeting would be.

He took the steps, two at a time. "Both your lives are in grave danger."

"Sure, they are. And if I just follow you alone into the forest, you'll make sure I stay safe."

His brow furrowed. "I'm not joking. This is serious. I saw you murdering Julian this very day."

CHAPTER THIRTY-FOUR
The Psycho Ex-Girlfriend

I was crabby, but I wasn't crabby enough to murder someone. I hated Julian, and I wanted him fired for his unprofessional conduct with a student, but I didn't want him dead. Much. Yes, I had an evil witch of a mother who had killed and tortured multiple people and blew up the school. But I had no intention of following in her footsteps.

"Baloney." My laughter came out as a wicked shriek that rivaled the Wicked Witch of the West. That didn't help my case of not being evil.

Pro Ro tried to say more, but I wasn't listening. I bent over, cackling so hard I wiped tears from my eyes.

Vega poked her head out of the doorway of the conference room. "Would you two fucktards hurry up? Principal Dumb-ass won't start until everyone is here. Some of us have places to be this evening."

A seat at the conference table was open next to Julian. He waved at me and smiled cheerily. I ignored him and took the seat between Vega and Jasper Jang. That put me across from Julian. I looked everywhere but at him.

My blood felt like it was about to boil. I was exhausted from the lack of sleep, my coffee was wearing off, and I wished I had asked Khaba for a special candy.

Now that I was in the room with Julian, I wasn't so sure I wouldn't kill him.

"Attention, y'all. Attention," Jeb said. "We ain't got time to waste. We need to discuss the stolen answer keys."

The room quieted.

"Darshan, would you kindly apprise us of anything new since we last

255

spoke?" the principal asked.

Something slid against my ankle. Julian was slouched low in his chair, probably so he could reach me to play footsie. I kicked him as hard as I could.

He grunted and moved his foot away. He glanced at Vega as if he thought she had done it. I smiled pleasantly. Thatch's head snapped up from where he sat farther down the table, looking from Julian to me. I wondered if Thatch had gotten a dose of pain magic just then.

Pro Ro coughed and tugged at his tunic. "I'm sorry to say, not much. For hours each night, I have divined using every method I know. Nothing new has resulted from my attempts."

My eyes narrowed. If only he spent half the time divining for answer keys as he did casting spells on people.

Pro Ro licked his lips. "As far as I can tell, the answer keys aren't missing at all. The students don't have them. I can't even see who stole them."

"So much for our divination teacher being able to divine," Vega muttered.

Khaba fiddled with the long line of his open shirt. "It could be powerful Fae magic." He shifted uncomfortably. "Magic so powerful I can't detect it."

I remembered my previous conversations with the kids. Hailey had insisted they didn't have the answer keys. Thatch and Khaba couldn't get any information out of them. I raised my hand and spoke before anyone told me not to. "Maybe the students don't have it because they never had it. Is it possible it's somewhere in your office? Or that a staff member like a brownie might have accidentally grabbed it, Headmaster?"

"Principal," someone corrected.

"What? That's plumb crazy." Jeb said. "We've looked multiple times."

His office was also extremely messy. It wouldn't surprise me if it had gotten lost in there.

Khaba wrote something down in a notebook. Maybe he would check into the brownies.

Jeb went on. "Besides that, I know where the answer keys have been hidden, thanks to Professor Thistledown. It's in the forest! Darshan, now that you know where to concentrate your efforts, you'll find it by hook or crook."

Thatch rubbed at the stubble on his chin. "Pray, Professor Thistledown, how did you come across this information?"

Julian squirmed under Thatch's scrutiny. "One hears things from students."

Josie and I made eye contact. Was this pillow talk between him and a specific student? I studied the principal. He didn't look in the least bit suspicious of Julian. Hadn't he read my goddamned note? Maybe he just had a good poker face, and he was going to take me aside after the meeting and talk to me about Julian. I fidgeted, kicking my foot against my chair in agitation until Vega turned to glare at me.

Pro Ro shook his head. "It isn't in the forest."

"Julian, will you share what you overheard?" Jeb asked.

"Tonight during the big game—during the pegasus polo tournament—some of the students are going to sneak away from the stadium and go into the woods. They will head toward the Morty Realm—away from the village. That's where we went wrong in our previous searches. We were looking toward Lachlan Falls. If we follow the students as they leave the game tonight, we'll be able to find the answer keys." Julian sat back in his chair, his grin a little too satisfied. His gaze settled on me.

Teachers all started talking at once. Anger exploded in the room, and this time it wasn't coming from me. I kicked at my chair, no one hearing the thuds now. The charge of emotions from the staff stoked my affinity like kindling to a fire. It took everything I could do not to fracture into a storm of rage.

Jasper Jang threw up his hands in disgust. "Not another wild-goose chase."

"I already have plans tonight," Vega said.

"We need to organize teams posted at intervals in the forest and outside the stadium to apprehend them," Khaba said.

"Not apprehend. Follow them," Julian insisted.

"Are you saying we can't attend the game? This is the last one of the season!" Silas Lupi said.

"How do we know this is a real tip, unlike the last one?" Grandmother Bluehorse asked.

I should have been more invested in the outcome of the search for the answer keys considering the fate of my job rested on finding them. A low murmur caught my attention. Pro Ro closed his eyes and chanted. A funny, fluttery feeling swelled and then died in the pit of my stomach. I focused on the energy in my core. It felt like an invisible string was attached to me, tugging at my affinity. A prick like a needle stabbed into my belly.

"Stop it," I said, my voice barely audible over the din in the room.

Pro Ro didn't stop. He chanted faster, louder. Jasper Jang and Vega turned to look at me.

I stood. "Stop it! I know you're casting a spell on me."

His eyes remained closed. He ducked his chin down. Josie stood, her wand raised and pointed at Pro Ro. The air crackled with static electricity. Red pain roiled in my belly.

Jeb's hair stood on end. Wind rustled the papers on the table and the robes of the staff members. Jackie Frost's witch hat went flying from her head. The breeze was warm, like it had come from the bowels of hell. My affinity threatened to burst.

A witch followed her instincts. The lucid-dreaming book had said I needed to decipher the truth in my heart from what my head told me not to believe. I couldn't keep quiet any longer. I had to show everyone what I knew in my heart.

"It's under his turban!" I said. The commotion of the teachers died down. "Her face is under the turban, and I'll prove it."

I launched myself across the table and tackled the turban like a football player. Pro Ro cried out as I wrestled it off him. It was attached better than I would have thought.

Pro Ro raised his hands, trying to defend himself. Julian grabbed onto my wrist. I got in a good punch to Julian's eye. Teachers unleashed a jumble of spells as they tripped over each other to get to me. Julian got the levitation spell probably intended for me, Vega received a restraint spell—which I suspected she secretly liked—and Jeb ended up domed off from everyone. My flailing arms and legs kicked a few wands out of nearby hands and knocked people into each other.

Thatch sat at the end of the table, drumming his fingers against the table with a look of bored indifference on his face.

"Look!" I said, still sprawled across the table as I tore the turban free of Pro Ro's head. "Loraline is under here."

Everyone froze. Wide-eyed horror spread across the faces of my colleagues.

On the top of Pro Ro's head was a bald spot. Not my mother's face. Fucktacular.

CHAPTER THIRTY-FIVE
Why Couldn't You Just Have Been Under There, Mother?

There are some things one cannot undo. Attacking a peer and accusing him of having the face of your evil mother instead of a bald spot is one of them.

Pro Ro stared at me in bewildered horror. "What? I've never even met the woman. Why would she be under my turban?"

"Indeed!" Jeb said.

"Oh my God!" Josie said. "This isn't *Harry Potter*, girl."

Thatch covered his eyes with his hands. He was shaking with anger, or more likely, laughter. Only someone sadistic would find this moment funny.

Josie grabbed the hem of my skirt and tugged it over my behind. Yep, not only had I launched myself at another teacher, but I'd just mooned everyone I had been sitting next to. At least I wore my striped leggings.

Khaba flicked his hand at me, and I slid backward off the table and into the chair.

"You did cast a spell on me. I could feel it." I pointed at Pro Ro, at a loss for anything else to say.

Pro Ro's nostrils flared. His cheeks turned crimson. "Indeed. At Jeb's request."

Jeb's eyes were full of pity. "A spell of protection, darlin'. To ensure your safety. Darshan has been having visions."

"We wanted to protect you," Pro Ro said.

This just kept getting worse and worse. I smoothed my pink hair out of my eyes and stood. People flinched back. Josie stared with wide eyes. She turned away. Khaba grimaced. One of my heels was missing from my shoe, and I nearly lost my balance.

I righted myself and walked out of the conference room with as much dignity as a drowned cat.

"Someone is getting fired," Vega said, none-too-quietly.

My heart plummeted even further. I didn't doubt it.

This was the newest worst day of my life. What I didn't know then was it was about to get worse.

CHAPTER THIRTY-SIX
The Turban Was for Religious Reasons. Duh.

I didn't know how I would live with my humiliation. I had just reaffirmed the view that I was descended from a crazy psycho bitch and the apple didn't fall far from the tree. I'd made wild assumptions about my colleagues and discredited myself as a source of reliable information. No one would believe me when I told them Julian Thistledown seduced minors. They would see me as jealous and unstable. Could I blame them?

And if I did show them the evidence on my phone, it would be another mark against me that I'd used the evils of technology on school grounds.

This had to be the moment representing the bitterest of bites in my prophecy chocolate. I had thought there would be way more sweetness this semester. Where was the creamy caramel that my prophecy chocolate had promised?

I passed Imani in the hallway. She sat at the feet of a suit of armor. A girl with green skin and elf ears sat next to her. A book was open in front of them, and they giggled. I wanted to smile for her, to be happy she'd made a friend. But I was too miserable with my own lack of friends. As close as I'd grown to Josie, I doubted our friendship would withstand my level of crazytown.

For no good reason at all, I had attacked a coworker. I had based my rationale on a freakin' dream—an obsession with a childhood book. If I was lucky, Jeb would terminate my position at the end of the quarter for "budgetary reasons" as opposed to the truth: religious discrimination and harassment of staff. All my fantasies of teaching at a magical school were over.

I couldn't bear seeing another adult and being asked to explain my fallible logic. The other teachers would be going to the game or out in the forest soon. I went straight to my room and packed my suitcase before Vega returned.

After I completed packing, I headed to my classroom to finish grading mid-terms and marking grade reports. I wrote detailed lesson plans for the next two weeks so that whoever came in to replace me wouldn't have to scramble to figure out what to do. The normal state of any art classroom was an environment of chaos. Not wanting someone else to walk into that mess, I packed all the pencils and chalk neatly in their containers, stacked the drawing paper, and made piles of student work to pass back. I organized like there was no tomorrow, mostly because I didn't think there would be.

My belly growled with hunger. Checking my cell phone clock, I saw it was an hour past dinner time. I didn't want to get anything to eat and risk stumbling into anyone. I should have grabbed a snack from my dorm earlier, but I hadn't thought about it then, and there was no way I was going back and risk running into Vega. I stacked my own personal supplies in a box on my desk and added my framed drawings on top.

In a stack of student art ready to be passed back, I turned the perspective drawings the same direction. Most were drawn on the recycled paper Khaba had given me from the office. One incomplete sketch displayed the worst perspective drawing I'd ever seen. The student hadn't used a ruler and for some reason there were two horizon lines. I turned it over to see who it belonged to. There was no name on the back, but there were a series of letters and numbers on the recycled paper. The top said: Spring Exam Answer Key, page 3.

I gasped. Was it really the lost answer key? On the back of a student drawing? I clutched it to my chest, not believing my luck. How had it gotten in a stack of recycled papers?

The papers had come from Jeb's office. I looked at the back of the other student art. Mostly they were memos, meeting notes, fiscal reports, and detention forms, but I found two additional pages to the answer key on the back of student art.

I could still save the day! Womby's wouldn't be fined. No one would have to be fired!

My heart sank again. Except, I would still be fired. A few hours ago I might have been a hero, but there was no way to redeem myself. I couldn't face Jeb and give it to him now. He'd think I had stolen it.

I placed it in the top drawer of my desk to keep it safe. I could ask Josie for help, but from the way she'd turned away from me in the meeting, I didn't know if she still considered me a friend. Perhaps I would never see her again after this.

I continued to pack my desk and tidy the classroom. My fairy godmother had taught me to leave every place you left cleaner than when you'd found it.

Next, I started on my posters. I didn't care about the motivational posters, but I wanted the Van Gogh, Frida Kahlo, Michelangelo, and the Leonardo posters that had cost me twenty dollars each.

I pushed a table up to the wall and stood on it, trying to hook my nails under the edge of the Sistine Chapel ceiling poster to peel it off. The problem was, Josie had used magic to put them up. I didn't know how to undo that.

"Hello, hello," Julian called from the doorway. His tone was annoyingly chipper.

I glanced over my shoulder at him and turned back to the poster. "What do you want?" A small edge of the paper tore.

"I didn't see you at dinner. I thought you might like something to eat. You did say lasagna was your favorite?" He set the plate on my desk.

"Aren't you supposed to be at the big game, hunting for answer keys some student told you was hidden in the woods? Funny how you convinced someone to tell you when no one else could."

"What can I say? He gives them the stick. I offer the carrot." He laughed at his own joke.

Ugh, that was probably a euphemism.

My affinity roiled like snakes inside me. Pro Ro might have been right when he said Julian was in danger of being murdered by me. I stared at the poster, forcing myself to breathe in butterflies and classical art and breathe out yucky thoughts of negativity and murder.

Julian strode over. "Say, what are you doing up there?"

My voice came out about as monotone as Thatch's. "I'm taking down all the posters Josie magically taped to the walls."

"Oh, let me help you with that." He flourished his wand in the air.

The air smelled of musky earth and wet wood. Green light glittered against the walls. All the posters floated down to the floor. My sweater unbuttoned itself and flew off as well. Fortunately, I wore a tank top underneath.

He offered me his hand as I hopped down from the table. I ignored him and retrieved my sweater from the floor.

"Oopsie," he said with a chuckle. "Did I do that?"

Fortunately for him, dirty looks couldn't kill. "Get out of my classroom." I shoved my arms through the sleeves of my sweater.

"I know you had a bad day. No one blames you. Josie said you were up half the night with worry about something. She implied she had evidence to support your suspicions. And Vega said you had nightmares." He stepped in closer, arms outstretched to hug me.

I put up a hand. "Don't touch me."

His eyes were hurt. "What's gotten into you?"

"No, not what's gotten into me? What's gotten into you? You act like you're interested in me, like we're dating, and this whole time you've been having sex with minors?"

He stared at me wide-eyed.

I snatched up my posters from the floor. "I don't want anything to do with you."

"I would never sleep with a student. Whatever those students said, they're liars."

I froze. *Students.* As in plural. "How many girls have you slept with?"

"None." He stood there awkwardly, shifting from foot to foot. A tight smile stretched across his face.

"Don't lie to me. I saw you having sex with that girl last night." Fury built inside me.

"Oh, that." He coughed. "There's a perfectly good explanation for that." He coughed again. It was a delaying tactic. I'd seen students do it often enough. "Someone cast a spell on me. I couldn't help it. I wasn't myself."

"Right." I plopped the posters down on a table. "And the other students?"

"Sweetie, you have to believe me. I only want you."

I fumbled for the key to the closet in my pocket, making my way around the horseshoe shaped enclosure of desks. "I don't have to believe you. I don't have to do anything."

I inserted the key in the lock, opened the door, and strode through it. He rushed toward me. I slammed the door in his face. It closed with a satisfying thud.

I used my phone as a flashlight as I made my way down the stairs. It crossed my mind I could walk all the way down to the dungeon with those stairs. Thatch had come up the stairs often enough, but I didn't want to encounter my frenemy, the dungeon master, in case he wasn't out looking for answer keys with everyone else. I stepped onto the landing to my supply closet and unlocked the door. The light illuminated my scant supplies. I took in a shaky breath, anger still rattling through me. I'd made it this far through the day without succumbing to hysterical sobbing. I could make it a little longer.

I set my phone on a shelf. The blue glow of light died away, but the closet wasn't dark. Green light glowed from behind me, casting my shadow on the wall.

The hairs on the back of my neck prickled. My energy spiked and dipped. A cramp shot through my core. The sensation of a string tugging on my ribcage stole my breath. It was like someone had hooked a line to my insides and was trying to lure me in like a fish.

The air smelled earthy and green with undertones of decay and rotting leaves. His breath was shallow, almost inaudible behind me.

"I told you to leave me alone. I don't want to talk to you." I whirled, freezing when I saw *him.*

Or maybe *it* would have been more accurate.

CHAPTER THIRTY-SEVEN
The Green Man's Monastery

The scream caught in my throat as I stared in horror. I had dreamed Julian was a demon, but this was so much worse.

The creature on the landing before me was Swamp Thing on steroids. Lacy moss and tufts of lichen hung from his body like clothes. A ridge of bark-like horns sprouted from the ferns and leaves of his hair. His skin was made of decaying wood.

His spine was hunched, bent like a snake curling over prey. His feet were more like the talons of a bird than anything human or plant. He was beautiful and dangerous, like a bog on a misty morning, waiting for someone to sink her feet into the earth to swallow her whole. The cramping in my belly grew stronger. A centipede crawled out of a knot in the wood that made up his face and scurried into his ear. He smiled, his teeth sharp points, uneven and rotting like the bark of his flesh.

"W-what are you?" I asked. Part of my brain, that logical analytic side chided me for my rudeness. That was considered an impolite question in this world. The other part of my brain was screaming incomprehensible gibberish.

I snatched up my phone and held it out protectively in front of me.

"Don't you recognize me, sweetie?" He chuckled. The voice wasn't quite Julian's, but close enough to recognize him.

"Do you understand now why one woman isn't enough for me, for a green man? I am a being of fertility and virility. In my blood flows the magic of ancient gods." He stepped closer. Vines grew out of his body, curling themselves toward me. One tickled my ankle.

I darted backward, away from him and into the closet. It wasn't ideal, but there was nowhere else to go.

He smiled. "My magic is stronger than Thatch or Vega or any Celestor at this school. I'm more powerful than Khaba with his limited wishes only to be granted when someone rubs his lamp. Even Jeb couldn't fathom the depths of my power. What a joke it was to play along with what the other teachers thought of me and pretend to be the blundering weakling who was too inept to even chaperone you to Lachlan Falls. You never stood a chance against my magic." Another tendril brushed my ankle.

I kicked at it.

"Neither did the other art teachers." He laughed wickedly. "I'm only surprised you were able to resist for as long as you did. But then, I can blame Thatch for that, always undoing my enchantments. What he called a curse, I call a gift."

Wings beat against the window, the light flashing in flickering shadows. I glanced behind me at the bird thud-thudding against my window. Was it Thatch's crow or the Raven Court?

"Stop. Don't come any closer," I said, holding up my phone. "I have this phone. I'm prepared to hurt you with it if I have to."

A vine shot out of his hand, grabbed my wrist and smashed my knuckles against the edge of the shelf. I cried out and dropped the phone.

I cradled my throbbing hand to my chest. "What do you want with me? Why are you doing this?"

"Do you really think I intend to work at this lowly school, making a poverty level wage for the rest of my life? The Raven Queen isn't the only one who wants you and is willing to pay for your life. She may employ Thatch to spy on you, to guide you to her side, but he isn't the only emissary working for the Fae."

My heart sank. Just when I had thought Thatch wasn't so bad.

Vines slithered around me, grabbing onto me and drawing me closer to him. "Of course that was before I had a taste of you for myself."

I screamed. The sound echoed in the stairwell. I tried to pull away, to push against his chest, but his vines held me there. I shrieked and thrashed.

His laugh was deep and throaty. "Who do you think is going to come to your aid? Jeb? The old loon is away. All the teachers are in the forest. There are no unicorns to save you. Even Thatch can't rescue you this time."

"Thatch?" I tried to yank myself free, but the vines held. "When did he try to save me?"

"He suspected there was a hex on your drink at the pub and attempted to use a counter curse to cleanse it." Vines slithered against my skin, exploring and prodding me.

I had accused Thatch of enchanting my drink, and he'd purposefully spilled it. For all his assholery, he hadn't been out to poison me.

"Wait, so Thatch didn't want to kill me because he wanted my job? It was all you?"

"He's been trying to keep you safe. But he's not here, is he? Could it be he's not half as good at divination as he claims?" Julian cackled.

The vines tightened around me, making it difficult to breathe. All of this was starting to make sense. Julian had thrown the spotlight off himself by blaming Thatch for everything. The last art teacher, Jorge Smith, had been snooping around, so he must have found out what Julian had done.

"Please, Julian." I shook my head. "You and me, we're friends. Don't do this."

"You don't know what you are, do you?" He licked my ear.

I turned my head away. The vines caressed my arms. One slid under my skirt, tickling behind my knee.

"I knew the moment Alouette Loraline had a daughter, you would have the same affinity. Jeb assumed you might be Celestor, but I knew the truth about what she was." He brushed the rough wood of his fingers against my cheek. "Your Red affinity solves the Fae Fertility Paradox. You'll strengthen my powers with your own."

Did he know about Thatch? About Imani? I prayed no one knew.

He purred against my ear. "Your body will make the perfect vessel to sire my heirs. You won't break like the other art teachers."

I screamed again.

"And the best part is, you'll have no choice but to enjoy it."

"No, I won't!"

I struggled against him. He clawed the sleeve of my sweater off one arm. He buried his face in my neck, nibbling his way across my skin and down my arm. Tingles pulsed over my flesh where his lips trailed. My face grew warm. His touch was like a drug. The more he stroked my skin, the more I lulled under his spell. Or was it under *my* spell?

Thatch had been right. I couldn't tell the difference between my own desires and someone else's. Even knowing this, I was powerless to stop it. I sank into his arms. Arousal flushed through me. I smoothed my hand over the frilly texture of ferns and moss covering his chest.

A sharp spasm of pain stole my breath. The hydra had said I was cursed. Perhaps it meant this pain, the spell Julian had cast over me, or perhaps it meant my willingness to give in to any man's desires that weren't my own. Derrick in my dreams had told me the same thing—Derrick, who I hadn't thought of in ages. Was it because of what Julian had done to me? He'd made me forget my vow to find my best friend.

Thatch had warned me not to let anyone know what my affinity was. He had told me someone might use me. Now here I was, about to become slave to someone else's will.

I closed my eyes, savoring the texture of wet wood kissing my face and the smell of earth. My body responded with yearning while my mind resisted. I had to think. I had to find a way to gain power over myself. But it was hard to focus. My body melted into his vines. My core throbbed with pleasure and pain. My affinity raged inside me like a storm.

Thatch had said it was dangerous to give my pain to someone else. I'd seen as much from what had happened with Josie. He had said I could kill a person if I wasn't careful. Jeb had feared what might happen if I gave in to carnal desires. The electrical explosion in the tattoo parlor had been evidence of that, as if my sordid past didn't offer enough examples.

I did the one thing I could do at that moment to combat Julian Thistledown. I kissed him with everything I had in me and sent my pain from my lips into his.

CHAPTER THIRTY-EIGHT
A Merlin-class Celestor's Divination

As my lips met Julian's and I gave in to desire, the energy inside me spiked, as did the pain. The air smelled sharp, like ozone right before lightning strikes. I visualized the angry red ball growing inside me. I pushed it out through my hands. Lightning exploded out of my core and through my body. I forced it into him.

He screamed and unfurled to his full height. Light crackled across my skin and shot into him. The magic slammed him hard into the wall. He writhed as pink-and-blue arcs of electricity sizzled into him. Desire was gone. The simmering heat of my own rage was all that remained.

I rammed him into the wall again and again with fingers made of lightning. Even after he was silent, I continued to burn his flesh. His crumpled remains fell onto the stairs. His body smoked.

I shook so hard I could barely breathe. I was smoking too. Slowly I slid against the wall, my knees buckling.

I sat, my legs curled up to my chest. The pain between my legs was so great it felt as though I sat on razor blades. I tried to move, but this only magnified the pain. Bleeding blisters speckled my palms. The charred flesh of my hands looked more like burnt meat than my own skin. My lips hurt. I trembled so violently my teeth chattered. Cold sweat drenched my back. The world was a tunnel closing in on all sides, growing darker. Colder.

The light from the window shifted, the orange rays of sunset falling on Julian's blackened face. I couldn't stop staring. His pants were down around his knees. It was hard to see where the shadows ended and the scorched remains of his body began. He no longer resembled the Julian I had known, only remnants of the monster he'd become. Charred vines and dried leaves lay scattered across the stairs.

The light coming in from the window faded, and I was left in darkness. I slumped sideways against the shelves, too exhausted to sit upright. The tremors slowly subsided. What I'd thought had been pain before was trivial compared to the growing agony inside me. The angry stabbing deep in my pelvis stole my breath away. Getting a tattoo was nothing compared to this.

Thatch had showed me how to control pain, to transfer that into energy inside me. But I was too exhausted to concentrate. I had only managed to shift energies when I'd been able to focus on my body without the pain. I didn't have the willpower now.

Something tickled across my arm. Probably a spider. I was too preoccupied with my misery to care. Every breath stabbed my lungs. The floor I sat on was wet. I wasn't sure if I sat in a puddle of my own urine or blood. Maybe I was dying.

The hallway brightened. A figure cloaked in shadows came into view.

My gaze fixed on the raven perched on the figure's shoulder. Someone from the Raven Court? His feet made no sound on the stone steps. I held my breath, hoping to go unnoticed. He crouched and waved a wand over Julian's body.

In the new light of his wand, I could see what I hadn't before, how Julian's eyes had rolled back into his head. Blood smeared the blackened wood of his lips. What remained of his clothes was ash, like mine had been after the affinity fire. The moss and leaves decorating his hair and clothes were brittle and dried. I'd done this. Newfound horror clamped down over me, making my breath come in ragged pants.

The figure stood and turned toward me.

Thatch.

My breath caught in my throat.

He stared calmly and coolly, his face an expressionless mask. He spoke, but no sound came from his lips. He lifted the bird from his shoulder, and it flew into the air. Khaba had been right. Thatch was working for the Raven Court.

CHAPTER THIRTY-NINE
Quoth the Raven

Thatch tapped the lightbulb above with his wand. The bulb brightened, illuminating the dust and cobwebs on the scant amount of art supplies more clearly than I had ever seen them. He stepped forward. Even when his foot encountered the scattered colored pencils, they made no sound as they rolled out of his way. The entire world lacked sound other than the pounding of my heart. I tried to move away, but my back was pressed against the wall. Pain flashed through me from that slight movement.

Thatch kneeled in front of me. His lips formed the shape of my name, but no sound came from him. "Miss Lawrence? Clarissa?"

His gaze moved from my face, to my hands to the half of the sweater fallen in the puddle. The puddle was pink. The space between shelves felt cramped with the two of us in there. His mouth formed more words, but I still didn't hear any sound. He stared at me expectantly.

He lifted a hand to my face. I flinched, my head hitting the shelf beside me. The bump to my temple was minimal compared to the new blaze of white burning in my mouth and hands and groin. A whimper caught in my throat. My vision blurred. He cupped his hands over my ears. I pressed my hands to his arms, trying to push him away, but this only brought on more agony flaring up my arms. His lips continued to move. He closed his eyes and chanted in silence.

My ears ached. Pressure increased and then lessened in my eardrum. A high-pitched tone stabbed into the sides of my head. Underneath the ringing, his voice surfaced, muffled at first, and then grew stronger. His words reminded me of a song, lyrical and deep. If I hadn't been so terrified of what he would do to me, I might have found the melody peaceful.

One of his hands shifted from the side of my head, fingers closing around my throat. I waited for him to squeeze, but he didn't. He palpated the tender tissue, finding the places under my jaw and tongue where it hurt the worst. His touch was cool, like an icepack on an inflamed wound. It was easier to swallow with his hand pressed against the fire of my skin.

"Clarissa, can you hear me?" he asked.

I'd never noticed how sultry his voice was before this moment. The calm of his tone reassured me. I tried to talk, but the desecrated ruin of my lips split open, and the metallic tang of blood touched my tongue. I choked.

He nodded. "Did you kill him on purpose or by accident?"

Behind him, I could see Julian's outstretched hand fallen across the steps. Oh God, I had killed someone. On purpose. The implication sank in. The trembling started up again.

Was Thatch going to tell Jeb he'd been right about me—that I couldn't control myself, and it was only a matter of time before I killed someone? Did he intend to turn me over to the Raven Court? Or drain me? I didn't know which fate was worse.

"Did you intend to kill him?" His voice was low and soft. The kindness in his tone made me hesitate more than the question itself. "Tell me the truth."

I stared up into the storm clouds of his gray eyes. I gave the smallest of nods.

"Good," he said firmly.

I blinked.

"I expect he deserved it." He lifted my right hand and sandwiched it between his own, more gently than I would have anticipated from him. He closed his eyes and inhaled. "Give me your pain. If there's one lesson I expect you've mastered, it's that one."

I closed my eyes. I imagined the pain traveling through my arms and out my hands. I pushed it into him, the red-hot flames and the razor-edged agony. He gasped. Little stinging drops trickled out my fingertips. My palm tingled and numbed.

"Give it all to me. All the pain. Push it out," he said. "Don't attempt to protect me from it. I'm not Josephine Kimura." He smiled at that.

I tried to release it all, but my head felt light. It was difficult to concentrate. The torture between my legs became blindingly strong as the other unwanted sensations left me. His fingers on my skin felt like straws, slurping up the sharp edges of unwanted bite. The blistered surface of my palm didn't hurt anymore. He set my hand onto my lap and held the other. His thumb smoothed over the back of my hand. A jolt of frigid cold rushed down my spine, making my body go rigid. I anticipated pain, but instead I grew more numb.

I opened my eyes to find him staring intently into my face. His skin was paler than a blanket of freshly fallen slow.

He hovered his hand over my arm and traced it up to my shoulder. The pressure of his touch was palpable even without his hand on me, making me wonder about the time I'd been on the cool steel of the table at the tattoo parlor, and I had thought I'd felt hands on me then. He had said it was all me. Perhaps it was, or perhaps it had been the curse. Julian's magic? I had seen a green man in my vision.

The pressure shifted over my head and down my abdomen. His gaze flickered to my lap. He lifted an eyebrow.

He shifted onto his knees, ignoring the puddle he kneeled in. One of his hands rested on my hip, his fingers like icicles through my clothes. His other reached under my legs. I didn't want anyone to touch me. I didn't want to be like I had been before, helpless to my affinity.

A burst of fury bubbled up out of me in a sob. I brought my elbow down on his hand, the force of the movement tearing something inside my core. My cry came out in a panting shriek that licked against the silence. It took me several moments to catch my breath.

"Miss Lawrence, I should think you would be intelligent enough to know—"

"No." My voice came out a raspy screech. "Don't touch me." My humiliation came flowing out of me. Now that I'd turned on the waterworks, I couldn't stop. I turned my face away so he wouldn't see my tears.

"I'm not going to touch you. I don't need to." His hand that had been on my hip was planted in the sticky puddle. I couldn't see the other under my legs.

He closed his eyes. His face was close enough to mine that I could feel the shallowness of his breath. His brow crinkled. My pain eased away. The burnt shards of my body cooled and solidified so that I felt whole again. Numbness washed over me. My own breathing came easier. Now that the pain was gone, exhaustion tugged at my frame.

His breath grew ragged. He leaned his forehead against the wall next to me, his muscles shaking in fatigue. I watched with detached interested. This was my pain inside him. He was willing to hurt for me. That didn't seem very evil. It didn't strike me as a Raven Court kind of thing to do. Had Julian been lying about Thatch? I didn't know what to think anymore.

When his eyes opened, the whites were gone. Instead I found myself gazing into inky blackness. He looked like the Raven Queen, Giver of Pain, when I'd seen her last. Maybe that was what pain did to Witchkin. I wasn't too out if it not to recognize how creepy he looked or how strange it was to see him resemble the Raven Queen. He blinked and slowly his eyes dilated back to normal.

He exhaled. A well of relief rushed out to him as tangible as water. "That was an incredible amount of pain." The pallor of his face flushed a healthy pink.

He slid an arm behind my back, the other hooked under my knees. I tensed.

"I advise you to remember, not every touch will be like his." He lifted me into his arms and carried me down the stairs toward the dungeon.

I leaned my head against his shoulder and sank into the sanctuary of sleep.

CHAPTER FORTY
Prince Charming

My bed felt as though it were made of clouds. I blinked my eyes open, disorientated when I took in my surroundings. Red velvet curtains hung from a wrought iron canopy bed. One side of the curtain was folded back so that I could see the room. Thatch dozed in the chair, a book on his lap. It was a comfortable desk chair, the one from his office.

A sconce on the wall lit the near side of the room, painting his face in a golden glow. His gray waistcoat was unbuttoned, the collar of the shirt underneath also unbuttoned. His navy-blue cravat was untied and loose around his neck. For the briefest of moments, he reminded me of a Gothic Mr. Darcy. I smiled, thinking of *Pride and Prejudice and Zombies*.

The room was larger than my own, with half a wall of bookcases. Most were fiction, ranging from William Shakespeare to Alexandre Dumas to Charles Dickens. He even had *Wuthering Heights* and Harriet Beecher Stowe's *Uncle Tom's Cabin*. I'd never thought of him as someone who read for enjoyment.

An oval mirror covered with a curtain and a wardrobe were pushed against the same wall. The shadows were too thick to reveal what art might be in the frames above the dresser or stacked next to the trunk along the other wall. I thought I remembered from the perspective of the mirror that one painting had sheep with a dragon and the other had unicorns. I'd run through the sheep painting and mucked it all up. Several large canvases were faced away, leaned against a wall.

Thatch stirred and stretched. He scooted the chair closer to me. "How about a drink of water?"

I nodded. He lifted my head and held a crystal goblet to my lips. The water tasted sweet in the desert of my mouth. There was something very surreal about this moment, even more so than walking into a painting. It struck me then.

"You're being too nice."

His eyes crinkled up in a genuine smile. "I hope you aren't going to get it into your head I'll be a softy later. One can't ever be nice if he's the dungeon master."

I laughed but stopped short when the lance of pain stabbed into my abdomen. I groaned and squeezed my eyes closed.

He smoothed a hand over my forehead. The pain in my abdomen decreased, whether it was because of his touch or because I remained still.

"Josephine Kimura told us about Julian. I wish you would have come to me."

I snorted. It hurt my throat to do so. "I thought you already knew."

"Do you actually think I would permit such behavior from one of my teachers?" he asked sharply.

"I didn't think you cared about anything."

His chair creaked. I forced my eyelids open.

His arms were crossed, and his nostrils flared. "You think I wouldn't care about some fertility pervert taking advantage of teenage girls by casting love spells on them? Girls came forward and reported his misconduct the moment he died and the spell was broken. You do realize that's what he did to you as well? Or what he tried to do. You're fortunate your magic resisted him. I'm guessing this resistance resulted in an increasing pain in your abdomen, which you neglected to tell me about."

I nodded in wonder. That's why I'd been experiencing affinity PMS?

He shook his head at me. "But instead of telling me, you kept this knowledge to yourself. Your reticence could have cost your life or someone else's."

"Craptacular. I just made his lordship of the dungeon angry." I realized too late I'd said it out loud.

"You and your insolence. You make it too easy to dislike you."

"Ditto." I closed my eyes again. A memory tickled my brain. Something important. My job. Did I have a job?

"The answer keys," I said, trying to stay awake. "I know where they are."

Thatch's voice sounded a million galaxies away. "Did Julian have them?"

"No. My desk. I found them on the back of student artwork."

"Bloody hell. You make everything one level more complicated, don't you?" He kept on speaking, but the lullaby of his deep voice carried me away into slumber. Everything was swallowed by blackness.

I woke again some time later, voices rousing me. I shifted, noticing the soreness in my limbs. The pain was a dull ache now, rather than the stabbing it had been before. My hands were bandaged. I wondered about the rest of me. Thatch stood in the corner with Jeb.

It was brighter now, the room illuminated with sunshine, though the lack of a light source was disconcerting. Perhaps it came from behind the red velvet curtain on the wall next to the door. I studied the art in the frames. The sheep painting was intact, no sign of students' misdoings there. One of the other framed pieces was a black-and-white ink drawing of Celtic knotwork. I was pretty sure I had seen the same piece in the lobby of the tattoo parlor, but I was too far away to tell for certain. Surely, this had to be his art. It was beautiful.

I tried to sit up. My insides cramped, and my vision swam.

Thatch appeared at my side, his aspect stern. "Don't move a muscle."

"Why am I here?" I could have asked that the first time I'd woke, but my brain felt less foggy now.

"You're somewhere safe and out of the way," Thatch said.

"Ah, there she is, the little darlin'," Jeb said. "How are you feelin'?"

"Like death microwaved with a side of hangover."

"See, I told you. She's nonsensical," Thatch said, a solicitous expression flashing over his face before melting back into his mask of calm. "Would it hurt to give her a few more hours to rest before you start questioning her?"

Jeb chewed on his mustache. "I'm afeared this can't wait."

I shifted in the bed, my breath catching at the pain of movement. "Am I in trouble?"

Jeb sat down in the chair next to the bed and patted my hand. "Of course you ain't, darlin'."

Thatch harrumphed.

Jeb waved a hand at Thatch. "Ain't you got some kind of restorative elixir you fixed up?"

Thatch went to the nightstand and held out a crystal goblet of amber fluid. "Drink this." Light filtered through it, casting golden shards across the blankets. The fluid looked like urine.

Thatch helped me sit up and shoved it into my bandaged hands. I glanced at Jeb. He waited, eyebrows raised expectantly.

"What is it?" I asked.

"Poison. What do you think?" Thatch snapped.

Someone had been restored to his normal, crabby self. I tried to hand the goblet back, but he wouldn't take it.

"It's a potion to restore your health," Jeb said kindly. "Felix insisted on makin' it himself. He's a true Celestor, sure enough, always thinkin' his magic, his remedies, his *everything* is better than all get-out. Thinks this potion is superior to Nurse Hilda's. Bless her heart. I do feel for her. She's mighty insulted."

"Let the old crone sulk," Thatch said. "Half her remedies don't work. The other half contain a suspicious amount of excrement. I don't know why you keep that incompetent oaf around. Students come out of the infirmary sicker than they arrived." He pointed a finger at me. "Drink your medicine. Now."

I held the goblet in shaking hands. I stared at the golden fluid, expecting it was going to taste like barf.

Thatch sighed in disgust. "Don't you think I would have found a more opportune moment if I intended to poison you?"

When I thought back to the way he'd lifted me into his arms and carried me from the stairwell with such concern and tenderness in his eyes, I didn't believe he would hurt me. I sipped the potion. It tasted like butterscotch, only with the kick of whiskey. I coughed. It warmed my throat and prickled pleasantly against my insides.

"All of it," Thatch said in his typical unsympathetic tone.

I guzzled it down, fighting the urge to belch. Cozy relaxation spread through my muscles. I wanted to sink into the blankets and go back to sleep.

Thatch poured water into the glass and handed it to me. I drank that too. My arms were weak, and I couldn't hold the glass for more than a few seconds. He took it from me and placed it on the nightstand before retreating to the corner.

Jeb patted my hand. "You poor dear. Can you tell me what happened?"

Thatch cleared his throat. "I already told you. Julian Thistledown cast a spell on Miss Lawrence, making her behave irrationally. She was then attacked by him in the stairwell of her supply closet. He intended to take her to the Raven Court. Fortunately, she'd learned enough from my teaching methods to stop him before he convinced her to leave the school grounds." He gave me a pointed look.

That was a slightly modified version of what had happened. I could tell there was something Thatch didn't want me to say, but I couldn't guess what. Perhaps he knew I had previously left school grounds with Julian. Or perhaps it had to do with what he had or hadn't taught me. Julian hadn't been under the orders of the Raven Court, he'd been under someone else's employment, but he hadn't said who. I didn't know if Thatch knew this or not, but I trusted Thatch.

"Yep, you said as much already," Jeb said. "I want to hear Miss Lawrence acknowledge the corn herself."

Who was the one talking nonsensical?

"How did you burn your hands, darlin'?"

I turned my hands over, staring at the white gauze. "Magic."

"Just so." Jeb chortled. "But really, how'd you do it? Do you know your affinity?"

Thatch watched me, his expression wary. Behind Jeb, he gave the slightest shake of his head. Apparently, the principal didn't know I was a Red.

"No," I said. "Julian said he knew what my affinity was. That's why the Raven Queen wanted me. Maybe why someone else wanted me too."

Thatch shook his head. Was it my affinity he didn't want Jeb to know about? Or that more Fae wanted me.

"I don't know what I am. Julian didn't say. He grabbed me, and I tried to push him away. I focused my energy and shot lightning out of my hands."

"Lightnin'?" Jeb leaned forward with interest.

"She doesn't mean lightning," Thatch said. "She means magic. Morties and new Witchkin alike often confuse the fractals of magic as something akin to lightning."

Jeb stroked his beard. "Perhaps. Or Miss Lawrence might be an Elementia or Celestor with a lightnin' affinity."

"It wasn't the right color for lightning, I guess. And there wasn't the smell of ozone." I lied, but I didn't know why I was lying. My intuition told me to trust Thatch.

Jeb asked me a few more questions. I yawned and closed my eyes.

Thatch crossed his arms. "See, you've fatigued her."

"You never cease to amaze me, Felix. I didn't know you had it in you to be such a devoted nursemaid."

I forced my eyes open, but the room was a haze.

"I'm not a nursemaid. I simply think that if I've gone to all the trouble of making drafts of medicine, it would be just as well not to interrupt the healing process so I'm not forced to waste even more of my time on such an ungrateful patient."

"Ah, yes, ever the practical one." The principal winked at me. "Never a kind bone in his body cuz that would be uglier than sin. It's all pragmatism."

Thatch nodded. "Exactly."

Jeb shifted to the edge of his seat and groaned as he got up. "Could use one of those restorative drafts myself." He looked to me. "I reckon you'll be well enough to be moved to the infirmary soon."

"It's far more practical to keep her here, away from students until she can return to her room. Let them think she's caught a bad case of the flu. That way she won't be associated with *his* death."

Jeb tugged at his beard. "Not a bad idea if it's just for a day or so. I can't have three teachers missing from their classes for long. Puck and Khaba can't cover for y'all."

"Oh no! My classes! What day is it?" I tried to sit up.

Thatch pointed his wand at me. "Lie down, or I'll bind you to that bed with magic."

I didn't doubt he would do such a thing.

Thatch turned back to the principal. "You needn't fret about overworking the staff. Miss Lawrence is near enough I can check on her easily from my classroom. I will resume my classes next period. I've taken the liberty of notifying her adoptive mother. Mrs. Lawrence will arrive this afternoon. I've made arrangements with Sam to escort her to the school."

The two men walked toward the door as Thatch and Jeb made plans.

My mom would be here? Oh boy. I didn't know whether to be grateful or afraid. I was going to be fussed over and pampered whether I liked it or not.

I sat in the bed, trying to go back to sleep, but I couldn't. My bladder was too full. I kept thinking about all Thatch had said—and what he hadn't wanted me to tell Jeb. Julian had used me and cursed me, made me forget Jeb's rules, my hope to find Derrick, and tried to force me to become his love slave. It all made me sick.

At last, Thatch returned.

"Why am I really in the dungeon?" I asked.

"So that I can ensure your safety."

Maybe that was the truth. Or maybe it was because he was a control freak.

"Okay, so I've been laying in a bed for an hour. You didn't give me any reading material. My bladder is about to explode, and I didn't know if it would be a problem if I wet the bed or you have a magical bedpan in here."

He glanced at the blankets and sighed in exasperation. "Did you urinate in my bed?"

"No. But I will pretty soon if you don't get me some kind of enchanted chamber pot."

He peeled back the blankets, revealing my purple Eeyore nightgown.

My eyes widened. "Did you undress me?"

"You never cease to amaze me with your insipid concerns. Of course, I had to undress you."

Ugh, my humiliation would never end. Thatch had seen me naked. He'd probably enjoyed it too.

He eased me forward. "If you could grasp the nature of what you did, you would be far more distressed to learn about your use of forbidden magic. I couldn't allow anyone to see your electrical burns."

"Why not?"

"Let's attend to more pressing concerns first, shall we?" He scooped me up in his arms and nodded toward the door on the far wall. "There's a water closet over there."

I slid an arm around his neck, securing myself against him. My face flushed with warmth when I thought about how close we were. He smelled nice, like dusty books and oil paints. "Please don't set me on a toilet. I've died of embarrassment enough times lately."

He chuckled. "Oh? More humiliating than tearing the turban off Darshan's head?"

"That's a hard one to beat, but yeah."

He exhaled against my cheek as he carried me. "What exactly went through your head that you thought that would be a good idea?"

"I was trying to follow my intuition."

"We can see how well that worked out for you." The warm wind of his breath tickled my hair.

It took all of my will to focus on his words instead of how close his lips were to my skin, how I wanted his lips on my skin. Probably my affinity made me want him. "You were the one who gave me the book on lucid dreaming. I dreamed my mother's face was under Pro Ro's turban."

He set me on my feet outside of the door and opened it. "Walk slowly," he said. He held onto my arm as if afraid I might flop over.

Shuffling was about as fast as I could go. My legs didn't want to move. The tile was cold on my bare feet. The sensation grounded me and woke up my senses. I held onto the marble counter for support. The bathroom was brighter than the rest of the dungeon. The stone of the walls and the floor was pale umber. Greek columns held up a domed ceiling decorated with Etruscan art.

"This is pretty swanky for a teacher's water closet," I said.

He remained at the doorway, looking like he was ready to leap forward in case I fell over. "I've lived in the dungeon for over thirty years. I wouldn't tolerate these rooms if I hadn't been able to incorporate my own renovations."

As I came into view in the elaborately carved frame of the mirror, I realized I didn't look as bad as I could have. My lips weren't blistered anymore, and my pink hair had been brushed. My hair had body rather than frizz and reminded me of Thatch's. Wherever he kept his magic hairbrush I was going to find it and try it out.

Through an adjoining door, I spied a fireplace. On the other wall, a waterfall trickled into a steaming pool. Tropical plants grew along the edges. It was lush and beautiful. I had never guessed Thatch had such good taste.

"I haven't got all day," he said.

I glanced over my shoulder. He closed the door between us.

His voice came through the door muffled. "I shall wait here in case you need assistance."

Great. Like my shy bladder was going to be able to pee now.

Ten minutes later I was back in bed eating a bowl of hot chicken and rice soup from a tray. Holding the spoon with bandaged hands proved to be more difficult than I'd imagined. I shoveled a spoonful in my mouth, dropping a chunk of chicken onto my lap.

"You're getting cock-a-leekie on my blanket," Thatch complained.

"Cock-a-what?" I burst into laughter. I didn't want to say what that sounded like.

He removed the spoon from my hand. "It's a Scottish soup. Really, you're as bad as the students." He said it with a groan, but there was a smile on his lips. He held up a spoonful.

I accepted the mouthful. "So, are you ever going to tell me why the burns and lightning zapping is such a no-no?" There had to be a reason he was keeping secrets from Jeb.

"Normal Witchkin cannot process electromagnetic energy." He shoveled another spoonful into my mouth. "They cannot channel lightning or cause electrical storms. There are few exceptions, but even Elementia with lightning affinities don't tolerate electronics, nor are they able to power technology through their energy. Human generated electricity weakens Celestor, Amni Plandai, and Elementia. It doesn't make them stronger like it does for those with the Red affinity."

I noticed how he kept saying "them" and "they." He didn't include himself in that list. "So lightning is *our* affinity? That doesn't make us a special kind of Elementia?" Lightning sounded like something that came from water, wind, earth, and air.

"No, electrical impulses are not the same as lightning. All Red affinities come from the body, whether your own or someone else's."

"I'm a conductor of electrical magic," I said. Now that he was being forthcoming, it made more sense. All along he'd been leading me down the right path, trying to test what I was, and giving me the knowledge I needed to figure it out on my own. Every book he'd given me, from lucid dreaming and developing intuition, to Elementia magic for lightning affinities or Amni Plandai fertility magic, it had all been meant to help me, not give me pointless reading to do.

Thatch set down the spoon. "There's something else you should know. Something you need to know." He wet his lips, the gesture uncharacteristically nervous. "The information I'm about to share is of a delicate nature. It would be best not to repeat it, as it will put you and others at risk."

"I won't tell anyone. I promise."

"Promises can be broken. It would be more pragmatic to bind you to your word with a spell. That way, I can ensure you never tell another soul what I'm about to tell you."

I swallowed. "I understand." After the way his trust had been broken before, I understood why he required this. "What do I need to do?"

He eyed me doubtfully. "You agree to a magical contract just like that, even though it could shatter your soul if you break it?"

My mouth went dry. I nodded.

"You're too trusting for your own good." He lifted another mouthful of soup to my lips. He shook his head. "You're too weak for a binding spell, and I don't relish the idea of making you worse and then having you here any longer than necessary. Your word will have to do." He fed me the last spoonful of cock-a-leekie. "Do you remember when I told you your body doesn't like pain?"

"Yes." I'd responded that no one likes being hurt.

He set my bowl aside. "Your affinity is touch, or more accurately, human electrical impulses transmitted through touch. Pain is the opposite nutrient your affinity needs, which is why you have an especially low threshold for pain."

"I just don't get why touchy-feeling magic is so bad. Is it all because Fae are jealous?" I asked.

"Touch magic is lumped into the same category as blood magic. When you think of tales of human sacrifice, can you see why Witchkin might be afraid of this? They shun anyone who might be capable of drawing power from others. They consider them dangerous. As if it isn't difficult enough being a Red and hiding what you are so that others don't shun you, you have an extra burden. You're Alouette Loraline's daughter. People already assume you're like her. It's only a matter of time before the greater Fae community discovers what you are. When they do, they might assume you are the key to all their problems."

"How would I be the key?"

"You have noticed you bring out the magic in others? You increase their powers. So it is with the Fae. They can use you to increase their virility and fecundity so that it solves their fertility problems. They can use you as a weapon. If they think you possess the same powers of Loraline's affinity, they will enslave you to do their bidding."

Just like Julian had attempted to do. He had been a fertility creature, wanting to increase his powers. A green man, he'd said. I shuddered, remembering his true form.

"People—Fae and Witchkin—knew my mother was a Red? So that means they're going to come after me?"

"Most Witchkin don't know what she was. Few Fae do. The Raven Queen has seen to it that the secret remains concealed. Certainly she must suspect you're Red, but she hasn't spoken of it. It is in her best interest not to draw attention to you. She won't want competition from other courts.

Should you side with any particular house of Fae, they will exploit you. I had hoped to save you from this by draining you."

"I don't want to be drained," I said quickly.

"I know. That's why I must teach you in secret." His brow crinkled with worry.

He would teach me? Truly? My heart could have soared out of my chest.

"This is why I have to keep it a secret?" I asked. "But Jeb must suspect."

"If he does, he hasn't said. The less he knows, the better." He swallowed and shifted in his chair, looking uneasy. "Give me your hand."

I flushed, remembering the last time he'd asked me to do that. His usually austere aspect was replaced by something softer and more vulnerable. He unwrapped the long strip of gauze from my palm. The skin was red and raw underneath, red scabs glossy with ointment. The charred skin was gone at least.

He unscrewed the lid of a glass jar and scooped out a dollop of thick cream. "There's only so much healing I can do with potions, spells, and salves. Your affinity, however, can do far more than I can." He dabbed the ointment on my palm. On my fingers there were no burns, but he massaged the cream into the unmarred skin anyway. It was relaxing, and I closed my eyes.

"Keep your eyes open." The sharpness in his tone startled me out of my complacency. "You need to be lucid and observant. I don't want you to later claim I . . . touched you elsewhere like you did in the tattoo parlor. If my suspicions are correct, your magic will make you feel more than . . . well, you'll see."

His touch was whisper soft over my injury. He smoothed his fingers up my wrist. My skin tingled. Warmth radiated from his touch. I sank into the comfort of it. The longer he stroked me, the more alive I felt. Another caress up the inside of my arm and my heart fluttered. My fingers twitched, and I noticed the burns didn't hurt at all anymore. The angry red sores on my palm darkened into scabs. The skin puckered and tightened, an uncomfortable itch tickling my palms. He massaged more salve onto the injuries. With his touch came the calm relief I needed. Tremors of pleasure shot up my arm.

I let out a breathy sigh. Cool blue energy pulsed up my wrist, over my bicep and radiated past my shoulder. The calm sank down into my heart and still lower into my core. The energy shifted, becoming red and hot. The muscles in my pelvis clenched. At first the sensation was a pleasant throb.

I stared up at the maroon canopy, trying to breathe through the pleasure. It felt like fingers stroking me between my legs, caressing places inside me no one had ever touched before.

Thatch's voice was stern. "Look at me."

I did. His hands remained on my hand. He only rubbed my fingers and palm. Like before at the tattoo parlor, his face was flushed with color. His eyes were dark, haunted. He glanced away, impatience twitching his lips into a frown. No, not impatience, embarrassment. I could see he didn't like this.

But he didn't stop.

After another moment, the pleasure intensified to the point of being overwhelming. Crests of ecstasy rose in me, rising like waves about to spill over a dam. The pressure between my legs became more insistent, faster. Tears filled my eyes at the undiluted exquisiteness of it. I felt full inside, too full. I wasn't healed enough for this. I didn't want to be touched like this. I wanted my will to be my own.

I yanked my hand away, gasping for breath. The heat inside me cooled.

Thatch hugged his arms around himself, shivering. His breath was labored, and he shifted in his chair, turning his body slightly away. I didn't know who was more uncomfortable with what had just happened.

"That was magic?" I asked. I stared down at my hand. It was greasy from ointment, but the scabs were gone. Pink patches remained where the blisters had been, but the skin wasn't even puckered. I flexed my hand, marveling over the lack of pain. "Your magic healed me?"

"*Your* magic. Your affinity," he corrected. "This is why you need your fairy godmother."

I laughed and shook my head. What he was suggesting sounded ridiculous. "So you're saying I need my mom for a magical orgasm? That's gross—it would be like incest."

"Once again you twist my meaning into something illicit." He tsked at me. "You need your mum because she will do the exact opposite. She will feed your affinity without drawing out sexual energies and overwhelming you. She will hug you and stroke your hair and coddle you in a way I cannot. Her touch will heal you far better than I can." He crossed his arms and stared across the room.

"Oh." That made sense. "Does my mom know what I am?" She had always been a huggy person and knew how to comfort me when I wasn't feeling well.

"It's unlikely. And you should see it stays that way. If she asks about your affinity, tell her you don't know."

"But why? She wouldn't use my affinity against me. I trust her. My fairy godmother has been my mom for my entire life. She *is* my mother, more than Loraline is—was." And I was certain she wouldn't judge me or think I was evil because I had a supposed "bad" affinity.

She had always tried to protect me from the Unseen Realm and those within it. She must have suspected what I was. I didn't believe it was a coincidence she'd kept me so sheltered, objected to me taking sex-ed classes, and tried to restrict my dating in high school. Unless she thought I was a fertility nymph or something akin to it.

"You're probably right. She won't use you. But it puts her in danger if you confide in her. That secret will be in her every gesture. It will be in her hesitancy to touch you. Imagine if the Raven Queen suspects she knows. Or others witness your interactions and the sudden change in how she treats you. The Raven Court will snatch her up to torture her. Is that what you want?"

I shook my head. "And me being this touch affinity, it's forbidden even if I don't hurt people with it? You said I don't like pain, so I should only use electrical impulses for pleasure, right?" Using it for pain had disastrous effects on my own body.

"It isn't called a touch affinity, even if that's what fuels the magic. We call it the Red affinity. It derives from older terminology of 'blood mages,' though I think the term is limiting in its inclusiveness. In some, this manifests as a necromancer or a succubus or Venus powers. Various ethnicities and mythology have other names for what the Red affinity does to you. A rusalka, leannán sídhe, siren, or Linin-demon or Lilith."

"That's your affinity as well?"

"Yes and no. My affinity works differently than yours."

"I never thought you were anything other than Celestor."

He inclined his head. "I work very hard to appear that way."

How horribly sad for him to hide who he was. And sadder still for him to go without touch for so long when he needed it. Knowing this about him made so much more sense.

"That's why you're so mean to Josie?" I asked. "You didn't want her to get close to you and find out what you are."

"That is none of your business." He bristled. "Many Witchkin have more than one affinity. One simply is the strongest, and that is the one we feed and harvest. For the few of us who are Reds, we disguise ourselves as Amni Plandai fertility nymphs, fuel the storm of our electricity as Elementia, or use the affinities of sky, moon or stars as Celestor. I use my powers as the head of the Celestor department to help Red students into other teams where they will be less noticed."

"Except for Imani."

He nodded. "I couldn't hide her affinity. She's going to need a mentor . . . a fairy godmother. You're going to have to master your powers so you can help her as she grows into hers. A female teacher would be more appropriate. Having a teacher of the opposite sex might cause . . . unhealthy attachments." The pain was raw in his voice. He swallowed and looked away.

"Was my mother your mentor?" I scooted closer and reached for his hand. My fingertips brushed against his.

He jerked back. "Don't pity me."

"I don't. I just. . . ." I didn't know what to say. "I care. I don't want you to hurt."

I placed my hand on his again. His spine went rigid. It must have been a long time since he'd allowed anyone to touch him.

He leaned forward and placed my hand on my lap. I didn't have to stretch to reach him now. He covered both of my hands with his own, dwarfing my fingers with the length of his. After a moment, he slid his hands back to his own lap.

"Mr. Thatch—Felix—would you please tell me the truth about something?" I tried to swallow the tight lump in my throat. "Are you my . . . father?"

A smile touched his perfectly shaped lips. "No. Thank Nimue, no."

That was a relief.

He wasn't touching me any longer, but he remained so close he could have kissed me. His eyes were intense, staring into mine. His breath brushed against my face. My heart skipped a beat. He was going to kiss me. Did I want him to kiss me? I felt connected to him, more drawn to him than any man I'd dated in years.

For the first time, I knew this desire came from me because he wasn't touching me, and I still wanted him. His lips parted. He leaned closer.

I lifted my chin.

His voice was so quiet I almost couldn't hear it. "My duty is to mentor you and be your teacher. It wouldn't be professional to cross that line. I am not going to touch you. I am not going to finish healing you. Do you understand?" He wet his lips. His gaze flickered to my mouth.

I nodded. There was yearning in his eyes. I wondered if he could see the longing in my own eyes, feel it tingling under my skin.

"It wouldn't be fair to you," he said. "And it certainly wouldn't be fair to me. I don't want to be in a relationship with anyone, most of all, not Alouette Loraline's daughter." The storm clouds in his eyes spoke of an eternity of past sorrows. "Do you understand me?"

The truth became as clear as water. "It was you. That time, in the wardrobe." That was why Julian hadn't been able to embrace me the same way. It had never been him. The way Felix Thatch had closed his arms around me had felt so right.

"I have no idea what you mean."

"You hugged me." He'd wanted me. I could see it in his eyes. He still did.

I closed my eyes and waited for him to kiss me. My Prince Charming. The sigh of his breath rushed against my cheek. He smelled of linseed oil and dusty books with a hint of cyanide. I'd never realized I liked the smell of poison.

The faintest whisper of a touch brushed across my face. I leaned forward, my lips meeting air. I opened my eyes.

He was gone.

That evening, my fairy godmother arrived. She fluttered about the room like a fairy on crack. I would have sworn she had wings from the way she moved. She fluffed pillows and tucked me in, planting a thousand kisses on my forehead and patting my face like I was an invalid. She unpacked art supplies she'd brought and stacked my favorite books next to the bed. Her words came out a mile a minute, fretting over me and my health. Like Mary Poppins, she removed an impossible number of items from her bag.

I felt bad for Satyr Sam. He'd carried both of her suitcases through the woods for two miles to the school.

She pulled out a Ziploc of earthquake brownies crusted with pecans and shredded coconut. My eyes almost bugged out of my head at the sight of them. "Thank you, Mom! You're the best!"

She set them on a plate. "That nice professor asked me to bring you brownies when he called. I take it you shared a few with him from the way he raved about my baking." She sat at the edge of the bed and set the plate on my tray.

"Raved? Wait, who was this?"

She tapped her fingers against the nightstand as if in thought. "Professor Thatch. What a sweetheart."

I nearly choked on a brownie. This couldn't be real. They hated each other. They'd battled. As if the surrealism of the moment wasn't enough, it was hard to imagine Thatch rant about anything in a positive way.

"Mom, you do know who he is, don't you? He tried to drain me before, and you sicked your familiar on him. Thatch hasn't erased your memories, has he?" I asked.

That was more of her kind of thing to do, but I had to ask.

"Honey, that's all water under the bridge. I've forgiven him for his misguided attempts to help you by removing you from my protection. What's important is that he's realized his mistakes. He called me so I could be here to take care of you."

Ah, so he'd appealed to her maternal instincts.

She patted my leg as I crammed the remainder of the brownie into my mouth. The coconut pecan caramel soaking into the brownie was heaven. My eyes rolled back into my head. I sank against the pillow in pure bliss. I hoped she didn't still enchant my food, but if she did, I was too much in heaven to care.

"Such a delightful man," Mom said. "You'll share some brownies with him, won't you?"

As if he hadn't had enough before. Still, it was the present that counted.

"And your friend, Josie?" Mom asked. "We should set some aside for when she comes to visit. She's been asking about you."

"Josie? She doesn't hate me?" I squealed.

"No. Why would she hate you?"

My heart warmed at the prospect of seeing her. I still had a friend. I smiled.

Mom unpacked potted plants from her bag as I ate another brownie. "As Mr. Thatch was showing me around, he told me a funny story about the principal. Did you know Mr. Bumblebub thought a student stole the answer key to some silly test? Apparently you suggested he should clean his desk and maybe he'd find it. Mr. Thatch snuck the divination teacher into the principal's office and they found it under a bunch of files in a box. It's just that it was too messy in there to find it, and all the wards were messing with the ability to divine it! So you had the right idea all along."

I choked on the brownie, shredding coconut going down the wrong hole. Mom rushed over with a goblet of water.

I gulped it down. "Mr. Thatch neglected to tell me that funny little story," I said.

I supposed he hadn't wanted the blame to fall on me for stealing the keys, though, Khaba had been the one to give them to me. He'd also been right about me finding it. Probably Jeb's messy office had been the original culprit, which is what I'd suggested at the teacher meeting, so Thatch's plan did make it sound like I had solved the problem. I laughed out loud.

"What do you say to getting more light in here?" Mom asked. She crossed to the velvet curtain on the opposite wall.

"We're in the dungeon. There isn't any—"

She tugged on the gold cords.

It wasn't a window. It was a painting. The woman was a fairy with shimmering purple wings and long red hair that cascaded down her back. She was nude, but tastefully posed. Her back was turned to the viewer as she glanced over her shoulder laughing. I couldn't tell if it was supposed to be me or my biological mother. Her hair was a darker auburn than my natural color, but much redder than Alouette Loraline's portrait in the hallway.

The more I studied it, the more I determined it had to be a painting of my biological mother. He'd painted his subject with such beauty and whimsical charm, there was no way he'd seen that in me—not with how he had treated me over the last couple months.

Even weirder was the idea it might be my mother. After all this time, after she'd used his affinity against him and tortured him, he kept her portrait up in his bedroom? He wasn't a sadist as I'd first thought. He was a masochist.

"Did Mr. Thatch paint this?" Mom pointed to the signature in the corner that she undoubtedly could read better than I could. She turned to me, her eyebrows raised in question. "You didn't tell me you two are . . . together?"

Not for my lack of trying that morning. Shame flushed to my cheeks. I could have kicked myself for my stupidity. He must have thought I was as bad as Josie. He was probably going to be majorly annoying and eat my prophecy chocolate to get me to hate him.

"We aren't together," I said. "That's someone else."

She gave me her best I'm-your-mother-and-I-know-when-someone-is-fibbing-look.

I rolled my eyes, feeling like one of my teenage students. "It's my biological mother."

She tilted her head to the side, examining the white squiggles in the corner of the painting. "No, it's not. He finished it two years ago. There's a date"

Two years ago? I stared at the painting, confused. He had been observing me, watching me more closely than I had known. Was this really how he saw me? A laughing sprite?

My prophecy chocolate had turned out to be true after all. The beginning had tasted bitter, only to be followed by a taste of something sweet.

I still had a job. At least until the end of the semester. My Prince Charming had ended up being a scoundrel. I guessed that was the bitterest notes of dark chocolate. The villainous dungeon master ended up being . . . well, I still didn't know what Felix Thatch was. I wasn't sure he could ever be considered the caramel center of my metaphorical candy, but he certainly was sweeter than I'd first thought.

I had learned some pretty good magic considering I was the most unmagical teacher at the school. I had learned my affinity and understood my biological mother.

Sort of. I had a feeling there was a lot more I had to learn about the Fae Fertility Paradox. I still needed to find Derrick. Most of all, there were mysteries I still needed to uncover. Particularly about Thatch.

And me.

THE END

Excerpt from Secondhand Hexes
Sequel to Witches Gone Wicked

CHAPTER ONE
The Sorcerer's Apprentice

There was one reason I was willing to visit Professor Felix Thatch and endure his snarky comments in the shadowy bowels of the school dungeon on a Saturday at seven a.m. I needed to learn to protect myself from being attacked again. I could only do that if I learned to conceal what I was.

I walked through the dank, moldy dungeon and into the hallway outside Thatch's office for my newest magic lesson, halting when I heard a woman speak. "I'm not going to do it. You've already ruined my existence enough by making me share a room with her. If you weren't my supervisor, I would poison you." The familiar voice made no attempt to mask the venom in her words.

I hesitated outside the door, not particularly wanting to face Vega Bloodmire, roommate evil-ordinaire. How odd that she would be visiting Thatch early in the morning, especially after staying out late the night before.

Thatch spoke slowly, enunciating each word with a crisp British accent. "You act as though a room by yourself in the tower is a right, not a privilege. It is a reward . . . you haven't yet earned."

"How can you say that? I've spied for you. I've reported Clarissa's behaviors and told you anytime she acted suspiciously. *You* said I could have my own room at the start of the new quarter. Now you're reneging on the deal."

Dread settled in my gut as I realized they were talking about me. Thatch hadn't forced me to share a room with Vega because he wanted to ruin my life; it was so someone could babysit me. I hated that he treated me like a little kid. I was a teacher.

Thatch coughed. "No. I said I would *consider* it. I have. You are not getting the tower."

"What did Josephine Kimura ever do to deserve the tower besides sleep with you?"

I gasped, clamping a hand over my mouth too late. What? My best friend had slept with the dungeon master? Josie hated Thatch. Then again, maybe this was why.

Feathers rustled, and metal rattled. Thatch's pet crow was in its cage inside his office no doubt.

"As you are quite aware, Miss Bloodmire, I do not form relationships with my subordinates. It would be unprofessional."

She muttered, "Who said anything about forming a relationship?"

I leaned against the wall in relief. I didn't know why it unsettled me so greatly that Josie might have slept with Thatch. It wasn't as if *I* liked him that way. It wasn't like I had been thinking about when he'd almost kissed me—most certainly I was not thinking about it multiple times each hour of each day. Every time I closed my eyes and imagined that whisper across my lips, I wasn't sure if it had been his magic that had brushed my skin or his mouth. Considering I was his subordinate and he was the aloof, professional professor, it was unlikely he had kissed me.

The idea of Josie having a past with my attractive frenemy only complicated my feelings for him. One minute I'd suspected him of wanting to curse me to get rid of me, the next I discovered my ex-boyfriend was behind all those deaths—and Thatch had been trying to save me from the same fate all along.

"Furthermore," Thatch went on, his sexy British accent enticing me to keep listening. "I have reason to believe Miss Kimura would make an unsuitable roommate for Miss Lawrence."

Vega snorted. "An unsuitable roommate for anyone from my experience with her."

Ire shot through me on Josie's behalf. She would make a way better roommate than Vega any day—and not just because she didn't hog up all the shelf space and hang nooses over my bed.

"I have need of you and your talents supervising Miss Lawrence a while longer," Thatch said. "I have compensated you generously for your troubles thus far. I shall continue to do so for as long as this arrangement exists. Will that suffice?"

He was paying her to babysit me? *What* was he paying her?

"No. You're expecting me to do even more work on your behalf now. It's bad enough you took away my prep and gave me Julian Thistledown's remedial History of Fae Studies. At least Jeb added a bonus to my monthly salary for that. Though, not enough for what I put up with. If you're going to pile additional duties on my plate, I expect more in return."

His tone was even, each word spoken crisply and clearly. "What do you want?"

"The price is four hours a week instead of two."

"Very well," he said.

"And I expect you to put in actual effort. You can't just sit there and watch. I expect you to enjoy it."

I leaned closer, trying to figure out what they were talking about. Did this have something to do with her staying out late? I wasn't sure I remembered her sneaking in at all the night before, and her bed had been made when I'd woken. What were the two of them up to?

"I never claimed I would enjoy myself, nor that you would find satisfaction in my company," he said. "I will continue to bring my sketchpad with me and draw while you torture me with these hedonistic excursions. I make no more promises other than to accompany you."

Vega huffed in exasperation.

Now I was really lost. What was he doing to pay her? Where were they going? Was she asking him to go to the graveyard with her or torture small animals? It had to be something morbid and magical, but I couldn't imagine what.

Thatch cleared his throat. "I have agreed to your terms. Additionally, if you do well, and you're able to keep Miss Lawrence from harm or getting into trouble, I will speak to Jeb on your behalf at the end of the year and ask him to give you the tower."

"By myself," she said. "I will have the tower *by myself* and not have to share with anyone."

"Indeed." He raised his voice. "Miss Lawrence, would you stop skulking in the shadows, spying like a delinquent student? Come in here."

So much for being sneaky.

I trudged into the room, trying to avoid Vega's glare. She lounged in the chair across from Thatch's desk, more at ease than anyone else in the world should be in a metal torture chair. She'd dressed in the equivalent of business casual for a flapper, the black cotton dress having a low waist that enhanced her slim figure. Upon first glance, it looked like she showed an indecent amount of leg, but the skirt was knee length. It just happened that Vega had outrageously long legs.

Not that I was jealous. Much.

Vega's dark eyes narrowed to slits. "How long were you listening?"

I shook my head. "A minute. Less than a minute. I wasn't skulking. I just didn't want to interrupt."

Thatch's perfectly shaped lips pursed like an old woman's. His severe features would have been beautiful if he had smiled, but he seldom did. I had a suspicion he knew I'd been there for more than a minute.

Vega smoothed a hand over her already perfect hair, the sides of the black bob curling around her elegant cheekbones. She remained seated. Not that I wanted to sit in the torture chair, but it was über awkward just standing there.

Thatch adjusted the white cravat around the high collar of his shirt. "Previously, Miss Lawrence, we discussed the need for you to expedite your learning so that you can gain control of your powers more quickly."

"Yes, I remember." My eagerness to learn magic soured in the pit of my stomach as foreboding swept over me.

There had to be a reason Vega hadn't left yet. My intuition told me I wasn't going to like the reason.

He gestured toward my archrival. "Meet your new magic mentor."

For the rest of the novel, go to Sarina Dorie's website for information about the next book in the series:
https://sarinadorie.com/writing/novels/wombys-school-for-wayward-witches

If you enjoyed this Cozy Witch Mystery *in the Womby's School for Wayward Witches Series* please leave a review on the online retailer where you purchased this collection. You might also enjoy free short stories published by the author on her website: http://sarinadorie.com/writing/short-stories.

Readers can hear updates about current writing projects and news about upcoming novels and free short stories as they become available by signing up for Sarina Dorie's newsletter at:

http://eepurl.com/4IUhP

Other novels written by the author can be found at:

http://sarinadorie.com/writing/novels

You can find Sarina Dorie on Facebook at:

https://www.facebook.com/sarina.dorie1/

You can find Sarina Dorie on Twitter at:

@Sarina Dorie

Seventeen-year-old Sarah's life changes forever when a man falls from the sky—and she falls in love. As if teenage romance isn't hard enough in the times of the Puritans, imagine falling in love with an alien!

Magic. Jehovah's witchnesses. Karmic collisions. . . .Two unlikely friends—a witch and a Jehovah's Witness—discover the magic of friendship, as well as real magic.

Gothic Romance. Mystery. Ghosts. Imagine a whimsical fairytale world with the feel of Jane Eyre . . . only working in a house of were-wolves.

For more fantasy, science fiction and romance, go to: www.sarinadorie.com

ABOUT THE AUTHOR

Sarina Dorie has sold over 150 short stories to markets like Analog, Daily Science Fiction, Magazine of Fantasy and Science Fiction, Orson Scott Card's IGMS, Cosmos, and Abyss and Apex. Her stories and published novels have won humor and Romance Writer of America awards. She has sold three novels to publishers. Her steampunk romance series, *The Memory Thief* and her collections, *Fairies, Robots and Unicorns—Oh My!* and *Ghosts, Werewolves and Zombies—Oh My!* are available on Amazon, along with a dozen other novels she has written.

A few of her favorite things include: gluten-free brownies (not necessarily glutton-free), Star Trek, steampunk aesthetics, fairies, Severus Snape, Captain Jack Sparrow and Mr. Darcy.

By day, Sarina is a public school art teacher, artist, belly dance performer and instructor, copy editor, fashion designer, event organizer and probably a few other things. By night, she writes. As you might imagine, this leaves little time for sleep.

CPSIA information can be obtained
at www.ICGtesting.com
Printed in the USA
BVHW042134270519
549414BV00017B/327/P